Alas, Ωmega

Book II

Other books from this author:

Jagged Grass (Volume I: Seminole Trilogy; paperback and e-book available online)

Sun God's Treasure (First book of the Sun God series; paperback and e-book available online)

Alas, Ωmega

Book II

James Tindall

Library of Congress Cataloging-in-Publication Data
Tindall, James
  Alas, Omega/James Tindall
    p. 522

ISBN: 978-0-9817037-8-7

Published by DTP Publishing, Denver, Colorado

Printed in the United States of America

10 9 8   7 6 5 4 3 2 1

ISBN: 978-0-9817037-8-7

Authors Note: *The Navajo Nation occupies all of northeastern Arizona, the southeastern portion of Utah, and northwestern New Mexico, near the 'four corners' area of the U.S. where the boundaries of Colorado, Utah, Arizona, and New Mexico meet. It is they and those they select, along with the united tribes of America, that can stop the fall of the Republic, which is the United States, in this, the fifth world! Although they will stop the Republics fall, they are unable to protect all.*

The map below is the Republic; it has lasted five decades longer than the average lifespan of 200 years for other world empires. The Republic is weak, crumbling, and corrupt. The burden is upon the Navajo and the United Tribes of America to save it, along with other warriors who would help protect the White Eyes. Seek the high ground. You will fight or you will perish. It is better to die on your feet like a warrior than begging on your knees like a coward! Sun God has left it in your hands. Choose ye sides this day. As for me, I will stand with Sun God!

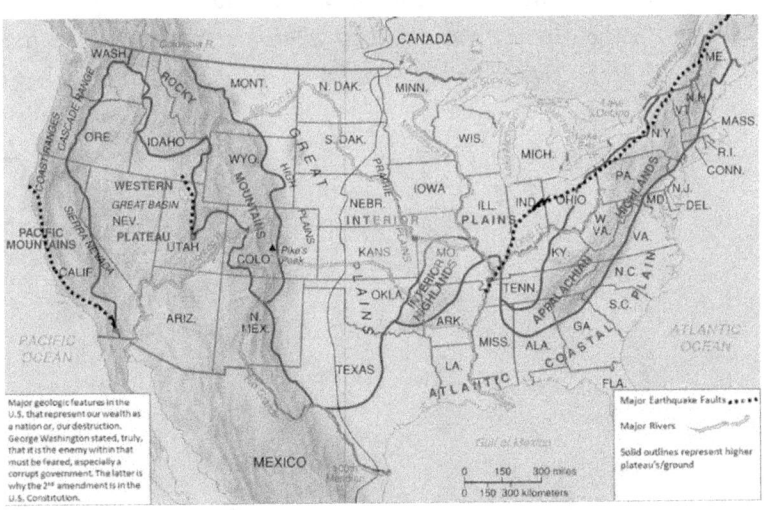

Major geologic features in the U.S. that represent our wealth as a nation or, our destruction. George Washington stated, truly, that it is the enemy within that must be feared, especially a corrupt government. The latter is why the 2ⁿᵈ amendment is in the U.S. Constitution.

Major Earthquake Faults ....

Major Rivers

Solid outlines represent higher plateau's/ground

Dedicated to

The Navajo and Seminole Nations

Felisha Scott, a loyal friend,

Ilasiea Gray

&

The true warriors in the United States who are unresponsive to political motivation and will do what is necessary to keep the United States free from its enemies — foreign and domestic.

Your call to act is here – now!

Disclaimer:

Many believe that what you are about to read will become a reality. It has been predicted for millennia; few have listened. Contained herein is a sequence of events, as correct as can be written, that will coalesce and bring the U.S. and its citizens to their knees; millions will perish. The United States will near its own destruction due to anger, hate, greed and an unquenchable lust of the elite for power.

The events will occur not because they need to, but because there are those who have forgotten the traditional ways of life and respect for the creator, whose only goals are control, power, wealth, and domination over the rest. You know who you are; it will be with finality that you witness your own, utter failure and demise.

In the end, while survivors may feel compassion, justice will be fulfilled – by the sword – the time for mercy has passed. If you are reading this, it is because it is through wisdom of Sun God, the Great Spirit, whether you call him by God, Adonai, Elohim, Yahweh, Allah, Brahman, Shangdi, or another name is irrelevant, for he who created us all is known to the faithful.

Despite your intentions to segregate and separate the people and to destroy the U.S., there are those among us – Wind Runner, Sky Thinker, G. Panther, Sun Bear, Walking Cloud and many others – who strive to reduce as much as possible the carnage that will soon befall this great nation, showing compassion to all who choose wisely. While a reprieve from the destruction is possible, it will not occur while racism remains the cry of the day from liberal fascists against those who would disagree with them and their ilk in control and because you fight against the Great Spirit. Listen well! The time to prepare is short — make haste. This is your final warning for Ωmega.

The locations mentioned herein are real, which are a part of the Sovereign Navajo Nation, other Native American Nations,

Prologue
The Mesa

Sun God and Monster Slayer peered down from Sun God's realm. Watching Tsosie and his son. Sun God had visited Tsosie many times and now, it was time to reveal himself to Tsosie's son.

"We need to begin the visit," Monster Slayer said. "I have judged the light of the people. The world becomes darker because the people no longer follow our way; they have been misled. We have reached the time in which the absence of light yields the authority to destroy that which you have created because the people have been blinded and corrupted through constant manipulation of the evil that governs."

"Yes, I agree," Sun God replied. "The lights of many have grown dim and they will pay the price, but many still glow bright; it is them we must save. It is not too late to turn others back to the path. Be patient for a little while longer. First, let us listen in on what our Medicine Man is telling the young leader on which the future rests for all."

Tsosie Yazzi was atop the mesa in the spot that had been so special to his father Totsoni, who had given up his life to become the mediator between this world and Sun God's realm. He came here often. It was now over four decades since the warning that a terrible time, when men and women would fail to keep the trust, would come, that

Wassaja, his grandfather, had predicted. Although they had kept and protected Sun God's Treasure, the time mentioned was at hand. He did not know precisely when but could feel it in his soul. As he gazed across Navajo Land, he began to speak to his son sitting next to him.

"The time that Wassaja, the Medicine Man, had spoken of has come my son. All the signs are appearing and coalescing. The U.S. and the world have passed through an extended period of economic growth, followed by a longer period of sluggish decline and now, of hateful division. As the years passed, the lower and middle classes have become accustomed to getting a little more; that is at an end. Our government is divided and inept, no longer able to manage the affairs of the people. While some feel guilty about being overly sympathetic to the lower classes, most have embraced greed and corruption as their master. Crime, corruption, immorality, mass murders, and shooting sprees continue to rise significantly from the top of the government to the lowest street criminal. There is increased rebellion and a separation of the young versus older generations to the point of labels, X-generation, Millennial's, E-generation, and others. And there has been a desertion of the learned ranks from the establishment due to politics because they no longer believe in the system or science. The indifference to politics by the general population has been accompanied by a loss of hope that has made it possible for small, well-organized elite groups to wield greater and greater influence and potentially take over, as Adolph Hitler did prior to WWII."

"But this has happened all my life father," Lusio said. "Isn't it just more politics than usual?"

"That is true my son, but do you remember your history?" Tsosie said. "In a way it is political, but far worse.

Politics have been the smoke and mirrors that have allowed us to reach our current state. The past has taught us that these signs preceded the American, French, Russian, and English (1642) revolutions, as well as the fall of the Roman Empire. All the signs we now see are perilously close to those events and others. There also has been a great reduction in the sanctity and dignity of the home and family. Taxes climb daily. Entertainment has become so vile, decadent, and violent that parents can no longer thwart the influence it has on their children. People of our time, rather than keep the promise of Sun God, seek money, fame, pleasure, and immorality. There is no concern for their neighbors. Why should there be when people do not know them? The U.S. and most countries constantly build their military and have at best weak leadership. There is a steady decay of responsibility at the personal level and a major decline in religious activity, excepting preaching politics at the pulpit. Further, no one is accountable; each blames another for the woes we now face."

"I have studied history all my life as you have taught me to." Lusio said. "This has been a constant thread in many countries. Is it somehow different today than it was yesterday or will be tomorrow?"

"It is," Tsosie responded, "I will tell you why. What I have just spoken are general trends as you have suggested but remember what Wassaja taught us. He said there were major signs that would signal the danger to the fifth world once more and for the last time. If you recall, these included increasing crime and lawlessness, which has become more and more prevalent among our government leaders who feel themselves above the law, as well as the people. The government and people in general have no concept of morality or of economic discipline. Our government has become an oppressive bureaucracy and there has been a continual decline in educational excellence, which started and that has continued since the "No Child Left Behind" act. In addition to that, the people have been deliberately divided by the government, which began with the former President and that has led to a substantial weakening of cultural foundations and preservations throughout the U.S. and the world. More importantly, there is gross immorality that has led to pure materialism and a decline in religious belief, as well as a significant effort to subvert it within our own government. Finally, we have reached a point where human life has been devalued and means nothing except as political talking points."

Lusio sat pondering what his father had said, staring across the vastness of Navajo Land. When Tsosie looked over at him, there were tears slowly trickling down his sons' cheeks. Lusio turned toward him.

"I know what you say is true father." Lusio said. "It is just that I do not want to believe it because that means I must face my own responsibilities, which are great."

"Yes," Tsosie said, "But you have been trained for this moment in time since before birth and you, more than anyone, including Wassaja, have been to Sun God's realm in preparation for your duties. Your task will not be easy, and we may all fail. In my heart, I know from where we are as a country, that millions will perish because they have and will continue to refuse the responsibility of their obligations; they are beyond help so dim has grown their light. In fact, most no longer have a clue as to what they were or should be. Come, let us prepare."

Night had fallen as Tsosie and Lusio readied themselves for what was about to happen. Next to a large boulder a short distance away, they built a small fire. Tsosie smoothed the earth and prepared an elaborate sand painting. It was one that Lusio had not seen before. The movements and symbols in the painting revolved counterclockwise in reminiscence of destruction rather than creation. The outer rim was a circle of turquoise on the outside and brown on the end, like a ribbon with a figure wearing a feathered headdress on the left and what appeared to be the world and the sun on the right. The inner part was as a tornado with four specific areas set apart by the same color lines as the outer figure, except the brown line was a bright red. Each end of the line in the four-part segment had a different kind of head on them that looked menacing and there were arrows, apparently having been dipped in blood that were placed strategically within the borders of the outer rim and four segments.

"I have not seen such a painting before," Lusio commented. "Why not? What is it for?"

"This is a special painting," Tsosie replied. "Only two that are living know it and it is shown to but few. It symbolizes destruction of the masses by Monster Slayer. The outer rim is Sun God's persona, all knowing and all encompassing. The inner segments are the four elements — earth, wind, fire, and water. The red color stands for Monster Slayer who will be loosed soon upon those who have lost their way and the red center is where he will begin. The people will be given but one more chance to prove themselves then, they are his to do with as he will. He will cleanse the inner vessel first. Is it not written in many religious beliefs, including our own?"

"Then," Lusio began, "this is to be a warning?"

"Oh, it is much more than a warning son," Tsosie replied. "This is a small depiction of what is about to happen. We cannot stop it; we can only help those who would follow the right path and more importantly, stop those who are and will continue to labor diligently to destroy our country. Many have called them the deep state, but they are far more insidious — more than you know."

Tsosie sat down, his back toward the boulder as Lusio sat to his left, beside him. For several minutes they had been chewing on peyote and each began to drift into a subconscious awareness of the spiritual side, away from this world. Tsosie slowly began to hum. Softly at first, which grew louder and turned into a chant. The chant was at first melancholy then, became ominous and foreboding. Both had slipped into that conscious state in which they could be fully aware.

As Tsosie chanted, a light, white mist began to cover the painting; slowly, imperceptibly, it changed to a light red that hovered over the sand painting. Instantly, a dual colored red and white column shot straight up to the heavens, so bright it looked like the midday sun around the two. As quickly as it had begun, the light changed to two personages who stood in front of and above them, in the air, their feet several feet above the ground — Sun God and Monster Slayer — about them was a white aura. The aura was so bright around the two that the only part of them visible were their faces, mostly their eyes. Sun God's eyes glowed a bright emerald green, Monster Slayers a dark, ruby red.

"We have been listening to what you have told Lusio," Sun God began. "Your words are true. The destruction you mention will be great for we know that most of the people will not change their path. Millions will be saved but many millions more will perish. The people have already chosen sides without realizing it."

"It will be so," Monster Slayer joined in. "The lights of many grow dim and I now have the authority to destroy them. However, I will let them do it themselves because their greed and lust require little help to complete the task."

"Lusio, Tsosie has been a faithful Medicine Man and has continued in their tradition," Sun God said. "Along with your mother Tara, as well as Audra and Musashi, you alone have been chosen by me to take on the responsibility that will help to save those who will remain in, or return to, the path. From this time forth, because of the important task forward, you will be known as Jeremy."

"Why must I change my name?" Lusio asked.

"Because it will be more acceptable by the White Eyes and it is that part of my people, the Earth Surface People, that you must help on a large scale," Sun God said.

"I understand," Jeremy said. "May I ask what the destruction is that you speak of?"

"I will tell you," Monster Slayer began. "When we created the fifth world, we knew that it would need to be saved first by protecting the gift, the treasure, which your father did admirably. While the protection of the gift was a trial for the first people and which they passed, the remaining peoples of the earth, also created by us, have had a different trial. The lights of the Earth Surface People grow dim. As to their destruction, they have brought it upon themselves."

"That destruction is quickly approaching," Sun God said. "The Holy People of the Navajo, such as Wassaja, Totsoni, and others gave to the Earth Surface People all the practical and ritual knowledge needed for their survival in this world and then, moved away to dwell in other realms above the earth, passing back and forth. Because of their continued interest and responsibilities in the day-to-day doings of the Earth Surface People, constant attention to ceremonies and taboos is necessary to stay in harmony with them. The condition of *hozoJin,* being in harmony with the supernatural powers — the two of us before you — is the single most important requirement that I have given the first people. Unfortunately, the Earth Surface People now make it impossible, due to their choices and the free agency I gave them, for that harmony to continue. It is, therefore, necessary to perform a cleansing so that the best of them can be saved."

"But you could just inspire them all couldn't you?" Jeremy asked.

"No!" Monster Slayer exclaimed. "That would remove their agency and responsibility and place it upon us. Therefore, the destruction of many is imminent. You asked what kind of destruction; it will be widespread. While I should personally destroy all and draw another line in the sand as I did with the Grand Canyon, the destruction of the Earth Surface People who will not return to the path will be uncompromising. They will face death from pestilence, natural disasters, animals, civil war, starvation, invasion, and myself. While I will destroy some, most have already destroyed themselves in a yet, future event. Unknowingly, the people have already chosen sides and soon, they must turn back to the path or die!"

"Let us plan the strategy," Sun God began. "It is time to put everything in motion and it will be many of your years in the making. There will be several key people that you will need to work with Jeremy. While you will have help along the way, you must develop and hold relationships with each for the time when they are needed. Some of these people include Sky Thinker's son, by the same name, Philip Weld, and General Jason Bardos, as well as others who will be made known to you."

Sun God continued as Jeremy listened intently about each individual he would need to cultivate a relationship with and hold it during the next two decades. After hours of discussion, they finished.

"I understand most of what you instructed," Jeremy said. "I also understand most of what I am assigned. For now, I have a question about one individual. Who is Philip Weld?"

"Philip Weld was foreordained by me to his future position with the Earth Surface People, like you to yours," Sun God said. "He is not aware of it and need not be for now. He has a big heart, is of strong spirit and body, and his intentions are commendable. In the terms of the Earth Surface People, he is a true patriot. To carry out your responsibilities, you will need someone in a position of authority so that preparations can be made to save those who will try to be saved in the physical and spiritual sense. Philip will become President of the United States. You must cultivate a strong bond and relationship with him!"

"Sun God wants to save as many as we can," Monster Slayer said. "Because of this, I will hold back my punishment for most, although many will endure my wrath. There is much to do that we will direct you on later. Think about what we have told you and ponder all these things. Time will pass quickly."

Sun God and Monster Slayer vanished, more quickly than they had come. Tsosie and Jeremy sat looking across smoldering embers of what had been their fire, across the mesa into a velvet, star-studded sky. Both were taking in what they had seen. After a while, Jeremy spoke. "There is so much to do father," Jeremy said. "How will I be able to do it all?"

"Tell me first, Tsosie began, "what you think needs to be done from listening to the Gods?"

"It is a foreboding task. As I understand it, I need to prepare millions of people for food shortages, natural hazards, pandemics, foreign invasion, economic collapse, power grid failure, civil unrest and civil war."

"That is about the size of it my son. But think not on how to prepare millions for it. They will make their own choices. You are preparing them for a continuity of life, of systems, of the best part of the people and government. You will not be able to protect them all. Most have already made their choices and they will end up where they may. Your job is to save as many as you can by helping them understand that their choices have consequences."

"Still, I do not know how I can accomplish it."

"There will be others to help you my son. It is what we are here to do and, as we protected Sun God's Treasure many years ago, so will we carry out his commands now. I will give you two scenarios; give me off-the-cuff answers about what you would do, assuming that you or those you work with will have the authority to make your decisions a reality."

"Okay," Jeremy said. "What is the first scenario?"

"You were told that we would be invaded by a foreign foe. If you were the invading force, would you drop nuclear weapons?"

"No! I would let some go off in the upper atmosphere so that communications would be destroyed and that my troops could then move in."

"Excellent, Tsosie said. "So, given that an EMP (electromagnetic pulse) from a nuclear blast in the atmosphere would damage most electronics, even some hardened military ones, what would you do to ensure that we would be able to communicate after the EMP?"

"Hmmmm, let me think," Jeremy paused. "I have it, the old communications technology using vacuum tubes would not be affected and if we could protect enough of the newer technology with Faraday cages, we would be able to continue good communications throughout hostilities of the invasion."

"That is correct and thus, you know what needs to start being done to ensure that aspect; in terms of war, establish a beachhead and communications. Here is scenario two. It is likely that for an invasion to occur that the enemy would wait until we are at our weakest, either through a large natural hazard, an economic collapse, or both, combined with a majority of our military being overseas or in armed civil war. How could you stop a foreign army without a large military force?"

"That would be exceedingly difficult, and I would hope we would have some sort of divine intervention if we were to have any chance at all. However, we would need to go to guerilla and asymmetric warfare and for that we would need to call in all militia's, assuming they would trust us, Sky Thinker and his trained sniper and warfare groups, as well as a person he knows that runs an STS Force, the Seminole Tribe and their transparency abilities, the Shadow Wolves of the Tohono O'odham tribe, Skin Walkers, and many other tribes and their warfare abilities. It would require tribes being united once again and cooperation with a special general of the White Eyes."

"That is the key," Tsosie responded. "You have the tools and the knowledge; the question is how to get what is needed done. For example, how will you unite the tribes?

Who will be our military strategist, and will he be able to work with a U.S. Army general?

"It is truly a daunting task," Jeremy said.

"Yes, and while there is ample time, you must begin at once. There is no time to lose. You begin your education at Harvard in a few months and it is there this fall, that you will meet Philip Weld. You must think about how to gain his trust. For now, it is time to begin working on all the related components for it will be twenty years from now when they will be needed; it will take that much time to prepare."

Four years had passed since that fateful night on the plateau with his father. Jeremy had done as Sun God had instructed and had through a quirk of fate, likely planned in his opinion, had not only developed a relationship with Philip or Phil as his friends called him, but had been his roommate the entire time at the Harvard. The two of them, under the tutelage of his father, Monster Slayer, and Sun God had developed a strategy that, if precisely followed would yield the needed results to save as many Earth Surface People as possible. But it was all up to Jeremy, to prove himself and perform his obligations. "Now, Jeremy mused, the real fun was about to begin." Another 15 years would pass before everything was in place.

Sky Thinker was sitting atop the plateau when Jeremy rode up. He was teaching long-range shooting to a dozen men. All had masks on so, it was impossible to identify who they were.

Most would call the training sniper training, but Sky Thinker did not like the term because he thought it was evil and presented the wrong perception among the less conservative. Sniper was a term based on killing rather than protection and thus, he preferred precision-sharpshooting. The goal of these trainees was to protect, not to kill even though they would need to. He was already preparing for that which was to come. Sky Thinker would be considered an unusual man by most. He was trained in all the fighting arts, yet he was a scholar, and spiritual as well. He had been trained by his father and had inherited his name because it was requisite for his calling and duties. Since birth he had been trained in guerilla and asymmetric warfare, military strategy, and martial arts. He had multiple black belts, was an expert with a knife, firearms, especially rifles, hand-to-hand combat, systems thinking, tracking, and various other skills. He had a bachelor's degree from the University of Arizona in psychology and had served as a Green Beret in the U.S. Army, conducting counter-insurgency operations in multiple Latin-American countries and in the Middle East.

To the men and women, he trained it seemed that he was everywhere and yet nowhere because he came and went at will. Many of his trainees thought he could vanish into thin air. Those who knew him, who were few, found him kind and compassionate. For those who did not, he was intense and cold — a matter-of-fact type of man who you intuitively knew was formidable and had zero tolerance for bullshit. At over six feet tall and very muscular, he was an intimidating figure. When he looked at you with his dark penetrating stare, it withered most and was, well, uncomfortable. Sky Thinker was all business and had no patience for small talk because he was about Sun God's business. Some called him a spiritual warrior. He was aware of Jeremy as he pulled up but continued to focus on training his men. He had already trained over 200 sharpshooters and his goal was to have at least 800 more for the time that was to come because, that is what Sun God had requested of him.

As Jeremy walked toward the firing line, he could not help but notice that Sky Thinker was in total command. No one moved or did anything without his watchful eye upon them. Jeremy did not know Sky Thinker very well but was aware of his reputation in physical combat and as what many would call a renaissance man. He had no reason to fear him or dislike him. They had met a few times and Sky Thinker had always been direct and friendly. Each of those times though, had only been in brief passing. Today would be different because Jeremy had been directed to meet and discuss future needs with this man, a true warrior if ever there was one. He could not help but wonder how much of what may come, that Sky Thinker was aware of.

"Good afternoon my brother," Jeremy said, extending his hand.

"Hello," Sky Thinker responded, shaking it with an iron grip. "What brings you out this way?"

"I'm not quite sure how to begin, can we speak a little more privately?" Jeremy asked.

"Certainly, just hold on one minute. Let me make an adjustment first," as he stepped up to a spotting scope.

"Number 2," Sky Thinker said. "Adjust up 1 and push 2 left (he paused a couple of seconds as the adjustment was being made). Send it!" He watched the round as it sought the target 1,500 meters away. "There, right on target. Keep up the good work. Number 1, take over for a while as I speak with our guest."

The two walked a short distance and had a seat upon a couple of smaller rocks jutting out of the ground. It was a nice feature in most of Navajo Land. One rarely needed a seat as there was always a rock to sit upon.

"How can I help you?" Sky Thinker asked.

"I'm not quite sure how to begin," Jeremy began, pondering for words. "I was instructed to come to you and discuss future needs about what I have been directed to do. I have been sent by Sun God and my father."

"Relax, I am aware. Monster Slayer instructed me on the basics."

Jeremy felt relieved that this warrior would not think he was nuts since many among his people did not believe in the ancient traditions and ways of the Navajo. Yet here before him sat a true warrior that was as enlightened as he, perhaps more.

"Then you know much of what I will ask of you," Jeremy said. "You are familiar with that which is to come in about 20 years and the fighting force you need to help develop? We must be able to work closely with the military and we also must help unite, especially the warriors, all the tribes so that we can stand as one against the invasion to come."

"I am aware of some of the major points but was told that you would give me greater detail."

"Okay," Jeremy said. "I'm not sure where to begin exactly, but here goes. From the timeframe I was given, we have 15-20 years to complete full preparations. It will require much effort from many people, all of whom need to understand the task at hand and be accountable."

"Let us cut to the chase," Sky Thinker interrupted. "I am a warrior and train warriors. From what I understand, foreign armies will invade this country. Is that correct?"

"Yes, that is correct."

"Then, what I need to know is do you know where the invasion will occur and if there is a location or multiple locations where a major land battle might occur?"

"I know both," Jeremy said drawing a map on the ground, which was a basic outline of the U.S., Canada, Latin America and the Atlantic and Pacific Oceans, emphasizing several land masses.

"The invasion will begin with these forces, as he pointed and continued to draw arrows on the map, the armed forces will be coming from this location and land here at these points. There will be two major groups. This will be the site of the major land battle."

"Where would you need my help?"

"The land battle will be the key. Although it is unlikely that we can keep them contained on the coast, once they cross here, pointing to the map on the ground, they will be at their most vulnerable point and will need to resupply and refuel. This is the best location to stop them. What I would need from you is a uniting of the tribes and your best shooters who know discretionary warfare, as well as guerilla and asymmetric tactics."

"Hmmmm," Sky Thinker mused. "This location is quite large, and shots would be further out than most of my shooters would be able to hit accurately; we would need to come up with a strategy for the overall defense. I know of only one man that could reach these targets from the locations you point out and he may be reluctant to become involved because he despises the government and politicians. Also, our rifles will be no match for tanks and armored vehicles."

"We have the latter covered, I hope. Regarding the other you mention, is he better skilled than you?" Jeremy asked.

"Who do you think trained me? I am the 'grasshopper', and he is the master. He is the best I know; his shooters are also. He lives and breathes this kind of scenario. He consistently shoots at two miles — one shot, one kill, and he and his force can consistently reach out to 1.7 miles, accurately. He is a brother and because of that, he will talk to you, but I would need to introduce you, else you may get shot as soon as you step onto his property. He trains not for the fun of it, but for just this scenario. He told me once that he has had a premonition all his life that this is his calling; I believe he is correct given our future circumstances. He's trained since he was small on the reservation where the Medicine Man of his tribe taught him to track and perform guerilla-warfare scenarios."

"Do you really think he could help, where you cannot?"

"Undeniably, for you see, his men are trained for the most adverse conditions. Not only can they shoot like hell, but they can remove sentries without a sound, and walk right into a crowded camp and sneak into tents where they will cut the enemies throat. But only one, simply to instill psychological fear in them. To make them so nervous and jumpy they never sleep, worrying that they could be next."

"Who is he?"

"He is called Lunadi, the short version. His name has a similar meaning to mine. It was given to him by his Medicine Man when he was a young boy as is their tribal custom. I would like to reiterate what I told you so that you clearly understand.

Lunadi's warriors are not just warriors, they are trained to be assassins thus, they train with great purpose in all fighting arts, survival, and camouflage. They can blend in anywhere, like a chameleon. If I did not know better, I would swear they are Kachina's. You must take care when you speak with him. He worked for the federal government and had great disdain, even a hatred, for their incompetence and stupidity. It comes from years of his being a heavy lifter. He did all the work, and they took all the credit. He finally quit as I understand it because the last couple of years all he thought of was how to kill all his colleagues and walk away."

"Do you think he could have done it? Get away with it I mean?"

"Most certainly. He would have left no evidence."

"Why do you think he didn't do it?"

"He told me once it was because they were not worth the gun powder it would take to blow their brains out, but I know better. He is a man of honor and the law and for now it is only the law and his beliefs that hold him and his force at bay. Thus, it is only Sun God's law *though shalt not kill* that saved his co-workers for we believe the same — there is no dignity in killing. Lunadi is a staunch believer in the constitution and has trained his STS Force for the time of which you speak. His has the gift of doling death, but only when Sun God releases him. His men will not waiver.

They will stare death in the face and do their duty. You know that I train warriors to fight and survive, right? Jeremy nodded. His warriors are trained simply not to kill without mercy, but to instill the greatest fear while doing so. He has trained them for when, as the White Eyes say, the shit hits the fan. At that time, he will unleash them, and he will welcome that day. It will be a time of economic collapse and armed civil war as you have described."

"Other than his combat skills, does he have other skills of value to us?" Jeremy asked.

"He is a complex individual but has the true gift of discernment of people and, he can see a decade ahead. I find it interesting that these plans are culminating now. I say that because Lunadi spoke at a military postgraduate school on the west coast around 2016, where he obtained a master's degree in international security studies. In that speech, he showed that Mexico would become a security buffer zone for the United States and that they would be more friends than allies; that two other specific countries would eventually establish military bases south of Mexico at Port Brito in Nicaragua and in Venezuela, as well as on the west coast of Canada and threaten our national security. With Mexico as a buffer, it would force the enemy to attack from the Pacific, Gulf, or Atlantic."

"Why do you think that speech was important?"

"Because my brother, the map you just drew on the ground is remarkably like the one he presented to the admiral, her aides and other officials. Hell, she was deputy director of National Intelligence (DDNI) and asked him if he had presented that to anyone else. She even invited him to speak with a new person in her office and get together to devise a more formal framework and added evidence to support what he had done. The new aid never called I am told. I suspect because they were envious and were certain Lunadi would somehow eclipse their knowledge and usurp their position, which he would have no interest in doing. Never underestimate the power of envy. Anyway, from what I could discern they were obviously baffled with what he had produced. The irony is that it has come true. Yet, they blew him off.

The real tragedy of the entire incident is that instead of them using his skills, other countries have sought him out. From teaching Presidential bodyguards in the Middle East, to training the sniper team for Turkey's Special Operations Police, to guerilla warfare to the military in El Salvador and other Latin American countries. Those people all love him and come back for more. Our own government pushed him out and he will have nothing to do with them, except to maybe kill them personally at will once the collapse happens. You see my brother, Lunadi is a three-dimensional thinker and teaches it to doctoral and other students; he is a polymath and is far above our plane in strategic thinking. He looks far out across a horizon, beyond that which we can see. And, you should know one more thing about him before you think about speaking with him in person. Although compassionate as a warrior, he has absolutely no empathy. If you make a poor decision, it is on you. Do you recall a couple of years back when about three dozen Hispanics, all illegal as it turned out, were gunned down in that shopping center in Texas by that lunatic shooter?"

"Of course, it made all the headlines," Jeremy said. "The anti-gun nuts came out in force."

"I will tell you what he remarked about it, and I quote," Sky Thinker said. "I guess when they came here to get all the free shit at taxpayers' expense that they were not counting on getting free lead!"

"That's a rather racist remark," Jeremy said. "I can see why the government pushed him out."

"No, it isn't racist if you consider the context," Sky Thinker said. "He is a minority and was married to a minority. It shows how much he believes in the law. If you break it, you pay. As he put it, those people made a conscious decision to come to the U.S. illegally, without legal paperwork, which is easy enough to get. In Lunadi's view, all decisions have a consequence and if they had not decided to come, they would still be alive. It is all about the law, but more importantly, about what is right and what is wrong. They made the decision to come and in doing so, they deliberately and knowingly broke the law. Thus, they were solely accountable for their actions. Of course, they just had no idea the consequences would be so dire. He has no empathy for people, regardless of race, culture, or gender who make poor decisions."

"I am not sure that we could work with him," Jeremy said. "He could be more trouble than we can deal with."

"I disagree," Sky Thinker said. "He is a brilliant strategist and totally unpredictable. That is why the government did not want him. They did, they just wanted to hide him away and take credit for his ideas. Let me ask you something. If you were shit on by your boss for twenty or so years, do you think it would change you?"

"Certainly," Jeremy replied. "I'd likely be beside myself."

"Then you have some appreciation for how he is the way he is. He and a colleague he works with constantly developed ideas and shared them with the government. From neural network analysis, increasing frequency of earthquakes, predicting mass human behavior, to reduction of the magnetic intensity of the earth's core and increasing problems with water, energy, and food security. They do, no, did all of this and every time they were correct and years ahead of others. They were questioned by military intelligence, the Strategic Air Command, Admirals, Colonels, and many others. What do you think happened?"

"I would assume their track record propelled them to a position of advising the decision makers."

"Quite the contrary. They were both ostracized, demeaned, and marginalized. Thinking back on it, Lunadi told me that a better approach would have been to make your bosses feel superior. He and his colleagues simply went too far in displaying their talents because they only wanted to help others. In going too far, they inspired fear, insecurity, and most of all, envy from their bosses — psychopathic narcissism — his opinion. So, instead of making their bosses appear more brilliant, they well, made them feel dumb, which they were. However, in doing so, it brought the wrath of the liboshits, as he calls them, down upon he and his colleague and they were swept under the rug. Unfortunately, they are the kind of people we need to pull our asses out of the coming fire. So, I'm not sure even if you begged if Lunadi and his group would help us."

"I only have a brief time to find out as I need to report to the President as soon as I can. You said his STS Force, what does that mean?"

"STS is an acronym for soft target suppression, which means to kill human targets. And his group is exceedingly good at it."

"I would like to talk to him, can you set up a meeting?" Jeremy asked.

"I can try, but will need to divulge a little of what you have told me if that is okay?" Sky Thinker asked. Also, you will need to go to him, he will not come to you."

"I understand; please set it up."

Congresswoman Susan Grisham of Michigan pulled her ringing cell phone from her pocket as she walked along the diagonal path in Ferris Park, two blocks northeast of the Michigan State Capitol. She cut across the grass and took a seat on a park bench facing the playground, Beacon soccer field behind her. Looking about and making sure she was alone, she answered.

"Hello,"

"You were chosen for a reason," the electronic voice said. "What is your progress?"

"I have planted the evidence and will lead authorities to it at the proper time."

"How incriminating is it?"

"It is a smoking gun and should tilt the congress to make the decision you wish."

"Good," the electronic voice stated. "We are counting on you and will tell you when."

Chosen for a reason my ass Susan was thinking. She got caught with her hand in the cookie jar, fucking an aid along with other allegations of federal fraud. No one knew, or so she thought, until one day, just like today, a voice, disguised electronically, called her on her cell. She often came to the park to think things out. They must have been watching or tracking her for the first call because she was exactly where she was this moment.

Tears began to roll down her cheeks. As a married woman she had cheated on her husband and fear of the outcome forced her to cooperate with these people, whoever they were. At first, for weeks she couldn't sleep. Then, she realized that she had something they wanted, and they would not divulge her indiscretions, which she was still doing. It wasn't every day you met a man hot after you with such a large manhood.

She pressed the cell phone against her lips, thinking back. As time passed, she had become accustomed to her newfound power and reveled in it, how she could coerce others to do her bidding. Her husband was none the wiser and these unknowns had not only made huge anonymous donations to her campaign for reelection they, had gotten her onto the speaking circuit, and she was quite the item in the news and on supporters' lips, as well as foes. She was an expert at treachery. More importantly, lots of money flowed in.

She couldn't help smiling and taking down a President she didn't like made it easier. Susan, like many other of the political class, rationalized that anything, even treason, was for the good of the people if it brought down the other party a notch or two and granted more control. So yes, she had come up with false evidence to plant against the President and have him removed from office. The Supreme Court was controlled by her people. They would make a mockery of the constitution in the trial, but in the end, they would side with congress because of the bribes, money or threats, and the President would be removed, rather quickly she gathered. She smiled even more in her lust for greater power and for something else, as she hit a number on her speed dial.

"Hey big rod, I need you. My office, twenty minutes."

It was a scorching summer day, pushing 100 degrees as their SUV pulled off the blacktop pavement and onto an old gravel road going west into what seemed a never-ending canyon; an isolated spot in southwest Colorado. The sparse grassland and cholla tree cactus quickly changed to rugged mountainous terrain, populated with juniper and cedar trees, over the next few miles. It was not much different from Navajo Land Jeremy thought as the vehicle, dust boiling up and obscuring it from behind, bumped its way down the road. What had been an open expanse was now ridges of rock and Juniper as he looked high above.

"You could probably keep people at bay with a good rifle here," Jeremy mused aloud, continuing to look up.

"Lunadi could keep an entire battalion at bay in this terrain," Sky Thinker said. "He already knows we are here."

The road began a sharp bend toward the left as Sky Thinker pressed the brakes and made a sharp right onto a spur road, directly in front of a small bridge with a white post on either side. It had a cable gate that had been lowered upon hearing their approach. As they started slowly across the bridge, a figure in a ghoulie suit appeared from seemingly nowhere directly beside them next to the driver-side window. Jeremy jumped, startled. All he could see was the man's eyes, dark and brooding, without expression as he stood close to the juniper tree from which he had emerged. Even standing close to the vehicle the man blended into the terrain around him.

He simply pointed and said, "Follow the road up about one mile. Do not turn off; do not stop or get out."

Sky Thinker nodded his head and tapped his left shoulder with his right hand in acknowledgement. Both noticed another similarly dressed man putting the cable back up and locking it as they started ahead.

"Damn," Jeremy remarked. "That guy scared the hell out of me."

"Get used to it," Sky Thinker responded. "They will be all along the path. Depending on their instructions some will be visible, others not."

The vehicle slowly crawled up the steep rocky road as it twisted and turned through the rugged terrain. Occasionally, a man dressed as the one at the gate would step to the edge of the road and point toward the direction they were going. Here and there, Jeremy and Sky Thinker could see others in the woods, barely visible to them and only because they were instructed to be so. Suddenly, Jeremy noticed two figures who were not camouflaged but wore brightly colored apparel, armed with sidearms and M4-carbines.

"That is odd," Jeremy said, pointing. "Look at those two. They are wearing brightly colored clothing but are barely visible."

"They are Seminole," Sky Thinker said. "The fiercest of all Indian warriors. They are from Lunadi's own tribe. They have worn the same battle dress for hundreds of years and fought the White Eyes in three wars. Andrew Jackson, the Indian hater, tried to drive them out of the Florida swamps to no avail; they never yielded or surrendered. They also never signed a peace treaty, only a cessation of hostilities agreement way back in 1962. Beware how you treat them. Do not offend Lunadi as I would like to return home. Just kidding, we will be fine, but mind your manners."

Jeremy nodded affirmatively as the SUV crawled up the hill. They had been going for about twenty minutes or so when they rounded a sharp bend and noticed a rifle range in the distance, high above the valley floor below. The road made a couple of sharper turns and they pulled into a small gravel clearing; there was a house off to the right. Standing on the open porch was Lunadi, who gave them a slight wave as he stood talking to whom Jeremy supposed were two more Seminole warriors. He abruptly walked out to greet them as Sky Thinker pulled the vehicle to a stop and they stepped out, approaching Lunadi.

"Greetings Sky Thinker," Lunadi called out. "You picked a nice warm day to visit. Who is this young man you have with you?"

"Lunadi, meet Jeremy," Sky Thinker said. "He is Navajo, son of Tsosie Yazzie."

"Ah, the Medicine Man's son," Lunadi mused, stretching forth his hand to shake theirs. "I have heard some of what you are doing. You will need to clue me in a little more so that I will know if I can be of help. For now, I need to go down and check on my group at the high-angle rifle course. Come, let us walk and talk."

"By high angle, do you mean shooting up or downhill at steep angles?" Jeremy asked.

"Precisely," Lunadi replied.

"So, I'm guessing that you would aim lower if shooting at such angles?"

"Well yes. You see, the exposure of the round or bullet to gravity is less when shooting up or down hill thus, the straight-line distance is shortened when the shooting angle is taken into effect. Sky Thinker, he is intuitive as you said, you must let me train him some."

"Yes, he is," Sky Thinker said. "And a quick learner."

"Tell me then," Lunadi said. "Why do you come so far to see me? How can I be of help to you both?"

Jeremy shot Sky Thinker a quick glance who nodded back as they walked through the Ponderosa Pines and Junipers. Jeremy was quickly thinking how to respond to the question. Then, it dawned on him to begin with a question of his own.

"Are you familiar with the legends of the Navajo and the turmoil that will occur in the fifth world as people lose their way with the Great Spirit?"

"Somewhat. Tell me more."

"One of the legends, which is true, because my father took part in it was the protection of Sun God's Treasure. The treasure was successfully protected so that Monster Slayer would not lay waste to the fifth world as he had previously to the first four. In a sense, we were able to have an extended reprieve. After the protection of the treasure, Sun God, whom you call the Great Spirit desired to save the White Eyes, the Earth Surface People, along with us, at least as many as will believe on him. Already that is looking grim. It has been made known to me that our future is dire. The lights that the Great Spirit gave to the people, individually, grow dimmer each day. If the lights grow too dim, we will all be destroyed. However, to test the people one last time so that all have a chance to redeem themselves, they will be required to fight for their lives by protecting the United States to determine if they are worthy to dwell with Sun God after the battles and threats have subsided. There will be invasions by foreign forces, and we will face a great many threats, which include earthquakes, floods, drought, famine and starvation on a mass scale, economic collapse, civil war, pandemics, EMP's, invasion, water shortage, terrorism, mass panic and hysteria, tsunami's, wildfires, solar flares, nuclear weapons, martial law, critical infrastructure failure on a wide scale, and the list goes on."

"One does not need to be visited by the Great Spirit to realize that these things are nearly upon us. I have attempted to warn many who do not listen. This includes the DDNI and various other high-ranking officials in the government. The narcissistic suck wipes rejected my research and advice. When I told them the country of Mexico would become a security buffer zone for the U.S., they ignored me. When I told them that global powers would build bases in Latin America to push a future offensive against us, I was ostracized and when I told U.S. NORTHCOM and STRATCOM leaders that the New Nicaragua Canal was a ruse for the purpose of China basing navy ships and military personnel in and around Lake Nicaragua and Brito on the west coast of that country, which would be their future staging areas, I was scoffed at. Whatever happens to them is therefore of little concern to me. They made their decision. I have made mine, which is never to work with those bastards again!"

As Lunadi spoke his temper rose and as it rose, his voice became louder and higher in pitch — if it were possible that acid could drip from a man's tongue — it was dripping, so bitter and vehement were his words. Jeremy suddenly realized he had touched a very raw nerve, but at the same time understood that here in front of him was a brilliant man who could put things together in a way he had not previously understood. He was astounded at Lunadi's comprehension of issues. It was uncanny that what he spoke was so remarkably close to what Jeremy had drawn on the map when he explained it to Sky Thinker. As they walked through the trees, Jeremy wondered if this man was in tune with the Great Spirit and if he was receiving visions by those from Sun God's realm, perhaps Sun God himself? "It seems that you have keen insight into the future," Jeremy said. "How did you arrive at your conclusions?"

"It's no dark secret," Lunadi replied. "Anyone with a brain should be able to put the scenario together. It is all part of a whole. The problem is the dunces in Washington have the IQ of a gnat. If you combine their collective brains, all 535 of them, into the rear end of a flea, they will roll around like a bb in a freight car. It is not my problem that they are unable to see that which is rapidly approaching; it will however, become their crisis. And I pay attention to our Medicine Man and elders. Let me tell you of a prophecy by one of our Wisdom Keepers, Buffalo Jim, who said "*The Creator made it so that Florida was shaped like the nose of a deer. One of these days soon the Creator will break the nose off the deer. Florida will break off and fall into the sea. Yes, you watch, it will happen. The time is just about here. Nothing can stop it. The people in Florida will all be dead.*"

It is not me that said that, but scientifically I can tell you it will happen due to a Tsunami from the east. It does not take a rocket scientist to put it together. I will miss the land when it is gone but will not miss the people who no longer regard that which is sacred and despise us, using imminent domain as a weapon to take our lands along with the lands of the poorer White Eyes. Should they wish to come here, this is my imminent domain — he held a rifle over his head as he walked that had been hanging from his shoulder — as for me, my men, and my friends, we will be pushed no further!"

With that, Lunadi fell silent. Sky Thinker did not know what to say and remained silent as well. As they fell silent, the sound of a light breeze as it flowed smoothly through the treetops fell softly upon their ears. Somehow, it had a calming effect on all three. Ahead of them, they could hear sporadic gunfire, which grew louder as they walked. Suddenly, rounding a bend in the trail, they found themselves overlooking a very steep canyon. Eight men were laying and sitting in teams in front of them, aiming rifles at distant targets that were barely visible with the naked eye. The shooters were dressed in blue jeans, hiking boots, and other casual wear. There was only one thing that stood out; all had on balaclava's so that only their eyes were visible.

Staring at the men, Lunadi could see that Jeremy was curious about the hoods on each of the men. Discerning what they were thinking, Lunadi spoke.

"Mine is a private school of survival. I teach who I will and whom I also vet. You are either invited or referred, there is no other way in. When you come here, your identity stays secret from all others. This keeps those from attending from naming classmates and keeps the White Eyes out of my business, which is to protect ourselves against their government. Excuse me please."

Lunadi began directing the shooters, correcting mistakes.

"I see what you mean about him," Jeremy said. "He may not be easily swayed to our course."

"You may be right," Sky Thinker responded. "However, he is more in tune than you think, and it depends on what you say and how you present it to him to get him to buy in."

The two began to watch Lunadi as he corrected his students and encouraged them. It was easy to see that he was a perfectionist and expected them to be as well, at least in the craft they were learning. He seemed the consummate teacher and despite his temperament, was compassionate.

"Number 3," Lunadi called out along the firing line. "You are hitting low, he was looking directly downrange through a spotting scope, watching the bullet trace as it flew along its trajectory, you must accurately range the target; up 1 and push left one-half."

A student had walked up and handed binoculars to the two visitors, "You'll need these to see the target clearly. It's below the ridge line directly in front of you."

"That's way out there," Jeremy said. "It's camouflaged and difficult to see. How far away is it?"

"I'd guess about 400 yards," Sky Thinker said.

"You have a keen eye my brother and are very close," the student responded. "I make it at a straight-line distance of 420 yards after shooting at it all morning. But, because of the steep angle is quite a bit further."

As they watched, the shooter made the directed adjustments on his scope turrets and fired. They could hear the metal clang as the bullet struck the AR-500 steel silhouette. They were impressed; a simple adjustment and the student was right on target.

"Remember," Lunadi explained as he unslung his rifle and

made minor adjustments to the turret knobs on his scope then, shouldered the rifle, "you need to be able to judge both distance and wind. If you can do that you can hit the target without fail and, you need to hit it from this distance while standing. Just accept the challenge and do it."

All the students watched as Lunadi assumed a standing position and leveled his rifle at the distant target.

"Can he hit it standing from this range?" Jeremy asked incredulously of the student next to him.

"Ummmm Hmmmm, watch. He is a master with his .338 Lapua Magnum."

The 420-yard shot seemed easy as Lunadi squeezed the trigger and the recoil from his rifle forced him back. About one-half second later, everyone heard the clang as a student yelled out, "direct hit center mass."

Lunadi, put the safety back on his rifle and re-slung it over his shoulder.

"Okay, gather round and let us discuss wind again. I will use an analogy. If we launch a rowboat across a river and wanted that boat to land exactly across from us on the far bank, we need to choose the best way to do that. Just as the rowboat is pushed by the current as it crosses the river, a bullet is pushed sideways by the wind. If you try to cross the river perpendicular to the flow of water, you will have the greatest force pushing on the side of the boat, except in our case, it is air pushing against the bullet. By the time you paddle your rowboat across the river, you will have been pushed downstream and will land, perhaps a long way past where you intended, no matter how hard you try. Thus, if you wish to land your boat on the opposite bank exactly across from your launch point, you must aim the boat upstream the proper amount so that the river's current pushes you toward your intended landing spot as you paddle across. This is exactly what you are doing in sharpshooting. You will launch the bullet into the wind, while compensating for the distance the bullet will be pushed or will drift, downwind from the target, for the time the bullet is in flight. And I need not remind you that in real battle, just as in this course, there are no windage flags so you must be able to accurately judge both wind speed and distance.

Additionally, you need to know the trajectories for four different calibers because battle is dynamic and unpredictable. As you are aware, these calibers are the 5.56x45 NATO, 7.62x51 NATO, 300 Winchester Magnum, and .338 Lapua Magnum. You will not always have time to fiddle with turret adjustments, so you need to move fast, think faster, and get accustomed to setting up on the run. We will talk about this later, on the mid, long, and extreme-range courses. For now, excellent job; go wash up for chow."

"You certainly made that shot look easy," Jeremy said.

"It just takes some good training and practice," Lunadi replied. "Sky Thinker can do it as well as I can. It's all about concentration."

"I'm not sure I could do it that well," Sky Thinker said, chuckling. "But that brings me to why we are here. There is something especially important that we need to discuss — in private."

"I understand and have been wondering what it is you seek," Lunadi said. "Let me get finished with today's courses and we'll sit beneath the stars later tonight; I will listen to what is on your mind."

Speaker of the House, Evelyn Rutledge, answered her phone. The electronic voice spoke softly.

"Our asset is in play. All is arranged as you required."
"Good, let's wait a while and I'll begin the show."

The meeting room was just another hotel room, although upscale, it served its purpose. The two men were out of their uniforms and had arrived discreetly at Sofitel Budapest the evening before. They had flown into two different airfields by private charter and driven over an hour to arrive. Checking in, they had been careful not to meet in the lobby where there were always prying eyes, listening ears, and cameras.

The two men could not look more different. One was almost a foot and a half shorter with black, graying hair, brown skin, slim and modestly dressed in business fashion. The other was well over six feet with white hair and very pale skin and dressed similarly. Their bodyguards had respectively checked the interior of the room prior to their arrival for electronic bugs and cameras and had given it the 'all clear' as the men had met in the middle, shaking hands.

"So, comrade," Li began, "I trust you had a pleasant journey?"
"I did," Panuftii Tyurin responded. "It was not bad, and I thought of our project throughout the trip."
The two men seated themselves so they could look across the Danube River, past the Széchenyi Chain Bridge, focusing on Buda Castle that overlooked Budapest. Panuftii, appeared a bit troubled.

"Do you ever have doubts about our planned project?" Panuftii asked. "Before you answer, look at the castle across the river. It reminds me of what we are going to attempt. Look at it, a multilayered building, preserving the traces of different centuries. Did you know it was first built by King Béla IV between 1247 and 1265? The oldest part of the present-day palace was constructed in the 14th century by Prince Stephen, Duke of Slavonia, the younger brother of King Louis I of Hungary. And now, we talk of instigating war. Let me remind you of what happened here. After the Battle of Mohács the medieval Kingdom of Hungary collapsed, and in 1541 Buda was occupied yet again by the Ottomans, who left the palace decaying. Eventually, it was partly used as barracks and a storage place and then, as stables. You catch my meaning? It was destroyed again in the great siege of 1686 when Buda was captured by allied Christian forces. In the heavy artillery bombardment, most of the castle and surrounding buildings collapsed and burned. In 1715 King Charles III ordered the demolition of the ruins. Time after time, that palace has been destroyed by one group after another until in 1791 it became the residence of the Habsburg Palatines of the Kingdom of Hungary. I think the last time it was fully destroyed was 1849 when the Hungarian revolutionary army of Artúr Görgey laid siege on Buda Castle. The Hungarians captured Buda with a great assault, but the palace completely burned. Finally, the last time it was rebuilt was in the mid-1850s."

"What is your point comrade?"

"My point is that palace is a small thing, yet many wanted it. And they kept attacking it, at very great cost until each of the conquerors obtained it. But what we're talking about is an entire country of vast expanse with many that will fight to their death to keep us from getting it."

"First, to answer your question, I have no doubts," Li replied. "Second, those who conquered that palace were not armed like we are."

"Still, what you are suggesting would appear madness, don't you agree?" Panuftii asked.

"I assure you, with our combined forces, waiting for the most opportunistic time, we will prevail."

Li unrolled a map on the coffee table in front of the sofa as they sat down to begin a basic-attack strategy upon the United States. Li Qiang was Shang Jinang, General of the Army of the People's Liberation Army Ground Force (PLAGF). A position equivalent to a four-star general in NATO. His career had spanned 30 years and if he were successful in this new venture, he would achieve the rank of Yi Jin Shang Jinang – First Class General, which rank had not been held in the People's Liberation Army since 1994. Throughout his career he had proven himself as a brilliant military strategist and logistician. He answered directly to the Minister of National Defense (MND) for this project and its feasibility. Qiang's position was one of raw power. He commanded The PLA with a ground force of 975,000 personnel, which accounted for almost half of the PLA's total manpower of around two million men. His ground forces were currently divided among five theatre commands stationed in China. In times of crisis, which he expected with the current project, his ground force would be reinforced by many reserve and paramilitary units. The PLAGF reserve component was about 510,000 personnel that were divided into 30 infantry and 12 anti-aircraft artillery (AAA) divisions. His infantry divisions alone could field 600,000-armed infantry. He was the go-to person for the Ministry of State Security as it began building up its technology, blue-water navy, and other military units. Recently he had overseen the establishment of two amphibious mechanized divisions in Nanjing and Guangzhou. Thanks to his strategies, 40 percent of PLA divisions and brigades were now mechanized or armored, almost double the percentage before 2015.

Although much of the PLA Ground Force had been reduced over the past few years at his suggestions, he had successfully led the charge in the rapid expansion of technology-intensive elements such as special operations forces (SOF), army aviation, surface-to-air missiles (SAMs), and electronic warfare units. It was he who had almost single handedly drafted the PLA's most recent operational doctrine of ground forces placing a much greater importance of information technology, electronic and information warfare, and long-range precision strikes in future warfare. He had watched the American's in Iraq, Iran, and Afghanistan and learned much from them. Older generation telephone and radio-based command, control, and communications, called C3 in the military, under his command, had almost all been replaced by his vision of an integrated battlefield information networks featuring local and wide-area networks (LAN and WAN), satellite communications, unmanned aerial vehicle (UAV)-based surveillance and reconnaissance systems, and mobile command and control centers. His was a carbon copy of those similar forces of the United States.

As part of military reforms, he had helped the MND create, for the first time, a separate headquarters for the ground forces. China's ground forces had never had their own headquarters until now and he was in charge. Before he was through, working with the MND, the navy, air force, and the newly renamed Rocket Force would report directly to him along with the Political Commissar. In the past ten years China's defense budget, thanks mostly to him, had increased three-fold. No, he was not concerned about the new project. He would plan and they would win!

Sitting directly across the small table from Li Qiang was a man no less his equal, Panuftii Tyurin, Chief of the

General Staff, Chief of the Army of the Russian Federation, who reported directly to the Minister of Defense (MoD) and the President. Russia, under Panu, as friends called him, had made recent steps towards modernization of the Armed Forces that was possible by Russia's economic resurgence based on oil and gas revenues as well a strengthening of its own domestic market and recently discovered gold reserves. And it was no secret that both China and Russia had been buying up global gold reserves to collapse the petrodollar. Panu was helping his President start a major equipment upgrade of their armed forces. Russia was currently spending about $200 billion U.S. dollars on the development and production of military equipment under the State Armament Program. This surge was a result initially of lessons learned during the August War in 2008 with Georgia. The State Armament Program, through the Prime Minister, announced that over $650 billion would be allocated to buy new hardware in the next decade. Panu was directing a growth of 70% of modern equipment in Russia's armed forces. Of course, he had admitted to the President that in some categories, the proportion of new weapon systems would reach 80% or even 100%. The Russian MoD planned to buy as many as 250 ICBMs, 800 aircraft, 1,200 helicopters, 44 submarines, 36 frigates, 28 corvettes, 18 cruisers, 24 destroyers, 6 aircraft carriers, and 62 air defense battalions. Naturally, several existing types would be upgraded.

In total, the Armed Forces received more than 30,000 units of new and modernized weapons and equipment, including more than 50 warships, 1,300 planes, over 1,800 drones, 4,700 tanks and armored combat vehicles. The Russian army also received, thanks to Panu's advice, 150-250 planes per year and over 300 short-range UAVs. Under his direction, Russia was also producing satellite-guided weapons, drones (including combat and kamikaze types and Quadro-copters), as well as electronic-warfare (EW) systems to counter them, cruise missiles, unmanned vehicles, exoskeletons and military robots and other military equipment. He had personally directed policy that allowed his armed forces, through support of the President, to adopt 35 types of weapons and military equipment and completed state tests of 21 more. The Russian MoD also had obtained the YeSU TZ (Yedinaya Sistema Upravleniya Takticheskogo Zvena) battlefield management system from Voronezh-based Sozvezdiye Concern. The YeSU TZ battlefield management system incorporates 11 subsystems that control artillery, electronic warfare systems, ground vehicles, air defense assets, engineering equipment, and coordination support, as well as other tasks. As if this build up were not enough, twelve missile regiments had been rearmed with Yars ICBMs, 10 missile brigades with Iskander tactical ballistic missile systems, 13 aviation regiments with MiG-31BM, Su-35S, Su-30SM, and Su-34 combat aircraft, three army aviation brigades and six helicopter regiments with Mi-28N and Ka-52 combat helicopters, 20 surface-to-air missile (SAM) regiments with S-400 Triumph SAM systems, 23 batteries with Pantsir-S self-propelled anti-aircraft gun-missile systems, and 17 batteries with Bal and Bastion mobile coastal defense missile systems [MCDMSs].

Two of America's enemies had and were continuing to arm themselves to the teeth. Even a middle-schooler could see that such an arms buildup was not defensive, but offensive in capability and intent. This buildup had not gone unnoticed by the U.S., NATO, and other allies. Frankly, it worried U.S. commanders and whether or not they could cope with the combined forces of these powerful enemies who had made an almost mirror-image duplicate of their own strategies and combat systems. Why not? They were the best. The irony is that many of them had attended U.S. military schools and cooperated in joint military exercises at U.S. military bases, RimPac, NATO, and others. The liberal elite in Washington had deliberately given the scepter of war away to enemies who were now planning to crush the U.S. If war did break out, it would not matter whose side one was on — millions would perish. There would be no winner, only losers. But those who lusted for power, control, and land were too arrogant and narcissistic to recognize it or to care.

The two generals had been planning the attack strategy for several hours and decided to take a break.

"I need to do some shopping and buy my wife a present," Panu said. "Come comrade, let us go see this street mall on Vaci u. It's only a few blocks south of us."

"Yes, I have heard it is quite good," Li replied. "Best of all, there are many people there so, we will be able to blend in." Li placed his map in a locked case. Then, the two men exited the room, leaving two guards behind as security, taking separate elevators down to the lobby.

It had been a long day at the range and survival course. Lunadi had taught the basics of the high-angle and mid-range (to about 800 yards) shooting courses, as well as emergency packs, fire, and water. Both Sky Thinker and Jeremy had watched all day, amazed at his skills. It was if he had been born with a knowledge of these things. The two had retired a short distance away deciding how to broach the purpose of their visit to him. He was just ending the class when they walked back to join him.

"I want to commend all of you for the effort you gave today," Lunadi said. "You did well. Tomorrow we will work on hand-to-hand combat and a knife-kill technique I developed called a 'pass by.' It is not difficult to learn but requires finesse."

"Where would we apply the technique?" a student asked.

"I will teach you tomorrow, but the short answer is in a crowded, public place. That is enough for now. Let us eat and retire so we can get an early start in the morning; 0600."

The entire group headed to the mess area. It was not much, just a few tables beneath a tarp. It was open and airy and best of all shaded, for which the men were grateful. A soft breeze helped cool them down. This was the first day of the course so, the food was already prepared for them. For each successive day, each student would prepare their own food, or they could choose one among them to prepare for all. The students chatted back and forth about the day's training. They were excited about what they had learned and were looking forward to the rest of the course. And why not, they had an expert instructor.

"They are excited," Jeremy said. "Are they always so excited?"

"Mostly," Lunadi replied. "These students are here for the second round of their training. All have been vetted and did well in their first course. And as I said, none are allowed to identify themselves to each other. It is the only way to keep prying eyes and ears out of my facility."

"Do you think that is necessary?" Sky Thinker asked. "You're not doing anything illegal."

"Yes, it is extremely necessary. I do not want any FBI or other government agents reporting back to their respective leaders. They perceive what I teach as a threat to them. It has always been so."

"Exactly what do you teach and what is your STS force?" Jeremy asked.

"It is simple to explain," Lunadi said. "I teach survival for all conditions, which includes six phases and forty separate training modules. Each time the students come they are trained in parts of three or four modules. It is difficult to take in at once, but important. The phases include all parts of survival from selecting shelter, building fire and treating water to hand-to-hand combat, knife fighting, guerilla warfare, counterinsurgency, asymmetric warfare, combat pistol, entry rifle, and extreme long-range shooting."

"That is quite a lot of training and impressive," Jeremy said. "What is the STS Force?"

"I do not discuss that with people, but since you are with Sky Thinker, I will briefly explain. One day and soon in my opinion, my force will be needed. We train not to kill, though we can do that proficiently, but to protect the underserved, those who cannot protect themselves, specifically the Tribes and those among the White Eyes who are deemed good people. I'm not talking about inner-city folks, but single mothers, tribal members and so forth."

"What does STS mean?"

"I will tell you, just as I did him, pointing to Sky Thinker, but you may not repeat it because it will give the wrong impression, especially to those, worthless as tits on a boar hog, Washington DC congress and senate idiots and liberal fascists. It means Soft Target Suppression. The military calls it soft target interdiction, but they refer to sniper fire for the most part at a distance; usually 1,000 yards or more. I refer to close-in combat and beyond. Our motto is *Death from Zero to 2,000 meters*. Every student you see here, waving his arm in an outward arc toward those seated around, are or will be an expert in dealing death within those distances, whether it be by hand, knife, pistol, rifle, bow, or other weapon. I have several that can deal death at 1.8 miles. Each student is trained to use every method of combat and to get extremely close to the enemy or, to operate at distance. They are my Death Commando's."

"You say that they will help protect others when they are needed?" Sky Thinker asked. "How will you call them?"

"It is all pre-arranged," Lunadi replied. "We have one simple verbal command that will be sent out to the commanders of the units who will then arrive here within 48 hours."

"But if you send that command can't it be intercepted by the NSA (National Security Agency) and de-ciphered in Salt Lake?" Jeremy asked.

"Yes, most certainly," Lunadi responded. "But it will do them no good because they cannot crack the code. Not even with their super-spy and listening facility in Utah."

"They are very good," Sky Thinker interrupted the conversation. "They intercept and decode everything. How can you keep them from decoding what you send?"

"To answer to your question, it is simple," Lunadi exclaimed! "You see, I used to work for the NSA. First, I am too small on the totem pole to make it worth their while. Second, I use a book cipher, what some refer to as a book code. It is a type of secret code that uses a quite common article, usually a book, as the key. All my commanders need to do is send the location codes that are needed to pinpoint specific words in a specific book; most of these books are rare and hard to find. If I use the same book over and over, NSA's super computers could possibly crack the code. To avoid that, I use up to 30 books.

One of the transmitted codes is the book number; each commander has all the books, scattered and with other than original book cover, so if you walked into all their homes, you would not notice they were the same books as in another commander's home. Thus, the book is the 'key' that is needed. Each commander has that key. If you do not have that key, you will be unable to crack the code. Most people that use a book cipher, transmit a message in groups of three numbers such as 14, 10, and 6. These are the coordinates that direct you to a specific word in the book. For example, the numbers I just gave would refer to page number, line number that you count from the first line, and the word number in that line. You could string together many sentences if you wanted to, but the more you do, the more opportunity there is to crack your code. You must be specific in choosing your book or books — they must be the same title and print edition. And, if you plan to send sentences, you need to choose a book that holds all the words that you need for your messages. Many people choose a dictionary, which I think is a mistake because if an agent breaks into your house, it would be a simple matter for him or her to compare the transmission with the words in the dictionary."

"But three numbers seem too simple," Jeremy said.

"And, you would be correct," Lunadi replied. "I also believe that which is why I use multiple books and, my code string is longer to denote two or more numbers in the string that are not used, i.e., they are dead. I send that by mixing a string of numbers so that the receiver knows which ones to ignore and where to begin."

"By doing this, could anyone crack your code?" Sky Thinker asked.

"I have not had one of my codes broken yet," Lunadi said proudly. "However, I send very brief messages and the code for marshalling my force is only two words, which I will not disclose. I also choose which key to use from a random number generator."

"I must say that is extraordinary," Jeremy said.

"I think it is just pragmatic," Lunadi replied.

"How many men are in your STS Force?" Sky Thinker asked.

"I have been building it for twenty years. Currently, these students round out the force to 1,000. In the STS Force are 10 commanders, each command one hundred men, although we do have a few women who are Peshawar and have significant combat experience. For each 100 men there are 10 leaders of a 10-member squad. They are loyal to me and will come when I request it, but that time has not yet arrived. They have been carefully chosen and all were taught by their mothers to obey the Great Spirit, Sun God as you refer to him, or they have a Christian upbringing. Thus, they are not blood thirsty, but will do what is required to protect all!"

"That is why we are here," Sky Thinker said, looking askance at Jeremy. "We would like to discuss it with you in private."

"Let's retire to a place where we can have complete privacy," Lunadi said. "But first, I need check on a few things and wash my face. Give me about 30 minutes."

Lunadi stood up and walked away, making a short waving motion with his hand. The two Seminole warriors they had noticed earlier, who always seemed no more than a few yards away from Lunadi, followed him to the front door, where he disappeared inside as the two warriors took positions on either side of the door.

The weather in Budapest was a balmy 81 degrees with a very light breeze from the northwest. The lobby of

Sofitel Budapest was unusual by American standards, it was sunken to street level with a surrounding upper level of lounges and restaurants that dropped down to the main level by wide chocolate colored, marble steps, directly toward the elevator. Across a white marble floor on red rugs, were deep brown and red chairs and sofas that were situated for guests and visitors to lounge about. It was in two of these, spread far apart across the lobby, that two CIA agents sat. They appeared to be casually reading a newspaper and magazine.

One of the agents noticed Li coming down the elevator, made of glass and gold, that afforded a clear view of the lobby area below. Li, no dummy when it came to surveillance tactics, carefully eyed the lobby and exited the elevator with his two-man entourage as the elevator abruptly went back up. The CIA agent at once, but slowly enough not to arouse suspicion, arose and began making his way toward the door that exited onto the street. He had his phone to his ear and spoke softly. Sam Malone was a CIA field officer; this was not his first rodeo.

"Dragon on his way," Sam said, glancing about and up. "Oh, Red Star coming down as well. Unsure of destination. Stay alert. Do not lose them."

Dragon and Red Star met up and climbed into a waiting car in front of the hotel. There was another car behind them with five men. The cars slid into traffic heading north on Apaczai Csere Street toward the chain bridge then, swung back south merging onto Jane Haning rkp. Two CIA vehicles were inconspicuously tailing them. The two generals had only gone about a half mile when the car turned left onto Március 15 tér heading east and abruptly stopped to let its passengers off at Váci utca, which was the start, heading back south, of one of Budapest's most popular street malls where only pedestrians were allowed.

"Yes,' Sam said, answering the phone. "I anticipated that they may go there as both have wives who want gifts from their journeys. Drop two agents and have them meet our other two agents just under the trees before the street mall begins. Use caution and spread out. Then, have the other four let off at the opposite end of the mall so they can do a waterfall. Remember, we are just to observe and discreetly take some photos. For this assignment, Sam had ensured that there were an equal number of men and women so they could team in pairs. After all, Budapest is a modern European tourist town and it would look more normal than two men or two women and thus, less likely to arouse suspicion.

Dragon and Red Star, along with six guards, went south along the mall in a loose box formation. They looked natural enough; only trained professionals would be able to penetrate to the primaries. And, unless you were seriously strapped, it would be an unwise move. It was time to report back, just a short message. A relay to Paris then, on to Washington over secure lines.

Austin Murray was director of operations for the CIA and if it involved intelligence and foreign affairs, he was immediately on it. His office was a few, short steps away from the Director Central Intelligence Agency (D/CIA). He was sitting at his desk when a soft knock came on the door.

"Enter," he said without looking up.

"We just received this sir, from Paris," his secretary said, placing one printed sheet on his desk as she looked at him quizzically.

"Thank you," Austin replied as she exited.

He picked up the paper.

It simply read, "Vacation going well. Picking up two books for you this afternoon. FRC."

Sitting back in his chair, Austin gazed at the ceiling. The two books meant Dragon and Red Star were meeting in person — they had done so in fact. The notation, FRC, disguised as initials, simply meant full report coming. It was something he, D/CIA, and the President only were aware of. For several years and these past few months especially, China and Russia had been building their forces far beyond anything needed for their respective country's defenses.

The bandits who belonged to the house of congress, had no clue and if Austin had anything to do with it, they would be kept in the dark since they could not keep a secret and they had a large list of names designated as traitors that seemed to grow each day. He often mused that several of his friends had been denied top secret clearances and were upstanding individuals yet, every congress critter had one and they ran their mouths constantly, especially the liberals. What an oxymoron. Anyway, back to the task at hand. There had been chatter here and there and while many had ignored it, the Triad as they called themselves had not. They had put three of their very best people on it, linking as much as they could to make sense out of what they assumed was the direction their enemies would take, while leaving room for flexibility. The chatter was beginning to leave a trail of breadcrumbs that the President already seemed privy to. He had told them that he had an insider and when the time was right, he would be revealed. Already, they had been preparing; it seemed odd in some ways but made sense in others. He picked up the phone.

"Stone,' Austin said bluntly.

"Yes Austin," D/CIA answered.

"It has started. A full report soon."

"Find me when you get it."

Concise and to the point, that was the D/CIA. A man of few words, all of which counted. Find me meant just that, no matter what, interrupt whatever was going on because of the importance of the matter.

The sun was beginning to set, casting an orange glow behind the two westward peaks about 20 miles away as Lunadi walked out the door carrying a small backpack. The two Seminole flanking behind him. Jeremy and Sky Thinker were still sitting at the table enjoying the views from 7,100 feet. They stood as he approached, the two warriors a scant three feet behind. Jeremy looked into their eyes. He was almost frozen, so intense and penetrating was their stare, as if they were looking right through him. His own people were easy going and though great warriors, these two were warriors always. There was no mistake, it is who they were. No wonder the Seminoles had the reputation for being the fiercest Indian warriors.

Although similarly dressed, they were quite different. Both wore mid-calf height moccasins that covered the bottom of buckskin colored leather pants. Jeremy guessed they were made from white-tailed deer hides. Other than the pants and moccasins, that is where the similarity ended. The one on the left, wore a multicolored, vertically striped shirt. Obviously handmade, it had a great many colors, but was predominantly red. The top of the warrior's hair was exposed above a red head wrap that ended just above the eyebrows. This was followed by black paint to the middle of his cheek bones that ran from ear to ear across his entire face. A similar band of black crossed his face, intersecting the bottom of his lower lip. Between the black stripes was a yellow stripe that traversed from the bottom of each ear to the other, intersecting the bottom of his nose. He wore two earrings that resembled drum tops made of metal. Under the top of his shirt was a bright blue scarf, covered with a short, red cape that draped to the bottom of his shoulder blades. The cape was held in the front by a crescent moon shaped, metal plate.

His shirt reached to the bottom of his front pockets. On the right hip was a small bag serving as a pouch, much like a messenger bag but smaller. It was deep red in color, trimmed in beads of yellow, with a floral designed, embroidered flap. The strap holding the bag was draped over the left shoulder. It was undoubtedly for shooting and survival supplies. Jeremy knew the old timers called it a 'possibles' bag. On the left hip the warrior wore a Bowie knife. In front his hand wrapped around the barrel of his rifle. It was as long as a black powder rifle almost, but modern. Jeremy was not familiar with it but knew instantly it was for extreme range.

The second warrior appeared to be the higher ranking one. He wore the same color and type head wrap and his shirt was of the same length, but a calico pattern, also predominantly red with a faded white, uniform pattern, geometric in shape. The shirt was trimmed with yellow frill where the sleeve attached to the shoulders and at the end of the cuff. Beneath the top of the shirt around the neck and shoulders was a buckskin cover. This warrior also wore a Bowie knife, but on the right; his shooting bag was on the left, black in color, trimmed with beads of green, also with an intricate floral pattern on the flap. Draped over his chest, he wore a large necklace composed of three, silver, quarter-moon shapes. Most interesting was his face paint. His chin was painted like feathers, but solid in a triangle tip ending at the lower lip. The triangle on his chin was trimmed in black. Beneath each nostril was a red stripe to the upper lip.

The arrow stripe ran right up the middle of his nose, between his eyes, with the tip of the arrow ending at the bottom of his head wrap. The gold arrow, as with the chin, was trimmed in black. Across his face, directly across the cheekbones, was a small black stripe joined by a white one about one-half inch wide followed by another narrow black stripe and a much wider red one, which, at the bottom, was trimmed with another narrow black stripe. The entire group of horizontal stripes were at least two inches wide from the bottom of his nose to just past halfway. He did not carry a long rifle, but an M-4 carbine cradled in his left arm. Their stares, unblinking and without emotion gave Sky Thinker and Jeremy a shudder. In some strange way it gave Jeremy more clues into Lunadi as a man.

Somehow, Lunadi sensed what they were feeling.

"Don't mind them," Lunadi said with a smile. "They will not harm you. By the way, your gaze gave you away as you stared at the long rifle. It is a Mark V Weatherby Tacmark in .338 Lapua Magnum. We customized it a little more and it is quite capable of shooting 2,000 plus yards."

"Are they part of your students?" Sky Thinker asked.

"Yes, but they work with me alone. I train them and they train my people. They are the best of my best. Come, this way."

They walked in the same direction they had that morning, but to the left of the high-angle course. After a short while, Lunadi motioned to the two warriors, pointing in two places. They stopped momentarily and he pulled a couple of bottles of water from his backpack along with a sack of pemican balls and handed them to the two warriors. The three nodded to each other politely and Jeremy turned back down the trail.

"No one passes," he said; the warriors nodded again in understanding.

They walked another ten minutes, coming to a rock outcropping that dropped into a ravine several hundred feet below. They could see the valley floor a couple of miles away. The small clearing had a ring of rocks in the middle and Lunadi quickly started a small fire. The faint glow from the setting sun was barely visible in the western sky as darkness settled. Above them, the sky was like silk, black as velvet, studded with millions of stars that were not visible in the city. They were spectacular. There was no sound except nature. It was so calm and peaceful that it was surreal, much like Navajo Land. They sat about the fire, but Lunadi kept his gaze in the distance.

"Why do you look so far off instead of at the fire?" Jeremy asked.

"It's a habit," Lunadi said. "Due to security; it keeps my night vision adjusted so that if something happened, I wouldn't be blind to the trouble."

"I understand," Jeremy replied. "Now that we are in private, I'd like to tell you why we are here. We came to enlist your help for what is likely to be one hell of a land battle and I have been told that we will be short of troops when it occurs. What we would need from you is, under your direction of course and working with others, to get the men you have trained to fight with us."

"Hmmmm, and just who would I be fighting for?"

"You would be fighting to save our people and our country. This would also require working with a general and his staff."

"I assume this general is a White Eyes?"

"Yes, but he is not like the rest."

"That is what they all say and like the news, it is always all lies with just enough truth to get suckers to buy in," Lunadi spoke softly, gazing off into the distance as he paused. The silence grew uncomfortable; as Jeremy and Sky Thinker looked at each other, the gap in the reply grew interminably. "I will not work with the White Eyes. For more than two decades they treated me like garbage until they needed something done, which they were incapable of doing. They are evil, especially the liberals who lie about everything and unfortunately it is they who control every government agency, every corporation, and every university. If they all died tomorrow it would not be too soon. Nothing of value comes from working with such people."

Jeremy was at a loss for words. As Lunadi had spoken, he continued to look across the distance, his voice growing softer. Then, he looked directly at both. Jeremy felt a chill go up his spine because the look was one of pure hatred toward those whom he had spoken about. He was not sure if he could convince the man that sat across from him to fight with them and knew that if he could not, failure was inevitable. He was saying a silent prayer to Sun God for help.

"I do not pretend to know how you must feel given the way that they treated you," Jeremy began. "But this battle and the strategy for it means our very lives."

"I know the battle of which you speak," Lunadi said as he smoothed the soil and began to draw a map of the U.S. and Latin America. "The battle will happen here. The enemy forces will stage and mobilize from here and here. I saw this ten years ago; it is how the dynamics are shifting. We will be stripped of men due to a war here and these enemies will launch an attack that we cannot initially repel."

Jeremy and Sky Thinker watched as he drew the map. It was detail for detail what they had talked about. They could not understand how Lunadi was able to possibly know such detailed information so long ago and Jeremy again wondered if Sun God or one of his Kachina's had visited him.

"How is it that you know of this?" Sky Thinker asked, reading Jeremy's look. "This was divulged to Jeremy by Sun God. Again how?"

"I am not privy to that which you allude, but I have a knack for putting things together. Everything relates — economics, science, war, supply lines, security, environment, all of it through interdependencies. It is not difficult to envision what may happen."

"Then, if you know this, you need to work with us," Jeremy blurted out. "You already have a knowledge of what is needed for us to be successful."

"Perhaps, but I have already given those parts to the admirals and their staff about the staging areas. For you see, the new Nicaragua canal wasn't ever meant to be finished, it was only a ruse for China to get a long-term lease with that country so that they could accomplish this very task. Before you ask, I will tell you. I first began seeing signs and put some comments together I had heard while teaching some Chinese officers and regular soldiers martial arts. It was on my mind since then and that is how I pieced it together. It was years ago, but the Chinese do not think in such short term as Americans. I was working with some scientists in Beijing on water issues, particularly their groundwater-pollution problems. One of the people at the meeting and workshops was a major who introduced me to another major from the Central Security Bureau, also called Unit 8341 or The Central Guard Unit, which is the chief security detail responsible for the security of senior Chinese government officials, Communist Party, and military leaders. They are a military bureau. And, like most things in China, are old. They were first activated in 1949, in Xibaipo, Hebei. What interested me was that this bureau is a completely independent PLA security regiment that does not report to the Beijing Military Region. Instead, they report directly to the People's Liberation Army General Staff Headquarters and are commanded by a Brigadier General of the People's Armed Police. Anyway, the major thought I was Mongolian since I was so dark from, by then, weeks in the summer sun. So, he began speaking Mandarin to me. My language skills were not so great. Long story short, he found out I was Native American and that I loved martial arts.

He naturally invited me to teach some of his officers and enlistees the type of martial arts I use in combat. To me it was more fun than sightseeing so, I taught about twenty men for a month, every evening and all day on the weekends. They were getting rather good too. We had a blast. In retrospect, it is something I should not have done, and I know some of the three-letter agencies knew or found out, which I do not care about. But I picked up information here and there while I taught them, mostly because my understanding of the language was much better than my speaking. So yes, I know of this plan. I presented it and my strategy was rejected. Had they listened; they could be better prepared. If they would listen now, they could still succeed, but politics, power, and control is their only interest. Why should I help these idiots?"

"This is exactly why we need you," Jeremy pleaded.

"Unless you are the Great Spirit, you may not tell a wall to get up and move three feet. These people are the same, you can tell them nothing because they already know all."

"My brother," Sky Thinker began, "it is for our people. Do not think of the White Eyes, but about us I beg you."

"There are few of our people who are unable to care for themselves. Those that are not able are the same as the White Eyes, worthless politicians. They are beyond help. I will not help you unless the Great Spirit himself stands in front of me and commands me; not much chance of that happening! Here, as he passed retrieved water bottles and pemican balls from his pack."

They were no longer comfortable looking at each other as they gazed across the valley, which was now well lit from a full moon that had risen while they talked. The two visitors were obviously subdued as they munched on their pemican.

The fire had burned down, giving off just enough light that they could see each other clearly. Lunadi was looking up toward the moon, which seemed to be getting brighter. Suddenly, he realized it was not the moon. Two large columns, one bright white, the other red, shot straight down and then away from them across the valley floor. Sky Thinker and Jeremy caught Lunadi's gaze and tracked the columns, which now made separate outward arches, first away and then back toward themselves. The two columns met again and were coming straight at them, having formed a shape resembling the heart. The speed was so fast that they did not have time to move and were about to jump out of the way when the columns shot straight toward the fire and stopped right in front of them, each column opening into a portal with a figure standing in it.

The portals merged quickly together into an even larger portal circled by a ring of blue flame, which crept past them forming the shape of an alcove. Both personages now standing directly in front of them had dark hair. One had green eyes and a blue painted face, from the bottom of his chin to the top of his cheek bones. The other had a black painted face in the same area with ruby eyes. Both figures wore turquoises head pieces. The three men looked in awe at the two figures standing off the ground in the portal entrance, about 40 feet in diameter. They could see past the figures as if looking into another world. It was indescribably beautiful, filled with wonderful flowers, gold pathways, and luminous light. Directly behind the personages stood vast columns of warriors. All aligned in perfect order. Suddenly, the portal settled over the three men like the end of a tube. They were looking around into a new world but could not take their eyes off the two personages.

The personage on the right spoke.

"I am Monster Slayer," he began. "I formed you before this world was. These are my warriors, waving his hand in the direction behind and all around them, the time has come for that which is to be, they will be of assistance to you. Hear and heed now Sun God."

"I am Sun God. Many call me by other names. Whether it be by The Great Spirit, Yahweh, Zeus, Jóhonaa'éí, Napioa, Tawa, Elohim, Allah, Ra, or other, it matters not for I am he. The time for war is close at hand. It is up to you all to help as many as will be helped. The Navajo have passed their test. The accountability falls upon you three and those who will help. This is my nation, and it will be swept. Save all that you can. You will receive no assistance from us until you have done all that you can do."

"Lunadi," Monster Slayer said. "You have a great hatred for the White Eyes, which is not without merit. I trained you in the life before this one. You were the greatest among all here. Do you not recognize them? It is you who trained all of these, waving his hand at those behind him, that you see under my direction."

Lunadi suddenly had his eyes opened, like a veil had been lifted, he recognized those warriors surrounding them on all sides in perfect columns. The warriors were smiling at him as he recognized each one, all of whom he had trained in his life before this one. An imperceptible tear rolled down his cheek as memories from the past flooded back. He did not know how, but they had been locked in his life in this realm. His heart felt like bursting as he was overwhelmed by the spirit of those he was gazing at.

"You must fulfill your responsibility and as you stated to Sky Thinker and Jeremy before we arrived, I command you to do so. You will give all your aid to this effort. Listen to your two brothers. It is because of Jeremy's silent prayer that we are here. It will be your force that will save all if such can be done. This I command you. If you will do all you can, I will protect your force." As Monster Slayer talked, Sky Thinker and Jeremy looked on in awe. They realized they would no longer need to convince Lunadi.

"Lunadi, my son," Sun God spoke. "You must rid yourself of hate and bitterness; you have such great compassion. Much more energy is consumed in hatred than required for love. Are you not here on this land training others because you received a premonition from me to purchase it and do so? Do you not remember Dallas Whitworth, Jeffrey Greene, and Edmund Parks? They were my servants. They told you that you were one of Sun God's chosen. You are. Do that which you know is right so that I need not chastise you."

With that, Sun God vanished, leaving Monster Slayer with the warriors around him. Monster Slayer stood, gazing intensely at Lunadi and then the others. It was not a harsh stare, but one of understanding, of compassion, almost gentle, but penetrating.

"You three have been called for a great purpose," Monster Slayer said. "Many millions are about to die, but through your efforts, millions of others can be saved. They have all made their choices, but those who will stand, and fight will need your help. Lunadi, you have a great force and an even bigger heart, though you deny it. They are the best trained of all in this realm. It is time to call them. Jeremy, continue working with the President. Sky Thinker, your role is to rally the tribes; all of them. Finally, Lunadi, look to your feelings and be accepting of the White Eyes general, whom you will work side by side with. He was, like you, created by me in the worlds before this one. You are great warriors both. The time is now upon you for final preparations."

Suddenly, Sun God reappeared beside Monster Slayer. "Lunadi, rise." Lunadi stood and as he did so, Sun God waved his hand slightly, projecting a soft beam of light across his head and shoulders. "You have your final anointing. Do you not remember that you have often prayed, asking my permission to 'get to gettin' as you call it and to destroy those you consider enemies of this chosen land? That time has come. War is upon us; now, my enemies are your enemies, and your enemies are my enemies. I command you to spare no enemy of mine and have no empathy. Before the start of final hostilities, we will send you the War Gods Ahayuta and Achi. They will help with the final strategy. Fulfill your duties!"

Sun God vanished again.

Lunadi realized this was not a request and his body sagged in complete subservience. He would finally be able to strike back at those who had destroyed and were still destroying the country and the Tribes.

"I do not desire to destroy this world, which is my right," Monster Slayer said. "Fulfill your duties and work together so that I do not need to." The warriors all around them waved at Lunadi, smiles on their faces.

As suddenly as they had come, they were gone. The portal closed, leaving the moon-bathed landscape in its place. The embers of the fire glowed red beneath the star-studded sky. For some reason, their bodies felt weakened as they sat gathering their thoughts. Sky Thinker was first to speak.

"We have our duties and must carry them out. We will leave early in the morning and begin strategic preparations. We must stay in contact with each other. Thus, we will use Lunadi's book codes to do so. Agreed?"

They all nodded their heads.

"I will be going back to meet with the President, behind the scenes as always," Jeremy said. "I will speak with him about the general commanding the last battle area and request a meeting between all of us."

"I will summon the commanders of my force," Lunadi said.

They sat for a long while, without speaking, contemplating what they had seen. There was no energy for other than that. The night sky was glorious as they each thought about what was ahead. After a few hours, strength returned to their bodies and they slowly walked back to the compound. No sooner than their heads hit the pillows than they were asleep. Dawn arrived quickly. The men in the compound had already dressed and were eating as the three quickly met, exchanged goodbyes, and Sky Thinker and Jeremy headed to the canyon below and out to the highway. There was much to do. Lunadi spent the early part of the morning with the students training on the high angle shooting range.

Once things were well in hand, he walked back to his home, selected a small book and put it in a bag, then made his way about one-half mile beyond the compound, entering a small, camouflaged hut that no one knew was there. The hut was solar powered with a bank of batteries that kept it ready. He turned on the small LED light then, his HF radio and other equipment. While it was warming up, he took out his book and wrote a string of ten, five-letter groups. His message would be short. Once his message was composed, he pulled his J-38 telegraph key, of WWII vintage, closer to him and began calling another operator in Morse code, repeating his call sign multiple times:

_._. _ _._ _._. _ _._ _._. _ _._ _·· · ··· _ ·_ _ _ _ ··· ··· _ ·_ _
_ _ ···

··· _ ·_ _ _ _ ··· _·_

CQ CQ CQ DE ST1S ST1S ST1S K
Calling, calling, calling from Sierra Tango 1 Sierra; Sierra Tango 1 Sierra; Sierra Tango 1 Sierra; end of transmission. Lunadi repeated this several times, waiting a brief interval between each repetition. Within two minutes a reply came back:

ST1S DE FD2A FD2A FD2A K
Sierra Tango 1 Sierra this is Foxtrot Delta 2 Alpha; Foxtrot Delta 2 Alpha; Foxtrot Delta 2 Alpha; end of transmission.

Certain that they were connected, Lunadi transmitted his message to Foxtrot Delta 2 Alpha. Then signed out, turned off his equipment, closed the hut, and headed back to the training area.

FD2A pulled out his call list comprised of ten individuals, the commanders of STS Force then, transmitted the message he had just received. Within a few minutes all ten had received and translated it:

Alas Omega!

CHAPTER 1

Future President

Jeremy thought back twenty years before. It had been a cool spring day in April, late afternoon when Philip Weld walked into his dormitory room on the third floor of Canaday Hall on Harvard Campus. Phil as his friends called him, had spent the morning in the HLS Library reviewing constitutional law cases. As he entered the room, he quickly shut the door, startled to see his roommate Jeremy meditating, floating about two feet in the air. He had seen it once before and thought he was going crazy, but this time, he was sure he was not.

"Damn," Phil said. "That freaks me out. Why do you do that and how the hell are you able to thwart the laws of physics?

"Because I can and because you need to learn to trust me," Jeremy said. "As for the laws of physics, it's just energy-wave manipulation."

"You know I trust you," Phil said.

"Yes, you do," Jeremy replied. "However, your trust is only to an extent. It will become especially important about twenty years from now when you become President of the United States."

Phil did not move as he stared directly into Jeremy's eyes, which normally brown, glowed blue green. He was not sure how to respond and became apprehensive as

Jeremy slowly descended to the rug on the floor then, stood. "Do you expect me to believe that you have a crystal ball?" Phil asked. "Or are you just feeding me a line of crap?"

"I have neither," Jeremy said. "I am in tune with the desires of Sun God for it is one of my purposes in this life."

"Okay, time for a test smart ass," Phil responded. "If you're so in tune, what have I been up to today?"

"Do you really think that will be a test for me?" Jeremy asked, without waiting for Phil's response. "I know exactly what you did. You arose at 6:00 a.m. as is your custom, ate a quick snack, worked out for an hour, attended the law seminar you discussed with me yesterday and then, went to study in the HLS Library."

"Anyone could guess that, especially you since you know my routine," Phil said. "You're so smart, what did I do in the library?"

"You reviewed constitutional law," Jeremy said, as he sat then, slowly gazed up at the ceiling. Phil looked up too, wondering what Jeremy saw, but did not see anything.

"Although you reviewed several cases," Jeremy continued, "Only one really stuck out to you and you have the same feeling about it that many others have had, because it is what liberals always bash conservatives with when they want to appoint another supreme court justice."

"What case?" Phil asked.

"Roe v Wade," Jeremy replied.

"How the hell do you know that?"

"You believe as do many others that if enough conservatives served on the supreme court that the case will be overturned. But you see, that will not happen. Why? First, because Supreme Court Justices do not typically go over old cases and overturn previous justice's decisions. That almost never happens. It has always been a scare tactic of the liberals who are takers, not givers. In this case you are looking at essentially the Ninth and Fourteenth Amendments. No case has been overruled for the Ninth amendment and only two for the Fourteenth, which is typically where Roe v Wade would fall. I find it interesting that the Fourteenth Amendment to the United States Constitution was adopted in 1868 as one of the Reconstruction Amendments. I wonder what happened to Indian rights in that process. It is one of the most consequential amendments and addresses citizenship rights and equal protection under the law. It was originally proposed in response to issues related to former slaves following the Civil War. The amendment, particularly its first section, is one of the most litigated parts of the Constitution, forming the basis for landmark decisions such as Brown v. Board of Education regarding racial segregation, Roe v. Wade regarding abortion, Bush v. Gore regarding the 2000 Presidential election, and Obergefell v. Hodges regarding same-sex marriage.

The amendment limits the actions of all state and local officials, including those acting on behalf of such an official. And, like I said, and perhaps more importantly, the justices decide the law and whether you believe it or not, follow the constitution rather strictly most times, despite their political leanings. The crucial point about Roe v Wade and why they will not overturn it is because to do so would remove the choice or agency and therefore the accountability, of the individual deciding to have an abortion. That is something the individual must decide and not the courts. They are in line with Sun God on that though they don't know that and thus, the law will remain as it is, if for no other reason than the justices know what is means to be accountable. Not to mention the fact that our government and people have been tending left and will continue to do so until our Constitution hangs by a thread and they will have packed the courts for more control to gain a one-party rule."

"How do you know me that well?" Phil stammered.

"How do you think a poor Native American can room with you at Harvard?" Jeremy asked. "It is one of my assignments and I have been shown your spirit. I have been waiting a while to tell you this. Now, we can have much more enlightening conversations moving forward. If you trust me enough, I will tell you all I know. In return, you must tell no one what we discuss because your future and that of the nation depends on it!"

"There is something quite different about you and it's definitely not what I expected from a Native American. "

"Then, let me enlighten you."

Jeremy began to explain the beliefs of the Navajo and other Tribes, from as far back as he could recall history. This included various battles of the U.S. Army with the Indians, including Custer's fall at Little Big Horn, the fifth world responsibility given to the Navajo and that which was to come that was the responsibility of the Earth Surface People.

"Philip, are you familiar with the Pueblo Revolt of 1680?

"No, I've never heard of it. Why is it important?"

"Let me tell you about it. In the beginning of the 17th Century, Spain controlled what is now the Southwest United States. The Spanish were brutal and forced the Pueblo to give up their religion. It is akin to the comments a past President made about Americans clinging to their religion and guns. The difference is that the Spanish enforced their rule with the sword. The Indians were primarily agriculturists and were subjected to Spanish economic and religious pressures.

Bernardo López, Spanish Governor of the area around 1659, required that various Pueblos give him salt, hides, and piñion nuts so he could resell them to fill his coffers. His Jesuit priests, servants of the Black Pope and essentially the right hand of Satan, invaded Indian kivas and flogged Indians who continued to practice their own religious beliefs such as dancing with formal ceremonial costumes, as well as masks of the Kachina Spirit belief. The Indians became virtual slaves of the Spanish, who flocked mostly to the Santa Fé area, with several thousand of them by the 1660s compared to ten times as many Indians. It was about this time that droughts became more prevalent in the west and that caused Apaches, Navajos, and Utes to raid the Pueblos.

The Spanish had promised to protect the Pueblos, yet six Pueblos had been destroyed, however, the Spanish still wanted their ill-gotten gain. Despite all this, the Pueblos remained patient, as religious persecution and greed of the invaders constantly increased. The Pueblos were not very friendly to each other, but they set aside their mutual hostility to cooperate and drive the Spanish out. They began talking to each other for a few years. Meanwhile, a new governor had assumed leadership from Spain, Antonio de Otermin. His rule became even more oppressive. He was warned of the consequences of poor governance. Yet, being the quintessential psychopathic narcissist, as is 99 percent of politicians, he ignored the warnings, believing that he could control any uprising that the Pueblos could throw at him. And, as is always the case, he was dead wrong. On August 10, 1680, the Pueblo revolt began when Jesuit priests murdered the well-respected Shaman Tesuque. It was the straw that broke the camel's back — the final limit.

The anger and ferocity of the Indians spread as fast as a wildfire pushed by high winds. They killed 21 Jesuits and 375 settlers. All around the area, the foreigners fled to Santa Fé. Otermin and his commanders were sure they had the uprising under control. They were wrong for you see, Indians had practiced guerrilla and asymmetric warfare for eons before the White Eyes showed up and even today, we are taught by our Medicine Men these tactics. What did the Pueblos do? They cut the towns water supply, forcing the remaining Spaniards to retreat to El Paso. The Indians were once again their own rulers."

"Why do you consider this important?" Philip asked.

"It is important because it relates to our day," Jeremy replied. "For you see, the governance of the Spaniards is like ours today. Our elitist government rulers have taken over everything, which has forced the working class and many others into a survival mode, and it will worsen with time. Both parents are forced to work two jobs and have almost no disposable income. Just as with the Pueblo's; as then, so today there is little hope. Do you remember a few Presidents ago, what was promised?"

"Yes, it was hope and change."

"That's right, but instead the working class received misery and despair as healthcare, allowed by those who sat at the table, drug manufacturers and insurance providers instead of health workers and doctors, to greatly increase the cost of it. The result was that our young men and women, most working at minimum wage jobs, had to take up the slack for those who would not work. Most of these young people, because of their financial situations ended up enrolling in Medicaid. And, it has gotten so much worse as these elitist push climate change, green revolution, seek to impeach their enemies, and other dark deeds. They use these issues as a ruse for their lust for more control and more power and to fill their coffers with money at slave wages from the working class. And because they know only how to take, not how to build."

"I still don't get your point."

"Let me ask you a question," Jeremy said. "Whose side are you on, the basic working class that made our country or the side of the elite politicians, mostly liberal suck wipes, that seek to destroy the very fabric of our nation?"

"I side with the workers."

"And you illustrate my point, which I'll now tell you. If you look across the country, people are mostly divided into three categories, republicans, democrats, and non-partisan; the latter grows larger daily. Those who belong to parties believe more in the party than the people. The non-partisans are the true patriots. They are the new, growing fringe group. The people have made their choice and are at a point where they will not change that choice.

This is where you come in. As I told you before, you will be our President and you will be walking a virtual gauntlet every day. One President called it the swamp, the deep state. It is neither; it is the bed of corruption managed by the Black Pope — it never was a swamp — it has and always will be a sewer. You cannot get away from the stench or the effects because it is like a virus that continually infects and will never die. You must begin to build trusted sources now that believe in the country more than parties so that you will be prepared to lead. Why? Because during your time as President two different nations armies will invade us.

Millions of our own people will die at their hand and from natural hazards. You must become immune as you seek the survival of the country and the few who will protect it. Yes, I said the few. You need look no further than the Revolutionary War. Only ten percent of the people picked up their arms to help General Washington. So, will it be also during your time, but this small percent will, along with Sun God's help, save the nation or, what will remain of it. Those who have chosen the wrong side will perish. But fear not, they perish because of their own decision, not yours. Unfortunately, as I said, the vast majority have already chosen. You cannot fight the greater will of whom created you. The time to pay the piper is quickly coming and the payment will be more dire than you imagine. Think about these things and tell no one. Shortly, you will receive incontrovertible proof of what I have spoken. I will return and then, I will take you to a special place where you will learn the greater truth of these things. Jeremy strode to the door and as he opened it turned, looking Phil directly in the eyes, "Remember, tell no one!"

Phil was stunned, as he sat looking at the now closed door. He was at a loss for words. He did not know if he should believe Jeremy or think that he had a loose screw. He began to think about all the history he knew, lessons from Sunday School many years ago, the global situation, how political parties no longer cared about people, but battled themselves for control of the government and he slowly began to connect the dots. Where in the world could a person make $200,000 per year and after a few years walk away a multi-millionaire —only from being elected to the Congress or Senate of the United States. Hmmmm, it did not take a rocket scientist to figure it out.

As promised, Jeremy returned in the late afternoon. It was a beautiful sunny day, and he was eager to finalize what he hoped would be the end of any doubts the future President may have about him or what he was trying to accomplish, and that Phil would be an integral part of. It was difficult to know what path would be left if Phil refused his part.

"Come," Jeremy said to Phil, "I have a place I want to take you."

"Is it far?" Phil asked.

"No, just a few minutes away. I have a taxi waiting for us; we will be there before you know it."

Phil knew there was no way to get out of what Jeremy had planned and since he had been studying all day, it would be good to take a break. So, he tagged along as they exited the building and climbed into the taxi.

"Where to?" the driver asked.

"Drop us at the corner of Dexter Row and Pleasant Street," Jeremy replied.

Phil was not familiar with the Boston area, so the street names did not register as being important or recognizable.

After about three miles the driver pulled to the curb and let them out. Phil stood looking around as Jeremy paid the driver.

"We could have driven all the way to where I am taking you," Jeremy explained, "But I wanted to let you get a feel for this place and talk a little before we reach our destination."

"Is that it?" Phil asked, pointing toward an obelisk about three hundred yards northeast of them, recognizing it as the Bunker Hill Monument.

"Yes, it is," Jeremy said. "I am sure that you recognize it."

"I do; I visited it my first weekend here before classes began," Phil replied. "It is quite historical, but history was never my thing."

"History is what we now need to learn from Phil, it is important that this afternoon, of all times that you listen carefully to what I am going to tell you. Can you do that for me?"

"I will try my best," Phil responded.

"Okay, let us head up the block to Monument Avenue and walk right up to the memorial. As we walk, I want you to have a silent prayer the first few minutes, that you wish greater understanding for this evening and that which is to come."

Phil nodded affirmatively, wondering what Jeremy meant, as the two men walked one block southeast on Dexter Row that led toward Boston Navy Yard then, turned left onto Monument Avenue. A strong breeze was blowing in from the Charles River as they walked. It was a long block, maybe two hundred yards as they neared the end of the street at the junction of High Street and directly in front of Monument Square and stopped, looking at Bunker Hill Monument.

Phil said, "I am ready."

The two walked between the concrete barrier posts, placed to keep cars out of monument grounds, and up the steps toward the center of the square. The elevation gave them a good view of the surrounding area, including the Boston Navy Yard about one-half mile away and the U.S. Coast Guard Base about a quarter mile beyond that to the southeast, adjoining the Charles River. It was then that Jeremy began.

"It is not often that people are reminded of what happened here on this spot so long ago. The battle was actually fought on Breed's Hill where we now stand. Bunker hill is about one-quarter mile northeast of us at the junction of Bunker Hill and Pearl Streets. While the preparations for the battle began there, Colonel William Prescott moved and built the redoubt here atop Breeds hill because it is closer to Boston and would be better for the artillery to bombard the British with. I will not bother you with the details of the battle as they are in the history books for all to read. But something particularly important was proven that day. Once the British saw that they were up against 1,200 Colonial troops, they launched three attacks. The first two attacks had 2,100 men to begin. Both attacks failed. Next, the British reinforced their ranks with four hundred more men and on the third attack, they took the hill. Although they defeated the Colonials, they learned an extremely importantly lesson and it is one that you must keep in mind when you are faced with what you believe are impossible odds as we move forward years from now.

The British learned that although they believed the rag tag colonials and patriots were not good soldiers, they were sobered by the fact that under good leadership, American soldiers were at least equal to their own, known then as the best in the world. Their spirit was indominable, they were courageous, committed, and they were fearless. This is what you will need to remember years from now — those who will help us save the country will not be formally trained military, but will have the courage, desire, and in many respects, greater skills to see the battle through."

They had been walking around the monument as Jeremy had been explaining the battle so many years ago.

Phil was looking down toward the shipyards as he responded. "So, what you are telling me is we will be underdogs when the time comes?"

"Perhaps even worse," Jeremy replied. "Come, let us go sit on the edge of the hill in the grass so we can watch the last light of day. Please be respectful and reverent to that which you are about to witness."

Phil did not know what Jeremy was referring to, but

complied as the two sat facing the shipyards, watching the rays of the sun bounce off the top of the small, cresting waves in the Charles river, leaving white froth in their wake. The water turned from blue to black as first, the sun's rays disappeared, the light began to fade entirely. Jeremy instinctively crossed his legs as he intently looked forward. Phil mimicked him, not sure what he should do.

The winds came to a complete stop, which seemed unnatural given the constant coastal breeze and, it became inexplicably calm. Without warning, a pillar of light descended exactly over their heads, which was brighter than the noon-day sun. The light descended upon them until they could recognize two personages standing above them in the air. It was Sun God and Monster Slayer. Both were looking directly at Phil whose eyes were wide in amazement.

"We come to you to solidify your trust with Jeremy," Monster Slayer said. "Hear and heed Sun God."

Sun God began by explaining to Phil the past and the future, affirming all that Jeremy had told him, and reiterated that what he had been told was all true.

"Philip, I knew you before this world was and through my grace you will be as Jeremy has spoken," Sun God began. "The future is perilous, but you will navigate it. Jeremy will be your advisor and guide. Trust no one else. Choose those whom you will work with wisely. Most are corrupt and have ulterior motives that are not in harmony with mine. They are disloyal and deny me and my power. You are a witness now and should no longer doubt because you both fulfill that calling to which you were born in this life. Go now, discuss this among yourselves and no others. Carefully develop your strategy. If you do all you can, Monster Slayer will aid you. If you do not, you, along with this entire nation, will be utterly swept and destroyed."

As the light turned to darkness, both Jeremy and Phil found themselves on their backs. It was an hour before they had the strength to move. As they looked into each other's eyes, they slowly arose and walked back to the university. This night would mark the beginning of many long and fruitful strategy sessions. Phil no longer doubted anything Jeremy told him and as the years passed their bond of trust became unbreakable. Jeremy, without realizing it, was already the future President's personal advisor and sounding board in all things and would remain so.

Years later, Lieutenant General Jason John Bardos, was taking his first vacation in over three years. He was known as a man who could get the impossible done in combat, despite that fact he was considered a giant pain in the ass by his superiors, he was 'the' heavy lifter. Even while at West Point, the Academy, the long-gray line as it was often called by the officers who had graduated from it and served our country well. He had always been the go-to guy for his classmates. The instructors and faculty considered him the intellectual leader of his class, able to see things that others did not. He had graduated at the top of his class and had a knack for and enjoyed figuring things out. The more complex the task, the more he enjoyed it. Jason had been transferred from one unit to another during his service because of envy of his commanding officers. Yet, every time he had been able to increase combat efficiency for infantry, armored units, special operations groups, and the U.S. Army Aviation Branch, as well as the U.S. Army Special Operations Aviation Command. The latter had been one of his favorite assignments as he worked to improve on the successes of helicopter attack formations in Vietnam and Apache success in Iraq.

As he sat on the rock, with his feet in the river beneath the sweltering summer Wyoming sun, he soaked in the rays and enjoyed the splendor of Shoshone National Forest. His face was fixed with a distant gaze, not seeing the trees in front of him, but a battlefield of the past that was a short eighty miles to his north where General George Armstrong Custer had been killed, along with over two hundred of his men by an overwhelming force of Lakota, Northern Cheyenne, and Arapaho warriors. It was not the rashness or arrogance of Custer that had gotten his entire force killed, though that was a part of the cause. The real reason was a clash of cultures and superior firepower. Had the army learned about the plain's tribes' cultures, much of the hostilities could have been avoided. The tribes had a long-standing spiritual tradition known as the Sun Dance ceremony; it was the most important religious event each year. The event was held away from outsiders and was a profound time for prayer and personal sacrifice on behalf of the villages and tribes and for making personal vows, not unlike New Year's resolutions, but with a much deeper spiritual intent to carry them out.

In the spring in 1876, the Lakota and the Cheyenne held a Sun Dance ceremony that was attended by quite a few "Agency Indians" who were called that because they had been confined to reservations, which they had slipped away from to attend the Sun Dance. During a Sun Dance on June 5, 1876, at Rosebud Creek in Montana, the main spiritual leader of the Hunkpapa Lakota was in attendance, Sitting Bull. He had a vision that he shared with Chief Crazy Horse of the Oglala Lakota and Chief Gall of the Hunkpapa Lakota of "soldiers falling into his camp like grasshoppers from the sky. Tragically, his vision would prove true before the end of the month. Ironically, at the same time the U.S. military was conducting a three-pronged approach with infantry and calvary to force the Lakota and the Cheyenne back onto their reservations.

What had been known as the Sioux Wars was inevitable because the Great Plains were the last Native American holdout and stronghold; a last opportunity for the Indian to control their destiny and not be subjugated under the thumb of a land-grabbing, greedy White Eyes, forked tongue government that sought to eradicate them. The large population of Indians along with the dry weather that was ever present across the plains had kept most people out. Then, the Civil War ended and with it the government granted ten percent of the plains lands to settlers and the railroads. The government in its ever-continuing pursuit for control and power allowed the settlers and railroads to kill every buffalo they could in the hopes of destroying completely the Native American livelihood. The more they killed, the angrier the Indians became, which led to brutal and savage attacks on both settlers and railroad personnel alike. The Sioux wars were brutal and continued as the anger from loss of life, land, and culture mounted on each side. The hatred of each side begat continual hatred of the other. It was into these circumstances that General Custer was thrust. Having had much success in the Civil War, he quickly discovered that those tactics were of little use against a foe that knew the land better than he, used fast ponies, and more importantly were persistent, resolute, ferocious, and focused. They fought not to kill, but to protect their families and way of life. Such opponents were not easy to defeat; every war fought by the U.S. had proven that, especially Vietnam and Afghanistan.

In addition to such resolute fighters, Custer faced the

Lakota leaders Chiefs Gall and Crazy Horse, who were battle-hardened. One skirmish led to a battle and so it continued until the end on June 25, 1876 when Custer and his 7th Calvary battalion met the encampment of Sitting Bull. In the end, it was not the culture nor necessarily the experience of the Native Americans that led to Custer's demise, but the fact that the Indians were much more numerous and armed with Henry, Spencer, and Winchester repeating rifles, as well as quick flung arrows from much practiced bows. The men of the 7th Calvary were armed with single-shot Springfield carbines and .45 caliber pistols. The battle was over before it began. Because none of Custer's men survived, there was no evidence to suggest accurately what had happened or how long the battle had lasted. Looking back through history, Bardos speculated that the battle did not last thirty minutes. Custer had simply been mismatched and his arrogance had made it worse.

The more he thought about it, Bardos wondered about what may have happened had the roles been reversed. For example, would Custer and his men have survived if they had the same weapons, but were in defensive positions against a superior force and if they had laid the trap instead of Sitting Bull and Gall? Looking at strategy the way he did, he knew the outcome would have been the same, there would have just been a longer battle with more Indians dead because none of the other 7th Calvary companies would have been able to reach Custer and his men in time to give aide before the battle ended.

It had been two weeks since he had talked to Phil, the new President. The meeting had been in secret, face-to-face and he had been commanded to produce a battle plan against superior forces that were traveling over plains bordered by mountains on either side. He was also directed to learn more about the culture of Native Americans and their beliefs, specifically the Navajo, Cheyenne, Arapaho, Hopi, Seminole, Crow, and others. Other than that, all he knew was that he was to prepare for a battle to save the nation if he could and to discuss it with no others until he had met with specific individuals that he was to work out plans, logistics, and a battle strategy with. It had intrigued him so much that he began reading everything he could about different tribes, especially their guerilla fighting tactics and prophecies. He was expecting the greatest challenge of his lifetime if what Phil had told him was correct and he had no reason to doubt it as they had known each other for over twenty years. From their very first meeting they had taken an instant liking to each other.

Since rank had its privileges, General Bardos had hitched a ride after leaving the President's office and brief about his meeting with Lunadi, from Joint Base Andrews outside Washington DC aboard a Gulfstream C-37A, a modified Gulfstream V. He had thought about the meeting all the way and about a variety of possibilities for a battle, which he did not know enough about yet to solidify a tentative operational plan for. The entire meeting was clandestine for which he had specific instructions. And he gathered that Lunadi did not care much for government officials or 'White Eyes' as he called them. It brought a smile to Jason's lips because he felt much the same. It was difficult to know whom one could trust anymore so; he did not trust anyone he had not known for fifteen or more years.

Jason would be with Lunadi for at least three days and so had packed a small leather duffle bag and dressed casually in a short sleeve shirt, jeans, and hiking boots. When the jet taxied to stop on Petersen Airforce Base, Jason quickly made his way through the small red brick terminal to the parking lot in front. There was a government sedan waiting for him. The driver, a sergeant with 10th Special Forces Group (Airborne) had been requested because Jason had worked with him multiple times and knew him from one of his earlier assignments. Thus, there was some trust between them, and special forces personnel were more apt to keep everything to themselves. The sergeant smartly saluted, which Bardos returned.

"Frank," Jason said, "Good to see you again." As the sergeant finished his salute and both reached out to shake hands.

"General, great to see you as well," Frank said. "What brings you out this way?"

"Ah you know, always some kind of business. I need you to drop me off here and this is strictly between us." Jason handed the sergeant a small piece of paper with an address – 1760 E Cheyenne Mountain Boulevard.

"Now you're talking General," the sergeant responded. "This is my weekly hangout, a coffee shop where a friend and I go a couple of times a week, just north of the Fort a few miles. It's about fifteen minutes away."

"A small world after all," Jason responded. "Just drop me there. I will be meeting someone to pick me up. I'll call you in a few days to come get me."

As they drove around and out the gate of the base, Jason could not help but note how sprawled out everything was. It was like one large suburban town under what he thought was the bluest sky he had ever seen, without a single cloud. The day felt warm, but there was a crispness about it with a touch of cool. Fall was in the air. Jason was still trying to get a feel for Lunadi from what the President and Jeremy had told him. He was so deep in thought that he did not notice the sedan come to a stop.

"We are here General," Frank said as he exited the car, walked back to the trunk, and took out the general's duffle bag. "Is there anything else you need from me?"

"No, you have been most helpful," the General replied. "Remember, tell no one. I will call you in three days or so and let you know when to pick me up. Oh, no salutes here." Jason didn't want to arouse any suspicions.

"Roger that," the sergeant nodded as he walked back, climbed in the car and quietly slid out of the parking lot, the General watching after him, admiring his efficient manner. Jason picked up his small duffle and walked into the north end of the coffee shop, which had a vestibule area with seating before going into the main section for ordering. Jason looked around and not seeing anyone, took a seat and waited.

He did not wait long. When he had pulled up one of Lunadi's men had been watching and compared the General to a picture he had been given. He pulled his black suburban around the side of the building, got out and walked into the seating area. A specific password was to be given in return to his greeting. His dark penetrating eyes instantly caught the General's gaze who felt just a little twinge of apprehension from the look. At last, he would meet those who were always fierce because as Jeremy had said, it was their nature.

"General?"

Jason nodded.

"What is your business in Colorado?"

"Free the oppressed," Jason replied, remembering the verbal code.

"Very well, I am Osceola Panther, Seminole Tribe of Florida, assistant to Lunadi. We must not linger here; please

81

follow me."

Osceola grabbed the General's duffle and walked briskly from the vestibule, the General following closely behind. Osceola unlocked his vehicle and opened the General's door then, threw the duffel into the back seat as he walked quickly around and slid behind the wheel. He was able to turn right onto Lake Avenue and was on I-25 southbound within two minutes. There was silence as the General studied Osceola.

The General could see that Osceola was determined and quick witted with an underlying attitude of aggression that emanated from him. It was like a permanent aura that most would not notice. His eyes were sharp, and he didn't miss much.

"It's about a two-hour ride to Lunadi," Osceola said. "You can recline your seat and take a nap if you wish."

"I'm fine," Jason said. "Why don't you tell me about yourself and your tribe."

"Very well. My first name comes from one of our most revered chiefs, Osceola. I grew up in the swamps all my life so, being in such an arid area is a little different for me. As you know, I am Seminole, which in our language means 'wild one'. It is said by many that our darkness lies just under the skin."

"What do you mean by darkness?" Jason asked.

"My people are warriors; we always have been. We have recognition of being the fiercest warriors of all the tribes. I do not know if that is true, but we are taught in warfare, tracking and other skills I cannot discuss with you, since we were very young, about 5 years of age. Our darkness is our sullen, angry nature given to us by the Great Spirit. As a warrior tribe, we have been taught to war, but there is no one to legitimately war against so, we hold the darkness in check. At least as much as we can. But it has a habit of sneaking out."

"And Lunadi," Jason asked, "He is also Seminole?"

"Yes, he is our mentor and teacher, a master of many things," Osceola said.

"What is he like?" Jason asked.

"It is difficult to describe him; you will find out for yourself. Some of the things I know I will tell you. He is unpredictable, yet compassionate and, he is a consummate teacher. He helps you become better, which he says is a teacher's job. He is an expert in many areas, some of which I am not familiar. The Medicine Man said he was one of the Great Spirits chosen ones and that he had a greater calling in this life. The Medicine Man told me that but did not say what that calling was. He is driven by a force I know not and for which I know not."

"Interesting," Jason mused. "Would you say he has a knack for figuring things out?"

"I believe so," Osceola replied. "One thing I do know is that he sees things far into the future or figures them out ahead of time. I do not know how."

Jason nodded as he looked out the window, trying to analyze the information he had been given. It matched with what Jeremy had divulged to him in his meeting with the President. He now believed that Lunadi would be a complicated individual and that if they did not get along, working together would be difficult. Jason secretly prayed that would not be the case.

Osceola was glancing at the General now and then, trying to read his body language and get a feel for his character. In some ways he was enamored with him because it is not every day a person gets to meet and speak with a three-star general. From what he could tell, the

General was sincere and focused, good traits to begin working with Lunadi.

"Tell me," Jason said, interrupting Osceola's thoughts, "I was told Lunadi trains people to be well skilled in warrior arts. Would you tell me a little more about it?"

"Yes, I do not think he would mind since you likely know some of it already. You see, he worked with the Feds for a long time, but was always a warrior at heart and all they ever did was put him down. Mostly due to envy, but you know their type better than I," Osceola said.

"Do I ever; go on."

"Anyway, Lunadi has been training people in survival, hand-to-hand combat, pistol and rifle shooting, strategy, and other issues for a long time, over twenty years, maybe thirty. I am one of his commanders and that is all I will tell you in that regard. He is expert in all these areas."

"I was told he trains assassins," Jason said.

"Well, the men he trains all have those skills, meaning they could go anywhere and take anyone out, but that is not the intent. He says the training is for the future when the chips for the entire country are on the line. So, while we could be assassins, that is not our role unless so ordered and when ordered as Lunadi says, we will become his death commandos." Osceola said.

"I have heard that you, his trainees are all good at long-range shooting and combat oriented skills. Is that true?"

"Yes; we can all shoot out to 2,000 yards with a rifle, use knives with great skill, track, infiltrate, and do hand-to-hand combat with the best. Most of us have the equivalent fighting skills of advanced black belts. We have had Navy Seals, Special Forces, and similar groups that we have worked with. To date, they have not bested us, although Lunadi has profound respect for them. He demands the best, teaches the best, and settles for nothing less from you. But you will get to experience this firsthand. Your rank will not influence his teaching or goals."

Jason looked out the window as the geology changed back and forth from rolling grassland to juniper dotted foothills and peaks. The hum of the wheels on the asphalt lulled him into a brief sleep. He was jolted awake when Osceola crossed over railroad tracks. They had left the freeway and were now going down the canyon, dust surging from beneath the tires, floating up behind them in great billows. Suddenly, Osceola turned a sharp right to go over a bridge where two figures stood in the middle with M-4 carbines, hands up, motioning them to stop. One walked up to each side of the vehicle, looked at the occupants then, motioned them onward.

"They didn't ask any questions," Jason remarked.

"That is because they were informed that I would be bringing one person with me and since they know me, they knew you were that person," Osceola smiled.

A few minutes later, Osceola pulled the vehicle to a stop in front of the house. On either side of the front door stood the two, ever present warriors. Both Osceola and Jason got out of the SUV.

"Hello, my brothers," Osceola yelled as he waved at the two warriors whose response was a small nod. "General, this is where I leave you per strict instructions. Please go to the door and knock. Don't mind my brothers, they will not scalp you; they know who you are," Osceola laughed as he walked away into the ponderosa pines.

James Tindall

CHAPTER 2

News from Afar

Austin, folder in hand, hurried down the hall to D/CIA's office entering the open door to find Peggy, sitting at her desk as busy as always, but also standing as a sentinel to anyone attempting to access the Director. Austin was a little short of breath.

Peggy was a trim, good-looking woman in her late forties who had been sought after by quite a few higher-level executives in the private sector but had chosen to work for the director. Austin had once asked her why she chose to be in intelligence, to which she had responded it was not the what, but the who. He did not understand and did not want to pry. She was an intelligent woman with a degree in human relations from Stanford. She cracked a smile as she looked above her oval shaped, primrose-colored glasses at Austin.

"Is he in Peggy?" Austin asked.

"He is, let me buzz to see if he's available."

"Director, Austin is here to see you if you have a moment." Immediately the inner door to D/CIA's office opened.

"Come on in Austin," Stone said, standing in the doorway. "Peggy, ensure we are not interrupted."

Peggy and Austin smiled at each other as he slid by her desk mouthing a silent, "thank you."

When the Director said no interruptions, it was clear to

Peggy there were to be no visitors or phone calls.

Austin handed Stone the folder as the Director walked around his desk motioning for him to take a seat. The Director breathed out a long sigh as he sat down in his chair, continuing to read the pages in the folder. He kept perusing through the limited number of pages, going back a couple of times and then forward. Finally looking up intently at Austin.

"My God," Stone said. "It looks like our fears are coming to fruition."

"I am afraid so sir. I have been racking my brain on how to handle this."

"Have you clarified these pictures as much as you can?" Stone asked.

"I have and only one of them was clear enough to identify with any kind of clarity." Austin replied, reaching his hand into his coat pocket, retrieving an 8 x 11 photo creased lengthwise. Handing it to his boss. "Only I, you, and the cryptographer has seen this, handing the photo across the broad desk."

The Director sat staring at the photo then, looked more intently with a magnifying glass he kept ever handy. He gasped aloud.

"This, this is the U.S." Stone managed to whisper, without removing his stare from the photo. "These lines are not clear, but the outline is recognizable enough."

"Sir, what do we do about this?"

Stone held up a finger for silence as he picked up his phone. "Peggy, set up an immediate meeting with the President, call me when you have it."

"Austin, this is what we have feared for a long time. I briefed the President a little about it, but just as a heads up. Oddly enough he did not seem surprised. Actually, …., His voice trailed off as his phone buzzed. Picking it up, he listened and said, 'great, tell them we're on our way."

"Time to go Austin, we have a meeting with the President in thirty."

Austin's mind began to whir as he was finally able to let the ramifications of the potential scenarios of what he had shared with Stone sink in. Before he realized it, they were already in a government vehicle headed for the White House. Stone kept looking over the document that Austin had presented to him. Both were so intent on what they were about that the short nine-mile distance from CIA in Langley passed quickly. As they stepped out of the car, they slightly primped as they headed into the White House.

They were quietly greeted by the President's Chief of Staff, Erin Shaw, a more than capable woman and a formidable adversary.

"Given the nature of this issue and its seriousness, the President will meet you in the JFK Conference room." Erin said.

They followed her down the hall toward the West Wing and into its basement. All put their phones in locked security boxes outside the room. The John F. Kennedy Conference room, generally called the 'Situation Room' was over 5,000 square feet in size and which the President and his advisors including the National Security Advisor, Homeland Security Advisor, Chief of Staff, and other administration officials such as Stone and Austin, used to monitor and develop strategy for crises situations, whether national or international. The room is a SCIF (Secure Compartmentalized Information Facility) that prevents outside intrusion or surveillance and has all the advanced equipment for secure, sophisticated communications to anywhere on the planet. More importantly, it allowed the

President to maintain complete control of any issue or to maintain control and command of the military around the globe.

The President and his personal advisor, Jeremy were already seated on the closest end, opposite side of the table. Austin had been here only once before. He and Stone grabbed the closest seats across from the President. As they sat, Erin spoke to the Secret Service agents outside the door, "No one in!" she said. She made her way around the other side of the conference room table. The dark mahogany and black chairs seemed fitting for the discussion.

"Let's have it." Phil said.

"Well Mr. President, I ...."

"Cut the bullshit Stone, we're all on a first name basis here."

"Okay Phil, I'll be blunt." Stone replied as he shoved the folder across the table to the President.

"I'll be brief. It appears that both China and Russia are developing invasion plans for the U.S."

There was dead silence in the room as Erin's eyes widened. Austin was watching as was his habit, neither the President nor Jeremy Yazzie blinked, as if they knew what the message would be. Austin was now curious, but his curiosity quickly evaporated as the President thumbed through the pages, looking askance at Jeremy.

"Okay, give it your best shot." Phil said.

"Briefly, we have followed Dragon and Red Star." Stone began. "They met in a Budapest hotel yesterday. Our man Sam Malone, whom you know, and his team were able to tail them and get some information, including photos taken from Buda Castle across the Danube River from their hotel and using a closer laser microphone, some of what they discussed. Concisely, they plan on joint operations against the U.S., in other words, they plan on attacking us here."

As Stone finished, he pulled the better photo from his inside coat pocket and pushed it across the table to the President, who quickly glanced at it and pushed it to Jeremy. Austin watched as Jeremy's eyes narrowed, a smile crossing his lips.

Erin was stunned, not knowing what to say she just looked back and forth at the men.

"As you can see," Austin started, "The map is clearly the U.S. but the detail is not fine enough for us to make out, what appear to be arrows on the map; movements of troops?"

"It is time!" Jeremy stated flatly, looking at the President.

The President sat straight up in his chair, leaning forward, looking from one face to another, several times. "How long have all of us known each other?" Phil asked.

"Almost twenty years," Stone replied.

"Then, we have trust so, listen. Jeremy, show them."

"If I may," Jeremy began as he took a marker out of his coat pocket and began to draw over the unclear lines on the photo, placing arrows at the appropriate ends. Then, he shoved the photo into the middle of the table for all to see. They were standing now, bending over for a better view, gasps coming from all but Phil and Jeremy.

Erin was quivering a bit as they reseated themselves, all eyes on Jeremy. Stone, began to open his mouth to speak, but Erin beat him to the question.

"How do you know what you just drew?" Erin asked. "More importantly, how long have you known?"

Stone and Austin were eyeing Jeremy warily, as if they considered him the enemy because their best intelligence agents were not able to discern what he had just drawn.

"I need not tell all of you the ramifications of what is now clarified from the arrows that were just filled in." Austin said. "Somehow, I feel like you have kept us out of a very important loop."

"Do not look at Jeremy with distrust," Phil said. "The reason that I asked you how long we have known each other is so you could think back on the trust we have developed. And, I have known Jeremy longer than the rest of you. What he is about to tell you, in answer to your question, is something that only a handful of people know and, excepting those present, none are in the current administration except for a general. So, listen carefully. While you may find it incredible, I have firsthand knowledge that it is true. And, we have not kept you out of the loop, we just wanted to make sure you were fully informed at the proper time because it is easier to objectively inform someone when the raw evidence is directly in front of them."

All eyes were on Jeremy as he began.
"I will start at the beginning and move quickly forward." Jeremy began. "I represent Sun God in this matter, and it is my responsibility to do all I can to help in this process, our very lives depend on it."
Jeremy related to them all that had happened since the Navajo's first trial they passed to save the fifth world. Now, it was time for the Earth Surface People to do their part. All that he had learned and seen he related to this group. From the role his grandfather Totsoni performed as mediator to the present.
The group, including the President were as if in a trance so interesting was the account that Jeremy portrayed. As Jeremy concluded, they sat speechless for a moment.

"If it were any other group we would probably belittle and laugh at the incredulous story you just told us." Stone said. "However, out of respect for and trust in the

President, I will say that while very skeptical, I accept your account. It seems truthful, but I must tell you, pretty far out there."

"I think that I speak for Austin as well," Erin spurted out, "But, it is difficult for us intel types to believe such things that we are unable to verify. Is there any proof that you can offer to back this up?"

"Don't be a doubting Thomas." Phil said. "I have witnessed it myself. I have seen Sun God and Monster Slayer of whom Jeremy referred."

Jeremy, squeezed the President's left arm, looking him in the eye.

"May I?"

The President nodded.

"I would not expect you to believe that which you have not seen. It is like faith that Christians speak of. "Faith is a hope for things that are true but that are not seen. However, because of the millions of lives that will depend on our actions, I will attempt to deliver some truth to you, which will require some faith on your part, right now, nothing doubting. Please be reverent and bow your heads for a moment."

Jeremy began a light hum followed by a blessing-way chant as he swayed ever so slightly back and forth then, suddenly spoke aloud, "Sun God I ask for confirmation for those who are putting their lives on the line to help the Earth Surface People." Jeremy began his chant again, very softly. Suddenly all around them could be heard the soft beat of drums and warriors chanting softly, "White Shell Woman duty calls." Over and over. Instantly the group was no longer surrounded by the situation room but were sitting on rocks at the top of a high plateau surrounded by

Ponderosa pine, juniper, and red sandstone cliffs. There was no sun, but near dusk and the sound of the drums grew a little louder. A white light appeared directly between the end of the group next to Erin and Austin; it was so white they had to shield their eyes to see. The brightness faded to reveal an exquisite woman and what appeared to be a male warrior standing behind her left shoulder. There was a soft white glow about the two.

Erin and the rest simply stared. The woman was dressed in white buckskin with a full head dress of white feathers that draped to her waist on the back. Her eyes were like flame. The headband at the base of the headdress appeared to be white leather with an X-style stitching at the bottom and the top where the feathers were attached with two to three inches of white thread having silver highlights. The headband had evenly spaced, triangular set pieces of turquoise upon silver broaches about an inch apart. From the white moccasins on her feet that were trimmed on the edges with lavender and red colored beads, to the top of her headdress, was pure simplicity. Her face had one marking that was a solid, narrow line just below her eyes from cheek to cheek on an opposite arc to her eyebrows with a silver marking within the line below the center of each of her eyes. Austin gasped at her beauty.

The warrior figure behind her was simply dressed in a tan buckskin robe, wearing a roach style headdress with three eagle feathers protruding upward from the back. From the top of his eyebrows to top of his cheekbones was a horizontal stripe of red that went from ear to ear. In his hand was a leather wrapped spear reaching to the top of his head ornamented with what appeared to be red animal hair drooping from the base of the spear blade to his mid chest level. Beneath the hair, where it anchored was also a small dream catcher. The groups eyes were wide in surprise as their gaze was fixed on the two. They looked incredulously at each other not knowing what to say and then, back at the two personages in front of them.

"Fear not and be of good cheer for I am White Shell Woman, and this, motioning toward the warrior standing next to her, is the Mediator. We have come at the request of Lusio, the one you call Jeremy, so that you will know of a surety that what he has told you is true. You are therefore bound to your duties and held accountable to Sun God. Do not fail him." She stood aside as the Mediator stepped forward.

"I am your bridge between the world of the Earth Surface People and Sun God's realm. When crises appear, I will help you if you do all you can. Do not fail Sun God." Mediator said.

"I perceive that you have questions and will answer the one foremost in your minds." White Shell Woman said. "You may not see Sun God until you have fulfilled your responsibilities! Listen to Lusio, he will direct you on your path. To prove to you that this is not a dream I will leave my mark upon you before I depart." Immediately she touched each one in turn on the middle of the left wrist. A peaceful and elated feeling crept over them — the two visitors vanished as quickly as they had appeared, leaving them in the familiar surroundings of the conference room.

Stone was the first to speak. "I never would have thought such a thing possible. It is more incredible than I could imagine but it felt like a dream."

"Remember what White Shell Woman said," Jeremy replied. "Look at your left wrists. All of you."

Each of them, including the President looked at their wrist and discovered a cruciform flower shape a little over an inch high, with petals at the 10, 2, 4, and 8 o'clock positions. Clockwise from left to right, the petals were ruby red, turquoise, pale yellow and white emanating from a ruby red center. Erin and Austin were rubbing the mark.

"It is permanent," Jeremy remarked. "It is a reminder that what you heard is true and therefore, your accountability is without question. Also, you are not to divulge what you just witnessed to anyone outside this room."

The arrogance of the Speaker of the House knew no bounds as she grinned, picking up her cell phone.

"Yes," the electronic voice said.

"Tell our asset to drop the first slur," Evelyn said.

"Are you sure that is wise at this juncture?"

"Yes, we need more time. The President will be fighting this rather than us."

"Alright. I will start the music."

"Remember," Evelyn said. "As with all allegations, he will need to prove he didn't, we do not need to prove he did. Make the innuendo." She was laughing as she hung up.

General Qiang was led into the office of President Jin by two armed soldiers who flanked him on each side of the chair he was motioned to sit in. The President motioned them away, indicating they were to wait outside his office door.

"So," Jin said, "How did your meeting with the general go?"

"It went very well, and we have been working more on the strategy of the invasion through secure channels using code words we developed."

Jin sat in his chair and swiveled to look out the window about their project. Like Li, he had come up through the political ranks on an exceptionally long road. His father had been a veteran, but during the cultural revolution had been purged and Li had been exiled to a small village where he lived in a cave so, he had plenty of time to think. If you cannot beat them join them had been a saying of his father and so, Jin joined the Chinese Communist Party (CCP) working as a party secretary and then, in various political offices around the coast. He served a stint as governor of a larger community finally caught a break when a Party Secretary was fired, executed, in Shanghai. The Politburo began to take notice of his abilities and he shot through the ranks, becoming Chairman of the Central Military Commission followed by General Secretary of the CCP and then, President of China. He swiveled back to face Li, looking deeply into his eyes. Li became uncomfortable because he felt that Jin was looking straight through him and he had nasty reputation of brutality that so far, no one had lived to talk about. If there was a face of pure evil Li thought, it was the President. Finally, Jin spoke.

"Li, if we fail you know that the Politburo will execute both of us do you not?

"President, we will not fail. All is coming along as planned; patience is needed, and we will achieve our goal."

"I need not remind you that while we will be as patient as possible, our people will soon be starving, we are rationing already as are other countries. The U.S. is no longer selling us the typical amount of grain due to agricultural shortages there, as a matter of fact, shipments from the U.S. are down eighty percent. Brazil and Africa, as well as Mexico and Europe are having similar problems." Li said. "We are running short on time. Is there any way you can press the timetable?"

"We can speed it up somewhat I believe," Li replied. "I will need to speak first with Admiral Dong."

"Very well," Li said. "Move as quickly as you can. One more thing, as Li leaned forward on his desk whispering, I know that we talked about launching during a favorable environmental scenario, but as a last resort, explode a nuke for an EMP about 250 miles up in the atmosphere. You determine the location or multiple locations. I will let you know how long we can hold out in the next week or so. We are analyzing the numbers now."

"General Tyurin and I have already developed a separate strategy as you suggest," Li said. "I am on my way now to speak with Admiral Dong."

"Very well," Jin responded, as he stood and pressed a small button on his desk, at which the two soldiers immediately opened the doors to escort Li out.

"I will keep you posted President," Li said as he exited. Jin had already turned, looking out the window, contemplating the path they were embarking on.

L i was working quietly at his desk as his transport flew south to Shanghai from Beijing. As general, it was his personally assigned plane, an extensively modified Xian-Y7-100, which had originally been built for transporting fifty-two people. It now had room for only fifteen, having been changed to a combined military command post and communications transport. General Qiang ensured it was always up to date with the latest technology. He specifically ordered during its first modification substantial sound buffering so that one could think over the sound of the twin, booster jet, prop engines. More importantly, it looked like and had the markings of a commercial airplane to avoid arousing suspicion. He let his thoughts drift from the task at hand.

He needed to talk to Admiral Leung anyway before proceeding forward. He was glad to be back from Budapest with his meeting with General Tyurin. He had been able to return home and spend some quality time with his family in Beijing followed by the meeting with his boss. Li was happy to travel to Shanghai to meet with the admiral; they had been friends for over twenty-five years, and they trusted each other, though often not agreeing on everything. The general smiled as he reflected on the path each of them had taken. Different from his, Admiral Leung had begun his career as an enlistee and worked his way up the ladder to a commanding officer of a frigate then, a frigate squadron and as commander of Support Base of the North Sea Fleet followed by President of the Dalian Naval Academy. Because of his strategic abilities, he was appointed deputy commander of the South Sea Fleet and then quickly to commander of all fleets. He had surpassed his dreams by rising to a deputy military region position as fleets commander. After two short years, he was promoted to admiral and commander of the Peoples Liberation Army Navy (PLAN). Li had no doubt his friend Wen could perform his own job and even that of the MND, but Wen's love had been and always would be the sea. He had been born and grew up in Shanghai, fishing with his father to put food on the table and earn a meager living.

Li's thoughts were interrupted as the plane's wheels bounced onto the tarmac of Shanghai Pudong International Airport, just across the Yangtze River from the navy shipbuilding yards. Due to his status, within a few minutes, General Qiang was in a private car with his two security guards from CCP Central Security Bureau (CSB), both dressed as businessmen and both very adept at hand-to-hand combat and firearms. Although not seen, it was certain they were armed with the Chinese QSZ-92 pistol. Their furtive glances did not miss anything. It took about thirty minutes to reach their destination as they traveled north on the Yingbin Expressway before turning right onto Shanghai Ring Expressway and then another right onto Hushan Expressway, crossing the Yangtze, at least the first half of the mouth of the river, called Majia Gang Bay. About a third of a mile before reaching Jiangnan Avenue, on Chongming Island, the driver took a quick right and proceeded southeast about a mile until he reached a security checkpoint.

They had not noticed the small car that had followed them and pulled into a parking lot to their left, cautiously observing. The checkpoint, though somewhat innocuous was formidable having multiple camera's, over half a dozen guards with pistols and JS-9 silenced submachine guns, loaded randomly with mixed ball and armor piercing ammo to stop both people and vehicles daring to pass without authorization. To the left and right were parking lots full of cars; no personal vehicles were allowed in the shipyard because it was full of classified equipment, weapons, and designs for ships. Everyone was searched and scanned before entering and when leaving. The driver rolled down the windows and handed the occupants ID's to the guard who stepped forward and looked inside. He had seen General Qiang on numerous occasions and smartly saluted, which was returned. The guard stepped back into the security booth and picked up a phone. Within seconds he directed the General's car forward and then made a circular motion overhead with his arm signaling a security car just in front to guide them, to their destination two miles down the yards to the area of the 'New Campus' where Admiral Leung was waiting.

General Qiang was always amazed at the productivity of the yards. Already, they had a navy of about 350 ships and their presence was daily being felt by the U.S. Navy whose size was just under 300 ships. Politics of the day with the liberals in control would soon enough become the death blow to the U.S. military he mused. They lacked in vision and were only about control and power, forgetting country and people. General Qiang wondered how the U.S. had survived so long.

His thoughts were interrupted as the car pulled slowly to a stop where Admiral Leung stood waiting. After he and his two security personnel had exited, his car and the escort car made a quick U-turn and headed back to the security checkpoint. Li motioned to his security detail to drop back. He smartly saluted the admiral and then they greeted each other in the traditional Chinese way that is seldom used today by cupping the left hand over the right and raising both hands upward to about chin level then, bowed slightly at the waist. Li stepped forward, grabbing, and shaking Wen's hand as they smiled.

"It is nice to see you old friend," Wen said. "We need to get together more often."

"And you as well, but duties keep us busy."

"Yes, they do," Wen replied. "Come let us walk, I have something to show you."

The two-security personal followed about ten steps back, just beyond ear shot of the soft-spoken tones of the two officers.

"So, how is our shipbuilding going?" Li asked.

"Better than expected, we are ahead of schedule and based on your initial timetable, will have three more 055 Renhai class, Guided Missile Attack Destroyers and two additional 052D Luyang III class, guided missile destroyers."

"That is more than I could have hoped for," Li said, surprise evident on his face."

"But I have another surprise for you," Wen said, chuckling.

"What?" Li asked.

"Oh, let us not spoil the fun, this is something you must see to believe. Think on your lake."

They had been walking past the fabrication and assembly shops and had rounded the first corner and nearing the end of the last shop where they turned left. After walking a few more yards, they found themselves overlooking the locks and a flooded basin that had been converted from agricultural farmland about ten years before. It was easy to see that General Qiang was pleased.

"Okay Wen, explain what we have."

"On the right, stern in, are two type 055 destroyers; the same as the one you see on your left so, three of those. If you will look further down on your left, bow facing us, are two type 05D destroyers. Let me briefly explain their capabilities so that your strategy can plan them in. The Type-052D are essentially air-defense destroyers, generally equivalent to the U.S. Navy's Arleigh Burke Class AEGIS destroyers. They displace 7,500 tons and can carry 64 large missiles including long-range surface to air missiles (SAMs) and cruise missiles capable of striking 1,500 miles out with high explosives, cluster, or nuclear warheads. The Type-055 Class ships as you know are also described as air-defense destroyers but verge on being cruisers in terms of size and fit. The 055's are almost twice the displacement and carry over 100 large missiles.

"So, you have seen only a part of the naval operations plan, what could you do with these ships from coastal standoff points?" Li asked.

"Let me give you an example," Wen began. "Suppose I

were in the Gulf of Mexico, off Houston say twenty miles, with the cruise missiles we arm the ships with, I could target American cities with our cruise missiles as far north as New York. Suppose we wanted to strike Las Vegas, Detroit, Chicago, Miami, Atlanta, Washington DC, Philadelphia, St. Louis, and other cities; we could strike them all from one location with just one of these 052D destroyers. And this yard is just part of a much bigger construction program of ships we are building."

"That is incredible," Li whispered, fearing Americans may hear him.

"That is not all my friend," Wen began. "The type of cruise missile we will use is the DH-10 land attack cruise missile (LACM) that launches out of its canister. It weighs about the same as the American Tomahawk cruise missile (1.5 tons) and can be launched from these ships. Each has a range of 1,550 miles and can hit a garage-door sized target. We can arm it with 1100-pound high explosive warhead, submunitions for attacking fighters on runways and tank columns, nuclear warheads, or fuel air explosives. We have equipped each missile with several guidance modes, including satellite navigation, inertial navigation, and terrain following, making it hard to jam or deceive. In my opinion, these cruise missiles are some of the most flexible, stealthy, and deadly weapons at our disposal. You are busy my friend and need to get out in the field more, these cruise missiles have several advantages over ballistic missiles; they can be updated during flight on battlefield changes and their low flight altitude makes them very stealthy against air defense radars. Best of all, the fuel-efficient turbofan engines make them lighter and cheaper than their ballistic counterparts in our arsenal; definitely the way to go."

"Alright, I'm convinced," Li said, his voice cracking with excitement. "I will need all the specifications you have for each ship as soon as you can get it to me."

"I will send them by courier next week," Wen said. "But there are some potential modifications in armaments and weapons we have been holding back on. But we are not done yet, follow me."

They walked a little further and Wen motioned Li onto and elevator attached to a crane. When they reached the top, they stepped out onto a small viewing deck. A brisk breeze was blowing from the east off the East China Sea. Li was looking across the shipyard at the magnificent new destroyers, so excited he almost forgot to breathe.

"Remember the problem you said you would have hiding your ships in a lake?" Wen asked.

"Yes, and it is still perplexing. I am not sure I have a way around it."

"Look below you," Wen said.

As Li looked below, he thought the new 055 destroyer had disappeared, he could not see it at first. When he did, he gasped in surprise.

"How did you do that?" Li asked.

"It is something I had our engineers working on and like everything else, we copied a lesson from the Americans. They came up with a multi camouflage idea for clothing. Instead of using greens like the military wears, we used mostly blues with small parts of pale green for the colors and applied it to our ships. We are unable to paint it on, so made it out of a plastic decal material in large roles and then, applied it to the surface of the ship. Heat from the engines and the wake of the ship while underway can still be seen by satellites and thermal imaging, but if parked, as you can see it is difficult to see."

"You are a genius friend." Li said, placing his hand on Wen's shoulder. "This will make it somewhat easier to carry out the plan."

"Yes, if you still want to proceed," Wen responded softly.

"What is troubling you Wen?"

"Li, you know that I am a staunch supporter of our party and country, and I would never do that which would be considered cowardice or treacherous to our leaders and all involved in this project, but I am worried. It is not about our ships for they are every bit as good as the Americans and with the ability of our new ships to handle these land attack cruise missiles (LACM) and even larger weapons, our ships have an edge over anything that sails the seas. What frightens me is we are going to go halfway around the world and execute a surprise attack on a non-suspecting foe and its people.

"That should not surprise you," Li replied. "It is war."

"Yes, it is war," Wen said. "But first it is going to be a sneak attack like Pearl Harbor and even more planned; secondly, unlike other countries, America has over 150 million armed citizens and among them more than 100,000 civilian and military trained snipers."

"I am not worried about them, why should you be?"

"Because we are attacking them and as much as most would clap to see us destroy the government in DC they hate, we are invading their land and they will not lie down and do nothing. Let me give you an example. You know that I have been to the U.S. and worked in the embassy for a while. The people are stubbornly independent. Historically, only ten percent of the people supported General Washington during the war with the British, which turned out to be more than sufficient due to their resolve. This happened in other countries throughout history too.

During operation Iraqi Freedom, the Americans who are quite good, with over a battalion of men, could not control one hundred terrorist fighters in Baghdad until their own people turned them in. Do you not think that this needs to be a part of your strategy?"

"I assure you that we have everything covered," Li said. "However, as your friend, I advise you not to confide this to others and, I will consider it more fully in our invasion strategy."

"That is all I ask," Wen responded. "I just do not want to be found wanting because we overlooked what could become a crucial issue."

As they walked back through the yard, chatting like old friends. Li knew that Wen brought up a good point and it was one he had not really considered as much he should. He would carefully consider it moving forward, but somehow knew it would be something that would need to be dealt with and not as successfully as he wanted. His old friend had mentioned an excellent point that could mean failure of the mission. As they parted and Li was whisked back to the airport, the problem kept gnawing at him as he forced it to the back of his mind to return to planning after he boarded his plane.

Erin walked briskly, determined, into the Oval Office, a newspaper in her hand.

"Have you seen this?" she asked, obviously pissed.

"I just heard," Phil said. "This is going to get ugly."

"You damned right. How can they stoop this low? It's that evil bitch the Speaker."

"What does the paper report?"

"A damn lie of course," she responded. "It says, and I quote, *an undisclosed source says the President has had an ongoing affair with his Chief of Staff Erin Shaw and that it led to the breakup of her marriage with a true patriot,* ... blah, blah, blah."

"I thought as much. We must nip this in the bud, shall we go?"

The two walked a short distance to the James S. Brady Press Briefing Room in the West Wing of the White House. They could hear the reporters clamoring for the press secretary who was standing behind the blue curtain, trying to gain her composure.

"Don't worry Jane, I have this. Both of you stay here."

The press was amazed to see President Weld emerge from the curtain. They were standing in front of their chairs, almost yelling to get the first question in. President Weld stood behind the podium, signaling with his hands to be seated.

"Let us compose ourselves people. Give us some quiet."

The reporters took their seats, becoming silent.

"I'll make this short and sweet the President said. I read one article this morning, which stated an undisclosed source. I'm not going to take questions but will tell you what is on my mind. First, I have not had an affair with anyone. Second, the report names an undisclosed source, which as you well know in this town generally means the beginning of a smear campaign. Third, the Chief of Staff's marriage ended long before the election campaign ever thought of beginning. Their breakup as far as I know was for personal reasons. Lastly, when this supposedly undisclosed source comes forward, I will be most happy to address you more seriously. As you know, this is just another attempt to focus my attention on something other than what needs to be done for our country."

The President exited the room as the reporters jumped

to their feet yelling, asking multiple questions at the same time, hoping for an answer.

CHAPTER 3

The General and the Warrior

Jason glanced at his surroundings as he walked toward the door and was struck by the beauty and peacefulness. Upon reaching it, the warriors very briefly nodded, their piercing eyes missing nothing. The general felt like a kid going to the principal's office for a scolding. As much of a warrior as the general was, he found himself a little intimidated by the two.

"No need to knock," Warrior 1 said. "He is expecting you, please enter."

Jason complied and was struck to see a blend of traditional with some contemporary design having great wood beams with metal supports and a large, stone fireplace. He was looking out the windows with almost a 360-degree view. He couldn't help staring at the mountain range to the west. He was startled when Lunadi appeared from the hallway that led to the back of the house. The general tried to size him up as was his habit. Lunadi was dressed simply in a pair of jeans and camouflaged sweatshirt. He was fit and moved like a graceful cat. As Lunadi put forth his hand to shake, Jason felt the same intimidation as with the warriors by the door. Lunadi's eyes seemed to pierce to the core and were brown like a stalking tiger. Without question, Jason thought, here was a true warrior.

"Hello General," Lunadi said, their hands shaking. "I've been anticipating your visit."

"And I, but please call me Jason."

"Very well, you may call me Lunadi. We are pretty informal around here except during instruction time. I presume you like coffee.

"Very much so."

Well, I've prepared some coffee and fry bread for us. Let's go upstairs to the deck and chat a little."

Lunadi grabbed a tray with coffee pot, bread and cups from off the counter. Jason followed him upstairs. Reaching the landing, he realized the house had two large wings joined together by a central, octagonal rotunda. He paused briefly as Lunadi walked out onto the deck and realized he had a view in every direction. Continuing, he pulled up a seat beside Lunadi. As he glanced across the horizon, he was once again struck by the beauty of the land. The plains lay below him to the southeast and then mountains for as far as he could see, a large range stretching south to north, and multiple peaks to the west. He immediately knew two things about Lunadi; that he had come here to reduce stress and that he was serious about security. The location had the high ground and only a novice would attempt to take it from those who occupied it.

Lunadi closely watched the general and had some understanding of what he was thinking as he surveyed the surroundings.

"So, Jason, tell me a little about yourself."

"Not much to tell really, my family immigrated to the U.S. back in the 1920s and we were fortunate enough to have the money to purchase a small rural farm where all of us grew up. The depression wasn't as devastating to the family as it was to most because the farm was paid for and there was plenty of water to grow gardens and raise chickens, pigs, and other livestock. The made it possible for my family to make it through the depression. We continued to farm vegetables and fruits to sell in nearby towns and made a meager living. Eventually, my great grandfather opened a restaurant, which became quite popular because we provided it with fresh produce for the menu and it became the go-to place for blue collar types. Anyway, I spent my youth gardening and waiting tables. When I had free time, I'd spend it riding my horse dad bought me for my 12th birthday. I loved school because that is where all my friends were. My high school idol was General Douglas McArthur and when I finished high school, one of my dad's patrons, a congressman, recommended me to attend the U.S. Military Academy at West Point. I had studied math, science, and physics during high school and had great analytical skills as well as Italian and Spanish Languages. I graduated top of my class in high school and fit the bill for the kind of person the Academy was looking for in an officer.

After the Academy, I served in one unit after another. My tours of duty were often short because no matter what I did I seemed to piss off my commanders so, they were happy to send me from one unit to another. The other units' officers and enlisted men loved me because I could fix things and saw things they didn't. Anyway, it has been fun overall, and I keep learning new things, adapting better strategies, and try to keep pushing the envelope, especially with the older technologies and manually operated equipment. The new electronic battlefield is fraught with dangers, especially inoperability should we get an EMP. Old school is best in my view. Ironically, we quit teaching it for several years until the upper command realized the new kids were incapable of continuity of operations if their new-fangled electronics failed so, they put manual training back in, thank God."

Lunadi had been watching the general as he spoke and realized they had quite a bit in common. When Jason had spoken about how his commanders has shuffled him off from one unit to another, he knew that Jason's work with the military was not vastly different than his.

"How about yourself," Jason said. "Tell me about your life."

"Strangely, my life seems somewhat like yours. I grew up on a reservation in south Florida. I am Seminole and a member of the Panther clan. *That would explain why he moved like a cat, Jason thought.* As a kid I wrestled alligators and broke horses with my friends. Like you, all my friends were at school so I couldn't wait to go every day. When I graduated, I went into the U.S. Army into military intelligence. I ended up working with the NSA and did quite a bit of work against spies with a .45, knife, and a camera. Afterward, I went on to earn three college degrees, including my PhD in physics and ended up working for the feds. I was, like you, a heavy lifter. But unlike you, did not get to transfer to different units, just ended up doing things for other groups. After a while, I was invited to attend a military postgraduate school in California, working on intelligence issues. It is where I earned my second master's degree in international and homeland security. My thesis was on developing a dedicated national intelligence network. I got through all of that and here I am. I had a premonition to buy this place and I did. It has helped relieve my stress and dissolve my keen hatred for the feds, at least it put it on the back burner so that I no longer think much about them. I'm content to train my people and those who need higher-level skills. Like you, I love the math and sciences and work on 3-D thinking and putting together strategies for problem issues."

"We are almost like two peas in a pod Lunadi."

"I suppose we are at that. One thing I have learned is to never underestimate the power of envy of those who pretend to be your leaders. It was a necessity to leave them behind and pursue my own path."

"I couldn't agree more," Jason replied, chuckling. "Time to focus on other things more important."

"I must admit, I do not find you as hostile as I was told you might be," Jason said smiling broadly.

"There is no hostility in me toward you Jason," Lunadi said. "I was told by a higher authority that I could trust you and since I trust him extremely, I will trust you."

"I appreciate that because without trust, we will not succeed in this endeavor. Since we are both warriors, we will put our all into it."

"Yes," Lunadi mused. "The warrior spirit never dies! Tell me Jason, do you know the warrior code?

"I am not sure what you mean in terms of a literal code, but a warrior does his duty to bring peace against all odds, not to take peace or to kill. Lately, I have been studying Native American culture and am reminded of the definition of a warrior by Sitting Bull, Chief of the Hunkpapa Lakota tribe when he said,

Warriors are not what you think of as warriors.
The warrior is not someone who fights,
because no one has the right to take another life.
The warrior, for us, is one who sacrifices
himself for the good of others.
His task is to take care of the elderly,

> *the defenseless, those who cannot*
> *provide for themselves,*
> *and above all, the children,*
> *the future of humanity.*

In a way, I find it ironic since he was among the chiefs who massacred General Custer, but on the other hand, he did so because he had to so that the children of the tribes could be ultimately protected."

"Quite right," Lunadi mused. "But when everything a tribe or nation stands for is about to perish due to lust for power and control and pure evil, warriors must stand forth. My martial arts instructor always said, *it is better to hurt than to maim, better to maim than kill for there is no dignity in killing* (Edmund K. Parker). But today we are faced with many enemies within who would destroy our country and the very foundation of our fabric. The enemies are paid by foreign actors and those who wish to see us fail. And, we have reached a point where if the warrior does not stand forth, our country will be destroyed totally by the enemies within. In that respect, while Sitting Bull was correct, it is time to unleash the power of the warrior within and the patriots.

As Native Americans we will defend the weak and our freedoms. And, as warriors we will make sacrifices so that all may live free. But, as is justified by Sun God, we will defend our country, lands, and families to the death. While we love peace, we live by the warrior code and will be your fiercest enemy. For the warrior, Native American or patriot, we live in honor, but are born to be warriors. The warrior spirit never dies!"

"That makes perfect sense," Jason replied. "As any

commander or soldier knows, none of us want to go to war because war is tragic and brutal and a great many innocents always perish. Collateral damage is far too often more than should be paid. But, as you have said, we have a great many enemies within who collude with our enemies and who wish to see us destroyed. Unfortunately, they will force our hand to become deadly and since they will not change, we must effect change upon them to protect our families and our country.

"Unfortunately, that which is coming is mostly to blame on the politicians who sit in Washington and who enable our enemy by accepting payment for doing the enemies bidding, somehow thinking they will remain in control once the enemy is upon us." Lunadi observed. "But, not understanding the enemy, when all is done, regardless of who wins, they will be executed. I hope the money was worth it for their treason."

"We are on the same page," Jason quipped. "I have been commanded by the President to come up with a battle plan involving a large valley, which I have done. However, I need to know more about the layout of the valley, location, etc. if I am to adequately help us prepare to stop them. Somehow, I sense you know the location, can you enlighten me?"

"Yes, I can; I presented part of it at the postgraduate school years ago. I was not sure how much to present so held back and am glad I did," Lunadi said as he began to unroll a large paper, that he had ripped from his Easel pad. "Let me start from scratch and think of Mexico as a security buffer zone for the United States. That will give you some idea of what to expect from invasion forces."

Lunadi began to draw a map of the U.S. and Mexico, along with the Gulf Coast and Latin America to include

Nicaragua, El Salvador, and the countries north and south of it.

Austin was sitting behind his desk with his back to the door, gazing out the window. Never in his wildest imagination would he have imagined what he had witnessed this day. He was not one to make light of his duties for they helped to keep the national security of the country and while he had always believed the U.S. was in control, what he had learned today showed him that the country was not. An uneasiness swept over him as he realized that he had an awesome responsibility to perform and that he was now, more than ever, accountable for it. Never having been a religious man, he also now knew that there was a higher power and that more than ever, he had to pull his act together. Ironically, he could not tell anyone what he knew and what had been brought to light this day. He was interrupted by a light knock on the door.

"Enter," he said as he swiveled around to see his assistant laying a piece of paper on his desk.

"Thank you, please hold my calls and visitors."

Sheila nodded in the affirmative as she walked away. Instinctively she knew that the paper was a coded message, but she did not know how to interpret it and didn't care to.

Austin looked at the paper carefully as he walked over and closed and locked the door. It was a message from his agent Su Kang in Shanghai. He next strode to a small table in the corner of his office, slid it sideways and lifted the carpet below it. To avoid noise, he carefully lifted the concealed door, which revealed a hidden floor safe. He had done it so many times that he had the safe open in mere seconds. There was a small red book among the contents by an obscure author in the 1950s. He grabbed it and walked back to his desk and began translating the code. The content of the message did not surprise him, but the timing did. He picked up his phone.

"Stone, do you have a minute? Okay, I'll be right there."

A few seconds later Peggy was ushering Austin into Stone's office, where he at once planted himself in a chair across from his boss. As Peggy closed the door, she saw Stone looking at her with an almost unnoticeable sideways shake of his head, meaning no visitors or calls of any kind.

"What do you have?" Stone asked.

"I just received a note from our man in Shanghai and I believe we need to interpret it."

"Give me the gist of it."

"Well, seems Dragon just flew in and visited Admiral Leung," Austin began. "He was there only a few hours and has returned to Beijing."

"Hmmmm," Stone mused. "The timing is rather quick given his return from Budapest. What are you thinking?"

"We know that he was home for a few days and that he visited with President Jin the day before he went to Shanghai," Austin said. "That is rather quick after the Budapest meeting."

"So, we need to guess, and I hate guessing," Stone hesitated. "A meeting with the admiral may mean he is adjusting and likely stepping up his timetable. What are you thinking?"

"We know that the Chinese are ramping up production of their new destroyers and that the admiral is personally overseeing the process," Austin said. "I would bet that he was checking on how many would be ready by a specific date. That is about all I can make of it since the PLAN will play a key role in the invasion."

"I believe you are correct," Stone responded. "Is there

any good news in this?"

"Only that our man Kang and his associate were able to place a tracking device on the generals plane."

"Damn," Stone whispered. "That could be dangerous."

"I agree, but it was done in the guise of routine maintenance check as a walk around. The mechanic was able to quickly put it into one of wings strobe lights. It will send a signal each time the light blinks. That will disguise and bury the signal so it will not be detected. Because it's on the outer part of the aircraft, it won't likely be swept for electronic signature."

"Outstanding," Stone responded, slapping his desk, chuckling. "Both risky and ingenious. What you're saying is that anywhere the plane goes, we can track them."

"That's right," Austin said. "However, given the limited flight range of the aircraft, it is not likely he will use it to travel out of country to meet with Red Star again, but it will let us know where it is parked at all times and thus, give us some idea of what he is up to and where he may be headed."

"That's good news," Stone said. "Nothing like a little good ELINT to replace HUMINT we cannot get. Tell me, do you think he will meet again with Red Star?"

"He will have to," Austin replied. "With our NSA facility and its quantum computing analytical ability in Salt Lake, they have learned their lesson from the ballot fraud and voting manipulation that they got caught in years back. Now, they all fear our abilities and have gone underground like terrorists, passing notes and verbal face-to-face rather than email and phone. We do know that when they traveled to Budapest that each was under a false identity and we know that identity and the passport numbers. I have already flagged them. We will do our best to track them before they leave, and we will have better luck with our HUMINT in Russia than in China."

"Very well," Stone said. "Keep me posted. Now I have another question for you, glancing up to ensure the door was closed. What we saw yesterday was nothing less than incredible and I wanted to know what you have been thinking about it so far? What I mean is, well I don't know what I mean because I'm still trying to filter it and understand the short- and long-term meaning."

"I have been thinking about it since it happened," Austin whispered thoughtfully, as if someone else would hear him. "What we know for certain is that there is a higher power. We need not have hope or faith anymore because we know for sure. On the other hand, we now have an awesome and inescapable responsibility to do our jobs to the best of our ability. I mean we always have, but now, well, we will answer to a higher power we cannot escape. I kept thinking about the appearance and then, after how weak I was and happy, almost without care."

"Yes, it is difficult to explain," Stoned said thoughtfully. "I felt much the same and questioned how they could just appear like that in a secure facility. It's not what I would have expected from my Sunday School and Bible Study experiences when I was a kid. Never-the-less it makes one think deeply. Do you think we should start praying?"

"I'm not sure what to think," Austin said, standing to leave. "However, I'm sure it would not hurt. *Turning before he opened the door and looking at Stone.* We need to keep contemplating on it and when we get a chance, ask Jeremy and the others in private, mostly Jeremy. For now, we need to be diligent because what we suspected is upon us and we will be lucky to live through it."

As Austin closed the door, Stone sat staring at it.

L unadi stood, stretching. "Okay, it is time for a break. Come with me. I want you to participate in a running shoot."

"What is a running shoot," Jason asked.

"You'll find out soon enough," Lunadi laughed. "I hope you ate your Wheaties this morning. It will be dark in a couple of hours, so we better move quickly."

The two walked downstairs and out onto the covered porch. The two ever-present warriors appeared carrying four small backpacks. Leaning their long rifles against the wall, they each donned a pack, while Lunadi and Jason put on the other two. The two warriors began a small trot with the general and Lunadi closely following. They rounded a small bend in the trail behind the house and were going downhill for about a quarter mile. The general was beginning to feel the strain as they followed the trail as it turned left and through thick pines and up and down small ravines. They had gone about one-half mile when Lunadi motioned to the warriors to halt.

"General," Lunadi smiled. "It looks like someone has been skipping PT."

"I wasn't planning on this, but I have been a little lazy lately," Jason remarked. "What do you have in this pack anyway? It seems to get heavier as you go."

"Each of these packs are full of survival gear and a rifle and pistol with 100 rounds of ammo each," Lunadi panted. "Take it off and let's go over some of the equipment because at the end of the run you will need to utilize the rifle and engage five targets within two minutes."

The two warriors stood nearby waiting patiently as Lunadi began explaining various items to the general.

"The main piece of equipment is a take-down rifle," Lunadi said, pulling the generals rifle from the pack in three pieces.

"You have the stock, barrel and handguard. When we get to the shooting range, you will need to pull out the stock and hold it in your left hand, resting the butt on your left thigh or ground and make sure you have pulled the charging handle back. Lunadi was demonstrating the process as he talked. Next, place the receiver end of the barrel into this hole and align the gas tube with this notch then twist slightly back and forth to ensure the barrel is seated properly. Tighten the barrel nut hand tight, screwing it all the way down. Finally, slide the handguard over the barrel and push this button through the notch and press this lever down. There, a fully assembled sniper rifle good to 1,200 yards."

"That's impressive," Jason said. "You put that together in less than a minute."

"That's right and the goal is one minute or less," Lunadi responded.

"Why the time limit," Jason asked.

"Suppose you have scouts that need to move fast and far to determine where the enemy is and then, to wait and support forward moving infantry," Lunadi responded. "The scouts carry this pack in my groups. It weighs 25 pounds or less, excluding the 12-pound, loaded sniper rifle. Once support or overwatch is needed, they can have their sniper rifle fully assembled in one minute and can engage five individual targets from zero to 1,200 yards within one minute. And, if an enemy group sees them, because the rifle is in their pack, they appear to be of minimal threat."

"Wait," Jason exclaimed! "You're telling me that these two men of yours, motioning to the two warriors, can run an extended distance, put this rifle together and engage five targets, all at different ranges within two minutes?"

"That's what I am telling you," Lunadi responded. "The

key is not only the semi-automatic rifle, but the scope, which has a dynamic targeting reticle adjusted at the factory for spin drift for every range, as well as wind speed to 25 mph and, it does not have a battery, so it is EMP proof."

"That seems like an incredible feat," Jason said. "I'm going to need to see it to believe it."

"Oh, you're not only going to see it," Lunadi began. "You're going to do it yourself. Now, let me explain the scope to you because it is the key to speed. But first, look through it at that boulder on the far ridge, pointing."

The general aimed at the boulder through the scope and exhaled.

"Interesting," Jason remarked. "The scope doesn't have the typical crosshair and seems to trend to the right. I'm guessing the middle vertical row is yards and the other horizontal rows are for wind?"

"Precisely," Lunadi said. "You use the middle row number to place on the known yardage your spotter gives you and the dots are marked in 5-mph winds left and right. For example, that boulder is level with us and is at 750 yards. You could just put the 750-yard marker in the scope on it and pull the trigger, but you would miss. There is a small adjustment you need to make for density altitude based upon the rifle you're shooting. Each rifle is given a nominal assignment value (NAV) based on the chronograph velocity of the ammo you shoot. The one you are holding has an NAV of four. To go along with that, you need to know density altitude. We are at 7,000 feet and 60° F; the graph on your scope says that 8.5 in thousands of feet because our air here is less dense. My hand-held weather meter says the density altitude is 9 at this temperature and elevation. So, let's use that in the simple shooting equation for the scope, which will give you a hold closer value. We write the equation as hold closer = NAV# - KDA# or $4 - 9 = -5K$. Look through your scope and on the far left you will see a sideways, lazy number at the 750-yard mark. What is it?"

"There isn't a number, but it is halfway between the 6 and 8 so it should be 7, right?" Jason asked, lowering the rifle.

"Good," Lunadi said. "Now we have our hold closer range, which is the -5K we just calculated times 7, giving us -35 so, what is the actual range to target based on our system?"

"Would it be 750 – 35 for 715 yards?" The general asked.

"Exactly," Lunadi said, smiling. "You're already way ahead of the pack because most people are not able to do it correctly the first time. Think about it as we complete the course."

They disassembled the rifle, put it back in the pack and were again on the way. The pace was increased by the two warriors. Not wanting to get too far ahead of the general, Lunadi held back and ran at a lesser pace. They covered the last half mile to the range quickly. The two warriors waited until they arrived.

"Begin," Lunadi yelled, blowing his whistle as he started his stopwatch. "Assemble your weapon as quickly as you can, the targets are in front of you and you have one minute, and fifty seconds left to assemble and engage. General, I will be your spotter. We will use 9 as our density altitude; use that for finding your hold closer distance."

The men were able to assemble and begin firing about one minute into the scenario. The first target was 350 yards away at the base of a tree. Lunadi was calling off distance as each of the men were making a mental calculation before firing. All hit the first target. To make it easier on the general, Lunadi called target ranges from close to far. The next target up was 520 yards. Once again, all hit their target. The third target was 745 yards. The general missed and shot over the target.

"Remember general, your gun has and NAV of 4 and we are using 9 as the KDA, which yields a negative number, not positive."

Realizing what he had done, Jason mentally calculated again and fired. The target was hit center mass. He could not help but smile, not because he was hitting the target, but at the fun he was having.

The next target call was 895 yards and again, all hit their target. The final target loomed far out; it was 1,150 yards.

"Watch it now," Lunadi cautioned. "The wind has started; I measure it at 5-mph from left to right so, push left to the first dot."

Both the warriors hit their mark, the steel of the target ringing from the impact of the bullet as it struck at about 1,100 feet per second.

"Dammit," Jason cursed, missing, just as Lunadi blew his whistle.

"Time," Lunadi shouted. "General, take one more shot, wind is still at five; use first wind dot to right of center stadia, your hold closer is 1,080 yards."

The general held as instructed and fired. The target rang once more from the impact of the round. The general was smiling at himself.

"Well done warriors," Lunadi said, smiling at them. "Jason, you were 15 seconds past the deadline, but you did very well considering this was your first time."

"I am amazed at the simplicity of this system and its lethality," Jason replied. "I have never shot that far except with a tank, but you made it seem so easy."

"With the system you are using that accounts for spin drift

of the bullet and for the wind proportional for each distance so that you can use the same dot for a 5-mph wind at 500 yards as at a 1,000, the shooter can simply concentrate on hold," Lunadi replied.

"I like the fact that you do not need to adjust the turrets for each distance or wind," Jason said. "It greatly reduces engagement time."

"Quite right and for clandestine operations, it is most efficient," Lunadi replied.

The group gathered their equipment together, put it back into their packs and headed back toward the house and compound. Rather than talking, each was in his own thoughts in the crisp fall air, the sun setting below the horizon, giving off a faint, orange-streaked glow with the last light of day.

The general was deep in thought about the process of the scope and wondered if it would be possible to replace current aiming equipment like the PASEO panoramic site. He mused that to maintain continuity during an EMP, that the hi-tech gun sights could be replaced on some of the older tanks with a version of the reticle used in this rifle scope and then, utilize separate rangefinders and thermal imaging capabilities. It was definitely something to think about. As he walked behind Lunadi, he couldn't help but think that they seemed to have quite a bit in common. Both were warriors and both loved their country, and they would do what was necessary to protect it until their dying breath. The general knew that the time for every patriot to step up was upon them. Every citizen who could wield a rifle would be pushed into service; there would be no other way. The liberals had left the gates of hell open on the American people that could only be closed permanently by bloodshed. The how would be left up to the President.

The general and Lunadi were on the upper deck, enjoying nature's splendor. A recent snowfall had bathed the Sangre de Cristo range in a pure whiteness that only snow could deliver; its tops shown like white pyramids. The sun had already set, and a full moon brightened the landscape almost as if it were day. If ever there was a scene deserving of a picture postcard, this was it. They were sipping coffee, both reflecting on the day and what lay ahead.

"Jason, do you think we can succeed in our endeavor?" Lunadi asked.

"I have been asking myself the same question," Jason replied. "I have always been able to deliver a lot with a little, but this is not going to be a picnic. After all, most of our forces will be tied up in the endless wars our worthless government sponsors for the kickbacks each of the politicians receive. More importantly, we are going up against enemies that have copied everything we do in warfare and have in many cases improved what they have observed and learned. It is much like what happened to America during the 1970s and onward when the Japanese toured our automobile plants and improved technology, eliminating bad quality to turn out a better car than we could make for several decades."

"I have had the same feeling," Lunadi said. "Let me ask you a question. I've been thinking they would want to keep the land and thus, the most likely attack would be an overhead nuclear burst about 250 miles up. If they did that, wouldn't they also suffer loss of communications and related breakdowns of much equipment?"

"You've been reading my mind," Jason replied. "I've done lots of research on that and talked to some experts. From what I have gleaned, I would say you are correct, so we need to get better with old school technology, just like what you teach here. High tech is fine, but you need a backup. The scope you had me use today, do you think it could be adapted to tanks?"

"I am not sure how tank aiming and sights work, but I do know the old Sherman's had an M70F telescopic sight," Lunadi said. "As I recall, lots of modern-day reticles were patterned after that. You would know how much such aiming systems have changed on tanks better than I, but if you could modify some of the current or even older tanks, using armor piercing ammunition, it could work. After all, a 105 mm tank is just a big rifle."

"I've been thinking of it since this morning," Jason said. "I think I know just the person to talk to."

The two fell silent again as the sun now completely gone and its last rays faded from the western sky, the full moon washed the mountains in a silver splendor. Lunadi noticed it first, a star, no it wasn't a star, it was moving directly toward them. The general noticing Lunadi's fixation, also saw it.

It was a light, changing colors, coming directly at them. At first it looked like two stars; it was and then they combined into one and the color changed from the typical dim to bright white to a faint blue. Almost in an instant their entire surroundings were bathed in blue-white light and then, the Sangre de Cristo range that was so beautiful in the moonlight, disappeared to reveal White Shell woman and the Mediator. Jason, mouth gaping open and gasping, looked toward Lunadi, who did not seem surprised and then, quickly back to the two gods, because that's what he thought they were.

Around the two, who stood in the air just above the deck railing, was a blue and red fiery portal. White Shell

Woman was dressed as before, her eyes looking directly upon the general. Behind them through the portal was the most peaceful and serene landscape one could imagine. There were flowers of all kinds and so beautiful, not like any found on earth.

Jason found himself caught up so that he was not conscious of White Shell Woman speaking as he was looking at what appeared to be a path the two were standing on; it was a combination of gold and turquoise. Suddenly, Jason was jolted back to the two persons in front of them as he heard his name.

"General Jason Bardos, I am White Shell Woman. I knew you before this world was. We come before you so that you will know your responsibility in that which is now upon you. This is the Mediator, pointing. Heed what he has to say and obey!"

White Shell Woman vanished, as if she had not been there. The portal remained open and in front of them stood the Mediator.

Astonished at the beauty of White Shell Woman, the general focused his gaze on the Mediator. He was a warrior figure dressed in a blood-red buckskin robe, not the tan he had appeared in before and wore a roach style headdress that was red with a light green border on the edge, with five eagle feathers protruding upward from the back to represent the five worlds. From the top of his eyebrows to top of his cheekbones was a horizontal stripe of red that went from ear to ear bordered in the same light green as his headdress. As before, in his hand was a leather wrapped spear reaching to the top of his head ornamented with what appeared to be red animal hair drooping from the base of the spear blade, which was covered in blood, to his mid chest level. Beneath the hair, where it anchored was also a small dream catcher. His eyes were a brooding red-black, and he was looking directly at the general.

"I am the Mediator," he said. "You will help my offspring fulfill their obligations. We have appeared to bear witness that what Lunadi and Jeremy say are true. Doubt them not. I am here to bridge this world to that of Sun God. Serve him, do your duty, and live. Or fail and perish. The choice is yours. But remember, millions of lives depend on your faithfulness to your calling. Your enemies are now our enemies!"

The mediator turned and began walking away, down the path he was on. The splendor was beyond the general's comprehension. The luscious beauty of the landscape suddenly changed and Jason and Lunadi were able to see thousands and thousands of warriors sharpening weapons and performing blood-curdling war cries as the Mediator walked into their midst. He beckoned them to follow him. They suddenly began floating in the air behind the Mediator. It was as if he had them in tow with some sort of invisible energy flow. They were led into a large building, the architecture was like none they had seen or could describe, except that it appeared to be in the shape of an egg cut in half. It was massive and pure white. Once inside, they were floating in the air. Looking down, the future battlefield was displayed before them.

"This is where the nations fate will be decided," the Mediator said. "Both of you have touched upon a key to your success, the old technology versus the new. Let me explain what you should look for and consider."

The Mediator began to explain all they should consider as they developed a sound strategy for the battle. We do not hear what is being said. When the meeting was concluded, Jason and Jeremy floated back through the realm, the warriors below them, cheering and chanting their names as they passed above, back to their seats on the deck, the portal closing behind them.

The general sat stunned. He could not move but kept looking toward where the portal had been, except now the mountain peaks arose again before him. He looked at Lunadi who was staring back at him. Despite the hardness of the general and the warrior he had trained all his life to be, a small tear rolled down his right cheek because he was just now becoming aware of the love that had emanated from the Gods and the incredible vision they had been shown.

"I did see what I just saw right," Jason's voice trembled.

"Yes, you did," Lunadi hoarsely whispered back. "It is a testament to our work and our duty so that you will know that what Jeremy tells you, as well as myself and others commissioned to do this work is truthful."

"It was as if the Mediator and White Shell Woman were looking right through me," Jason Stammered.

"They were, they know your soul better than you do and they can read your intent, thoughts, and character at-a-glance."

"So, what am I supposed to do now?" Jason asked.

"You will do that which we are planning to do," Lunadi spoke softly. "You and I, and the others will do it to the very best of our ability or millions of our fellow Americans will die and we along with them."

"You really know how to cheer a guy up," Jason replied.

"This is not a happy matter," Lunadi said. "The Mediator was dressed for war and it is to war we will go, likely overmatched and outgunned. Come let us go to bed and think about this. Tomorrow we will pull together additional plans and as you know, we will need to present them to the

President, Jeremy, and the others as soon as we can."
The two stood and took a long look at the beautiful, moon-bathed mountains, before heading downstairs. The night proved to be restless as each reflected on what they had seen and heard.

Sky Thinker sat in the office of the President of the Minnesota Chippewa Tribe. The tribe was a part of six reservations around the area, not including the Turtle Mountain Band of Chippewa in North Dakota. Their name meaning 'first people.' He was contemplating how to introduce the situation and whether he would be received openly or not. One issue that was sure to arise was the eventual work of the Chippewa, formerly called, and some still called them, the Ojibwa, with the Lakota tribe from Pine Ridge Reservation. Dating back to 1740 – 1858, the Ojibwa were at war with the Lakota and at the time the Ojibwa proved to be one of the most powerful war forces in North American history. Early history had put their home territory near Sualt Ste. Marie, Michigan. Geopolitically, they inhabited a part of the major transcontinental waterway and were, as a result, involved in the fur trade, as well as inter-tribal conflicts and rivalries. They were aided with arms by the French and their expansion as a tribe, particularly the southern Chippewa, caused significant hostility with the Lakota Tribes who were pushed ever westward.

The Lakota were pushed out of their territory around the headwaters of the Mississippi. Aided by the Cree and Assiniboine allies, the Ojibwa moved west into Minnesota as hostilities between the two tribes increased. Knowing that the French were supplying the Ojibwa with arms, in 1736, the Lakota killed a party of French on Massacre

Island, near Fort St. Charles on the Lake of the Woods. The area was strategic since Fort St. Charles could control the southern parts of the Hudson Bay river-basin system and the headwaters of the Mississippi and was an entrance onto the Great Plains. Not long after, the Ojibwa retaliated, seizing control of the upper areas of the Mississippi, and moving toward the Red River and the Great Plain. The Lakota were forced out and moved westward. There still appeared to be grudges between the tribes. A hornet's nest to jump into if ever there was one.

"The President will see you now," as she led him back to the office. Such a pleasant voice he thought.

President Ferni Martineau stood up from behind his desk and walked around it to shake Sky Thinker's hand bidding him to take a seat.

"Call me Ferni; you have come a long way Sky Thinker of the Navajo," President Martineau said. "What can I help you with?"

"Well, I'm not sure quite how to begin this," Sky Thinker paused. "Are you familiar with the Ojibwa and Chippewa legend of Nanabozho about the creation?"

"Certainly," Ferni said, "We were just talking about it in our cultural and religious studies last week."

"That is great," Sky Thinker said, breathing a sigh of relief. "It is along those lines that I have been commanded to come here and speak with you. Let me begin at the beginning."

Sky Thinker began to explain the legends of various tribes, including the Navajo and the first through fifth worlds and relating them in terms of not only legends, but current geopolitical events. Ferni sat entranced as the history from the past unfolded into current events and what was expected of the all the tribes and the legends passed down through generations, which were not legends at all but facts. He laid out from the creation to the present and how all the tribes had been divided from one to the many there were today. Separated so that the government of the White Eyes could control them. As separate nations they were much easier to control. The government and those who sought control over them knew that united, the tribes would no longer need to suffer at the hands of a brutal, lying government. United, the tribes would be an unconquerable force. And yet, all the tribes had bought into the storyline that was a complete lie of the White Eyes. Sky Thinker illustrated the truth of what was and what currently is, making note of various environmental issues such as the big pipeline project, water compact agreements by various tribes with states and private owners and the various acts passed by the government in Congress to maintain control of tribes, including how the government has treated the northwest confederated tribe in relation to their fishing livelihood and dam spanning the Columbia River. And finally, how the tribe had controlled much of the waterways of the Hudson-Bay River Basin, which was the gift of life to the White Eyes and how, because of the value of those waterways, all tribes had been driven further away with no say about how they would be used. More importantly, why had the tribes not benefitted from them?

Ferni sat there looking at him, astounded at the account, but which he was familiar enough with many of the issues and problems to know that they were true. As he sat contemplating, he began to wonder why Sky Thinker of the Navajo had come.

The two men had gotten up early to begin completion of their plans, which they would present to the President in a couple of weeks' time. The first order of business was strong coffee so that they could ponder what they had carried out thus far. Lunadi placed cups, cream, sugar, and an entire pot of coffee on a tray and carried it up, sitting it upon a table positioned between two chairs.

"Damn," Jason exclaimed! "That mountain range is as majestic as ever. I could look at it all day. It's so quiet and serene here."

"Yeah," Lunadi replied. "I never tire of the view or the setting. The best thing of all is that there are no prying eyes that can see anything of significance going on."

"Well, what are your thoughts so far?" Jason asked.

"From what I can tell we will be in for a ride, despite our best efforts," Lunadi answered. "Our government is fractured, the constitution is dead, the courts are against the President and the people, most of the politicians are on the Chinese payroll and the country is generally unhinged, ready for armed civil war. I have always thought that this could be a possibility but have always managed to push it to the back of my mind. Now, it is a reality that is being pushed more toward fruition each day."

"Agreed," the general said. "As a military strategist, we are almost ready for their invasion. A combination of natural disasters and or splintering of the people into civil war would provide the advantage they need to initiate. We must make haste in our plans. Given what has happened so far, I have already arranged much of our needed armaments from tanks to helicopters, planes, and trucks, as well as men to be at the appointed places. It is in the guise of a basic military drill so, even the top brass is not paying attention to it. And until further notice, no one is allowed off base. Once we begin the final preparation process, all cell phones will be confiscated so that we have a total information blackout from the site. Let's continue armament and personnel placements on the map."

The general unrolled the map on the table as they bent over peering at it.

"I took this from the Library of Congress," Jason began. "It is new enough to show all the components we need to discuss, but old enough it did not draw suspicion. This is where our gun emplacements will be initially. We know that the main Chinese force will have to come from the southwest. My guess is that since they own Long Beach Port that they have some weapons in place there already that will be sufficient to repel our forces. Also, they will dock their supply ships there and that will be the start of their supply line. We must also watch for potential Russian forces coming in from the southeast from the direction of the Mohave Range and Sacramento Valley area because they will be able to cross the Colorado River from that direction. All the other bridges over it, pointing at multiple locations, we will have wired and will blow them at any sign of enemy encroachment."

"Will you be able to camouflage everything so the enemy will not see it?" Lunadi asked.

"We already have," Jason replied. "And we have considered an EMP attack so most of the equipment is underground. "They will attack Nellis and Creech Airforce Bases without a doubt, as well as Area 51. Therefore, I have contingencies to move all that equipment here, pointing to four separate locations. Additionally, we will place two decoy airports here and here. The planes will be older ones, but they will be mostly covered so that when they strike them, they will believe they have taken out our air defenses and feel they have superiority."

"So, you're going to bait them in?" Lunadi asked.

"Yes, we are going to lay a mouse trap and hope they take

the cheese," Jason chuckled. "I will have maybe one division to command, otherwise, the traitors in Washington will come snooping and China will know by end of business day. Tragic, but a reality. How many men can you provide?"

"Sky Thinker is working with the tribes now," Lunadi said. "He will not fail and will have, I believe, Sun God's help. I conservatively estimate that we can find 50,000 warriors. If Sun God or his servants help convince them, we could have as many as 150,000 whooping warriors who have been itching to fix this problem since they were placed on reservations. And I will be able to give you nine hundred extreme long-range rifleman who will not miss and are trained in all forms of warfare including guerilla, asymmetric, and explosives."

"I thought you have one thousand men," Jason said.

"That I do," Lunadi responded. "But Sun God told me in person that my enemies are now his enemies and vice versa. Therefore, that one hundred, will be commencing *Operation Dead End* in two weeks' time. The time for treason has come to an end. The many heads of the snake that has put us in this position will be cut off, one-by-one. They will move around the country in six-man teams."

The general knew what he meant; it was unmistakable. He also knew that the Russians would sweep up the east coast and kill many, among whom there would be traitors. They would not be able to get away because they would not have the support of the people. He would think upon it later because he was sure he could add some names to the list that surely must exist.

"General, I believe we have all the basics," Lunadi said. "Let me get you something, walking back into the house and returning with three books written by obscure writers in the 1970s. We will stay connected now via ham radio and book codes; I have put my call sign inside the first cover on a small scrap of paper. Please memorize and destroy it. We must not use any electronic means and when we do, it must be very innocuous. It is probably best if we do not contact each other directly by phone as much as we may want to."

"I agree," Jason said. "I am familiar with book codes. I have a confidant that I will reach out to, he will give me a secure handle so that we can talk. We'll put some finishing touches on this and finalize it when we meet with the others. But I also need something from you if you have it. Do you have a picture of the reticle that I used?"

"Yes, let me get a user manual for the scope."

Lunadi walked downstairs and returned shortly, catching the general gazing at the mountains.

"Here you go," Lunadi said, handing over the manual. "This has all the information you will need."

"Thank you, I'll make good use of it."

The two men contemplated their next steps as they leaned over the rail, reflecting upon that which they must do and what was to come. Inexorably, their gaze was drawn to the grandeur of the snowcapped mountains to the west. The general would miss this place.

General Bardos faced a long trip home as he pondered all that would need to be done. His sergeant had picked him up at the coffee shop and taken him back to Petersen Airforce Base. Sitting on the plane, he pulled out a small bound, pocket sized notebook and began making notes to himself in shorthand. A long-lost art except for court stenographers for the most part, but a practice he had begun using years ago to keep others from reading what he wrote. He would later transfer his notes to the map he and Lunadi used and to his memory. Only those with a need to know would learn only what they needed. He picked up the secure phone on the plane and dialed a number, taking photos of parts of the manual Lunadi had given him as he waited.

"Major Roth, this is General Bardos. Do you remember the old M70 through M76 telescopic sights on the old Sherman tanks? Yes, those. I'm going to send you a picture of a new, dynamic reticle we can obtain that will negate EMP effects. I'll also send instructions on how it works as soon as I land, as well as where to procure the reticles. I want you to work with the armorer. I'm fairly certain we can retrofit or replace the current Paseo sights with it. If so, I want all our armor outfitted with this reticle immediately and begin training the crews with it. Get back to me when you can."

The President was sitting on one of the sofa's across from Erin, he was looking at the latest reports from the U.S. Department of Agriculture. Food supplies were quickly dwindling. So far, few had noticed but at some point, as store shelves began to show more and more spotty shortages of various goods, the news would make the press. "Damn, this is going to be a crisis of epic proportions," Phil said, looking across at Erin. "Have you spoken to the Secretary of Agriculture (SoA) about this? How did this happen?"

"Yes, I told him to stay quiet," Erin said. "He agreed. From what I can tell this scenario has been building for a few years. He says the climate-change advocates have swept under the rug the fact that the weather patterns have been cooling since 2005, which is also why we have had fewer and fewer hurricanes in the gulf. They've ignored the facts to push their agenda."

"Big surprise," Phil murmured.

"Essentially, as the weather cooled, this past winter brought severe temperatures across the Midwest before there was a blanket of snow to cover the winter wheat. That wheat was exposed for too long and died. SoA said the loss was at least fifty percent of the crop. To make matters worse, unseasonably wet weather hit just before planting in the spring, which prevented farmers from getting into the field to plant on time across most of the Midwest, as well as many other parts of the country. Due to the delayed planting, the final blow was the early winter, which killed almost sixty-five percent of most crops."

"Talk about rubbing salt into the wound," Phil said. Who knows about this?"

"Most of the farmers who were affected, but it is not political enough to get coverage from the press," Erin replied. "Other than that, Nick and the SoA."

"Hmmmm," Phil mused, looking up at the ceiling. "This explains why the Chinese are contemplating what they are, maybe. They need food, right?"

"I would think so sir," Erin said. "On another note, it looks like the affair smear has hit the skids. Thank you for what you did."

"No worries," Phil said. "Glad we nipped it in the bud as fast as we did. You would think these people would be busy enough managing the affairs of the people rather than manipulating for power. Anyway, keep this under wraps. I'll call Nick and get his opinion on it. Maybe he can make an offer to get the Chinese to be more cooperative, at least stall them."

"Yes sir," Erin said, as she left the room.

The President was quickly on the phone to the Secretary of State.

"Nick, Erin just gave me the rundown on the potential shortages. I need you to work with the SoA then, see what kind of food we can spare for the Chinese."

"That may not be so easy sir," Nick said.

"Why?"

"Because Africa has recently been hit with the worst locust disaster in over two hundred years, Brazil is in a major drought, as is most of South America and Mexico, and if that were not enough, there has been major flooding in India and Europe."

"So, you're telling me the entire world is going to have short supplies of food?" Phil asked incredulously.

"Afraid so sir,"

"Well, do what you can to assist the Chinese. Starving people become angry and irrational."

"Yes sir."

The President was beginning to feel overwhelmed as a multifaceted crisis was developing for which the country and its people would have little control. The future looked dimmer each day.

President Martineau was looking directly at Sky Thinker, finally he was able to begin to understand the entire history that this warrior from the Navajo Tribe had presented to him. He was not sure where it was going or what the purpose was, but he would quickly find out. As he leaned forward the wall of his office began to change. Imperceptibly at first, but noticeable none-the-less. The walls turned opaque and then a light sky blue. Almost at once the walls of his office completely disappeared; the floor had become transparent, as, looking at Sky Thinker's piercing glance, he quickly leaned back in his chair, afraid to move.

"I do not understand," Ferni stuttered as he sat looking down and all around.

The two were now standing, as if in the air, the entire office had vanished. They could see the earth far over horizon and below them was Navajo Land. Ferni recognized it from his visit long ago. The fear he had originally felt had melted away as the excitement he had known as a small boy crept in.

"This is incredible," Ferni managed to whisper. "But how? How do you do this?"

"I did not do this," Sky Thinker replied. "He did, pointing."

Ferni looked but did not see anything so, he began looking all around nervously and then back to where he had started. It was then that he noticed a set of brooding red-black eyes peering at him with such a penetrating gaze he had to look away. When he looked back, the eyes were gone. Suddenly, as if walking through a wall, a personage stepped through from another dimension. It was the Mediator. Ferni began gasping for air as he started hyperventilating. Sky Thinker stepped forward and put his hands on Ferni's shoulders.

"It is alright," Sky Thinker whispered.

"But isn't he one of your Kachina's?" Ferni asked, a trembling hand motioning toward the Mediator. They appear to those who are about to die."

"He is not here to harm you but to instruct you. Fear him not."

"How is it that the faith of our people's leaders has grown so weak?" Mediator asked. "Had you even a speck of faith, we would stand beside you in your time of trouble, but lo, you have forgotten us. You have forgotten Sun God and that which you have been entrusted to do. Pay you no heed to your own tribal legends? It is they that show you the path and yet you trod after the Earth Surface People who have led you to the very edge of destruction. How is it that you bow to them and think not for yourselves? That you go along with their treachery to invite the enemy into our gates? An enemy that will slaughter the White Eyes in this land and our own people. They will sweep as locusts across the land, killing men, women, and children, replacing ours with their own as has been their habit for over 10,000 years. How is it that I must appear before you and chasten you so that you will perform your duties? You and your fellow leaders are as children who wist not what to do. But fear not, I shall remind you for the last time."

Ferni and Sky Thinker felt like slinking away except there was nowhere to go, no one to cry out to; they shook like reeds in the wind as they realized their own failures throughout their life. The gaze of the Mediator was inescapable. At once it was fearsome, penetrating, angry as a tempest at sea, but it was also compassionate and as Mediator spoke, they began to take some courage and became captivated at what he was saying.

"Like you, I lived among the Earth Surface People and made good friends and like you there are many among them that are courageous and giving, both kind and gentle, with warrior hearts who will fight to the death if necessary, to protect that which they believe is right. Those same traits are in abundance among our peoples, yet they have become dormant under the yoke of bondage as the people have turned against each other because of what the leaders of both exhibits. It is not the people that should be blaming each other; the people should be blaming the leaders who are exceedingly corrupt at every level. They care not for the will of Sun God nor his teachings, whether among our people or among the Earth Surface People. How is it that you have not compared the teachings and legends between the two and have gone so far astray that you worship that which has no spirit or meaning? Sun God will gather his people in this place for the last time and those who will not honorably perform their duties will be swept away under the feet of thousands of warriors that will. For those who will not pick up their weapons of war and fight for Sun God and for their lives, liberty, and country – this hallowed land, they shall be put to death with no mercy.

Most are not worthy to be graced by the presence of Sun God therefore, I am here in his stead to instruct you and guide you to places you thought not, to attitudes you thought not, to the warrior spirits you possess, but so apathetically submit to others who would cower at your gaze. Fear must no longer be a part of you. It must be shed totally like the skin of the snake that inhabits the rocks. You, pointing at them, and those that you gather under my direction will be true warriors, ready to leap upon command and take down the enemy who is encroaching as I speak. They will learn that the people of Sun God, both you and the Earth Surface People of this nation, will not back down regardless of the consequences or the innumerable number of the enemy that will come. It will be shown to them how fruitless it is to fight against an enemy they know not that they comprehend not, and that they cannot see. There is much I would tell you, but you are not yet ready thus, it must be that you simply do that which you are now commanded and what is that you ask? I command you, under the authority of Sun God and Monster Slayer to gather the leaders of our tribes together in this place six weeks from today."

Mediator pointed to Chaco Canyon that had been frequented many times by Wassaja and Tsosie and by him when he had lived among them. It was a place of the ancients.

"Some may refuse to come, and misery will await until so much misery has been heaped upon them that they will be compelled to obey. Here is your mark that you may always remember this day."

They each felt a sharp pain as they looked at their left hand. Between the thumb and forefinger was now a red and turquoise tattoo of a spear with three feathers grasped in the fist of an unseen warrior.

"Go now I command you. Gather the leaders. There we will await them at the appointed time to give them instructions. Show them your mark. Fail not and fear not!"

As soon as the Mediator had finished, there appeared a clockwise rotating wind spout in the middle of the room that stripped the grandeur of the place they had been show away and they were both sitting in the same position as when the vision had started. Both were breathing excitedly as they looked around, wondering if they had been daydreaming. Then, in unison, they looked at their left hand to the mark that the Mediator had left.

"This was not a dream was it?" Ferni asked.

"I'm afraid not," Sky Thinker responded. "Jeremy told me that this kind of event would happen, but I sort of passed it off."

"Who is Jeremy?" Ferni asked.

"He's one of our tribal members that serves as confidant to …." Sky Thinker's voice trailed off. "It's not important right now, I'll tell you about him later. Right now, we have been given a task that we must fulfill, and we have only six weeks to gather the leaders of 574 Tribes."

"We need a plan, and we need it quick," Ferni said.

They cleared the top of Ferni's desk and grabbed a large easel pad from its stand and began making a plan on how they would approach the largest tribes and their leaders and then, filter down to the smaller tribes. The schedule would be a tight one, but if they split their efforts and got the larger Tribes leaders to help, they felt certain that they could carry out that which they had been assigned.

The ten commanders of the STS force had arrived in the mountains. All were present at what was a very private meeting. They would divulge only that which was necessary to the one hundred men under each of their commands. Lunadi's commanders were all Native American from various tribes and took their command seriously. That which they had prepared for over years was close at hand.

Those present included Lunadi and his commanders — Panther, Oconee, Guale, Mikasuki, Yuchi, Yamassee,

Agnew, Jumper, Freeman, and Ponchin.

"Men, we have discussed the main battle strategy and all that I and the general have discussed," Lunadi said. "Are there any questions?"

"Sir, I have one," Commander Yuchi said. "What is the best way to prepare our men?"

"You may bring your men here for more training if you wish," Lunadi said. "Or, they can practice the drills we have devised at home or close to them. But they must remain sharp."

"Will we have notice of when to meet at the location?" Jumper asked.

"We have a tentative plan to meet at least two to three weeks prior to when we anticipate engaging," Lunadi said. "Once we get there, we will drill daily until combat commences."

The men looked at each other with the realization that this was no longer training exercises. They were about to put their lives on the line.

"Any more questions?" Lunadi asked. "Okay, let me know if you need anything. Follow contact protocol. You will be hearing from me soon."

CHAPTER 4

Plan Unveiled

Sam Malone had gotten word that Dragon had been tracked to Shanghai where he boarded a flight to Tokyo's Narita airport. The agents there had confirmed that he had booked through with a stopover at Dallas Ft. Worth. He made a few quick calls and within minutes, was on a military jet, disguised as a small transport to Managua. When he landed, a fellow agent he had worked with many times was waiting for him, along with a local asset.

"Bob," Sam shouted over the noise of the traffic. "Good to see you."

"You as well," Bob said. "This is Ramon, he'll be our guide and language expert. We had better get going if we want to get anything done before dark."

They jumped into a small truck and were off.

"We'll be going to Chontales," Bob said. "We hid a small inflatable skiff down by the lake to see if we can find anything. Yesterday I spotted an 055 destroyer, but it just up and disappeared on me."

"How could that be?" Sam asked. "The lake isn't that large is it?"

"It's about thirty-five miles across on average and almost one hundred miles long so yeah, it's big. If you recall from our work in Miami a few years back against the Cubans, you cannot see land once you're about eight miles from shoreline, at least flat land. There will be a few landmarks you can see further here, but still, it's a large lake, about 3,200 square miles."

"I didn't realize it was that large," Sam said. "That's certainly large enough to hide a ship or lots of them. How much shoreline are we looking at?"

"Almost two-hundred forty miles," Bob replied, yelling due to the sound of tires on asphalt and wind coming through the open windows.

They continued to talk and plan as they made their way to Chontales. The road was narrow, not nearly as wide as roads in the States. Sam couldn't get his mind off the heat. Even in early October it was sweltering. The only breeze was coming through the window and he felt like he'd been swimming with his clothes on. The truck turned off onto a narrow dirt road by a small farming community. It was choked by jungle and led steeply downward. Here and there was a small farm with buildings made from wood boards and metal roofs that seemed to barely stand, young children and old men and women going about their chores to support a meager existence. It was obvious the road was not a major thoroughfare; they did not meet another vehicle for the 13-mile trip to the lake. Near the end of the road, they pulled into a small grove of trees, completely hiding the truck. Looking around, the terrain was now less steep but full of volcanic rock clearings and hills, surrounded by dense undergrowth and jungle. The air was stagnant as sweat dripped from the men's brows. Ramon took off his hat and tied a bandana around his forehead to stop the dripping sweat then, replacing his hat, smiled at them. It seemed like a good idea, so Bob and Sam mimicked him.

Ramon began speaking to Bob in Spanish, pointing here and there as they walked. Without warning, they had reached the lakeshore where they maneuvered to a vantage point behind the crest of a hill made of jumbles of small volcanic rock. It concealed them from anyone that may be about.

"What did Ramon tell you?" Sam asked.

"He was explaining that this is one of the more remote areas around the lake, but that it is patrolled day and night by rigid hull inflatable boats that appeared to be performing visit, board, search, and seizure (VBSS) exercises. He said the boats each had three men, a driver and two armed military personnel. Lately, there has been a rash of disappearing fishermen. Ramon said if you get too close to certain areas that they will stop you; there has also been quite a bit of debris from sunken boats. The locals no longer venture out after dark."

"Where is one of these areas he spoke of?" Sam asked.

Bob spoke to Ramon in whispered Spanish, who pointed in a northeast direction. Following his lead, Sam trained and focused his binoculars. The sun was behind them, so they didn't need to worry about glint from the glass giving their location away as they began to scan the shoreline and the lake.

The lake was dotted here and there by small fishing boats that seemed to just float along, frozen in time. The air was so still that the lake was almost like glass, barely a ripple.

"Where did you see that destroyer?" Sam asked.

"It was in this same direction, but I'd say it was a good two miles out," Bob said.

Sam kept staring through his binoculars, each of them were scanning back and forth for any sign of a ship that was large enough to be a warship.

"Come to think of it," Bob began. "That ship was being

towed by a tug, why would they do that?"

"Is the lake too shallow to safely maneuver the ship," Sam asked.

"It shouldn't be," Bob said thoughtfully. "It's eighty-five feet or so away from shore and as I recall in my training, a destroyer such as the Arleigh Burke-class has a draft of about thirty-two feet, which should be like the 055 which is copied from it. Most aircraft carriers have a draft of only around thirty-five feet."

"Hmmmm," Sam mused. "I think I may know why. When did you see that ship and when does our satellite fly over?"

"I saw it around dusk," Bob said. "That's about an hour before the bird flies over on its flight path. Oh, I got it. They're trying to hide the heat plume!"

"That would be my guess," Sam said. "By towing it there would be no wake and no thermal image. Pretty ingenious. Was there anything peculiar about the ship itself?"

"It was hard to see," Bob said. "Not because of the light, it just seemed to really blend in. The masts of the ship didn't stand out, almost as if they were not there, but I passed it off because I figured it was just the minimal light."

Suddenly, Ramon interrupted their conversation pointing and saying, "Mira!"

Sam and Bob saw it instantly through their binoculars. It was an 05D destroyer, almost a mirror image of our own Arleigh Burke-class. It was being towed by a tug. The sun was still up, not yet dusk and they could see it clearly. The bottom of the ship was a computerized multi-cam blue and from the main deck upward, it was a multi-cam gray, sky blue, and white.

"Damn," Sam muttered beneath his breath. "That ship is almost invisible. The hull blends with the water line on the horizon and the masts disappear into the sky, almost as if they are not there."

"That must have been why I had a tough time seeing the ship yesterday," Bob said. "They would need to go to great lengths to paint a ship like that."

"Yes, they would," Sam responded. "But wouldn't you if you were planning a sneak attack on the US? Besides, they have covered work areas at the Chongming Island navy yards in Shanghai. Come to think of it, our last satellite photos could barely make out ship outlines in the docking area. If I had to guess, I would say that the ship is camouflaged from an aerial view as well. This is most concerning."

"I think we should take the skiff and get closer," Bob said. "We will need to be careful to avoid their patrol boats. Hopefully, we can get a few photos to send back to Langley."

"Agreed," Sam replied, motioning with his hand to leave.

The three men crept toward the shore where their boat was hidden. It was a fast inflatable with two outboard engines and was quiet. They moved swiftly across the water at about forty knots then, slowed as they began to see the shadow of the hull against the skyline. They cut the engines and drifted closer. Sam knew the ships radar wouldn't pick them up, but keen eyes could. They maneuvered their camouflaged boat next to the ship's hull. Since it was being towed by a tug there was no danger of being pulled beneath it. Bob took out his camera and began taking close-up photos of the painting on the hull. It was just like the multi-cam U.S. troops wore, with blues instead of greens. There was no way to get close-ups of the mast, but Bob took what he could get from their position as they moved away from the hull. They let the ship drift past. Once it was a few hundred yards beyond, they started the engines and headed back to shore. No sooner had they began to move, than they heard a thud, like the sound a mortar makes; a flare lighted off to their left. They gunned the motors, but it was too late, another flare burst directly above them; it was like midday. They could hear and dimly see the shadow of a patrol boat coming in from their right flank about six hundred yards away.

They were able to outrun it as they made a slant to the left for a short distance and then back to the right. The ship was sending up more flares, but they were in the wrong direction now. The patrol boat, having lost sight of them, in a last-ditch effort, began shooting in a swath, hoping to hit them. The 12.7 mm rounds from the boat began hitting all around them as they zig-zagged back and forth. Ramon was hit in the left shoulder; Bob hastily grabbed the wheel as Sam tended to him. They managed to make it to shore, ditch the boat in a hidden spot and make it up a slight hill, disappearing from view. The patrol boat, spotlights on, was looking for them near the water line, still spraying everywhere with their machinegun fire. Just as they were cresting a small hill off the shore, a bullet struck Bob in the right arm, knocking him forward as he and Ramon tumbled down the other side. Sam, grazed in the right leg, fell on top of them. Their adrenaline flowing, they were attending to Ramon to stop the blood flow from his shoulder wound. It was then they noticed he had caught another round in his lower back above the waist. It had gone completely through. Ramon was dead. Without speaking, both grabbed him as they hobbled off to better cover.

Sam dressed his wound quickly and tended to Bob. The bullet hadn't broken a bone and went through clean.
"Can you hold out for a minute?" Sam asked.
"Yeah," Bob muttered. "Get this off to Langley, handing the

camera over."

Sam downloaded the photos to his phone and was able to get a signal and sent them directly to the analysis group who were under the direct supervision of Austin Murray for this assignment. It had been so classified that they were on their own. Finding the truck, Sam helped Bob into the passenger side and then, went back to get Ramon. It took him several hours over the rough terrain, but, breathing heavily and sweating from every pore, still bleeding, he finally was able to haul Ramon into the back of the pickup bed and cover him. They listened carefully for over an hour. Sure, the Chinese were not following them, they cranked the truck and headed off to their safehouse in Managua, arriving just before daylight.

The electronic voice always gave the Speaker the shivers. There was just something unnatural about it. The worst thing was that she didn't know who it was. A promise had been made to put her in power and not to pry, they would do the communication and blackmail. That was the only way to describe it. Her contribution was politics and manipulation.

"The plan failed to do any damage," the electronic voice said.

"True, but it served the purpose," Evelyn said. "It put the President under suspicion and his staff."

"What do you suggest as next move?" the voice questioned.

"Now that he is under scrutiny, the press will dig harder," Evelyn said, smiling to herself. "Now we up the ante. Tell me, what are you and I doing right now?"

"Colluding," the electronic voice replied.

"Exactly, so now we deflect," Evelyn said. "Tell the asset to plant a little trail of the President colluding with the

Chinese and maybe Iran."

"Very well."

As the phone went dead, she wondered who exactly she was dealing with. She knew it had to be the Chinese, but which group? Well, she wouldn't worry, both would get what they wanted in the end. The day was turning out better than she thought.

It had been several weeks since the General and Lunadi had met. All the while they had been exchanging short notes using book codes to ensure secrecy of their planning. Finally, they had put together all the basics of the plan and were ready to share it with the small cadre of professionals who would make it a reality. The General had Lunadi meet him at Petersen Air Force Base in Colorado Springs where they hopped a private military plane to DC. As the only two passengers, they settled in for the short three-hour flight and kept working on their plan, tweaking it as much as they could until more eyes and opinions were laid upon it.

Erin Shaw had quietly met everyone and led them down to the JFK Conference Room as they arrived. Present for the planning meeting were the President, Jeremy, Erin (Chief of Staff), General Jason Bardos, Lunadi, Austin and Stone and Secretary of State Nick Fabiani. The SoS had not been able to attend the last meeting due to an overseas assignment in Europe but had been filled in by the President and Erin. Nick, like the rest was a true warrior and had known the President for eighteen years. He was fiercely loyal, and his black mane of hair fell across his forehead toward his almost black-brown eyes giving him a sinister appearance. It was said he only had two looks, he was either smiling or he was not and when he wasn't, he looked mean as hell. At six foot three inches, he was an intimidating specimen of a man. He was fit and young enough so that his black hair was just beginning to show little specs of gray here and there. Lunadi, having not met him before, was sizing Nick up. Jason had given him a brief on him. Nick caught his eye, approached him and shook his hand.

"You must be Lunadi," Nick said, smiling as he shook hands.

"Yes, that's right," Lunadi said. "And you're the Secretary of State?"

"Yes but, call me Nick."

"The general tells me you served in special forces in Latin America; what group were you with?" Lunadi asked.

"I was with the 7th Special Forces Group."

"Ah, I'm familiar with them. You worked on guerrilla and insurgency warfare ops with the El Salvadorans, Guatemalans, and Hondurans, right?"

"You know your groups," Nick replied. "I worked with most of the countries south of Mexico, including Panama. That work was a lot more fun than this job. Got to be so damn congenial and professional when you'd really just like to beat the shit out of some of the people you work with, especially the politicians, both laughing."

Lunadi couldn't help but like Nick, but then, the few people in the room were all warriors and warriors, while often disagreeing, generally put differences aside to solve problems, if for no other reason than their lives and those of the men and nation depended on their ability to do so. The general next introduced Lunadi to Austin and Stone who somehow looked slightly familiar to him.

"Since we're all going to be on a first name basis," Jason began. "This is Austin our Director of Operations with the CIA and this is Stone, Director CIA. This is Lunadi. I'll leave you gentleman to get acquainted."

"It is a pleasure to meet you," Austin said, shaking his hand. "Both of us have heard quite a bit about you from Jeremy. He says you're the epitome of warriors."

"I wouldn't know about that," Lunadi replied grinning. "I just try hard. I am honored to meet you both, despite the circumstances."

"I'm not sure if you remember us or not," Stone said. "But we attended the presentation you gave to the Admiral and colleagues at the presentation meeting at the military postgraduate school some years back. Given the current predicament we find ourselves in, it is a shame she didn't listen instead of mocking your brilliance. We would be much further ahead in this mess. And damn, what a mess."

"Right, I was thinking you both looked familiar," Lunadi said. "I was supposed to begin working with another PhD in the Admiral's office afterward sharing ideas, but the call never came. Guess they thought I was a quack."

"No, it wasn't that," Austin said.

"It was pure envy," Stone joined in. "They just didn't understand how you came up with the fact Mexico would become a security buffer zone for the U.S."

"Yeah, and since they didn't think of it because they weren't smart enough," Austin said. "They did what all politicians do, they blew you off."

"Tell me," Stone whispered, leaning closer to Lunadi. "Is it true that you have advanced black belts in five systems and teach guerilla-warfare tactics to other Tribes?"

"Yes, it's true," Lunadi said. "I had a premonition years ago, which has recently come true or I wouldn't be here, that those I teach will help to save us."

"Jeremy told us that you have trained one thousand expert marksmen," Austin said. "What is your typical range?"

"I have two groups that work in teams just like other sniper teams," Lunadi said. "The requirement to be in either group is to shoot 90% efficiency at every range, known or unknown. One group concentrates from zero to 1,000 yards, the other focuses beyond 1,000 yards out to 2,000 yards. A few can shoot accurate several hundred yards beyond that."

"That is most impressive," Stone responded. "I used to love shooting at distance, but it was only out to about 800 yards. By-the-way, we can't wait to see what you and the Jason have come up with for the initial plan."

"We have been fine tuning it," Lunadi said. "But it will need all of your input to see it through. Excuse me, will you? I need to talk to Jeremy before we get started."

The two eyed Lunadi thoughtfully as he walked away.

"Did you notice his eyes?" Austin asked.

"Yes, they missed nothing and appeared as though they were looking straight through us," Stone said.

"If I didn't know better," Austin said. "I would say they were lie detectors with the ability to tell if we were truthful or not."

Stone nodded affirmatively as they each grabbed a coffee and donut.

Jeremy was talking with the President.

"Hello Jeremy," Lunadi said, tapping him on the shoulder. "I want to thank you for inviting me. I must say that I am impressed with the quality of these people."

"Ah, Lunadi," Jeremy said, taking the coffee cup from his lips. "I knew you would not let me down. Come, let me introduce you to the President of the United States, turning around.

"Phil," Jeremy said, prodding Lunadi to step forward.

"This is Lunadi of the Seminole Tribe of Florida via way of the Colorado mountains."

"Mr. President," Lunadi said, thrusting his hand forward as the two shook. "It is a great pleasure and honor to meet you sir."

"Not at all," the President said. "The honor is mine. And please, call me Phil. I'm not much for formality in such private circumstances. Jeremy has spoken very highly of you. I hope that you and the general can get us out of this mess alive."

"I won't guarantee anything," Lunadi said. "But I'll give you every ounce of effort in my body."

Erin knew everyone in the room very well except Lunadi. As he was introduced to the others, she had kept her eyes on him, noticing how he had carried himself. He did not exhibit the awe of most who met such high-ranking officials but was at great ease around them. Instead, he was the epitome of professionalism. She had researched him through the intelligence group. He held four college degrees including a PhD in physics and engineering, had attended the U.S. Military postgraduate school, authored a great many journal articles and a couple of textbooks, had apparently mentored over sixty doctoral students who thought the world of him, and was skilled in, from what they could discern, many physical arts, all of them deadly. She discerned that here was no ordinary nerd type of man and from what she had discovered about his work, was quite remarkable. She eased over toward he and Jeremy for an introduction.

"Ah, Erin," Jeremy said. "I was just going to come over. Permit me to introduce you to Lunadi. This is Erin Shaw, the Presidents Chief of Staff. Nothing gets done around here without her being involved."

"Pleased to meet you Lunadi," Erin said, shaking his hand.

There was an immediate spark as their eyes locked. It was thrilling and captivating at the same time, like magic. There was an immediate chemistry, almost like electricity as their fingers touched. Both their eyes widened slightly. Surprised at the moment, Jeremy noticed it as well. Neither wanted the handshake to end and neither had expected the feelings they were experiencing. There was an immediate chemistry and what would become a lasting connection.

Erin was aghast at her feelings, which she was able to quickly hide, driving them back into her professional demeanor. Lunadi's eyes were still locked onto hers. At her average height of five feet six inches, he towered over her with large hands and broad shoulders. In what was only a few brief seconds, but what seemed to Erin an eternity, he spoke.

"A privilege Ms. Shaw," Lunadi said, his voice cracking just a little, as he had felt the same connection she had. "It is Ms. isn't it?"

"Yes," Erin replied, Lunadi still shaking her hand with his left hand covering over the top of her and his right hands. "Please, call me Erin. Let's get better acquainted later, it's time to get started. We have a lot to do."

"Agreed," Lunadi said, dropping his hands.

"Everyone," Erin said. "We need to get started on this project. I think we have all been introduced now, so let's move on and gather around. I'll turn the presentation over to General Bardos and Lunadi."

General Bardos and Lunadi, pulled a rolled map that Jason had precisely detailed through their discussions and everyone would see it for the first time.

"Normally, we would present this via electronic means,"

Jason began. "However, given the critical nature and to prevent prying eyes and ears from having it, this is the only copy."

The map was unrolled atop the conference table. It was eight feet long and four feet high.

"Please push your chairs away toward the wall," Jason said. "The map is too large to see by sitting down. We're just going to need to stand and view it as we discuss each area."

"Also, we need your input," Lunadi said. "There are too many components, and we must not overlook a single one. Any, and I mean any, ideas that you may have, we want to hear them."

"I'll give a brief overview first," Jason began. "Then, we will get into the nitty gritty of what we need to do. Lunadi presented the idea a few years back at the military postgraduate school to one of our admirals, telling her that Mexico would serve as a security buffer zone. Indeed, he was correct. If not for the simple reason that these invading forces would have to slug their way through the arid, rugged landscape of that country fighting both the people, the Mexican military, and supporting U.S. forces. It would be an insurmountable task for any military. They would simply get bogged down and pummeled by the opposition. Because of that and the visions Sun God has allowed us, we know that this is the route they will take. There really are no other good alternatives."

"That is correct," Lunadi joined in. "We know that the Chinese obtained a 100-year lease on what is called the New Nicaragua Canal. However, for ten years they have done nothing except cut a canal with locks like the Panama Canal from Port Brito on the west coast into Lake Nicaragua.

Evidence is showing that they are massing in that area and hiding their ships along the perimeter of the lake. This is from information collected by the CIA if I am correct."

"You are correct," Stone interjected. "Our field agents have been tailing both Dragon and Red Star, you know who they are from the brief, that we believe are leading this objective."

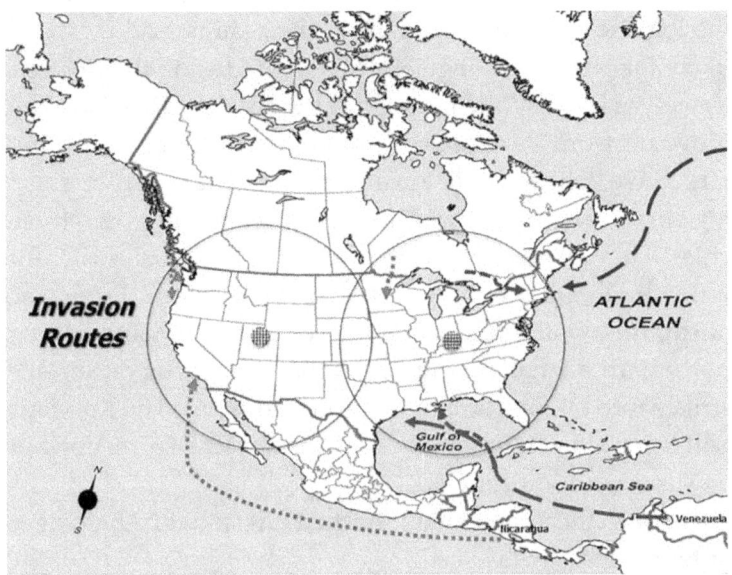

"If I may," Austin said. "Stone is correct. I have not had a chance to complete the analysis yet, but one of our best field agents sent me a note this morning. He reports about 150 ships there so far. We lost a man when they were discovered surveilling."

"It is as we suspected then," Jason said, glancing around the table and at Lunadi.

"There is so much to fill in with all your experiences," Lunadi continued. "For now, let's get through this portion and we can do that as we continue to fine tune our defense. As you see here, everyone bending over the map observing all the major points and routes, Jason and I believe that the Chinese will come from the north out of Canada against the main target objectives of Seattle and Portland. From the south, they will target Long Beach Port and then move inland — both from the Pacific coast. We conclude it must be the port as the first objective because they own it, it has the logistical capability to harbor their ships, and they will likely take-out San Diego Naval Station during the process, as well as LAX. While they are doing that, the Russians will move up from Venezuela, through the Gulf of Mexico and target, we believe, Houston and New Orleans, for the same logistical reason as the Chinese targeted the other three cities. They all have major ports making their task easier for offloading equipment, troops, and supplies. From the north, they will likely move into one of the Maine fishing ports with a smaller contingent that will focus on missile strikes into DC to decapitate the government. The Russians will come at us from the east or Atlantic Ocean direction out of Maine and Venezuela."

"What are these two small, hashed circles with the bigger outer circles?" Erin asked.

"Very observant," Lunadi replied. "The general and I believe that for their plan to work, they will need to not only wait for the best time to strike, but to be successful, they will need to take out our communications. Those circles represent EMP strikes above Salt Lake City and Louisville, Kentucky. We could be wrong about the initial placement but given the effects The EMP strikes would come somewhere along the lateral of those two cities. The effects cover the large outward circle and as you can observe, two EMP detonations about 250 miles up, will disrupt all communications, at least for a time."

"That would be catastrophic," Erin gasped. "We would be

sitting ducks, wouldn't we?"

"I'll turn this over to the general for more precise information on that," Lunadi said.

"You're correct Erin," Jason said. "If we are correct, we will lose many communications and could be blind to what they are doing."

"Can we do anything about it?" Stone asked. "This is very disconcerting."

"Yes, to an extent," Jason said. "Lunadi and I both suggest going old school, working with equipment that is not affected by EMP. Although no real tests have been done other than those in late 1950s and early 1960s by the U.S. and the Russians, we must assume that we will lose communications in the digital world, just as with the Ariel-1, affected a few days after the experiment Starfish Prime in September 1962. Only this time, the effect will likely be immediate. The satellite still worked, but the communications it put out were gibberish."

"So, you're telling us that our electronic warfare (EW) battlefield operations are unlikely to work here?" Phil asked.

"That's correct, sir" Lunadi said. "The general has been working on defeating their plan with that issue. And if you recall history, Starfish Prime was exploded 250 miles above the Pacific and the EMP pulse was strong enough to disrupt global radio communications and even blew out streetlights on the ground in Hawaii, as well as created a temporary radiation belt around the Earth."

"I have come up with some alternatives," Jason said. "They are not as effective as our EW policy lays out, but we can still support them, defend our assets, and attack."

"So, essentially, you're telling us we need to go old school on these bastards?" Phil queried.

"That is about the size of it I'm afraid," Jason said. "But fear not, I believe we have it well in hand."

"There are so many of the Congress in the pocket of the Chinese at this point that we will have a difficult time getting things through for the funding we need," Stone said. "They will fight us at every turn."

"That is of no concern," Phil said. "Jeremy and I have been siphoning funds for the past four years, as well as making assignments for various military groups with the help of Jason so we should be good to go. There are still some things we need, but let's look at those after we finish the basic strategy. Continue if you would Jason."

"Right," Jason began. "Because the Russians will likely land near or at Houston, the Chinese must come through the I-15 corridor through Bakersfield into Las Vegas. Cutting through that area will give them control of Washington State, Oregon, California and Arizona if they succeed. Their northern forces will move through into Idaho, take Salt Lake City, and likely Denver. They will have control of the entire west coast. So, we need to stop them here, pointing to an area on the map."

"Don't you think that will be difficult if we go old school?" Stone asked. "I mean, without our equipment being able to use advanced technology, we will be at a disadvantage, won't we?"

"I was thinking the same thing until I met initially with Lunadi," Jason replied. "But after him showing me what they could do with a newly designed scope, I began asking around with some of our combat engineers and armorers; we can put the same kind of sighting system on our tanks, which will not be affected by an EMP and still give us incredible accuracy. We already fitted an M1-Abrams with a mockup of this sight and were able to hit seven targets per minute with an M256 hard target and anti-tank round from one-quarter mile out to two plus miles with 95% accuracy. We disengaged the fire control and aimed manually. The tank was like an army sniper; it is really something to see. We have been able to extend the range and are currently training commanders how to use the manual system."

"Wait a minute," Nick chimed in. "You're telling me you went manual, got better range and better accuracy than our high-tech equipment can do?"

"Exactly," Jason replied. "Sometimes old-school methods are the best. You know as well as I do that many of the top staff are taking kickbacks from the defense contractors who oversell their weapons. They have pulled the wool over our eyes for a long time. Also, there is something else to think about. The Chinese are also vulnerable to an EMP so, we may have some surprises for them."

"What can we help you with," Jeremy asked. "It's obvious you are both brilliant strategists, but what can the President do to help expedite preparations? Obviously if the Chinese are as close as you say we don't have much time."

"The general has been doing a lot of the heavy lifting," Lunadi began. "While we have concentrated on the land battle, we need some sea assets. The problem is, you need an admiral and excuses for why you need him, along with his ships. These must be highly capable, anti-ship types. A few submarines wouldn't hurt either."

"We will work on that," Phil replied. "Nick can bring some pressure to bear so he, Jeremy, and I will delve into it over lunch."

"May we break for lunch?" Stone asked. "Austin and I would like to get back to the report and analysis from Nicaragua. I'm sure it will be important to the rest of the planning this afternoon."

"Certainly," Erin responded. "Let's break. Jason, roll the map up and take it with you. There are too many eyes and ears around to leave it lying about. The general nodded as he rolled the map up, put it back in its tube and slung it over his shoulder. Let's meet back here at 1:30."

All of them stood up and proceeded out the door to their respective offices. Only Erin and Lunadi were left.

"There's a small café up near H Street a couple of blocks from here," Erin said. "Why don't you let me take you to lunch and I can show you around a bit before we resume."

"That would be great," Lunadi said. "It's not my first time in DC, but it has been quite a while. Besides, DC was never someplace I wanted to hang my hat."

The two had made it outside and rounded the treasury building heading up 15th Street.

"Tell me, Lunadi, "Erin said. "I've read your background file and you have many accomplishments and skill sets. How is it that you have never worked for our more clandestine groups full time or with State?"

"I wanted to," Lunadi began. "But every time I tried to venture into those areas, I was held back. A friend here said my agency had blackballed my file for no one else to hire me. At one time, I was accused of being belligerent by our security head and he denied my TS-SCI clearance, despite CIA having cleared me. I was applying for other jobs that required it and well, it stopped any chance I had of moving on. I was forced to end my career where I was. I had always thought I could beat them, but that is not so. The well is poisoned against you with each new director coming in."

"That sounds exactly like politics in DC," Erin smiled. "It's not funny but something you need to learn to negotiate. Few warriors can do so because they are not inclined to bend their will to the narcissists that invade Capitol Hill each election cycle. The problem is that narcissism and lust for power have become the overriding factors in character now, especially with the Washington elite."

"How have you survived here?" Lunadi asked.

"Oh, that's easy to answer," Erin replied. "I'm the Presidents Chief of Staff and I take no prisoners."

Both were laughing at the comment as they walked into an old-style lunch joint. The owner caught Erin's eye and motioned them over.

"Ah, you brought a friend today. Have a seat, motioning to a small table with two chairs in the corner that had a reserved sign on it, I'll send a server right over."

For some strange sense he couldn't explain, Lunadi felt at ease with Erin; he was excited at the same time. It was something he rarely felt when around women, his manhood stirring. Perhaps it was because she too was a warrior like some of the Peshawar women fighters he had trained. And he was sure Erin was just as formidable if not more so. His thoughts were interrupted as she handed him the lone menu on the table. A single piece of paper to be disposed of after use due to the recent virus the political class had used as a weapon of control against the working class. For a brief instant, her hand brushed his in the transfer and there it was again. It was like sparks, a feeling of excitement and of familiarity at the same time. Their eyes locked momentarily, and it seemed to last an eternity. It was as if they had known each other their entire life, but at the same time there was that curiosity of the unfamiliar. Wanting to speak, but not speaking.

"Excuse me," the server said, standing next to the table. "What will you have?"

"I'll have the chicken sandwich with a bottle of sparkling

water," Erin said, turning her gaze to the server.

"Let me try your cheeseburger, with a side of tomatoes and a coke," Lunadi said.

"Coming right up." The server walked away.

"Do you mind if I ask you a personal question?" Erin asked.

"Not at all," Lunadi said, grinning. "I'll answer any question you want as long as it's not one I don't want to answer."

"Jeremy said that you are single," Erin began. "Has there ever been a Mrs. Lunadi?"

"There was once," Lunadi said. "She was killed in an auto accident in Miami. We never had kids. After she died, I transferred out west and threw myself into my work. It was a dark time, but I got over it."

Erin was looking at him intently as he spoke, trying to read his thoughts and character.

"Have you had relationships since then," Erin asked, leaning forward slightly.

"Oh, I've had friends, which is what I tend to become with women, but as far as something long term, well, I must admit that has escaped me. My friends tell me it's because I'm too intense, but such is my nature. I can live with it."

"I heard you could have taken a job in DC after you left the Feds in Denver," Erin replied. "Why didn't you?"

"That's simple to answer," Lunadi said, his eyes narrowing. "I was the heavy lifter and did my job to the fullest. Yet, the liberals who ran the agency treated me like garbage, as if I didn't exist. If they had a problem, they wanted solved they relied on me; called me the 'fix it man.' But when they didn't need a dog and pony show, I was shoved back into a dark corner. That, combined with the constant backstabbing made me too weary and angry to ever work with the government again."

Erin could sense the hidden anger welling up within him, yet he was able to control it. It was not difficult to assess that here in front of her was a man of great worth and compassion. An untapped resource any government could benefit from.

"What about yourself?" Lunadi asked. "How did you come to this place?"

"I grew up on a farm in Delaware," Erin began. "My parents always wanted me to work in government and after visiting DC almost every week due to my dads' career with the U.S. Treasury, I began to picture myself serving the people in some capacity or other just like my dad and so, I attended Princeton where I earned a bachelor's degree in political science and then, went on to Yale for a master's degree in international relations. There were a couple of relationships, but they never worked out, it was like I was their competition.

I worked here and there as a researcher and consultant, including with the RAND Corporation and the Congressional Research Service. It was after a few years with the latter, presenting my research in brief, to members of congress and the senate and their committees that I got my big break in the form of recognition of my work and worth. When Phil began running for office before his first term, I worked for him doing everything from cultural demographics, managing his staff, negotiating with both sides, due to the connections I had nurtured and just kept busy. When, he won, he appointed me his chief of staff."

"Impressive," Lunadi remarked.

"I heard that you moved to an isolated area after you quit the service," Erin began. "Why did you do that?"

"No big secret," Lunadi said. "I grew up in the Florida Everglades and being in a natural setting like that always gave me peace. The tranquility relaxed me. I had always wanted a studio for my work overlooking the ocean, but after the military school in California, staying in a hotel down by the beach, I decided the view was great, but getting to sleep with the surf pounding the beach all night, along with the wind, which made the building creek constantly, I decided against it. I had thought about buying land because I was teaching martial arts, shooting, and survival in my off time quite a bit, but I kept putting it off. Finally, one night I got the unmistakable premonition I was supposed to get out of the city for security purposes. So, I started looking at different properties, about a thousand of them, and finally chose the one where I am. I teach my survival school full time and am secluded. At 7,100 feet I have picture postcard views and my closest neighbor is a mile away. The town is small, few know me, and I keep to myself. I have no guests that are not invited. All my life I felt there was something that I was called to do, now, I no longer wonder what it is. Look at these pictures of my property."

Lunadi handed her his phone and Erin perused the pictures and a couple of short videos. There was a longing in her eyes, something far away. Lunadi understood what it was for he had many times had the same.

"These are awesome," Erin sighed. "They remind me of when I was a kid with no worries. It seems like an eternity ago."

She handed the phone back to Lunadi. Unexpectedly, as he grabbed it, he cupped her hand between his. The chemistry was instant as they looked into each other's eyes.

"At the risk of being too bold and being direct as is my nature," Lunadi whispered, leaning forward. "There is something about you that makes me contagiously attracted to you. I was wondering if I could get to know more about you other than the professional side."

"I.., I don't know what to say," Erin stuttered. "I feel the attraction as well. While we do not know each other very well, we will be working together some. Yes, yes, I'd like that very much. And I would love, when this thing is over, to visit your place and enjoy the serenity that it displays in the photos."

They were smiling at each other as the server returned with their food. They continued chatting like school children excited for the first day of school.

General Li Qiang's plane lifted off the runway of Aeropuerto Internacional Augusto César Sandino airport in Managua on the first leg of his flight to Istanbul. He was somewhat troubled by the report that several men in a skiff had been so close to a PLAN destroyer a few nights before. It concerned him more that they had gotten away without a trace. However, as his commanders had told him, the occurrence was common, and they had sunk and killed the occupants of quite a few such boats already. Still, it troubled him that this skiff was fast enough to outrun his gun boats that were on constant patrol to keep their secret. Despite the reassurances of his commanders, the incident gnawed at his consciousness. He pushed it to the back of his mind as he pulled out a small spiral bound notebook not much larger than the palm of his hand and began scribbling notes in Mandarin about the project. Flying first class under an assumed name, wearing civilian attire, he was certain no one recognized him. He had a little over twenty-four hours to get his thoughts together before meeting with General Tyurin. They had communicated only briefly about the meeting and one issue of ship deployment for the attack.

They would resolve that in person.

Li kept scribbling as thoughts came to him about the overall strategy and how it would be implemented, when they would mass, and how they would handle logistics, which was a major concern. After all, laying seize to the headwaters of the Indus River with troops and equipment was one thing because the area was contiguous to his own country. Moving equipment and troops 10,000 miles with the element of surprise against a tech-savvy enemy as strong as the U.S. was something else entirely. He wished there was another way. He had talked to President Jin about cooperating with the Americans and putting away some of their issues due to the rising food shortage. But as President Jin had made it clear, this was the beginning of continually declining global food resources thus, they needed a larger supply so that 1.4 billion Chinese did not starve in the future. It would not be as dire, but because the country had lost one hundred percent of its agricultural crop in its 'breadbasket,' the Yangtze River Basin due to six weeks of flooding resulting from an atmospheric river, they would take America, kill its citizens while imprisoning some and it would become ChinaA. The goal was colonization! For its part, Russia would obtain food supplies as needed for the foreseeable future and access to the highest-level military technology the U.S. had. He drifted into an uneasy sleep.

Li was jolted from his sleep as the wheels of the plane touched the tarmac in a stiff wind. Instinctively, he grasped the arm rests of his first-class seat. His knuckles turned white from the grip as he found himself breathing sharply. Slowly, he relaxed, realizing where he was and what he was about. Looking out the window, aside from the wind, it was a nice sunny day in Istanbul. He and his two security personnel of the CSB, deboarded the plane and made their way to customs. He could have used his official status and went through very quickly, but because passports were globally tracked and Turkey was still presumably allies with the U.S., Li and his men went through the same ritual as all other passengers. Although he had been here multiple times, it never ceased to amaze him how busy it was. Waiting in line for the customs booths, all he saw was a sea of passenger's heads from one side of customs to the other. It took over an hour to get to a booth. Once through, one of his security detail went ahead to meet the car that would be picking them up. The other stayed just off his left shoulder to his rear. Finally making it out of Atatürk international terminal, Li breathed a sigh of quiet relief. With a stiff breeze and a pleasant temperature of about 70°, the air felt fresh, blowing in from the north, off the Black Sea. As he stepped into the car, a non-descript sedan, followed by his detail, Li found himself excited about the meeting. They would put the polishing details on their plan and strategy. He had no way of knowing the Americans were currently doing the same.

Stone and Austin were sitting going over the reports from Nicaragua. Tragically, they had lost a field operative and had already made arrangements to help the family and take care of them for the foreseeable future. Ramon would be difficult to replace. His would be the first of a very large body count.

"This is most concerning," Austin said. "These photos show a remarkable technique in camouflage. Very ingenious."

"Agreed," Stone replied. "So, from all the information, it looks like about two hundred ships ringing the lake and these satellite photos do not show them. Well, if you look closely, you can make out one here and there, but you cannot tell they are warships."

"It appears that they are not that far away from complete readiness," Austin said. "We need to share this with the others."

"Yes," Let's head back."

The lunch break was much needed by the group. Now it was time to get back to the final changes so that field implementation could be finished. The group arrived at the same time to find the President and Jeremy hovering over some notes they had made.

"Ah," Phil said, looking up. "You're all back. Good, we have some suggestions for you."

Once again Erin commanded the secret service agents at the door to admit no one as she closed it behind her. General Bardos was unrolling the map again, placing it on the table. "Jeremy was just going over some items that will be brought into the final plans," Phil said.

"Yes," Jeremy said. "Most of you do not know it so I'll just give you some small details. My colleague, Sky Thinker, is gathering warriors from all the tribes. We will know in a few days approximately how many. They will be commanded by General Bardos onsite."

"How many are you expecting?" Nick asked.

"Somewhere between 50,000 to 150,000, hopefully," Jeremy said.

"That's much more than I would have guessed," Nick said, whistling.

"Well," Jeremy began. "They will not be as well trained as Sky Thinkers 1,000 men and Lunadi's 1,000, but they all know how to shoot pretty well, and most will be experienced in guerilla warfare."

"I have 900 that will be on site for the general," Lunadi said.

"Because of what Sun God told me, I have another 100 that will be carrying out Operation Dead End, which I'm not prepared to discuss at the moment."

The others around the table were looking at Lunadi, wondering what Operation Dead End was, but knew he had divulged as much as he was going to; they let it slide.

"General, how many men will that give you total?" Phil asked.

"I can have 12,000 along with two armored divisions and one wing routed from the air force, that's about 200 planes. I also have pulled in enough Apache helicopters to do the job, as well as several combat aviation units including the 1st Battalion, 211th Aviation Regiment out of Utah, the 3rd Battalion, 140th Aviation Regiment from Buckley Air Force Base in Colorado, and the and the 1st Aviation Brigade out of Fort Huachuca, Arizona. I will get others if I can but will need to use caution not to present a red flag to the traitors we have amongst our government. Total, given the other forces mentioned, we should be able to field 50,000 men, perhaps more."

"Do any of you know how many men the Chinese will have," Nick asked, looking around the table.

"We have satellite views of most of their cruise ships," Jason began. "Those have been coming and going, as well as troops based out of Canada; we have been watching them for several months, particularly the logistical supply lines. In our estimation we are looking at a force of somewhere around 100,000 men, but it could be far more because we do not know how long they have been preparing. It is possible the number could be as high as 300,000 or more. About 75 percent of the number of what we think they have are based along the Canadian border north of Seattle. Those will sweep from the north into

Seattle and Portland, likely securing the ports and then, sweep across Idaho and down into Salt Lake City.

The force we will need to stop, will be the bulk of their carrier-based planes along with the armored divisions, will come from the Port of Long Beach. They will spearhead to take Las Vegas with a contingent of Russians swooping through Phoenix. Once they have taken that, they will likely proceed to Denver, taking down our second capital and controlling the entire western states. We are fairly certain due to my intelligence that the Russians will attempt to take the state of Texas and the eastern seaboard, although bypassing it would be faster. They could do that because of their presence in central Canada near our border. We do not know how many are in Ottawa and the region west of it near Thunder Bay as depicted by the arrows on the map, north of the Midwest above Minneapolis."

"Do we even have half a chance?" Phil asked. "The congress has stopped funding to the military for almost everything and has overridden my vetoes on almost every single issue. Intelligence reports say they are communicating directly with the Chinese. We're working to counteract that, but they've been planning this for years apparently and have key players in all the right places."

"Yes," Jeremy interrupted. "I need not remind you of the visit we had. If we do everything we can, we will have the help we need."

"I agree," Jason chimed in. "It's not pretty, but we do have sufficient manpower and we have arranged lots of surprise parties for our unwanted guests. The biggest problem we will have is the Club systems the Russians deploy, and that the Chinese copied. These could cripple most of the country before we get started and its likely they will attack with those just prior to the invasion."

"What systems are you talking about?" Erin and Nick blurted out in unison.

"They are quite devious," Jason said. "Essentially, they are like our land transported anti-ship missiles the Army and Marines are now deploying, but instead of being pulled behind a truck on a launch trailer, they have designed them for 40-foot cargo containers. Each container can be remotely operated and has four missiles in it capable of a 900-mile range with a 1,100-pound warhead, much like our Tomahawk cruise missiles."

"My God," Nick whispered, "We would be sitting ducks."

"They could take out the power grid, communications, and all our military bases, as well as our warships in port, everything," Erin muttered.

"That is precisely the point," Jason said. "Mr. President, I need your permission to perform search and destroy raids on each of the units we can find."

"Do whatever it takes," Phil replied. "Do you have enough men to carry out such a mission?"

"No," Jason stated emphatically! "And that's the problem. We need more trained groups because we need to do this quickly since we have many places to search and then, keep our eyes open for potential new arrivals of these systems."

"Are you thinking of the Navy Seals for the job?" Phil asked."

"Absolutely not," Jason said. "They have been compromised by traitors inside the joint chiefs. "I want to go with the 10th Special Forces group out of Fort Carson and then, supplement them with enough personnel to cover all the areas we need to cover first. Plus, I can control them and assign them to the rest of the supposed training exercises we are doing."

"I see," Erin mused. "Tell me, we hear about the seals all

the time. What's so special about the Special Forces and what is it their patch means. I've seen it around here, but never understood those things?"

"Interesting you should ask," Jason said. "I'm sure most of the others could answer your question, but I'll try to be brief. The Navy Seals are trained for aggression and do a great job. The special forces are trained for operations behind enemy lines for an extended length of time such as to gather intelligence, take out strategic assets, and stay hidden while doing their job. And now, we need that exact skill set. The meaning of the Special Forces shoulder patch comes from fundamental, yet complex attributes that mark the soldiers who wear it. Jeremy will appreciate this aspect; the teal blue arrowhead alludes to Native American's basic skills in which Special Forces personnel are trained to a very high degree, i.e., living off the land — survival. The dagger represents the unconventional warfare nature of Special Forces Operations, and the three lightning flashes reflects their ability to strike rapidly by air, land, or water. The Special Forces Motto "De Oppresso Liber" that essentially is translated to: "From oppression we will liberate them. Regardless, I need more men to make this work. Preferably men already with good experience in guerrilla and discretionary warfare."

"Ideas anyone?" Phil asked, glancing around the table. "How many men are you thinking?" Nick asked.

"Let me see," Jason said, thinking. "Let me do some math as I talk out loud. There are 364 commercial ports that serve the U.S. To hide these systems, the enemy would want to use the larger ports. That would include the ports of South Louisiana, Houston, New York and Newark, Beaumont, Long Beach, New Orleans, Corpus Christie, Tacoma, Portland, Oakland, and Texas City. That's a dozen ports and then, there are 250 free trade zones that are mostly associated with ports of entry. These are geographic zones designated specifically to store imported goods. As you may recall, many of these are now Special Economic Zones (SEZ's) and are growing in number rapidly. These zones are a class of SEZ; a geographic area where goods may be landed, stored, handled, etc. under specific customs regulation and generally not subject to customs duty or inspection until they need to go through customs if being sold or admitted into the U.S. They are mostly organized around major seaports, international airports, and national frontiers — areas with many geographic advantages for trade. This creates a manpower problem. We will need about fifty, four-man teams or roughly two hundred plus operators. And this needs to be done now before the enemy decides to move."

"How soon can you move if you had the men?" Phil asked.

"Immediately."

"Any ideas?" Phil asked, glancing around the group.

"I could get you squads of eight men each from Mexico, El Salvador, Brazil, Chile, Columbia, and a couple of other countries," Nick volunteered. "If you do this in the guise of a training operation, they would be eager to help. That would give you more than fifty personnel. I could probably get them to come up with a dozen each. What ruse do I give them for the training?"

"Tell them port security," Jason replied. "That's of big interest nowadays."

"I could give you at least eighty men," Lunadi said. "They are all prior special ops people from special forces, navy seals, marine raiders, six prior Delta Force, and prior special tactics airmen who served in the air force."

"Excellent," Jason said excitedly. "You are lifesavers. Could you get on the calls immediately? I want to get them training within the next couple of days. I'll mix them in with the 10th Special Forces operators and we should have around 220 personnel. I think we may be able to scale down to 3 or 4-man teams and we can get these areas inspected right away."

"How are you planning to take these systems out if you find them?" Erin asked.

"We can find them through electrical radiation from some equipment we've recently modified, even though they are dormant," Jason said. "Once found, we will disable them with M14 TH3 thermite grenades. We already have a unit we were able to get and know precisely where to cut a large enough hole in the container to drop it in so that it will destroy the operational console and uplink and we have already come up with a plan to be able to get into the ports and other sites as part of various inspection teams so that we do not arouse undue suspicion. Another plan we are working on is by one of our hackers. A couple of them think that we can quickly develop a comm module for it so that we can launch the missiles back at them. Unless that fully materializes, I'll be going with the thermite."

"But won't the thermite give them a heads up before they invade?" Nick asked. "Seems like it would be better to sabotage them to go off when they initiate launch or is that too complicated?"

"Hmmmm," Jason mused. "You bring up a good point. We can alter the thermite to a plastic explosive planted inside so that they go off when the container is opened during initial launch operations. We will devise a plan for that; it will give us three options."

"Do you think you can get all of them?" Phil asked.

"No sir. At best, we will probably get 80 percent, maybe a

little more." Jason responded. "They will still have some that will do major damage. We are just trying to limit that. I have gotten some intelligence that they will generally strike our power and communications. Also, the capitol building in an attempt to disrupt government. But that's fairly standard strike points. Not much different than what we've done from WWI up through the Middle East wars."

"Getting the capitol building while those traitors are in session would be no big loss," Nick grinned. "I've had my share of their treason."

Everyone chuckled.

"Seriously though," Nick said. "We need to get as many as we can. I don't think there is much more I can contribute here. Excuse me and I'll start contacting those groups."

Nick, nodded at everyone and exited the room, closing the door behind him. He took his phone from his pocket as he walked and dialed his counterpart in Mexico, the first on his list.

"What do you want or need from me?" Phil asked.

"I believe the best thing would be to provide access to some hidden funding away from the prying eyes of the congress," Jason said. "From now on, we must not trust any of them until we find out how deep the treason goes. Also, we need to come up with a ruse for additional training so that the operation will fall under that umbrella."

"Hmmmm," Erin contemplated. "You know, we have had those explosions recently at some communications hubs and manufacturing plants that have gotten the attention of the media. We could always list specific training under the guise of domestic and transnational terrorists potentially cooperating with each other."

"Very good," Phil said. "That sounds plausible. What do you think general?"

"That works for us," Jason said, rolling up the map. "As long as we have the funds for training, logistics, munitions, etc. it should work admirably. I forgot to mention it before Nick took off, we are calling this Battle for Nevada for our small group but for the terrorist training to pull in the other groups, let us go with Operation Safe Haven. The latter is what we say to everyone who may have a desire to know. Because ports are so important, it will throw them off."

"I would like to add one more thing," Jeremy chimed in. "It is extremely important that no one talk of this on the phone. Lunadi is more secretive than most of us and so, he uses book codes to communicate. I suggest from now on that we be very tight lipped."

"Excellent point," Phil said. "Jason, can you and Lunadi find the most efficient way for our group to secretly communicate via code words, book codes, whatever you think we can quickly put to use? Your contact will be Erin who will communicate to the rest of us."

"We will do that Mr. President," Jason said, standing up. "We can meet briefly one more time and by then, I'll be able to let you know final status and if we need anything else."

"Very well," Phil said. "Anything else?"

"We would be remiss not to update you on Nicaragua," Stone replied. "Austin and I received a disturbing report and were able to look at the final analysis over lunch. We lost one of our CIA assets there due to machinegun fire from a Chinese patrol boat. The two men with him were able to get away but took some disturbing photographs. As you may know, the New Nicaragua Canal has only been started at Port Brito, where the Chinese have amassed a massive amount of supplies. They have been sneaking in their ships one by one, having them towed by barges and tugs so the heat plumes do not show up during the satellite pass, which is during the early evening hours. Look at these, *passing the photos around the table*."

"I don't see anything but a lake," Erin said, staring at a photo.

"Same here," Phil joined in.

"Look closer around the edges of the lake," Austin said.

"I, ...," Jeremy began, his voice trailing off. "Wait, are these faint outlines of ships?"

"Good eye," Stone said. "Yes, they are currently the bulk of the Chinese Blue Navy. Roughly two hundred ships, give or take and I suspect more are on the way."

"They're not even visible to the eye," Phil said. "How the hell did they pull that off?"

The rest of the group was casting glances at each other, nodding affirmatively.

"Our best guess Mr. President, is that they have found a way to camouflage their ships with a multicam like we do troops." Austin responded. "At least that's what our agent thinks and he's one of our absolute best. Even during daylight, he said it was difficult to spot the ships, which is why our asset was killed. They had to get too close to the target."

"Will the incident draw suspicion?" Jason asked.

"We do not believe it will," Stone replied. "According to our sources, they have had frequent disappearances of small boats, mostly in the evening around these parts of the lake, *pointing*."

"This is cause for concern," Phil said. "General, you may want to consider advancing your timetable."

"Yes sir," Jason said, looking at Lunadi. "We're already on it."

"Great," Phil said. "Let's adjourn and if you need anything, contact Erin and she'll speak with the rest of us."

Everyone filed out of the conference room. Erin and Lunadi lagged behind the others as they walked down the hall.

"I know that your schedule is very busy Erin," Lunadi said. "But I was wondering if you could come spend the weekend sometime soon out at my property?"

Erin was gazing into Lunadi's eyes. There was something there, something special about this man. She was not able to put her finger on it. The thought of him, despite their short acquaintance, pulled at her heart strings. She got chills thinking about the trip.

"I cannot promise anything in terms of dates," Erin replied softly, almost a whisper. "But I will try to arrange something as soon as I can. If I cannot, would you be willing to come back?"

"Yes," Lunadi replied. "Training will ramp up heavily now, but I will see what I can do as well."

"Great," Erin smile. "Let's see what we can come up with." The two walked just a little too close to each other as they followed the others.

Jeremy had glanced over his shoulder and caught them out of the corner of his eye speaking in unintelligible low tones. Ah he thought, the heart of the warrior softens with compassion. It was the compassion he knew that Lunadi had, despite his distrust and extreme dislike of those who managed the government. He would die on his feet before he would surrender to those who sought control over all Americans. For this woman, he knew that Lunadi would bow on his knees to her. Funny thing what love can do.

CHAPTER 5

The Dragon and the Bear

General Qiang's car was stuck in a traffic jam. The accident slowing them down had been caused deliberately so that CIA operatives could get into position to tail him. They knew his assumed identity; his passport was flagged the minute it left Nicaragua and again in Istanbul. Behind him about sixty-five yards, among the jumble of cars waiting for the accident to clear, was an agent on a motorcycle. She blended in with the traffic. Even though the general's security guards and driver attempted to spot tails, they completely overlooked the motorcycle, scattered with over a dozen others amongst the cars. People were beginning to become impatient and signified it by blasting their horns.

"Send a message to Tyurin," Li said, talking to his security guard. "Tell him we will be delayed due to traffic."

Li sat patiently waiting, after all, there was nothing he could do to affect the outcome of his current situation. Despite the noise of the traffic, they rolled the windows down for some fresh air. There was a stiff breeze blowing in off the Sea of Marmara as they sat stuck on Kennedy Cd that ran mostly eastward along the waterfront.

Finally, much longer than anticipated, the traffic began moving again. Off to the right Li could see ferry boats, cargo vessels and motorboats that effortlessly glided across the water. They passed the Yenikapi Ferry Terminal off to the right and a little further down, the driver made a U-turn to go back the opposite direction so he could pull off onto Aksakal Sk heading north toward Beyazit Square and the Grand Bazaar.

He could have taken an easier route but wanted to make sure no one was following. The agent on the motorcycle kept going along Kennedy as a small sedan in front of them turned onto the same road. The road twisted and turned as they wound their way up the hill. Suddenly the sedan stopped, letting a female passenger out. Li's driver hit the brakes and horn. Staring at the driver as he passed, he yelled, "Идиот." It meant idiot in Russian. The driver shrugged his shoulders as a way of apology and pulled back onto the street continuing in the same direction. The occupants of Li's car did not know that it was a ruse for the car to pick up pace behind them and pull into the same parking lot for the Bazaar as Dragon.

Let's see the American's watch us in this place Li mused. The Grand Bazaar consisted of a sprawling network of narrow streets and over 4,000 shops peddling jewelry, rugs, leatherwork, clothes and just about anything one could imagine. It was always crowded and today particularly so because it was Saturday. The one thing the general didn't count on was that because it was so crowded, it was difficult to spot surveillance teams. In a lucky break, knowing the affinity for the generals to pick up gifts for their wives while traveling, Sam Malone had estimated where his teams needed to be. Because it was such a tourist area, all the teams, again, were men and women from different cultures; they had picked up Dragon the minute they left the parking lot.

Dragon and his security detail were walking through a

covered section of shops in a particularly crowded area when they entered a shop about fifty feet in front of Sam and his female Istanbul asset, the same one that had been on the motorcycle. They instinctively moved to the other side of the narrow street as they passed. Sam could see the two CSB security guards, but there was a curtain at the back of the shop, and he supposed Dragon had went through it. His female companion tapped him on the shoulder indicating she would go in and do some shopping. He knew she would snoop around. Nodding affirmatively, he spoke into the mic hidden beneath his shirt, requesting another team come up and position themselves for listening. This team had a laser microphone that would be able to pick up voices in the shop. Whether they could discern them afterward would be another issue.

His companion still in the shop, the other team arrived and with the male turning his back toward the shop, his female companion, pretending to whisper to him and show him a little attention, trained the laser mic onto a table filled with very colorful Turkish pottery situated on the right side of the black curtain. She gave a small thumbs up to Sam who, his companion returning, walked off. They would get what they could but knew this meeting would be short and might not yield worthwhile intelligence.

When they had entered, Li nodded to the shop keeper as he strode past, glanced back and eased through the curtain. The place was small, but adequate. Seated at a small table sipping Turkish coffee, was Red Star.

"Ah, Li my friend," Panu said. "We must stop meeting like this. What is so important we had to meet again so soon?" It broke the ice as they both lightly laughed.

"How close are you to being ready?" Li asked.

"I have been going over the plans based on our last

meeting," Panu replied. "Theoretically in six to eight weeks. We are creating an announcement to have military training exercises with Venezuela which should discard any suspicions the Americans have. What about yourself?"

"The President has told me that he will come up with an appropriate date," Li said. "But he has not been keeping me apprised of what the committee is deciding."

"And that concerns you?"

"Yes, because it could delay launch and give away our advantage of surprise."

"What are you saying?" Panu asked, concerned.

"We had an incident recently in which a skiff came up next to a destroyer," Li said. "Ordinarily, I wouldn't think anything about it, but it outran one of our gunboats. Although such incidents have happened before, those boats were slow. What concerns me is that they may have discovered more of our ships and how we have been hiding them."

"Hmmmm," Panu nodded thoughtfully. "If they discover you before we launch, the advantage of surprise will be gone. That is most concerning. What would you suggest?"

"The best scenario would be to push our timetable," Li said. "But to do that, President Jin needs to give me the go ahead. He's so control minded that I doubt he will. We have already had multiple disagreements and he has never budged."

"Then, we continued as planned," Panu said. "You sure you don't want some coffee?"

"No, I prefer tea," Li replied. "Besides, that stuff is unfiltered, it'll wake the dead."

Panu grinned and snapped his fingers twice signaling one of his bodyguards. The guard leaned over as Panu whispered something in his ear. While he was thus engaged, Li pulled a smaller version of their invasion map from the small attaché case he had been carrying. It was neatly folded down the center to hide its contents. The curtain briefly opened as the guard brought in a tray with both coffee and tea, sat it down and disappeared.

"Thank you," Li said, as he began pouring himself a cup of tea. "You know, the most crucial element will be timing. We must work in unison and be on station off Long Beach and Houston at the same time."

"It would be best if we could pull off their navy first," Panu said.

"Yes, that would give us a better opportunity for a foothold," Li replied. "If we could do that, we would be able to set up our anti-ship missiles and would be able to defend against any troop landings they could make."

"We already have our container missile systems set up in ten of their largest ports, as well as sitting in small lots around the country. Push the magic button and their power and communications go away within a few minutes."

"Agreed," Li said. "But we must not get ahead of ourselves," Li explained. "We must wait until just prior to invasion before we do that."

"Do you think those systems will remain hidden?" Panu asked. "I shudder to think of the consequences if they are found."

"Relax," Li said, grinning. "Do not worry my friend. We have had most of the American politicians on our payroll for twenty years and keep recruiting more. If something happens, I'll be the first to know. They are currently making a drive against their President to accuse him of an affair, colluding with foreign governments, whatever they can throw at him to keep him occupied. When you are looking at the buzzing flies above your head, it is difficult to keep track of the snake crawling through the door. With that, our primary asset whom we've paid millions to over the past decade, will be in charge."

"I have met their President," Panu said. "He is a warrior and those that follow him are also, at least most of them. If they become involved, I do not think we have the military might to deal with millions of them."

"We may not need to," Li replied. "The asset, once in primary position will circumvent their second amendment and confiscate all guns. That will allow us to do whatever we want. Besides, even if that timetable does not work and Weld remains in office, once we hit them with the first salvo, it will be too late."

"How do you figure that?" Panu asked. "If the patriots as they call them, remain armed, we will be drawn into a long-drawn out war. Even if we move in more troops, our supply lines will be greatly extended and vulnerable. We must not be overly confident. Might I remind you of history? The Germans captured Rostov in WWII, their supply lines were overextended, and they consequently lost the town, it was the first time the German advance had been successfully repelled. And it was for the same reason that Napoleon lost 100 years before that, they both outpaced their supply lines."

"I understand your position my friend," Li responded. "However, I assure you that nothing they plan will go unnoticed by us and that we will prevail. Once we begin, our transport and supply ships will be on the way and, we have stored vast amounts of munitions, equipment, food, numbers of personnel, and other supplies in western and central Canada, right under the noses of both governments and their intelligence groups. If we gain the element of surprise, there will be nothing they can do to win. More importantly, China is hemorrhaging money due to pay outs to all the American politicians. Once the battle begins, I will have our primary asset call an emergency meeting of their senate and house. And as the Americans would say, I will give them a big surprise."

Panu was not quite sure he understood and didn't want to. His only concern was to hold up his end and make Mother Russia proud.

"So, you see my friend, you worry too much."

Panu was nodding his head, his thought wheels spinning. Being a general, Panu had always thought about the upcoming attack as a military matter to accomplish an objective for his country and people, after all, everyone needed food. It was not until now that he realized just how brutal the Chinese would be. Thinking back on history, he was reminded of the invasion of Russia by Hitler's German army. By the skin of their teeth and the start of what became a brutal winter, they had miraculously emerged the victor against a superior foe. Now, their timeline for attack was mirroring that of the Germans against Russia. If they got trapped in the U.S. during winter it was entirely possible all their well-laid plans would go out the window.

"Regardless of your plans Li," Panu began. "We will need to contend with their navy in the Gulf of Mexico, as well as ground forces moving to the coasts. And while we can take down the communications temporarily, it is unlikely we will take down military communications."

"That is so," Li responded. "But all we need to do is blind them temporarily until we have a foothold."

"Hmmmm," Panu pondered. "I see what you mean, but how are you proposing to do that?"

"Explode an EMP in the upper atmosphere, likely two," Li said emphatically!

"That will also affect our communications somewhat," Panu began. "Although it won't knock them out, we could get glitches at critical times."

"True," Li replied. "We will just need to live with it. Nothing about this invasion will be perfect. We just need to work around the kinks."

"So, let's run it down by the stages," Panu said, pouring himself another cup of coffee.

Li, looking about to ensure there were no prying eyes, unfolded the smaller map. Using a dry erase marker, red for China, blue for Russia, he began marking as he went.

"Let us go over our plans again," Li said. "Once orders are given, we will depart Nicaragua to Long Beach Port twenty-four hours before your warships sail. It will take us about three and one-half days to reach launch position, it should only take you about two and one-half days. At this point, we will set off the EMPs. The effects will cover the entire U.S. within milliseconds. Two hours after the EMP's we will give command for all units to engage regardless of where our ships are at zero hour. This includes, launching missiles from all ships. Container launchers will be launched at our to-be-determined zero hour before the EMPs are exploded. We do not want to risk a communication glitch due to the EMP so, they must be launched prior to that. This includes all of them; those moved around the U.S. and in free trade zones. All total, combined with yours, we have a total of two hundred containers: 800 missiles. You need to select alternate targets in Russian sectors in event you are out of range for primary targets. This will ensure redundancy since many missiles in the container launchers are keyed to primary targets as well. Our troops will move from near Ottawa southward to New York City and Philadelphia on into Washington DC."

"Let me make a suggestion," Panu began. "It is likely going to be difficult to supply the troops logistically. Why don't we have supply ships shadow the coasts to keep food, munitions and fuel moving to them. On the west coast in your sectors, that would be U.S. Highway 101 that twists and turns through Washington, Oregon and California. On the east coast in our sectors, that would be U.S. Highway Route 17 from Florida through Virginia and then, I-95 north from Virginia to Maine. Perhaps it is not the best way, but the supply lines would be harder to cut."

"Excellent idea comrade," Li said. "That would be like bypassing controlled territory as General McArthur did to the Japanese, which worked flawlessly. It would make their resistance irrelevant. As a matter of fact, once we begin, we will look for pockets of resistance then, move past and flank them. It likely wouldn't work for large groups of several hundred men and their equipment but would be quite effective for smaller groups."

Li was looking at the wall, staring into an unseen distance. Panu instinctively knew that Li was playing various scenarios over in his head and applying strategies to each.

"You plan should work admirably," Li said. "We will have our engineers and logistical staff begin working on the specifics as soon as we get back."

Sam and his fellow agent had walked about thirty yards further, just enough distance to maintain contact with the two agents handling the laser mic. One of them gave Sam an imperceptible thumbs up indicating they were able to hear the conversation. With the signal, Sam walked further down where there were few people along the Bazaar walkway. Pulling a satellite phone from his backpack, he made a brief call.

Austin was busy going over the last report from Nicaragua and examining the photos with a magnifying glass for any details he may have overlooked. He glanced up when he realized there was a soft knock at the door.

"Sam on line one." Sheila said.

"Thank you," Austin said, reaching for his phone, eyes still glued on the photos. "How's your vacation going?"

"Quite well," Sam replied. "Caught two big fish by luring them in. I'll send you some pics soon. Anything you want me to pick up for you while I'm here?"

"Yeah," Austin replied. "How about some of that coffee you were bragging about?"

"Roger that," Sam replied. "Peggy is coming back early so will send it with her."

"Great," Austin said. "I'll look forward to getting it. Have fun and let me know when you'll be back."

Austin clicked down the receiver. So, the Dragon and Red Star were in another meeting. Luring them in meant they had a signal of the conversation, which would be transmitted via secure satellite relay they affectionately called Peggy. He picked up his phone again.

"We'll be receiving a transmission shortly from Peggy about our friends,"

"Should prove interesting," Stone said. "Our eyes only, lets meet in the SCIF as soon as you have it."

"Roger that."

Panu was pointing with his finger at the Canadian portion of the map.

"This is a large gap to leave between Ontario and British Columbia."

"Yes," Li replied. "However, there is little populace across those states. The only real threat is from a few air force bases, which are used mostly for heavy bombers to strike you, a relic of the Cold War and, which we have targeted with our container missiles. There's no real threat to our armies that will be moving south."

"Then," Panu began. "Moving out of Ontario, we will have the age-old problem of logistics."

"Correct," Li said. "But that should not be a problem as the supply line will be following the troops in timed increments. There is always the risk of overreach, but that should not be a problem in our case."

"The rapid advance should shift the war effort to our favor," Panu said. "Just like the Germans in WWII, we will use the blitzkrieg principle and overwhelm the enemy before resistance can build up. What are your plans for movement?"

"We will push straight south from Ottawa down 781 to 81 for short, circumvent Baltimore and drive to DC," Li said. "Our fleet and missiles will be bombing major infrastructure along the way in Boston, Philadelphia, New York, and Baltimore and your ships offshore will be of great assistance. We will hit all the military installations, communications, and power hubs before moving. The goal is to drive the roughly 500 miles in twenty hours. Once we are dug in, it will be difficult to get us out."

"From our landing near Houston, we will take I-10 to Mobile," Panu said. "From there, we will travel up through Atlanta, over to Charlotte and on to Richmond. I have several columns set to branch off along the way to take mop up after bombardment, the troops at Ft Campbell, Ft Bragg and Ft. Jackson."

"What about the naval base in Norfolk?" Li asked.

"That will be done by submarine launched cruise missiles," Panu said. "How will you implement your plan of attack?"

"You already know about the west coast components," Li began. "Along with those we will use several divisions to branch off from Seattle and move along through Boise, picking up Interstate 84 into Salt Lake. From Long Beach, we will make a push through Victorville and Barstow along Interstate 15 into Las Vegas. Once we have Salt Lake and Las Vegas secured, we will take Denver from both the north and south."

"That fits with our planning well," Panu remarked. "That will give us the major control points to consolidate power after victory. One thing still worries me and that is the so-called American Patriots. You do know that many Americans refer to Texas as the 'State of Guns' and they are not fond of their government. Bypassing them could be a mistake."

"Yes, it could be," Li said. "But they are too busy fighting their own government in a war of words. Besides, they are clueless of what's really going on. After all, our social-media campaign of limitation and censorship has caused so much distrust that they believe nothing the mainstream media puts out. We need not worry about them."

"Do you need additional support from us?" Panu asked. "The plan looks too textbook and will work only if all goes perfectly. I've learned through years of NATO games and the Americans Middle East tactics that we must not assume we will have no hiccups."

"I feel much the same," Li said. "As long as we keep the element of surprise, we should be fine. The one hiccup I see is if we do not take Las Vegas. It is isolated but will take us a few days, perhaps a week or more, to move enforce."

"Hmmmm," Panu thought. "I can lend you one, perhaps two divisions, which should be sufficient. We may lose the element of surprise but could pincer the city with you coming in from the west and us from the south. I'm almost certain they will blow the Hoover Dam bypass. That leaves us only with the opportunity, to save time, to move through Texas then Arizona via Phoenix and we can combine forces and drive in together. Circling around to come in from the northeast or north requires too much time."

"Correct," Li said. "I do not have a map on me but have been thinking of this problem for a while. When you get back, consider coming across as you have said to Bullhead City and driving into Las Vegas from the south. As I recall, the road runs parallel to what is called the Black Canyon so, if you run short of water, you should be able to replenish it from the Colorado River. Come, I am starving. Let us take a tour of the square. Afterward, there's a good restaurant I heard about that is only a short drive away."

The two men casually left the shop, strolling along the covered walk in the Bazaar. Sam's group were able to follow them with comparative ease without being detected. Dragon and Red Star strode a short distance to Beyazit Square, which was much less crowded than the streets inside the Grand Bazaar. This allowed both of their attentive security detail to observe their surroundings and determine if they were being followed.

Sam had his men drop back so that they blended more with the crowd, which they would occasionally slip behind, remove a coat and then, put on another one of different color so that they remained unnoticed. On several instances, different members of the team would perform a waterfall to remain blended with other people in the scattered crowd as they kept a watchful eye on their targets.

The Beyazit Square was home to the Beyazit and Nuruosmaniye Mosques. The generals decided to go inside, which required removing their shows and putting on disposable foot covers. This made it difficult to watch them, so Sam only sent in one agent to keep eyes on them. He knew that the two generals would not discuss anything of significance and that any tidbit would be guarded. He was certain he had gotten most of what they would be able to garner from this meeting, but he would keep at it until the meeting was finished.

"What is this tower?" Panu asked.

"It is the Beyazit Tower," Li replied. "Many years ago, it was a lookout tower for fires in the city. Both men were in deep thought as they walked, contemplating that which was to come. Abruptly, Li stopped, they were standing in front of the main gate to Istanbul University.

"Isn't the gate magnificent?" Li asked.

"Yes, it is quite beautiful architecture," Panu responded.

"Have you ever been inside the gate and the classrooms?"

"I never told you, but this is where I obtained my master's degree in international relations and security studies." Li said.

"You speak Arabic?" Panu asked, surprised.

"Oh no," Li chuckled. "The courses here, most of them, are taught in English because it is the global language of business. Our own universities have followed the same pattern. Most of the major universities in China such as HoHai, Beijing, and others offer all their courses in English as well because most of the students speak it."

"Ah yes," Panu said. "We too have followed suite to gain more of the international students. Quite of few of our universities teach courses in English for a degree, but only at the master's level. An acquaintance of mine in NATO earned his master's degree in aerodynamics at the Moscow Institute of Physics and Technology. Don't you think it is ironic that we seek to destroy that which we mimic in our own cultures?"

"In some ways I suppose," Li said. "But it is a necessity to keep America from constantly imposing their will on the rest of the world, toppling governments as they desire, and imposing economic sanctions on whom they will, all to get them to fall in line behind their corrupt government."

"But it is the government," Panu said. "It is not the people, for they are much like any people from any nation. Look around us and the number of nationalities we can identify. There, *pointing*, is an Arabic couple, and there, a European couple, American, Asian, and more. All of them are enjoying life, taking pictures, having a vacation and having fun. I doubt any of them are thinking of overthrowing a country. In my travels I have found that we all have much in common. Most taut a love of music as a common thread, but there is a love of children, similar experiences in jobs, and typically a dislike of their own government, among other commonalities."

"Yes," Li commented. "All true and I would not disagree. The problem would not be just the sanctions or bullying but using food as a weapon is crossing the line. Since they are unwilling to meet our demands, we will take this route."

"I suppose you are correct," Panu replied. "However, their Secretary of State has contacted us and is outlining potential aid packages. Our intelligence says that they have the same problems with the shortages that we do. I had not followed the environment issue, but the cooling, along with awfully bad weather for winter, spring, and fall has affected us all."

"Yes, Fabiani has also spoken with President Jin and our Politburo as well," Li said. "The issue is we do not believe them."

"Why?" Panu asked. "Our intelligence shows they are as worried as we are and have given much aid already, leaving them with considerably less food and other resources than they typically have. I'm not on their side mind you, but they generally give much and seem to be doing so now. Our agriculture minister says their numbers correlate with what we are seeing in terms of overall foodstuffs."

"Yes, I know," Li said. "We are also aware of the massive flooding, droughts, locusts, and other production aspects globally. The food shortage now is nothing compared to what it will be in a few months and who knows what next year will bring. That is why we need to move now. We need to capture and control America's food and other resources. Any nation starving will eliminate aid to others if they have their own shortage. That is why we cannot afford to set back and let America dictate our supplies. They have much, we have little. Do the math."

Panu contemplated what Li had said. Overall, it made sense, but the risk to success was great. And Panu knew one thing about Americans, in spite of their hate-mongering government, they were a very giving people.

"Look there," Li said. "The front of the mosque. If we were high enough, we would be able to see the Ayasofya Camii that is directly southeast of it. Come, let us go to dinner."

The sun was beginning to hover near the horizon as the mosque cast long shadows over the Grand Bazaar. Cirrus clouds filled the sky as the sun sank in a bright orange ball, creating a swirl of multiple orange colors from bright to dark, filling the landscape with subtle yet bright hues. The splendor was indescribable, and it seemed to bring a measure of peace to the two men. Before long they were in their cars and headed toward Taskim Square. Panu was enjoying the ride. He mused to himself how Li knew Istanbul so well. Studying at the university had given him an in-depth knowledge of the city. His car was passing over the water now as they crossed it on Galata Köprüsü merging into Kimeratlti Cd. The Bosporus straight that linked the Sea of Marmara with the Black Sea was on the right. The deep blue of the water by day had turned to black. The lights surrounding the straight shimmered off the water's surface. Panu was in a trance because it reminded him so much of home and Moscow. This city indeed had a historical past. The car began to slow as it followed Li's car off the main thoroughfare and wound down smaller streets toward the square. The traffic was rather crazy, cars would pull out in front with just the fender portion blocking the way as they forced other drivers to slow and dart into a spot in front of them. Getting out of the cars near Istiklal Cd., with the customary two-person security detail, the men made their way down the street, the detail taking up a box formation defensive position, common in bodyguard work for dignitaries thus, going unnoticed to those not experienced in such matters.

Panu, walking alongside Li, marveled at the number of shops, restaurants, cafes, and street shows. There were trams like those in San Francisco.

"Is it always this busy," Panu asked, speaking loudly to make himself heard above the din.

"Always," Li said, grinning. "This is the most famous street and entertainment area in the city. I used to come here to unwind after a test."

"Where are we headed?" Panu asked.

"We have a few blocks to get to Asmali Mescit," Li replied. "It is the dining and wining street."

Panu laughed.

"Seriously," Li said. "If you enjoy night life and great restaurants, it is the place to go. You'll see."

Li seemed to take great pride in showing Panu his old stomping grounds from college and the fact that he knew the city like the back of his hand. He did not tell the general about the Chinese intelligence safe houses in the city and how they collected data on people and countries that did business in it. On the one hand, Istanbul was a beautiful city, but like all major cities, the daytime view stood in stark contrast to the darkness that hid so well, the dark dealing of men. It was only a few minutes later that they reached the restaurant that Li had selected. It was obvious as soon as they entered why he had.

"Greeting Li Qiang." A man spoke loudly from halfway across the restaurant. "It has been a long time."

"Baris," Li exclaimed, nodding and shaking hands. "So good to see you again. Come, this is my friend Panu. We're visiting some other friends and will be leaving tomorrow."

"Oh, so soon," Baris said. "Well, at least you came tonight. What will you have?"

"Do you have a quiet table in the corner?" Li asked. "We need to discuss a few things. Also, our men here, can you hook them up with something they can eat at the bar?"

"Of course," Baris said. "Right this way."

The two were seated at a table along the front of the establishment, but away from the door next to a wall where they could observe people on the street. Baris waved over a server and left the two men alone as they ordered a drink then, had a look at the menu. By the time their drinks arrived they knew what they wanted and ordered, looking out the plate-glass window at the busy scene outside.

"To you my friend," Li said, raising his glass, as they each bumped drinks in the toast. "May success and fortune come our way."

"Yes," Panu smiled wryly. "To us and our project."

They talked of friends and family and what the future may bring as they ate. Their security detail was positioned around the bar in the center front of the restaurant, constantly attentive to potential security threats.

Sam's team of agents outside, along the street, kept tabs on Dragon and Red Star who remained unaware of their presence. It was late when they wrapped it up. Listening in on the conversation, there was nothing mentioned of the attack that Sam would bet his small CIA salary on, would not be long in coming. The team trailed them back to their hotel and the next morning to the airport.

As soon as the two had departed, Sam was on a satellite phone to Austin.

"Update on our vacation," Sam said.

"Hope you're having fun trapsing around," Austin responded. "Time to get back here and get to work."

"Understood," Sam said. "Fun time here is over anyway. Will see you tomorrow."

It was early the next morning when Austin got a knock on his office door. He looked up to see Sam.

"I have the information," Sam said.

"Great, one moment please." Austin said, holding up a finger. "Stone, he's here. Okay, on the way."

"Let's go sit with Stone," Austin said. "He's eager to see what you have for us."

A couple of minutes later they were led into Stone's office.

"Shut the door will you Sheila," Stone said. "I'll let you know when I'm available again."

Once the door was shut, Stone wasted no time as the two

took up chairs in front of his desk. "What do you have for us?"

"It's not pretty but here's the gist of it," Sam began. "The attack routes are as you had suggested to me earlier, walking to a map and pointing to specific points on it. They mentioned blinding us with an EMP before launching their attack, moving forces out of Canada to support the west coast attack and taking out our power and communication just before. Also, they have someone inside, in the congress, but plenty of congress are taking their money – trust no one. I'm not certain who their primary contact is."

Stone and Austin glanced at each other, nodding understandingly as Sam continued.

"We have also ascertained that they intend on using container-based missile systems to launch at least 800 missiles just prior to invasion. They were not specific, but my guess is they will launch the missiles then, the EMP's followed by the attack. They are also working up a plan to deal with our navy in the Gulf of Mexico and attacking our shore-based troops. With the number of missiles they discussed, I'm supposing this will be done with those. But as I recall, their new destroyers can have sixty to a hundred missiles each. It's a real mess and if I must say so, fairly brilliant. They discussed victory as long as they kept surprise. Even without it, this is going to be a real shit fest. All the information is on this recording."

Sam pulled a compact disc from his messenger bag and slid it across to Stone.

"We were fairly sure about the container-based missiles," Stone said. "However, we did not think there would be that many. Did they mention where they may be?"

"Yes," Sam replied. "Here is a transcript of the conversation from both the meeting in the Grand Bazaar and the dinner meeting later where they just chatted about friends, life and stuff."

Sam handed each of them the transcripts of the conversation the generals had.

"Austin," Stone said. "Do you know where Jason is?"

"He's actually at Andrews," Austin said.

"Call him and ask him to come over ASAP," Stone said, turning to look out the window, concern on his face. Abruptly, he turned back, glancing at the conversation transcript.

"Did the Dragon and Red Star mention when this attack may occur?"

"There was no specific date given," Sam said. "Only that it was up to President Jin to confirm when with Dragon. Apparently, the Russians are ready and waiting on a go from the CCP."

"That makes sense," Stone said. "Russia does have a navy better equipped to transport troops. Austin, hand me one of those U.S. maps behind you."

Austin turned around and on a small table behind him was a stack of U.S. maps with just an outline of each state, Canada, and Mexico. There must have been several hundred of them.

"You sure you have enough of these," Austin said, grinning as he handed Stone the map.

"I thought they may come in handy for our planning sessions," Stone replied. "I'll go through the transcripts and you mark the locations of where they say the container missiles are."

The two carefully plotted all the locations mentioned and double checked them against the locations mentioned in the transcripts. They were just finishing when Jason arrived.

"Ah Jason," Stone said, introducing him to Sam. "We

have come across some intelligence we need your expertise with, especially the tactical side."

"You mentioned before you would be using teams to detect the container missile systems the Chinese would be using against us," Austin chimed in. "Would you mind marking the locations on this blank map?"

"I would rather not as it could compromise the mission," Jason said, eyeing them carefully.

"Please," Stone said. "It's vital."

"Very well," Jason said as he began marking locations his teams would be searching for. Finishing, he pushed the map in front of the other three men.

"It's almost identical," Sam whispered.

"Identical to what?" Jason asked.

"To this," Austin said, pushing the map they had just created next to the one Jason had drawn.

Jason looked at both maps, exhaling loudly.

"Where did you get this?" Jason asked, voice cracking.

"Tell him Sam," Stone said.

"We have been following Dragon and Red Star, code names for two generals from the CCP and Russia. They have met several times in out of the way locations. So far, we have been able to conceal our surveillance efforts. This map was produced from a conversation they had in Istanbul two days ago. The only difference I can see is that you missed a couple of locations but have added a few more."

"How were you able to get close enough to them to listen in?" Jason asked. "I mean, are you quite certain this information is legitimate?"

"Quite," Sam responded. "We have tailed them everywhere we could, collecting all the HUMINT possible. We gathered this using a laser microphone and the quality was pretty good."

"Here's a transcript of the conversation," Stone said, handing it over.

Jason perused the transcript quickly, glancing at the map and back to the transcript.

"There's something else you should know," Stone began, as Jason put down the transcript. "Sam and his team have found 150 Chinese warships, give or take, camouflaged, in Lake Nicaragua. The go ahead for launch will be given by President Jin. This means they are not ready yet. We have also informed you of CCP troop movements in Canada. The sixty-four-dollar question is, in your opinion, how long do you think we have before they initiate war?"

"That's difficult to answer," Jason said. "But if I were to hazard a guess and based on what I know of their military numbers and strength, I would say we have three to six months."

"You really think we have that long?" Stone asked.

"Yes," Jason replied. "It is not the numbers that are of the biggest concern for an operation like this, but the planning and coordination that make it possible. If logistics are lacking, defeat rather than victory is inevitable. Sam, have you been collecting intelligence on their troops in Canada?"

"We are just beginning to look at that," Sam said. "I lost a man down in Nicaragua getting the intelligence we have to this point. Now that it is burgeoning out of control as it were, we are beginning to focus more field efforts on that piece of their operation. I have several teams up there now. Do you have any specific requests?"

"Certainly," Jason said. "The most important would be their locations, numbers, armaments, and likely supply mechanism and routes. It appears they have been up there far longer than we realize making their supply chains somewhat evident. I'm sure the locals know more about

James Tindall

them than they would like, especially since the Canadian Prime Minister invited them in to help protect their assets. A ruse of course, but too many left-wing pansies believe everything they hear on the news. Also, look particularly for any missile systems and aircraft. They are good at mingling them with private aircraft scattered here and there, likely tucked out of the way, so they are unnoticed."

"We can certainly do that," Sam responded. "Anything else?"

"Yes, Stone has pictures of the missile container systems they have. We have developed an alternate plan to defeat them. However, in the event you find some and we cannot get up there we need GPS coordinates so that we can destroy them using our own missiles."

"Understood," Sam said. "Stone, if you and Austin don't mind, I'd like your permission to begin this operation at once. We are growing short on time."

"By all means," Austin said. "We must move with haste."

"Do you have a code name you want to use for it?" Stone asked.

"Hmmmm," Sam mused. "I would go with Operation Maple Tree, but that would be a dead giveaway. Let's call it Operation Eider."

The other three men raised their eyebrows.

"It's a small species of duck prevalent to Canada. The male, although brightly colored blends right in, which is what we'll need to do."

They all had a good chuckle.

"I'll be on my way gentlemen," Sam said, walking to the door. "I'll relay my information to Austin as usual."

"Oh Sam," Stone said. "Be careful, these guys bite."

"Roger that sir, closing the door behind him."

The congress woman was sitting on her favorite bench in the park, awaiting the call. No sooner than she had sat down, her cell rang. She looked about, wondering if this person or those who may be associated with the voice had eyes on her. With a trembling hand, she raised the phone to her ear as she continued looking furtively about.

"Hello."

"I have spoken with our friend," the fluctuating electronic voice said. "The initial plan did not do the damage needed. What are your next steps?"

"I anticipated this," Susan said. "We increase the pressure."

"How? We are paying you a large sum, specifics by my superiors are requested. Begin!"

"We have tainted the President with the initial story. The sharks are circling, now we add blood to the water. The next step will be accusations, supposedly emanating from the State Department that the President is colluding with the Chinese and that evidence will soon be forthcoming. I have already planted that evidence with falsified emails and phone calls. And, we have a rogue CIA agent that will verify the calls and emails."

"Excellent. How effective do you think this will be?"

"By the time they uncover that the story has lots of holes, the President will have been impeached and out of office," Susan said quietly, still looking about. "I hope you are ready because once it begins, it will pick up momentum quickly."

"Understood."

The line went dead as Susan, making sure no one was around, slowly rose and began walking back toward the state house. She knew that she would be taken care of, so far, she had been overwhelmed by the amount of donations to her campaign, quite a bit of which she had siphoned off for personal use as she continued to build her power base. The mere thought of it began to excite her. Still, she wondered what was in it for this mysterious voice and for the Speaker. It had to be the Speaker because she wielded the big stick if the President were ousted. Apparently, she had lots of dirt on the VP involving child pornography and drinking the blood of children. There was now a large group, especially among the elites who tortured and terrified kids to build adrenochrome in the blood then, drink it to reduce aging. Such evil she thought but it was a proven fact that in past societies, human sacrifice helped bolster differences in social status, reinforcing social stratifications and hastening the development and separation between layers in that status. If the VP were involved in such, even the inuendo would have the entire country calling for his head. My God she thought, that's the Speakers play. She is next in line for President if she can get both out. She was certainly shrew enough to execute such a plan and succeed.

Sky Thinker and Ferni had spent the past few weeks on the road, flying and driving, and had met with Tribal leaders in over twenty central and eastern states. Surprisingly, they had met with much greater success than they had hoped. Of course, a little divine intervention here and there didn't hurt. They had flown to California and had met with the federated tribes. The twelve bands included the Chelan, Chief Joseph Band of Nez Perce, Colville, Entiat, Lakes, Methow, Moses-Columbia, Nespelem, Okanogan, Palus, San Poil, and Wenatchi. It had been an interesting meeting with too much yelling and screaming until the Mediator appeared. All differences were set aside. As they visited each Tribe, new recruits were sent to other tribes so that their recruitment numbers grew. They were making good headway considering the obstacles in dealing with Tribal governments. Along their western route, they would visit the Agua Caliente, Alturas, Tule River, Quechan, Gila River, Lakota, Hopi and all other western tribes. Their last stop would be the Navajo Tribe because it was on their land, in Chaco Canyon, that the council would be held for all the tribe's leadership and warriors. The President had already closed the location until further notice upon advice from Jeremy.

"Do you think we will be able to keep our time schedule and fulfill the command given us?" Ferni asked.

"It will be close, but we will," Sky Thinker replied. "I must tell you that I cannot remember a time when I've been so excited. The warrior path has been my life, but never did I imagine serving Sun God in such a capacity."

"I understand exactly," Ferni said. "To think for hundreds of years that our people, scattered over the land on many reservations would have the chance to save the nation that had been so savagely and brutally taken from them."

Ferni let out a big sigh. Sky Thinker glanced over at him briefly from behind the wheel. There were tears running down his cheeks.

"Finally," Ferni said. "Our people will be able to take their rightful place in this country. When this is finished, we shall no longer be subjugated to the state and federal government nor will we suffer the overseers of the BIA. Some of us may not live through this to see it, but it will come."

"Yes," Sky Thinker said. "A new era is dawning, one with great responsibilities and great satisfaction and reward. I do not remember a time that I looked so forward to the future. It is ironic that both our warriors and those of the Earth

Surface People have trained all our lives and have not had the opportunity to war. Now, we will fight the war that will potentially end all others. I wish my father and our ancestors before us could be here to witness it."

The weather in Thunder Bay, Ontario was getting quite cold. Weather reports about a brisk breeze blowing off the bay was an understatement; it was downright bone chilling. This area was much further north than Sam and his team, Samantha and Rob, wanted to be at this time of year. The town wasn't exactly a thriving metropolis. They had been riding around the province and seen quite a few CCP military vehicles around, but no clear indication of where they were going. They had covered the area down by the waterfront, across from Pie Island and along Thunder Bay off Lake Superior. Next, they had driven around a little, getting out and walking several blocks at a time doing a grid search. Mixing with the few other pedestrians who were braving the cold; they blended well and brought no attention to themselves. After investigating the waterfront with no luck seeing additional CCP vehicles, they opted for local intel. The locals would know, they always knew everything so, time to go fishing. The three had parked a half hour before, split up and walked several blocks and walked into a bar and grill along Mountdale Avenue. Each took separate seats around the main room. Sam, warily surveying the joint when he walked in, noticed a man by himself at the bar dressed modestly in jeans and shirt, without a tie, but wearing an upscale winter coat. He sidled up next to him on a free stool and ordered a light beer. He was softly humming to himself.

"What's that tune you're humming?" the man asked. "Sounds familiar."

"I don't know," Sam replied. "Some damn commercial I think; it just entered my brain and now I can't get it out."

"I know what you mean," the man said. "I'm Scott by the way, *offering his hand.*"

"Sam."

"You're not from around here, are you?" Scott asked.

"What gave me away?" Sam asked.

"Your shoes and your coat," Scott replied. "A little too light. American?"

"Yes," Sam answered. "My boss is trying to expand north of the border with wholesale pricing on distribution of oil and gas and related products."

"I'd be all for that if the price is cheaper than the rip off we pay now."

"Well, I'm working on it," Sam began. "Say, what are all these vehicles I've seen with the red star on them."

"Well, haven't you heard?" Scott asked sarcastically. "Our great Prime Minister invited them here to protect their assets. What assets is what all the people are asking?"

Scott leaned closer to Sam whispering.

"They are all over and I'm guessing several divisions," Scott remarked. "The troops are everywhere. I actually saw them unloading tanks and planes right off the bay. Put the damn things on flatbeds and hauled them away. After a couple of times doing that they stopped and then, only do it at night. Hell, damn trucks make so much noise can't get any sleep. Every twenty minutes like clockwork from midnight until about 5 a.m. Been doing it several months now. I tell you; I think they're going to take us over. Hell, maybe even invade you yanks."

Scott was out of beer, Sam picked up the tab for the next one. The more Scott drank, the more information he volunteered. Glancing around the bar, Sam could see that both Rob and Samantha were pumping others for information.

"Tell me," Sam began. "Did I hear you right? You think they have several divisions?"

"Maybe more," Scott said. "The Prime Minister let them build a base out near Dryden. They even lengthened the runway there in payment for the base. I travel the country selling insurance and see them everywhere. From what a fellow salesman tells me, they have similar bases set up in Quebec and British Columbia. He told me he got onto the base by mistake and they ran him off. He has a friend that is in the RCAF and he's seen everything they have over the country. Always up in the air flying. This guy told my friend there are at least ten divisions in Canada with supporting fighter squadrons and tank battalions. He may be overexaggerating a little but seems like an awful lot of firepower for protecting assets."

"Yeah, I guess," Sam said. "What's the RCAF, *feigning ignorance*?"

"The Royal Canadian Air Force," Scott said. "Yeah, my friends' friend is a military man. But get this, he has a fellow officer in the Canadian Rangers, and they have been practicing mock guerilla operations against these Chinese bases to increase their skill level. I'm sure the Prime Minister and the Chinese would blow their tops if they knew."

Sam was contemplating how much people were willing to divulge to a stranger when they were buzzed and pissed at the same time.

"That's a lot of troops you're talking about," Sam said, *thinking to himself that it was about 100,000, far too many to protect assets.*

"Yeah, well, my buddy says more arrive every day," Scott

retorted.

"You know, I've always been fascinated with flying, but never had the time," Sam began. "I'd love to talk to your RCAF buddy. I bet he could tell a lot about flying jets."

"I'm sure he wouldn't mind," Scott said. "He loves to talk flying. His name is Nathan and I'll be seeing him tomorrow. He usually hangs out around the officer's club in Moose Jaw, with the 431st Squadron. They fly sorties all along the border. He comes in here every Thursday or Friday. A right talkative chap if I must say. Loves to tell his stories about the commies."

"I take it he doesn't like them," Sam queried, as he made a mental note to have a female agent on site when the pilot showed up.

"Hell, none of us do," Scott said. "The Prime Minister shoved them down our throats and when there's quite a few of them around they treat us like crap and like to bully us. It's as if we cannot do anything about it and they know it. I'd like to pick up a rifle and take pot shots at them."

"I'm sure it will work itself out," Sam said. "It was nice meeting you. I need to run but will be back in a couple of more times during this trip. Perhaps we can have a cold one then."

"No worries," Scott replied, as Sam slid off his stool, shook hands and was out the door.

On the way out, he noticed Rob and Samantha were still talking. He continued through the doorway knowing they would excuse themselves when they could without arousing suspicion and slip out at separate times. Sam had hit a veritable gold mine of information. But right off, he knew that he would need more teams to gather intelligence. As he got back to the truck, he reached into the glove box and retrieved a Sat phone, dialed a number and waited for someone in the ops division to pick up. It only took a couple of rings. Sam immediately recognized the voice.

"This is A2C1Z," Sam began, using phonetic alphabet. "I need a reservation for lunch in Ottawa tomorrow."

"How many in your party sir?" The female voice asked.

"We have a group of ten," Sam replied.

"Thank you, sir," The voice said. "I'll take care of it. A confirmation number has been sent."

Almost immediately, a number appeared in his text box. It would be called to confirm the meeting location just before arrival. Had anyone been listening in on his transmission, it would appear like what it was, a common luncheon reservation in Ottawa for a group of ten people. In reality, it was for a meeting of ten, three-member HUMINT teams just like he, Rob, and Samantha comprised. They needed to get going. Sam climbed into the pickup and cranked the engine to warm it up. There was a gas station right down the block, so he gassed up quickly and returned back to his parking spot. He didn't need to wait long. Samantha appeared from the shadows as it grew dark and climbed in. After about ten minutes, Rob showed up and they were off, talking as they drove. It would take them about sixteen hours to reach Ottawa. Once out of town, initially picking up Highway 11, they began exchanging notes. Rob pulled out a small bound journal and began making bulleted notes of their combined intel.

"I think we have real problems here," Samantha began. "The woman I was speaking with was an RCAF pilot. She retired full time about six months ago, but still flies as a reservist. She told me that at almost every small municipal airport along the U.S. border, that the CCP had placed either half or a full squadron of fighter jets. She said they were mostly Chengdu J-10 carrying TG-100 GPS guided bombs. They can fly missions around the clock. With a combat radius of about 900 miles, they could reach as far south as Charleston. Hell, even the fighters flying from near Thunder Bay could reach Denver, St. Louis, or Kansas City with ease."

"That's a serious problem," Rob whistled. "Any other information?"

"No, that's all I was able to get," Samantha said.

"What about you Rob?" Sam asked.

"Well, you're not going to believe this," Rob began. "The guy I was talking to was an RCMP. He works with the main headquarters in Ottawa. Turns out the Canadians don't care much for the Chinese being here and there are increasing tensions between them. He didn't give me any information in terms of aircraft, but one of his duties is to tour the various locations and report tensions and how to better work with the community. There were two items of particular interest. First, he listed ten bases the Chinese have and where they are. I scratched them down under the table as he mentioned them here and there and what was happening. I've been jotting them down as you two talked so they are all clear. When we get a chance, we can plot them on a map. The other thing seemed strange to me, which is why I made a mental note. He told me that at each of these sites were around ten containers, you know, the CONEX that you see on container ships at most of our ports and pretty much used for storage everywhere you go."

"Why did he think it was odd?" Samantha asked.

"He said that all of them were lined up in neat rows about thirty feet apart, and that they were all pointed in the same direction, south." Rob replied.

"How does he know that?" Sam asked.

"He said at first that he didn't notice it," Rob began. "But as he worked around each of the sites, he began to notice that a typical CONEX only has double doors on the end. These all not only had that, but on the south end he noticed they all had doors about the size of a house door. He passed it off as an access door that is easier to get into than opening the double doors at the back. The other odd thing he noted is they are all the same color, painted in camouflage and for months, he has not seen anyone around them at all. He thought that was strange if they were for storage, which he suspects. One day he said he began walking toward them to take a look out of curiosity but was immediately stopped by two armed soldiers who motioned him away. This was near the base they built near Fort Francis airport, which is west of Thunder Bay, about two hundred miles."

"Damn," Sam swore under his breath!

"Anything else?" Sam asked.

"He mentioned that the more remote the area where the troops are based, the more unfriendly they are," Rob said. "Seems like they want control of everything because we've seen this scenario before."

Rob was referring to incidents in Afghanistan and the Congo to which both Sam and Samantha nodded.

"You swore about the containers," Samantha said. "What gives?"

"I was going to tell you later," Sam began. "Since you bring it up, those are portable missile systems with four missiles each and a range of about one thousand miles. Essentially cruise missiles that can fly ten to fifteen meters above deck."

"Holy shit," Rob said, looking from one to the other. "You're telling me they could just push a button and obliterated DC or any city within that range?"

"That's what I'm saying," Sam responded. "This means we will need to gather intelligence like we've never done before. I've called in additional teams that we'll meet in Ottawa. From there we will scatter to the four winds and map every one of these sites. Rob, you may as well start drawing and making a list. For each site, we will need to know the GPS coordinates, number of troops, equipment, locations, and specific GPS coordinates of each container. Collect any helpful information."

The mood grew somber. Rob pulled a notebook from his backpack as they began discussing details of an expanded Operation Eider. They drove through the night on a mix of paved and unpaved roads toward their destination.

James Tindall

CHAPTER 6
The Council

Sky Thinker and Ferni had headed out of Los Angeles, picking up interstate 15 northeast toward Barstow where they merged onto Interstate 40. The trip to Gallup, New Mexico was a long one. Finally reaching Gallup, they checked into a small motel about midnight. They were feeling good about their progress and had talked the entire way about the spiritual side of their undertaking and what they might expect to experience in Chaco Canyon. Early the next morning they picked up Highway 264 north to Yah-ta-hey, New Mexico and then circled back west heading to Window Rock, Arizona, the main Tribal headquarters of the Navajo Nation. On the way they had already made an appointment with the Tribal President, Ken Little. Instead of meeting President Little in his office, they were directed to the Navajo Council Chamber building where he was finishing a meeting with the twenty-four delegates of the council — representatives for the Navajo Nation. Ken met them outside the building entrance, a broad, beaming smile on his face for Sky Thinker was his friend who had taken up the warrior way. Ken was a warrior himself, but more of the paper pushing, wordsmith type. But his roots ran deep. He was named after his grandfather who had served as a code talker in World War II.

"What brings you out this way my warrior friend?" Ken

asked.

"It's a long story and we've been pushing hard," Sky Thinker replied. "Meet President Martineau of the Ojibwa tribe."

"Call me Ferni."

"It's a privilege," Ken said, shaking hands. "Come on in and we'll chat. Do you mind if a few of my delegates listen in?" Sky Thinker and Ferni glanced at each other. They both knew it would be difficult to convince this one man, who was tribal leader of the largest tribe in the U.S. But they had come this far, and it was the last stop on a long road of convincing. What the hell.

"What we have come to discuss is of a sensitive nature," Sky Thinker said. "We need all the help we can so, yes, they may stay and listen and then, spread the word for what needs to be."

"By the way," Ken said. "Jeremy will be here shortly as well."

Sky Thinker looked at Ken, surprise obvious, but he realized that with Jeremy here to help convince him, they just may have a chance. After all, no one would believe the story they were telling without proof and maybe, just maybe, Jeremy would be able to provide it. As they walked into the council chambers the two travelers were filled with anxiousness and excitement.

The chamber was quite large with a speaker podium at the far end, surrounded by four flags, two on either side, that overlooked the delegates seats. Ferni couldn't help but think how much it reminded him of the congress in DC. There were seven rows of semi-circular chairs, with a continuous semi-circular desk for each row that faced the podium. There was also another set bordering either side of the middle running vertically away from the podium.

Ample space Sky Thinker thought for a discussion. Five delegates had decided to stay and listen. The group all sat near the front of the chamber as they began.

"So, my friend," Ken began. "Tell us why we are here and why it is so important."

"Alright," Sky Thinker said. "I will be brief. We were sent by Sun God, Monster Slayer, and the Mediator to convince tribal leaders of the peril we face and to gather our warriors to fight what I think may be the last battle."

"I see," Ken responded, looking around at his delegates. "If this were coming from anyone else, I would tell you the discussion is already over, but because I have known you all my life, I will listen, however, I must tell you that you will need to be quite convincing and of course, proof would be welcome."

"I can provide that or my account of it," Ferni said. "I was the first to be contacted. And like you, as President of the Ojibwa, I was extremely doubting. The doubt disappeared in short order when the Mediator appeared. I still do not know if we were in his realm or if he just gave us a vision of it while he spoke."

There was a hum of conversation among the five delegates, looking back and forth at the other three men. Suddenly, one of them spoke.

"What you are saying sounds a bit preposterous," the delegate said. "I'm afraid the President is correct; you will need to provide more proof than the words of another. We mean you no disrespect President Martineau."

"None taken," Ferni said. "However, no matter what happens in this life or the next, I assure you my account is true. And I would tend to agree if I were in your position. But after I saw the personage, I could not help but think how far we have drifted from the Great Spirit."

"Is there any other proof that you have?" Ken asked. "I mean something more tangible. It's going to take more than this to convince our tribe to do what you ask."

Just then, the double doors at the back of the chamber opened, bathing and illuminating the chamber from the bright sunshine outside. A single shadow was visible in the doorway that momentarily disappeared, as the doors closed the group heard footsteps approaching them.

"Jeremy," Ken spoke loudly. "I'm glad you're here. We were just entertaining a story by our friends."

"It is not a story; it is truth," Jeremy commented. "Like it or not, it is time to step up or step off and, for those who step off, there will be no place in Sun God's realm in the next life."

The group just sat staring at Jeremy. He was so blunt and matter of fact they did not know how to respond.

"We would all like to believe you my friend," a delegate said. "But this is a tall order without proof. You are a member of our nation and one of its most respected and while we believe your words, getting the nation to believe them is, well, going to be difficult."

"Yes, it is," Jeremy replied, looking at Ferni and Sky Thinker. "These men have been to most of the tribes and have managed to convince them to join us. How do the scriptures put it; a prophet is not without honor save among his own? These men tell you no lie, which is why I am here. Our tribe is the lynch pin of this entire operation. Do you still desire proof?"

"Yes, we demand it," another delegate responded.

"Very well," Jeremy said. "Know then, that this demand has consequences. Once you know of a surety due to the proof, you will be fully accountable for your decisions. If you decide to step off, you will never enter the realm of Sun

God when you have gone the way of all the earth. If you agree, stay. If not, depart and your accountability will be no more."

All present nodded affirmatively as they leaned forward in their chairs in anticipation of what might happen. Jeremy began to hum very softly, which ever so slowly turned into a chant, increasing in intensity as he continued. The sound of drums began, war drums, as the delegates and other men began looking around to determine where the sound was coming from. The drums grew louder and louder as the walls of the chamber began at first vibrate and then, turn a glowing white, brighter as the noon sun. The flags on either side of the podium began blowing toward the men who looked up, wondering where the wind was coming from. As they looked, the only thing visible between the flags was a large plaque of the Great Seal of the Navajo Nation, which was directly behind the podium. Without warning a personage walked right through them. There was a great brightness surrounding it, but not so bright the group could not see what the figure looked like.

A dreadful look came across the men's faces as the figure gazed down upon them, standing in the air in front of the speaker's podium. Immediately, the group recognized it as a Kachina, and their eyes widened in horror. They wanted to run but were so paralyzed with fear, they could scarcely breathe.

The figure had a black face and yellow patches beneath the eyes, a spear in its right hand. light from the personage's aura caused the spear tip to glint, making it difficult to see him. All they could see now was the spear and the eagle feathers attached to it where the tip joined the shaft. Suddenly, the figure was gone; the group felt relieved. But just as suddenly, it reappeared, not three feet from them. It was now clearly visible. The blood drained from their faces as they fully realized what they were seeing. In addition to the black face and yellow patches beneath the eyes, the figure wore a series of eagle feathers that protruded vertically from a head piece in a fan like fashion. The head piece was a mixture of blue, black, red, and yellow colors, elaborately painted in triangular shapes. The figure wore white buckskin and brown moccasins with a red, black, and yellow border about the ankles. The buckskin was trimmed in red pyramids about the edges and ended just above the knees like a skirt. Around his waist, the figure wore a red sash about four inches in width. The sash was trimmed in black and had insets of square and diamond patterns, trimmed in turquoise, silver, and gold. Around the muscular biceps of the figure were fashioned ornate silver and turquoise armbands.

They had all heard the legends and were intimately familiar with this personage. Medicine men long past and currently, had told them of it many times. And now, they were not laughing. It was the Kachina, merchant of death as legends proclaimed — those who see it are about to die. The men swallowed hard as sweat beaded on their foreheads. Still frozen in fear, the men knew not what to do.

"Fear not, I am your proof delegates and Presidents," the Kachina said. "I come directly from Sun God. I am the appointed mediator. Do you understand?"

The men nodded in unison, unable to look away.

"I was chosen mediator to protect the 5th world and our medicine men and warriors did their part. Now, the peril upon you is great. Look at me, do you older delegates not recognize me? I am Totsoni Yazzie, son of the great Medicine Man Wassaja Yazzie who saved us all. Jeremy is my grandson. Do you not see? The three men before you have been made accountable by Sun God. Hear them and do as they instruct. If you fail, this world will be destroyed, and you will never see the realm of Sun God. Heed my words and obey! The Mediator waved his hand and slowly, memories from long past, came flooding into the men's minds. At once after his last word, bright light washed the room, making it impossible to see then, the light gathered directly around the Mediator as he shot straight up through the ceiling in a beam of blue-white light, disappearing. He had scarcely gone when he returned.

"If you decide to step off, when next you see me, I will take you."

With that he vanished again.

The men were stunned, so physical and mentally drained they could not move as they sat looking around at each other for several minutes, trying to regain their composure and to gather their thoughts.

"Words cannot describe what I am feeling," Ken began, small tears rolling down his cheeks.

"Delegates, are we in agreement of the truth of what we have just witnessed and of the words of Sky Thinker and Ferni?"

"We are," the delegates said in unison."

"Okay, my friend," Ken said. "Tell us what it is that we must do."

"As I mentioned before," Sky Thinker began, "We are only messengers. What we told you before is true. Every tribe is to bring its leaders and warriors to Chaco Canyon, to the Pueblo Bonito site to meet in council. You are to dress for war in your formal headdresses. The meeting is of great significance and will be spiritual in nature."

"Who will be at the meeting to instruct us," Ken asked. "Is

it the three of you?"

"We will be there," Sky Thinker said. "Jeremy and a few White Eyes will be present as well, including a general but it is not they who will be instructing us."

"Who then, if we are to prepare so formally?" Ken asked.

"Sun God and Monster Slayer, along with other deity will be the ones giving the instruction. That is all I can tell you because that is what we were instructed."

The delegates gasped at the thought of meeting Sun God, but they trembled in fear as well, feeling they were unworthy as guilt of their vices and weaknesses swept over them. Jeremy sensed what they were thinking.

"Do not fear my brothers," Jeremy said. "Sun God chastens those he loves. Prepare yourselves through personal rituals of purification and prayer. If you feel it necessary, ask for forgiveness for those things not adhering to spiritual beliefs in your life. We need all of you and, your desire to help is more important than your small sins born of human weakness."

"Ken," Jeremy said. "We must begin preparations so we will leave you. You and your leaders and warriors will meet us at Chaco Canyon at the appointed time."

"That is six days from now on Sunday at dusk," Sky Thinker joined in.

"I trust you will not be late," Jeremy said emphatically!"

"There is no way we are going to miss this," Ken said. "We will be on time and in force."

The three men stood to leave, walking briskly toward the doors of the council chamber. As they opened the doors to exit, Jeremy turned and called softly across the chamber.

"Remember, you must prepare spiritually for that which you will soon experience. Your warriors must prepare as well. See to it!"

The doors closed immediately behind them as they walked to their vehicles.

The Speaker and her small team were in an industrial section of south Baltimore. They were standing behind two-way, bullet-proof glass. On the other side of the glass sat a man, in a chair on a bare concrete floor. Next to him was a table, on it was a single monitor with a split screen. He was dressed in suit and tie, but cords kept him secured to the anchored chair; duct tape was wrapped around his mouth and head so he could not speak.

"We know of your weakness, but that is not how we will persuade you to help us," an electronic voice spoke to him. "Behold,"

As the man looked, he saw a figure in an alley, running away from two men who cornered the figure at the dead end. When the figure looked up it was a man. It was his cousin. The two assailants drew pistols and pointed them at the cousin's head, one had a cell phone to his ear. The man in the chair eye's widened as he attempted to free himself from his bonds, shaking his head and talking into his gag.

"You will help us kill the President!"

The man in the chair shook his head no, looking as if he was screaming into the gag, the resulting sound only a loud murmuring. The two assailants shot the man in the head, the lifeless corpse now fallen, blood flowing onto the cement.

As the two assailants walked away, the split picture on the right side of the monitor revealed a new scene. A man and woman were parked at a stop light; two men wearing hoods from a car to the rear got out and walked up to either side of the vehicle. Pulling out pistols, they pointed them at the occupants inside the car.

"Last chance," the electronic voice said. "You will help us kill the President."

The man in the chair tried to jump up and down, freeing himself, obviously screaming under the tape around his mouth as he shook his body from side to side and shaking his head no. The cords around his wrist cut into his flesh as blood began to drip onto the floor. The Speaker nodded; an instant later the occupants of the vehicle were gunned down. The monitor continued to show the cousin dead in the alley; the head of the male behind the wheel of the car slumped out the driver window, his face clearly visible. The man in the chair, slumped down, his shoulders sagging, almost lifeless. The team behind the glass could see he was trembling and crying.

"You have one last chance," the garbled voice said. "You have lost your cousin and your brother and his wife. Look at the monitor please."

The man looked up at the monitor. It showed a single, full picture of a nice room in a suburban home; not his. The camera panned to reveal a sofa where his wife and two young children sat, surrounded by three males, guns obvious, but not in plain sight. His wife was looking directly into the camera, tears on her cheeks, trying not to cry in front of the kids.

"Honey," she whispered, *turning so her children did not hear, reading from a paper in her hands.* "These men will kill us if you do not do what they ask. They are going to keep us until the task is complete. Please do what they want."

The sound on the camera went dead as the picture remained. His wife was hugging their children close to her, protecting them as best she could. The man in the chair slumped, all resistance gone. On his waist was the badge of the U.S. Secret Service.

"Will you help us?" the voice asked.

A hooded figure walked up to the Secret Service agent in the chair and ripped the tape off his mouth.

"I will do as you ask," the agent murmured defeatedly.

"Indoctrinate him, drug him, whatever you need to do to ensure he complies," Evelyn said.

Ninety miles later, the three men pulled into Chaco Canyon in preparation for what would become a life-changing event for them and the world, although the great majority would never know about it. It was still early in the day with a light wind blowing from the southeast; cool, but not cold as they walked their way through the ruins to Pueblo Bonito. A great many scholars and archeologists has attempted to describe what the ruins were and how they operated. Located in the deep deserts of northwest New Mexico, these extensive ruins of what many had called the greatest architectural achievement of the Northern American Indians, were believed to have been the main social and ceremonial center of the Anasazi culture. The word *Anasazi* is Navajo, meaning "the ancient ones" or "the ancient enemies." It was believed among the Navajo that the Anasazi had split up primarily into the Hopi tribe then, spread throughout Arizona and New Mexico. From the legends and history handed down by the Medicine Man and his father, it seemed logical to Jeremy. Both Jeremy and Sky Thinker had been here before. The ruins were massive compared to most Native American ruins found in North America, a stunning collection of advanced buildings, akin to city monuments, and dwellings.

The three men had walked through the national park to the ruin of Pueblo Bonito, which was closed for maintenance until further notice, at least that was the story to the press, who could care less anyway. It's not like the park would be any kind of mainstream story. President Weld had seen to it for Jeremy. They had the park to themselves and would until the council was over in six days' time.

"What are you thinking?" Sky Thinker asked.
Jeremy heard the question and was contemplating what he was looking at as he stared north northwest across the ruins.

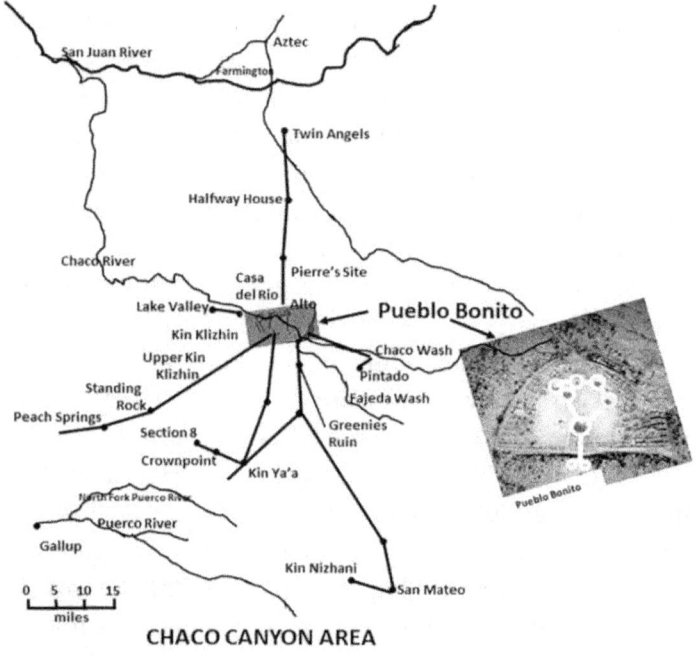

CHACO CANYON AREA

Having been here several times with his father, he began remembering his teachings. This was the main house of the Chaco's. It was a 'D' shape holding thirty-six kivas, about 700 connected rooms; archeologists had theorized that some of the buildings around it were five stories high. This had once been the center of life for ceremonies, astronomy, storage, and even burial.

"Let me show you something," Jeremy said. "Walk carefully."

They were not supposed to, but they carefully walked the great Kiva near the end of the ruins. As they looked down, they could see a low bench all the way around the Kiva with four masonry squares, to hold the four main posts made of wood and stone, that supported the roof. In the middle was a square firebox. A ladder through the roof supplied the entrance into the kiva. Along the sides of the walls were holes that had at one time held beams that supported the next story above the kiva.

"Wow," Ferni said. "This is impressive. What was it used for?"

"It is a kiva," Jeremy said. "It was used by the Chacoan tribes for religious rituals and community gatherings to decide issues. Most of the religious rituals were based on the Kachina belief system. My father, the Medicine Man, told me many legends about this place. Many years ago, he had spoken with some Cahokia tribal people who were Algonquian speaking. They were members of the Illinois Confederation and once lived in what is now the Midwest. One of their beliefs was routed in the stars because they believed that was where the Great Spirit lived according to their ancient legends. More specifically, this Cahokia Medicine Man visited here with my father and pointed out to him several things that came as a surprise to my father. Let's get up a little higher so we can see better, and I'll explain."

They took the path around the pueblo to the east and traversed some of the old, more collapsed portion on the northeast corner so that they were about twenty feet above the pueblo floor. It wasn't as high as they would have liked to be, but enough so that they could clearly see most of the thirty-six kivas below them. It was quite interesting. The breeze had stopped and although it was about 45° F, the warmth of the sun brought welcome relief.

"Look at those three kivas across the top to our right," Jeremy said. "Draw an imaginary line hooking them together and then, hook each end to the large kivas just below them. Now, see the large kiva we were looking at, draw a line from each end to that one and then, one line from that one in a southerly direction about twenty yards or so past the entrance; imagine two kivas on the end of that line. Like this."

Jeremy had been drawing as he explained it and showed them his illustration.

"It looks like a constellation of some sort," Ferni said. "I used to study astronomy in school."

"Very good," Jeremy said. "We believe this is the Pleiades constellation, also call the Seven Sisters and Messier 45, which is an open star cluster in the northwest of the constellation Taurus. It's close enough to earth to see with the naked eye."

"So, you're telling us this pueblo was built for a specific purpose," Sky Thinker said.

"I believe so," Jeremy said. "The question is for what purpose? Look way out about 700 yards to the south southeast, you can barely see it. It's that small hill and just toward the right end is a circular shape. That's what we call the Casa Rinconada, which is actually an armless Kachina. It has many meanings. What the Hopi call the star visitors, we know as Sun God and his related deity. There is a story of serpent gods, often referred to as a Kachina riding a cosmic serpent that some believe to be a wormhole through space that brings aliens, as it were, here to earth. But it is deeper than that. I'll show you later, but around the ruins, in places most cannot go, you can see petroglyphs of lizard like humanoids. The Hopi believed it to be an entity that kept the tribes at war with each other, as a form of control. It is much like the belief many now have with our governments that keep people agitated with all other groups, so they have more control, which is true.

There have been many skeletal remains here that were obviously sacrificed and some cannibalized by extremely large teeth. The serpent rider as we call him, had the ability to shape shift. While many believe that it was an alien, a real serpent, it was Monster Slayer, trying to get the people to rekindle their faith in Sun God. They had been left alone so long that their light of faith grew dim and it was their hatred toward each other that drove the continual war; tribe against tribe. Their stories can be found on the sides of the canyon wall. One set of drawings in particular shows women and children running from warriors who killed them because of their lust for murder. In retaliation for such evil, Sun God sent his winged warriors who decapitated the tribal warriors, ripping their heads and spine from their bodies as their entrails fell to the earth. Were it not for the evil being displayed, the winged warriors would have remained observers only. But there is an entity that rides the tunnels of space that spreads evil and has the ability to influence humans. I suppose the White Eyes would call it the devil, but there is much to the realm after this one we know nothing about."

"Do you think we would find a drawing of him here?" Sky Thinker asked.

"Most certainly," Jeremy said, pointing. "It's off in that

direction."

"What does it look like?" Ferni asked.

"The drawing depicts it as a dinosaur type creature," Jeremy said. "It has a semi-long tail, a swollen abdomen, long claws and teeth and was very large. Oh, and it had a helmet with a visor."

"Hmmmm," Ferni grinned. "These guys must have had a big imagination."

"Perhaps," Jeremy responded thoughtfully. "But a thousand years ago no one could have imagined a helmet with a visor that had not been invented yet. Come, darkness is falling, we need to prepare."

Jeremy had brought a small charcoal grill and plenty of charcoal. He had also brought whole ears of corn, short ribs and a variety of drinks. As he prepared the grill and got it going, Ferni prepared the corn for roasting while Sky Thinker made a batch of Navajo Fry Bread blending the right proportions of flour, water, salt, and baking powder. After a short while the grill was ready and they sat back watching the stars, occasionally seeing one shoot across the sky. There was just a faint tinge of light blue in the western sky when Jeremy pointed.

"Look there, to the southeast," Jeremy said. "See Orion's Belt? Draw a straight line through the three stars and a little way out is a bright star call Aldebran, keep going along the same line. That cluster of stars is Pleiades; where Sun God lives, supposedly."

It was surprising how easy they were to see if you knew where to look. The food was done and served up. They ate quietly as they chewed the short ribs, eating fry bread and corn on the side. It was a hearty meal and well enjoyed after a long and exciting day. They had covered the grill as they sat close to feel its warmth in the chilly night air. Many miles from the nearest town, it was pitch black except for the stars set like jewels in the night sky. A peace fell over them as they gazed upward and absorbed the quiet; it was interrupted occasionally by the howl of a coyote. They had been sitting about an hour, enjoying the serenity when they heard the faint sound of drums. It was difficult to pinpoint the direction of the sounds.

"Look there," Ferni exclaimed, pointing!

The sound of the drums was coming from the Pueblo Bonito. Erie shadows of warriors were cast against the inner courtyard from the glow of a burning fire. Sometimes the shadows were the shadows of men, at other times, the shadows appeared like a serpent with a large belly, long tale, claws like a lion, and teeth like a giant dinosaur, with a helmet or visor on its head. As the shadows began to circle the wall, the beat of the drums grew louder and louder until they were deafening in the still night air. At first, the three men were afraid and then, taking courage, they began inching closer toward the pueblo. When they finally reached it, entering from the south entrance, the sounds had stopped, but there was still a fire about two hundred feet in from the south entrance, adjacent to a straight-line edge to the last two large kivas on the north end of the pueblo.

The men were nervous as they crept forward toward the fire. It was deathly quiet when they reached the fire; there were no seats and the fire was not burning from logs, but directly from the ground with a pure orange red flame that flickered and rose about three feet from the pueblo floor. The three became even more nervous, not knowing what to think or do.

"What kind of flame is this?" Sky Thinker asked. "I have never seen anything like it."

"Evidently, it is of the gods," Jeremy said.

"Look," Ferni said, pointing. "There is where someone has been sitting, several men from the looks of it."

"You're right," Jeremy stammered nervously.

"Sit," a voice from out of the night air said. "Sit by the fire. Now!"

Looking nervously about, the three men did as commanded. Instinctively, they sat facing the entrance from where they had come as the fire suddenly and without warning, grew at least four times larger. As they sat looking around and at each other, they began to notice, rainbow-colored columns. The intensity and brightness were more than they could describe. The columns rose from the kivas to their left and right and also from the two larger kivas at an angle to each other just forward of them. Unexpectedly, a much larger column appeared atop the largest kiva near the entrance and two more behind it outside the pueblo. The columns started to swirl like a tornado, the rainbow colors changing to a bright blue, white. The swirl stopped to reveal seven personages in place of the swirling columns. Six of them were dressed identically and appeared to be warriors. Each wore three feathers protruding from the back of their heads behind a bristly roach. Their faces were painted white as snow, excepting a wide black band across their face where their eyes were. It stretched from the top of the cheek bones to just above the eyebrows. On their cheeks were three stripes of red on either side and they were wearing large necklaces of what appeared to be bear claws, hanging to the center of their chests, separated between the claws with several turquois beads. Each held a buckskin shield in their right hand with depictions of the four elements on a pale-yellow background, with an image of Sun God in the center. In their left hand, each held a silver tipped spear, dripping in blood down the shaft. The site was both terrifying and exciting at the same time.

The light on the largest kiva directly in front of the men, about one hundred feet away, slowly started to dissipate and then, washed outward over the entire pueblo to reveal a terrifying figure. Much unlike the others, he was at least forty feet tall wearing only a silver loin cloth trimmed on the edges in gold, his feet were bare and six toed. He was more muscular than any person they had ever seen. Standing erect, his hands were resting on a sword, palms down. His presence was so commanding that they pushed themselves away from him as they sat on the dirt. About his biceps were wide bracelets of silver and turquoise with similar ones about his wrists. Around his neck was a gold collar embedded with rubies in the center. His face was painted pale blue with one bright red line about an inch wide going from the hairline to the bottom of his chin on either side of his nose. His hair was pulled behind his head into a ponytail they could not see. But it was his eyes that were the most prominent part of his personage. They were staring directly at them, penetrating to the core; uncomforting. His eyes were not solid in color, but were as a rolling, bright orange flame that never stopped moving. They were so enthralled with the personages who appeared that they were unaware of the drums that continued to beat louder and louder and louder and as the large figure in front of them revealed himself completely, the drums suddenly stopped.

The figure stood staring down on them; they were so small in comparison. He slowly waved his right hand from his left to his right in a small arc, resting it again atop his sword, which appeared to be at least fifteen feet long. Atop each of the remaining kiva's appeared the same unnatural flame they were sitting by. The brightness was now like noon day and the personages were clearly visible, revealing even more detail than they had noticed before. But they could not remove their gaze from the large figure in front, who kept staring directly at them, without blinking. He finally spoke with a voice like soft thunder, not too loud, but penetrating.

"Do not be afraid," the personage said. "I have been sent by the war gods who will be in council with you soon. I am called Aichu, but it is of no importance."

"Why have they sent you," Jeremy asked, trying to control his cracking voice as fear crept in.

"I am to remind you that you have a great responsibility," Aichu said. "You must prepare for receiving the deity in the next few days."

"How should we prepare?" Sky Thinker asked.

"Prepare through ceremony as you have been taught," Aichu replied. "Do not fail!"

"There is much to do in so short a time," Jeremy said. "We will do all we can."

"That is not good enough," Aichu responded sharply, raising his sword in his right hand and pointing it directly at them. "You must fulfill your duty else you will walk as I have, in penance, for thousands of years hoping that you get a second chance to prove yourself worthy or be cast into ch'įįdiitah hodook'ą́ą́ł, the hot place."

The three men verbally gasped as they realized what Aichu had said as he lowered his sword again and rested his hands atop it. They had heard it spoken in their legends, which they thought were the tales of elders who wanted attention as they neared death. Funny how people tend to push things off as just tales, not wanting to believe it because the belief of it would place a burden for them to respond.

"The pain and anguish you know not," Aichu continued. "To think that you could be with Sun God had you simply performed your duties. The hot place of hell is not as most of you would think. It has long been depicted as a place of fire and desolation, but it is more than that. It is a burning, a mental torment and anguish that never ends as you think about what could have been. The fire that surrounds you in that place is insignificant compared to the searing mental anguish."

"I have always had doubts about my abilities to perform what I need to," Jeremy said. "It seems too much to bear at times."

"We are all called to do certain tasks," Aichu said. "As long as we do all we can, Sun God will provide help. Fail him not. Do not look back on it and think what could have been. Remember my words!

At once, the personages disappeared, fading into the darkness of night, along with the unnatural fires. The three were left sitting on the earth, staring at where Aichu and his warriors had been, past them into the stars twinkling in the black, still sky. They didn't realize how late it had become as they began to discern the faint glow in the eastern horizon, a witness to the soon rising sun.

"My immediate duty is to get my leaders and warriors here who have been preparing," Ferni said. "I must return to them now. Let me know if there is anything you need from me."

"We will let you know," Jeremy said as Ferni walked off.

"Come, there is much to do," Jeremy said.

"I am not a Medicine Man, so just tell me what you need," Sky Thinker said, as they began walking back to the truck.

"The first thing I need to do is a special sand painting,"

Jeremy said. "Come!"

Sky Thinker could not believe what he had seen. Following Jeremy across the ruins, his thoughts drifted to the past as he recalled the teachings of the Medicine Man. Most of his life he had passed them off as legend, myths to keep the people in line so they would obey the principles of Sun God. He realized that all legends are born from truth. He began to feel more exhilarated as he followed Jeremy and could not wait until the council with the Gods.

Erin had been able to get a free weekend and arranged a visit to Lunadi's place in Colorado. It was only for a couple of days but promised to be a good getaway. It was early morning and Lunadi had prepared coffee and fry bread, sprinkled with cinnamon and powdered sugar on the upper deck.

"This is so beautiful," Erin said. "What is that mountain range?"

"It is called the southern front range in Colorado," Lunadi replied. "It is the Sangre de Cristo mountain range, the Blood of Christ by the Spanish of the ancient west."

"It's like a picture on a post card," Erin whispered as she sipped her coffee and ate her fry bread. "I bet you wished you could stay here all the time."

"I do mostly," Lunadi said, gazing deeply into her eyes. I mean, I teach here and rarely go off the property unless I need to shop or make visits like the one in DC. I have no reason to leave except of necessity."

"Yes, I can see why," Erin said softly. "No one fighting for parking spaces along the street to watch football games at your neighbors and no sounds except the breeze and the birds. It is so serene and peaceful."

Erin was gazing across the mountains, in awe of the

nature's beauty. It was obvious she was in deep thought.

"Do you ever get lonely living here alone?"

"Not really. I stay busy most of the time with teaching and writing. When I want a break, I take hikes around the area, go on a road trip, or go to Denver for shopping and dining, sometime to Pueblo or Colorado Springs or overseas to teach SOGs. There are all kinds of animals to see such as coyote, fox, bear, mountain lions, deer, turkey and others. It's fun to just watch and enjoy them in their natural habitat."

"Yes, but still, it's isolated here. I'm not sure if I could handle it on my own. Do you ever date?"

"You're funny," Lunadi said, laughing. There's no one in the small towns around here to date. The women are either taken, or well, very unattractive. So, no, like you said, it is too secluded for most. I have a friend who runs a guide business. He got married last August. They seemed to get along well."

"What do you mean, seemed?"

"Well, she grew up in a small town about twenty miles from here. She complained where he lived, just up the road a few miles, was too secluded. They got divorced in October after only two months of marriage."

Erin started laughing hysterically. "That has to be the world record."

Lunadi was laughing with her.

"Tell me about yourself," Lunadi said. "I only know the professional side."

"There is not a lot to tell really. I'll give you a synopsis. I was raised not far from Washington, DC as you know, on a small farm. But since my father worked with the Feds, our family would go into town quite frequently. There's so much to do and see there and it was convenient for my mother and I as we waited on dad to finish work on the weekends. The history of the place, especially the people who built it, the founding fathers, the monuments, all grew on me. I came to realize that I could make a difference and so, began working on doing so. I have always been impressed by the large number of people willing to lay down their lives for our country to keep it free and to keep the constitution alive. They are far different from the elected cowards we have in office today; the political elite who believe they are above us and the law but are also afraid of their own shadow. I suppose that is why we are in the mess we find ourselves. Anyway, I went off to college like most of my friends, did very well in all my classes and here I am."

"Was there a boyfriend, a husband, lovers? I don't mean to pry."

"Sure, I had a couple of boyfriends and was married for a couple of years to a vice admiral in the navy. It was fun and we got along well. I found out he was cheating on me with an ensign aboard his carrier. Having no kids, we went our separate ways. I haven't spoken to him for years. Now, my work with the President keeps me more than busy enough to keep my mind off such things."

"I'm sorry to hear that but it looks like you did well despite the setback."

"I don't think I would even call it a setback. It was more like a revelation. It taught me a lot about how to judge people and discern their inner self, which has been a tremendous help in my duties working with Phil. Besides, most of the men in DC are wimps, not like the warriors who have given their lives for our freedom. However, I find you quite different. Jeremy said you would be, and he was not wrong. He said, and I quote, you're the greatest warrior he has ever met."

"That's flattering, but in reality, I just work hard."

"Oh, I think it is more than that. According to my dossier, you grew up on a reservation, was trained by your Medicine Man in guerilla warfare, tracking, shooting and survival, and in the transparency along with your brother Billie Panther then, you went off into the military to become the epitome of warriors, working against spies with a pistol, knife, and a camera and somehow managed to survive when others did not. I heard you were called the specter. Then, as if that wasn't enough punishment, after the military you got several degrees and continued to work for the government."

"That about sums it up, pretty bland isn't it?"

"Not quite. Tell me, why did they call you the specter?"

"It all came about on a mission that I was on with two others. We crept into an area surrounding a Russian submarine base to get pictures of a new sub they were building. Satellites could not get the job done and so, they sent us. One of our group was gravely wounded and they were hunting us down. There was no other choice, either we revert to guerilla warfare and take them out or they take us out. We could not outrun them with a wounded man. So, I split away from my fellow soldiers and circled back behind our pursuers and began my work. It was a moonlit night, which gave me the upper hand. I crept up behind them as they were closing in and took them out one-by-one with my knife and hands."

As Lunadi related the story, he was looking across at the mountains, a distant look upon his face as he remembered every detail of that night so long ago.

"You took out an entire unit?"

"It was just a squad of eight men. Not a big deal. Besides, it was them or us and I made it them. Because of my training,

I have a knack for disappearing in the woods whenever I need to or want to."

Erin sat there looking at him. She couldn't help herself from staring.

"I would say Jeremy was right then, you are a great warrior."

"I'll tell you a secret Erin. All my life I have been trained to be a warrior. From the day I first met the Medicine Man to now. I have never stopped training. I have never been truly tested. Even the squad I took out was easy for me."

"Somehow, I think your time has come because we will all be lucky to make it out of this alive. Come now, *grabbing his hands and snuggling up to him as they gazed off the deck*, let's talk about the softer side of you as she leaned close and kissed him full on the lips."

They quit talking as they hugged each other tightly, kissing, their tongues probing, staring into each other's eyes, becoming aroused. Finally, Erin thought, here was a man's man, not the wimps of DC, but a real live warrior. She could feel his manhood growing against her as he slowly slid his hands up beneath her blouse, cupping her breasts as he stroked her nipples and kissed her fervently, letting his hands glide around to her back and down behind and beneath her jeans as he cupped her amazingly shaped ass in his large hands. Stepping back, he could see she had closed her eyes. He was trying to fight that which there was no fighting, an attraction he could not explain. It was a feeling he had known only once before and as hard as he was, he did not want to let it go. They were interrupted, both their phones ringing. As they stood back and looked at them, it was the same message, from Jeremy.

"Come at once!"

"Well, I guess we will have to pick up where we left off at another time," Erin said, *smiling as she cupped his face in her hands and planted a big wet kiss on his mouth.*

"I'll look forward to it," Lunadi replied, *bending her backward with a long kiss, his left hand fondling her breasts.*

"I guess we had better get going then," Erin said. "I know he told us where we would be meeting but have no clue as to where it is."

"Come," Lunadi replied. "It's about six hours from here. I'll take my truck and we can continue our conversation along the way."

Within a half an hour, they had packed lunches and Erin's bag, along with hot coffee and other needed items and were off. After crossing Raton Pass on Interstate 25, it was smooth driving.

In the bottom of the largest kiva, Jeremy and Sky Thinker cleared the earthen floor so that is was smooth and level. They had been preparing it for the better part of the morning. Jeremy was preparing a sand painting, a part of the Encircling Guardian ceremony as he explained what he was doing to Sky Thinker.

"I'm not sure what you are doing my brother but will do what I can to help," Sky Thinker said.

"The preparation of the area was all you were qualified to do," Jeremy said. "I mean no offense, but you're not trained as a Medicine Man so, you'll just have to watch."

Beside him, Jeremy had placed a variety of colored sands, crushed stone and dried plants, and powdered chalk in heaps adjacent to where the sandpainting (iikááh) would be. It took him hours to complete it as he continually explained to Sky Thinker. On a pale-yellow background were four of the same figures representing fire, earth, air, and water at the 12, 3, 6, and 9 o'clock positions, respectively. Surrounding the figures in a near perfect circle was a lightning bolt. At the six o'clock position the bolt was open beneath the 'air' figure. In his tribal tradition, the air figure faced east, the direction of the rising sun, which is sacred to the Navajo. The lightning bolt protects from all directions except eastward, which is protected by the Encircling Guardian. It is through this opening that healing energies enter into the ceremony.

Between the figures were intricate designs. One line from 8 o'clock to 2 o'clock began with a long spear having seven feathers evenly distributed down its shaft and that pointed at the 8 o'clock direction and ended in the exact center, from which a mountain range ran to the 2 o'clock position. From the 10 o'clock to 4 o'clock position, right next to the lightning bolt on either end was a single tree representing light at 10 o'clock and darkness at 4 o'clock.

"I will not describe the other details to you brother because they are sacred to the Medicine Man whose responsibility is to lead the people in faith," Jeremy said.

Finally finished, the two packed up all the materials used for the painting and put them back into Jeremy's truck. It was getting close to dusk as they made it back and started a small fire near the sandpainting.

From a small bag in his coat pocket, Jeremy took two pieces of peyote. As they slowly chewed the plant they began to drift off, their surroundings becoming surreal. Still staring at the flames of their small fire, it seemed to dance uncontrollably, bending in a ninety-degree angle and circling the floor. Almost as suddenly as they drifted off, they were wide awake from the soft beating of drums coming from the sandpainting. They did not know if they were awake or dreaming as they stared at each other.

The sandpainting began to change into a clockwise circling form and as the four colors in it mixed like a swirl cake, the painting turned a soft opaque blue from which a column of green light shot straight up, changing at once to a light red. The light of the column burst across the kiva to reveal the Mediator, who stood above them in the air, a soft white aura surrounding his personage.

The Mediator gazed down upon them with orange eyes. At first Jeremy thought the stare was very piercing, then realized it was one of compassion. They stared at the Mediator in amazement, afraid to speak. With full realization of who the personage was, from their cross-legged position, both bowed their heads to acknowledge subservience and gratitude, not daring to look upon the face of Mediator until allowed to do so.

"Be of good cheer and lift your heads," Mediator said. "I have come to assist you in your time of trouble. Life in the fifth world is never easy for Sun God's chosen, but the joys along the way will overshadow the labors. I sense you have many questions to ask of me."

"We do," speaking in unison.

The two of us have been given a difficult task that we do not know if we can accomplish," Jeremy said.

"Besides, it begins in two days when we are supposed to prepare ourselves and those coming for the council," Sky Thinker interrupted.

"Have you tried the best you can so far," Mediator asked?

"Yes, we are working around the clock to do all we can," Jeremy said.

"Then, that is all Sun God requires," Mediator said. "You two, as well as the others are doing important work. The foundation you have laid will come to fruition in the next two days."

"How do you know that?" Sky Thinker asked.

"Because, you have already succeeded where others failed in the previous four worlds," Mediator replied. "You have not succumbed to the serpent god, the purveyor of evil. Have you not examined the history here? This place was one of Sun God's chosen places, the people were his chosen people. They had been brought across the great deep, away from those in the vast desert that perverted his laws. But alas, they too became wicked as they turned their back on what they knew to be right and slowly, they drifted to the side of the serpent, the evil one. You have already done much to repair that. By performing this ceremony, you have cleansed the evil that last dwelled here."

The Mediator took his spear, holding the complete length in his outstretched, right hand. He slowly turned in one complete circle until he returned to his starting position. Then, he lowered his spear, next to his foot. As soon as the spear stopped, a green-white light rapidly spread in a circle going outward as far as they could see. Dark shadows could be seen fleeing the light, apparently lingering demons whose time was up. As the light caught them in mid stride, they burst into a blue flame, the cinders from their body racing upward as the last sparks of their ashes fell to the earth and were doused. The two were in awe at what they were seeing, mouths agape.

"Where Sun God is, the serpent cannot come," Mediator said. "You were asked to prepare yourselves, which you have now done. This meeting place of the council is cleansed because of your faithfulness in performing your duties. You can rest from that part of your labor. Now, you must make ready all needed for the many who will arrive during the next two days. You must also prepare them prior to Sun God's arrival. All must be clean and pure in heart. Doubt not."

"How is this so?" Sky Thinker asked.

"All of you were chosen for this battle from before this world was," Mediator replied. "You were chosen from the beginning and you have conducted yourself well. Because of you, our people will prosper again as they turn to the side of Sun God. Endure to the end. You have shown love and compassion and have done everything in your power to ensure that you have followed the principles and the concepts of the ways of the great Medicine Men before you. I am Totsoni Yazzi, your grandfather. You hold a special place in my heart as do your friends. Look and behold."

The walls of the kiva turned into a visual portal as they witnessed the Kachina standing in the road, his jeep going off the cliff, and Totsoni's spirit flying through the air with the Kachina.

"I was reminded of my promise and my duties in this life," Mediator said. "Once I remembered my past, it was easy to pursue the future. Go now, do that which you are commanded, and all will be well. Perform in honor"

The Mediator stretched out his hand as he waved goodbye. It was as if he stepped slowly into another dimension for, they could see the walls of the kiva as the last part of his hand sparkled like gold flakes in the sun, leaving them alone by the small fire. The sandpainting had vanished along with the Mediator.

The final two days passed quickly. Jeremy and Sky Thinker had frantically prepared as much as they could. Thankfully, Jeremy had made a call and the entire team was present and doing all they could to assist because today was the day. The decision had been made due to growing numbers, that only tribal leaders and the leaders of the war clans and their best warriors could attend, which proved to be quite a large group, as the attendees had been gathering since the end of the Encircling Guardian ceremony. The ground was now hallowed and those attending had been instructed to spiritually prepare themselves. All was in order. No one would be present except those invited. The rest of the team had been gathered most having arrived with the President who had come via a small motorcade of inconspicuous vehicles. Traveling on Air Force One and Marine One would draw too much attention from traitorous enemies in Washington and the press. No, this was a time for absolute secrecy.

"Mr. President," Jeremey exclaimed, shaking hands as the entourage walked into Pueblo Bonito. "It is so good to see you again sir."

"Great seeing you as well," Phil said. "You sure know how to throw a party, especially out in the middle of nowhere. How is it that you chose this place?"

"I did not," Jeremy stated. "Sun God instructed me that this is where we should meet. Given the nature of our meeting, it is suitable in both function and location. Besides its remoteness, it has specific spiritual meaning from what I am told by the deity."

"Could you explain?" Stone asked.

"I'll try my best," Jeremy said. "Sky Thinker and I grew up near here as boys. This always has been a hallowed place for the Navajo and the Chacoan people who built it. There are many legends, and as you can see looking around you, the buildings, although incredibly old, have an architecture unlike anything during the time they were constructed. Despite our high elevation at over 6,000 feet where Chaco Canyon is scorched in the summer and bitterly cold in the winter, the early inhabitants date back to 2900 BC, yet look at the architecture. We still marvel at their competence and skill, which is far beyond ours."

"But I thought this was built by the Anasazi," Austin said. "I mean, they were hunters and nomads as I understand."

"It was not built by them," Sky Thinker said. "They inhabited that which was already here, although you are correct about the latter."

"It is said that intensive construction occurred in the canyon from about 900 to 1100 AD," Jeremy joined in. "But I suspect the construction was much earlier than that according to legends passed down by our Medicine Men. The sophistication of these old communities proves that."

"There must be a specific reason Sun God chose this location," Phil mused.

"Oh," Jeremy began, "I'm sure there is. Let me give you a quick rundown of the rest of the history. As you know from your readings, this pueblo has over 600 rooms and was up to five stories high in some areas. Archeologists suggest a population of around 1,000. As time went on, the Chacoan's abandoned the site. Some say it was because the sacred kivas were burned. The question is why were they burned? No one knows. The odd thing is that although the Chacoan's left, they did not take their possessions with them."

"That is very odd," Stone said. "It points to something significant happening. Fleeing from war perhaps?"

"I quite agree," Jeremy said. "We have never figured it out. Still, the history of this place points to some high-level spiritual events. It is said around 1300 AD, most of the Anasazi in this area moved south, east, and west to the areas of the Hopi mesas along the Rio Grande, Rio Puerco, and Little Colorado Rivers. The tribes in these areas consider themselves descendants of the Anasazi. Sometime during the sixteenth century, Athapaskan-speaking tribes, known as the Navajo, today, moved into the San Juan Basin, and took up the agricultural techniques of the Puebloans that still lived here. No long after, the Spaniards moved in, which as you know created many intense conflicts with all the tribes. They were like locusts. They stripped the natural resources and sent them to their settlements in the south, suppressed tribal religions through conversion to Catholicism, and organized a slave trade, the slaves being tribal members. Despite this adversity, the Navajo remained and have went through great trials in the process. Through disease, famine, and warfare we have managed to survive. Even when Mexican and white ranchers began encroaching on our lands in competition for water and grazing of our cows, we remained. The Federal stock-reduction programs developed by the White Eye's government sided with those ranchers, applying the reduction of cattle herds only to the Navajo. And yet, we remained."

"I had no idea," Phil said. "You've went through hell and it was deliberate. Do you think any of those in Washington were aware of the spiritual influence this location could make?"

"Let me answer that," Sky Thinker said. "Years ago, I met one of the BIA agents assigned to the tribe. He was plundering around out here and even then, thought that tribal members should stay away. It was as if he knew something we did not and did not want our tribal members influenced by something out of his control. He would not say what, but I knew it had to be. People in your government know something that we do not."

"Quite right," Jeremy continued. "Let me finish the

brief history and perhaps we can make sense out of it before the council tonight. You see, radiating out from this complex is a mysterious series of straight lines that extend anywhere from ten to twenty miles into the desert in each direction. But they are not random because they are as straight as an arrow, even going over mesas, as well as up and down vertical cliffs, which would make them impractical for human travel. The ancients here would not have had the technology to do that. It is presumed the roads lead to other settlements, but I would guess that is not true due to the straightness of these roads. In our history, we have legends of out-of-body travel, especially the ancient Medicine Men."

"You mean like the Seminole Transparency?" Lunadi asked. "I know personally that can be accomplished."

"Yes," Jeremy said. "It must be similar or even the same in some respects. And it makes sense in my view because many of the lines or roads leading from this place end at small shrine-like structures. This is a type of what we have also seen in the Anasazi region. What is surprising is that there are more than five hundred miles of these lines. Looking at them from a variety of maps, or sketches of them since many have eroded, gives them the appearance of specific star constellations. Perhaps they were used to travel, worship ancient gods, or represent other deity or entities from these places; it is unclear. possibly this evening we will find out more. But enough of the history. It's time to complete preparations for tonight. Excuse me for a while. I must go speak with the tribal leaders to set up a location of each of the tribes and arriving warriors."

As Jeremy walked away, the eyes of the others followed, not sure what they should be doing.

"Don't look so lost," Sky thinker said, grinning. "The first thing we need to do is dress you in suitable attire. It's sort of like going to church on Sunday, dress your best for you will be in the presence of deity. Come."

Sky Thinker and Jeremy had anticipated the problem and had a changing area set up surrounded by blankets on poles to block unwanted looks. One by one he instructed them on the basics of Navajo dress and helped them select suitable clothing for the ceremony. Before long, they came out dressed appropriately for the occasion. Most were in simple Navajo fashion. Erin was dressed in a one-piece dress, dark gray in color with black horizontal stripes across the top of the chest and diamond shaped patterns below it. She wore a simple belt girded about the waist with, turquoise earrings and bracelets, and her hair pulled back. It was quite modest. Over her left arm was draped a common, woven jacket of Navajo design. The men, excepting the President, were all dressed the same, white leggings with a leather belt having silver, circular amulets tied at the waist over a thick canvas shirt. Their only adornment being a three-stranded white bead necklace and a wide, red headband. The President was dressed much differently.

"Are you certain this is appropriate?" Phil asked. "I am not one of your chiefs."

"No, you are not," Sky Thinker replied. "You are chief of our chiefs for you honorably lead the nation."

The President was adorned in full length buckskins with multicolored beads running vertically from the mid-shoulder on each side to the bottom of his coat and on each side in the center of his leggings. Around his neck he wore a four-rowed, alabaster necklace with short, two-inch lengths, ending in silver tips hooked to a vertical piece of leather. Upon his head was a full headdress of eagle feathers attached to a white beaded band with red thread securing the attachments. The band had alternating vertical bars and pyramids that were strangely reminiscent of the great pyramids of Egypt. The vertical bar in the center was gray, with yellow bars on either side then, red and finally blue. The pyramids were the same, excepting the small doorway depicted at the bottom center was blue, surrounded by pale green, then red, and finally blue. From the edges of the headdress hung leather strands with turquoise and rubies attached near the bottoms in alternating patterns. Upon his feet were beaded moccasins, ankle height.

When the others saw him, they gasped. He looked every part the Navajo Chief and carried himself with dignity.

"I will do my best not to disappoint you," Phil said. "It is an honor to wear your traditional clothing. I will not disrespect it."

"I know you will not," Sky Thinker said. "It is who you have always been."

"Is this appropriate?" Lunadi asked. "I brought my own traditional clothing."

"It is quite sufficient," Sky Thinker responded. "All the other warriors have done the same."

Lunadi was wearing a typical Seminole warrior outfit. On his head was a multicolored headband of red, blue, yellow, orange and black color, appearing as one fabric with several dark turkey feathers protruding above his right eye and one long, blood red feather. Around his neck was a red scarf tied at the back, which protected his neck from a beaded band of a necklace that held two, heavy, quarter moon shaped pieces of silver. He wore a long-sleeved, calico type shirt that was a pale tan with vertical blue stripes. Across the top of his shoulders were dark blue wavy frills, as well as at the juncture of the shirt sleeve and shoulder seam and around the wrists. Across his left shoulder hung a possibles bag, with such an exquisite design it is difficult to describe. His pants were tanned buckskin with leather strands hanging off the bottom covering plain moccasins. Just above each knee was tied a Seminole beadwork length of belt. His face was painted blood red with a wide black strip across the eyes. He looked ferocious. Erin, glancing at him realized, this was the real Lunadi. A warrior's warrior whom she wanted to know more. Her heavenly chamber moistened just thinking about it.

"Come, let us join Jeremy," Sky Thinker said.

Jeremy was meeting with all the tribal leaders and warriors. They were standing just south of the entrance to Pueblo Bonito; he was waving his hands across the area south of the entrance to gain their attention to it.

"This area is where we will be seated; we need to fit all into it," Jeremy explained. "We have little time left for preparation. You will notice the structure is about 550 feet wide. According to our Medicine Men of the past, the community gathered here for religious instruction. What we need is three blocks across with ten-foot aisles between them and the same for the depth. So, we will have nine large blocks where leaders and warriors will sit. The leaders and warriors of each tribe should sit together. If you cannot, find a seat wherever you can. We will all sit cross legged. So, we need to get rid of any small stones and bushes that will hinder us from moving about and seeing the pueblo. Any questions."

"Do you think we can all fit here?" a leader asked.

"I do not know," Jeremy said. "Just in case, if we cannot, let's clear the areas of the southeast and southwest corners. Also, let's make sure to keep the road to the south clear, no vehicles, only people."

Talking amongst themselves and waving their hands, the leaders and warriors dispersed to make sure the area was cleared for the ceremony.

"Look at you," Jeremy said, surprised and laughing. "I would have never thought you would look so indigenous. Seriously though, this is a solemn occasion. Phil, could I ask you a question?"

"Certainly," Phil responded.

"Let's walk over here."

The two walked a short distance so the others could not hear, looking at the group occasionally, smiling.

"You have two secret service agents with you," Jeremy said. "Do you trust them with your life?"

"Actually three," Phil said. "And I do. They have been with me for five years except the newer guy, nodding in his direction, he has only been with me for three years but has been trustworthy so far. Why do you ask?"

"I have been so busy I did not notice and did not discern a threat," Jeremy said. "However, one of the Iroquois leaders indicated the same agent you just mentioned and told me earlier that he had a dark spirit. I just want you to be aware of this. With so many people it will be difficult to monitor them all. I can only trust that we are in good hands as we move into what will be one of the most momentous nights in tribal and U.S. history."

The two walked back to the group as nonchalant as they could. They had changed the topic of the discussion to the ruins so no one would know what they had discussed.

"What's up next on the agenda?" Jason asked, as the two

walked up.

"The tribal leaders are preparing a place for everyone to sit once the council begins," Jeremy said.

"When will that be?" Lunadi asked.

"The Mediator told me to have everyone gathered together by dusk," Jeremy replied.

"That's about an hour from now," Austin said. "I guess that makes sense because there are no lights out here."

"Well, we do have one last chore to take care of," Jeremy said. "We have already placed bundles of wood by each of the kivas, we now need to light the fires. They need to be burning when darkness falls. Come, let's do the first one, the large one just inside the entrance."

The group climbed down one by one into the large kiva just inside the south entrance. A few bundles of wood were bound and laying just off the center in the dirt. Jeremy smoothed the floor with his hands and then, shaved some of the logs. He took the shavings and placed them directly in the middle, looking up overhead to ensure placement then, added more small kindling and struck a match as he held it beneath the shavings.

"Hey, I thought you guys were experts at survival," Jason chuckled. "Isn't the match cheating?"

"Sometimes you find yourself in a hurry," Jeremy said, grinning. "Besides, we can't all be like Lunadi and Sky Thinker."

The group laughed, knowing exactly what Jeremy meant. Within a minute or so the fire was burning brightly.

"Great," Jeremy said. "This looks good. Okay, all of you split up and light each of the kivas in the main inner courtyard. There are eight on the north end, and another just behind us. Also, we will have one in the southeast and southwest corners. Lunadi, why don't you and Erin do those. Let's go, it will be dusk shortly."

The group split up as they lit one fire after another. Erin and Lunadi went to the southeast corner first and repeated the process that Jeremy had just showed them.

"What do you think will happen tonight?" Erin asked. "I mean, the visit of the Mediator and White Shell Woman in the SCIF was incredible, but I must admit, a little fearsome."

"I'm not sure," Lunadi replied. "I had a visitation by Sun God and Monster Slayer on my property. They chastised me in front of Sky Thinker and Jeremy. Not in a severe, but a loving way. It is still fresh in my mind."

"I have never really thought about God the way I probably should," Erin said. "I mean like lots of people I went to Sunday School and church and all, but was never the religious type, especially as I got more involved in politics."

"Understood," Lunadi said, as he got the first fire going and they began walking to the next. "I grew up doing the same but have always been mindful of Great Spirit. Although I never talk about it much, it has always been a deep belief. After the visit recently, I have been thinking more and more about it and find myself praying about doing the right thing."

"You don't strike me like the praying type," Erin grinned as she touched his hand.

"Strange thing about warriors," Lunadi said. "Of all people they are the ones who I have found have the most compassion and a love for others, despite their training. They always seem to try to do the right things through simply helping the elders and service. It has always been our way. A true warrior helps the people. Is that not what you do?"

"I never thought of it like that," Erin said. "You're right, I think. I have always had this driving passion to help others and help our country. It just seemed to be the right thing to do and now, we need more help than ever."

"Exactly," Lunadi replied. "There are traitors in our midst, a great many, and they may yet bring about our downfall as a nation."

"Agreed," Erin said. "Phil and I often wonder who we can trust in DC and it is so difficult to know as we have little trust as it is. The problem is, it is affecting the entire country because we need to keep secret plans that will potentially save us because most of the left-leaning congress is on the payroll of the Chinese. We have evidence of all of it, but there is nothing we can do yet because the constitution is basically dead. Everyone is on the take it seems."

"Yes, they are," Lunadi said. "We cannot change that, we can only prepare for what is to come and somehow, bring those to justice. Someday, I will tell you about Operation Dead End, which is currently underway. It will help, but we need to worry about this first."

The two finished building the last fire and walked back to meet the others, Erin's hand on the small of Lunadi's back, butterflies in her stomach. The last tip of the sun was falling behind White Rock and Little White Cone peaks. Darkness would fall quickly. They caught up with Jeremy and the others at the entrance and were surprised to see that all the warriors and tribal leaders had already gathered and were sitting quietly, in solemn assembly. Not only were the nine blocks the leaders set up already filled, but there were also warriors and leaders sitting on all sides and behind, as well as across the road south of the ruins.

"I never thought there would be this many," Sky Thinker remarked softly.

"This is the result of all your hard work my brother,"

Jeremy said, looking at Sky Thinker with the compassion and the love of a warrior. "You and Ferni, who is over there, in the front."

The two waved in acknowledgement. Ferni understood the wave and smiled, waving back.

"This is intimidating, makes me feel like a fish out of water," Phil said.

"What do you think will happen tonight?" Stone asked.

"My friends," Jeremy began. "I do not know, but I suppose you should buckle in as they say and enjoy the ride. Go, take your seats. I have a short announcement to make."

Ferni had saved some space for their small group and waved, motioning them over. They walked softly to where he was and took a seat.

"It is good to see you again brother," Sky Thinker said as they took their seats. "How many do you think are here?"

"Based on the seating as directed by the tribal leaders, chiefs and Presidents, I was thinking we could squeeze in about 8,000, but looking at all of them, I'd say we have at least 15,000."

The two stood looking quietly for a moment at all the warriors, many of whom gave a soft wave, nod, or smile. They returned the acknowledgements and sat down, both feeling relieved that they had done what was needed from them. All eyes were on Jeremy as he stood in the middle of the south side of the pueblo, gazing out across the crowd, a megaphone in his hand. The air was so still and calm one could hear a pebble drop. It was as if they were sitting in a large natural Amphitheatre. Perhaps that is why this place had been built; to teach the people.

"My brothers," Jeremy spoke in a soft, firm voice. "I am not one for long speeches and you know why you have been summoned here. Welcome. This night will be a night you can tell your children and grandchildren about. As you know, our nation is in grave peril and we have been asked to help save it. I do not know what will happen here tonight in the home of our ancestors. All I know is that deity has requested our presence. As we wait, please have patience, and reverently meditate. And thank you, thank you all for coming.

The sky to the west had turned from the last streak of orange overlain by a light blue to a faint blue hue as the stars replaced day in the night sky. Jeremy bowed his head, his eyes closed as he placed his hands on his knees. Upon seeing it, those around him emulated his reverent manner, which spread through all the warriors. He began to lightly chant, the same thing over and over. The rest of the warriors and leaders copied him as they all joined in unison, over 15,000 warriors chanting softly.

One could physically feel the spirit. Now dark, the soft chant echoed loudly against the canyon walls as the dim light from the fires within the kivas and inner courtyard of the pueblo, cast their shadows against the ruined, still standing walls of the pueblo. Suddenly, a soft voice pierced the chant. Everyone stopped and looked about; they saw nothing and then, the voice came again; they could not understand it then, there was the soft beat of drum from the large kiva. After just a moment they stopped, and the voice returned. This time, it was clear, coming from above them. "Prepare yourselves and fear not. You are the faithful — welcome!"

The drums beat again, very softly, accompanied by chants that stopped momentarily as the warriors began looking about once more. At once everyone turned their heads toward the east as a bright light appeared, seeming to stretch from horizon to horizon, but it was not far away.

It quickly moved toward them, a huge wall of blue-white light. As it reached them, it stopped at the edge of the warriors and then, encircled all of them as it burst into a white fog settling on and all around them. As they looked, the fog separated back to the circle of light it had been and then, shot straight upward, one long column with the stars visible inside. Instantly the column closed and fell back toward them, forming a huge dome of white light. It was now bright as midday inside the dome. Everyone was looking in amazement as they began to see soft blue flashes like small lightning bolts, but not as bright, all over the pueblo. Sand began to shift, and stones began to move as the pueblo in front of them changed before their very eyes. Within a couple of moments, the pueblo was fully restored to its original form. The group sat spellbound, gasping in amazement, wondering how this could be?

As the warriors sat watching, everything was still, calm, not a sound. They could no longer see the stars; all they saw was the dome of light that encircled them. They could not see out and presumed that no one could see in. The silence so still only their breathing was heard. A red column of light shot down from the top of the dome onto the far-left kiva. It disappeared as quickly as it came, revealing a personage standing above the kiva in the air. It was a woman wearing an exquisite white blouse with a waist length gold necklace. On her head was a V-shaped headdress of green feathers and arch of pure gold flames around her head, above which sat four semi-circular rows of white pearls.

"I am Soul Searcher. I come to search your souls, whether they have courage or cowardice."

Another red beam shot down atop the kiva next to her. And again, another personage was revealed, a fearsome looking man with a face as white as snow, red around his eyes and mouth and a breastplate of green and red stone. In his hand he held a stone tomahawk. His eyes were black and brooding.

"I am Masauwu, the death Kachina. You will serve Sun God or die; the choice is yours."

One by one, from left to right a shooting red column was replaced with a personage.

"I am Changing Woman."

"I am White Shell Woman."

"I am the Mediator."

"I am Ocatu, leader of your lost tribes."

Ocatu wore a breast plate that held twelve stones, each representing a tribe. Medicine Men had long spoke of him.

The warriors sat, unable to speak. The white dome began to change as it opened, and the star-studded sky became visible. It subsided to form a wall around the gathering about five feet high. The stars in the sky were now clearly visible and the personages had a white glow about them. Suddenly, directly in front of them, in front of the pueblo, Monster Slayer materialized, as if he just stepped from thin air; he stood in the air with his feet above the ground. His eyes, a dark ruby red, with feet as pure turquoise. In his hand was his ever-present spear, now glowing red, like an ember in a fire. First appearing as a normal sized man, he changed his form until he was fifty feet tall. The warriors gasped, for the first time, fear fell upon them as Monster Slayer's eyes pierced each one to the very core.

"Do not fear me," Monster Slayer began. "Tonight, I bring you good news. You have gathered as strong warriors and because you are willing to stand and fight, to serve this hallowed land, we will be here to help you. Marvel not and prepare yourself. Dig deep and find the reverence necessary to receive the visitation of a god. Please, bow your heads and close your eyes."

The warriors did as commanded, fervently saying silent prayers as they contemplated that which they had just seen and that which was about to happen.

"Awake, my brothers in arms," Monster Slayer said.

No sooner had he said this than there was again the faint beat of drums and from the large kiva directly in front of them a large red column of light appeared shooting down from the sky, which cast a red hue all around, much like a red flashlight that saves one's night vision.

The color and hue on the rocks around and within the pueblo was intense. The drums began to beat a little louder and a second column appeared next to the first, this one was green. The intense red hue now changed to yellow and the intensity grew. The drums began to beat even louder, and a chant began, originating from the back of the pueblo, the warriors beating the drums could be seen against the backdrop of the mesa, above the heads of Soul Searcher and the other deity. The language of the chant was foreign, not recognized by those present. Abruptly, the drums and chant stopped as a third column of light shot down and mixed with the first two, creating a bright white column.

The column shrunk to the height of a man and then a personage materialized out of the light as the column gave way to the aura of Sun God, standing in the air above the kiva with eyes as flaming fire, and feet as though shining gold, wearing white buckskin, a turquoise headpiece and a silver earring, along with a turquoise and silver necklace. His face from the top of his cheeks down was a bright blue and protruding from behind his head were four white eagle feathers. His presence was awe inspiring. The group of warriors had gone from cross-legged to bowing on their knees, their faces on their hands, afraid to look up.

"Raise yourselves, for I am he," Sun God commanded, as the warriors resumed once again their cross-legged position. "I am he who created all things. I am he whom you worship by many names. I am Sun God!"

Sun God gazed across the group of warriors. A gaze that was both withering and piercing, his eyes flaming in a circular manner, like a tornado. Finally, his gaze came to rest on Jeremy and the President, before once again taking in the gathered warriors and other deity circling behind him. The silence was unsettling. What was but a few seconds, seemed an eternity to the warriors before Sun God spoke again. Without realizing it, they became acutely aware of the presence of his spirit as it comforted them and the fear and trepidation they felt, left them. All eyes were looking upon Sun God whose compassion toward them was evident.

"Look around you my people," Sun God said. "Do you not recognize this city, like that of old when you were graced by my presence? How have you fallen so far in this the Fifth World? I have tried so many times to help you remember that which you are through the tradition and passing down of my laws by the Medicine Men but alas, you would not listen.

Many times, have I spared thee and yet, you still would not stay on the path and repent of your sins and return to me with purpose of heart. And now, the dwellings in your midst have become like this place, desolate. But it need not be. The time has come for you to fulfill your covenant with me and standing as witnesses are the deity behind me. You will fulfill your oath, or you will die. This is the written law."

When the warriors heard these words, tears began to roll down their faces as they were allowed to remember some of their past and what they had promised to do in the Fifth World. They were looking around at each other, realizing their friendship and relationships in worlds and times before this one. It made them feel small for they knew they had fallen from the path.

"Fear not," Sun God began again. "There is ample time to fulfill your bargain. This country will be swept for the last time because many of the tribes and Earth Surface People have neglected my ways but be of good cheer for you and those you labor with shall be spared ch'įįdiitah hodook'ą́ą́ł if you now fulfill your oaths. You will not be hewn down, drowned in the depths of the sea, nor burned by the fire of my breath and that of Monster Slayer. Have I not told you of these things through my Medicine Men, all of whom have been faithful to delivering my message, but you would listen not. Nor would the Earth Surface People listen to the prophets sent among them by my hand and whether by me or the mouths of my servants, it is the same. A sweeping of this nation you want and a sweeping ye shall receive for you would not adhere to my words.

You have chosen the side you are on because you are here. These are my servants, pointing to Jeremy and his group. Now, ye shall be my servants for in your hands rest the lives of millions. Like you, the Earth Surface People have chosen. Many millions will perish because of the side they have chosen. Pray not for them for they are the wicked but pray and be reverent for those who fight alongside of you in the near battle. I could give Monster Slayer alone the authority to sweep this nation, but then, you would not be able to fulfill your oath and obligation, it would remove your agency and free will then, I should be no different than the serpent god whom you call the devil. All must choose whom to follow, either into eternal light or eternal darkness.

Has not my many servants testified to you of these things and you would not listen. Their testimony is true, as are my words of life and death are true. Because you would not listen, I myself will relate unto you from whence you came and who you are. Behold those in penance, the Rephaim."

The earth began to tremble as if a great earthquake was happening when the warriors noticed white hued shapes running toward them from the north. There were seven figures who jumped down from the hundred feet high ledges behind the pueblo and encircled it. Two positioned themselves at the front corners of the pueblo, the remaining four were equal distant in a semicircle ringing it, behind the deity. It was Aichu and six others like him, all dressed the same and at least forty feet tall. Having taken their place, they were standing at attention with their hands palm down on their fifteen-foot swords. So sudden had been their approach that the warriors pushed away on their hands and butts as the dust from the giants settled around them. Like the deity, there was a white aura around each, but not nearly as bright. The warriors were looking at these seven personages in awe because of their size.

"These are they who are working their way back into my presence as I have agreed," Sun God began again. "They are the last of their kind here on earth who realized their wrong doings in time to earn penance. Their penance will be fulfilled, and they will again be allowed to enter my presence by helping you in the coming battle. Eons ago, a group of my angels, sons of God, rebelled against me. They were banned and fell to the fifth world. After their fall, they began to take human women as child bearers, which was forbidden. As they began to manipulate the DNA of the Earth Surface People their evil was before my face continually and I caused the great flood to destroy them. Some survived and these are the last of their kind. In this very place, those who fled left everything behind for they were fleeing certain death. The ancestors of these remaining seven ate human flesh, an abomination before me. I will not answer the sins of their fathers onto them. The people before you, fell to the great serpent god, the devil and began worshipping him. The Rephaim attacked them and the survivors fled to build their dwellings high up in the cliffs, attempting to survive. These seven knew what their ancestors were doing was wrong and they alone remain, from angelic parentage. They will now prove themselves in the final struggle.

I am well pleased with some, but the works of man have been disappointing. Time after time you have failed me when you should not. And time after time I have gathered you as a hen gather her chicks. Knowing your nature, I have foreseen the evil that men do. Thousands of years ago, I brought you out of the city of Zech because of wickedness, to this land of promise, my hallowed land, to establish a righteous branch who would follow my word. I established the Medicine Men to guide and teach you and still, you have wandered down strange paths. I reserve that of mine unto me for I see what is to come. These are mine. Ten tribes who follow me as they should."

Sun God turned and waved both hands in an outward arch. On the north side of the pueblo a huge dimensional portal opened with flaming fire as its borders. Thousands upon thousands of warriors could be seen in ten large columns across rolling hills and mountains. At the head of each column stood a single individual, dressed like the variety of the warriors present, a mix of all the tribes. These ten men floated forward in the air, standing five on each side of Sun God, their dark eyes peering down upon the warriors in front of them. Speaking not a word, they turned to gaze upon Sun God then, in unison said, "we are ready." Immediately they floated back through the air, the heads of their tribes.

"This is my land, it is hallowed land," Sun God said. "I will no longer let my people dwell in sin and trod under foot that which I have created." As Sun God spoke, he floated through the air to stand above the ground in the center of the warriors and then began to slowly circle each row, letting them touch him. As each touched him, they were quickened to the core by his spirit. Never had they felt any emotion so strong as to know that he was and that despite their short comings, they would answer the call and stand as men among men to help keep the country from being swept from within and without. To protect it against the traitors in Washington who paid lip service to their office, but who secretly made treacherous deals against the people with foreign adversaries.

Sun God continued to circle the rows of warriors and finally stopped directly in front of Jeremy and his group. "Lusio, Philip, Jason, Erin, Stone, Austin, Nick, Sky Thinker, Lunadi, Ferni — arise and stand forth to face your fellow warriors," Sun God said. "Fellow warriors, these are the people who will help lead you against the treachery from within. I created them from before this world was to carry out the duties they now inherit. They were chosen by me because of their great hearts and courage. Heed them as you go forth to fight the enemy within and from without."

As Sun God had been talking, he was slowly floating back from the air to the center of the large kiva where he disappeared, shooting skyward in a column of white. The white column shrank and then, separated into the three colored columns of red, yellow and green, which dissolved away to reveal the fire still burning in the kiva. Without hesitation, Monster Slayer and Soul Searcher floated forward, directly over the center kiva. Soul Searcher was saying something to Monster Slayer, nodding toward the warriors. There was now great apprehension in the warriors as they stood facing these deities. Soul Searcher floated forward toward the Jeremy's small group and stopped directly in front of them, hovering about six feet off the ground. They had not noticed before, but her eyes were bright yellow, having a small black center and penetrating gaze.

"There is one among you plotting treachery," Soul Searcher said. "This is not allowed within the presence of Sun God. It is you, the one with the dark heart." She pointed at one of the President's secret service, the same whom Jeremy had indicated earlier.

"That's right," the agent said. "This fake President will never succeed but we will, we will take this hallowed land and control it as we have been plotting for two hundred years, *drawing his pistol and beginning to point it directly at the President.*"

As the pistol raised, Soul Searcher shot yellow energy beams from her eyes, freezing the agent in place as the gun dissolved to powder. The energy surrounding the agent began to turn him translucent. The warriors felt large thuds and a slicing noise. Aichu had stepped forward and chopped through the agent with an outward slice, so rapidly that the sword sang as it swept through the agent and over the warriors. The agent looked like a sparkler as the sparks emanating from the energy blast of Soul Searcher swept out over the warriors; the agent was no more. Aichu, stepped back, assuming his position, his penetrating stare watching all.

"Disobedience and treachery will no longer be tolerated," Soul Searcher said. "Keep your hearts pure and your thoughts clean! Death is the immediate punishment if you do not."

Soul Searcher glided back, next to Monster Slayer who was staring at the warriors.

"You don't see that every day," Erin whispered.

All the warriors were aghast. They had been trained as warriors all their life, but never had they seen a display of supernatural power over an enemy. The remaining two secret service agents were on either side of the President, blocking him from approach of others.

"You have no need of protection here Phillip," Monster Slayer said. "We protect those who were chosen before this world was. My brothers, my warriors, this is the President of the United States. He, along with his group before you, will help you plan the final battle defense. Work together and you will achieve victory. These men before you are like yourselves, pure in heart. Indeed, they regale themselves of no higher stature than you, my fellow warriors. If you will do what you can, we will help you. Now that you have witnessed our power, you must have some understanding of what we can do."

"I can see the darkness of one's heart," Soul Searcher chimed in. "The fallen one had a darkness no less than the devil himself. Beware, lest you succumb to the power of that evil one. Behold."

"God help me keep a pure heart," Nick whispered.

A giant portal opened before them, progressing through the history of the Chacoan's who had lived here centuries before. The warriors were in awe. It began with a vision of the ancient people and how they lived and worshipped Sun God. Two of the kiva's were ceremonial, the others were used as fisheries to provide food for the people on a constant basis due to the climate, still others were used for food storage, and cisterns to store water for crop growth, raising small animals, mostly goats and chickens, and for drinking and bathing. Jeremy and Sky Thinker marveled at what they saw, for unlike the artist renditions of what the pueblo probably looked like, it was truly a community living place. Water from the tops of the mesa were channeled into a box canyon a few hundred yards east where the Chacoan's had a small surface reservoir diked just behind the ruins of what had been Chetro Ketl. From there the water had been channeled into a large handmade furrow down to Pueblo Bonito fill all the kiva cisterns in the pueblo, Chetro Ketl, and Pueblo del Arroyo just to the west about four hundred yards.

It all finally made sense. Two main Kiva's in the pueblo had been used for ceremony, all the others were used for agricultural and water purposes. As Soul Searcher waved her hand, the portal changed, showing the areas outward from the pueblo to an exceptionally large kiva-like structure about seven hundred yards south, southeast of the pueblo. It was known among some as the 'headless Kachina.' They could see the Chacoan's laughing and splashing in the water as they sat, dipping their feet into clear water. It was like watching a home movie. Finally, the portal moved back to a view of the pueblo where they could see members of the small community growing crops, gardening in the two main areas of the pueblo. While there were living spaces all throughout and everyone fulfilled a task. They had been a self-contained community and it was easy to understand how they survived so efficiently; everything was inside the pueblo for the most part to protect crops from birds and other pests and the small animals from the bands of coyotes that roamed about, some of whom they had heard earlier as night fell. His thoughts were interrupted by a voice.

"What happened to the ancients that lived here?" Erin asked.

Soul Searcher looked directly at her, as if it were forbidden to speak, but her stare was not one of admonition but of approval for the interest.

"They fell away, as is the nature of those who betray Sun God," Soul Searcher said, as she spoke, the view into the portal began to show the history of the canyon. "The old Medicine Man of the tribe went the way of all the earth and a younger Medicine Man took his place. He knew the people would listen to him so, he began to slowly lead away their hearts to worship the serpent god. First, he began to sabotage the harvest, then the water supply and turned the people to the way of darkness. After a while, they cared not for the right path. Their hearts were darkened to the point where they had no light left in them. Because of their sins, the holy one who sent the Rephaim upon them. But it did not need to be so. Had they repented and followed the path, Sun God would have taken them unto himself."

As she explained, they could see the Rephaim come upon the pueblo and surrounding units as the sun hit its zenith. The people had no time to pack anything as they fled for their lives. They could not outrun the Rephaim who caught them and devoured them alive. Many had been trampled under their feet as they ran and only a few were able to get away, the rest perished within an hour. The scene was so gruesome that Erin and Phil had to turn away so they would not see. The others cast their eyes downward, astonishment on their face.

"Now you understand," Soul Searcher said. "Those who do not what they are commanded by Sun God will perish quickly because they deny that which they know to be just and true. Our people were placed in this harsh land to test their faithfulness. It is often told among you that the faithful are used to punish the wicked, so too is it true that the wicked are used to carry out Sun God's judgements upon all."

"You have seen enough," Monster Slayer intruded. "The time of final preparation is at hand. All of you warriors will prepare for battle. If you are hewn down, then we have prepared a special place for you. There is no need to fear, action is now required. Jeremy, you and your group step forward please and then turn and face our mighty warriors." The small group did as Monster Slayer commanded them.

"These are those who will plan the defense against your enemies and will work with the chiefs to make sure all is in place and that each tribe and their warriors knows what is expected of them. Trust them, for as Sun God told you, they were prepared for this very event. Mediator, step forward. *The Mediator glided from the background taking his place at the side of Monster Slayer.* The Mediator will be the messenger between you and us. Listen and heed. President Weld, many of the warriors are wondering why they should help after the federal government has treated them so poorly. You will finish this battle, purge the traitors from government, the only penalty being death. You will enlarge each tribe's land by seven-fold, ensure the trust responsibilities is carried out by the federal government and not the states in which they reside and finally, you will appoint a Native American Intelligence and Progress committee that is autonomous from congress with the power to ensure my people are treated as they should be. Jeremy, gather these leaders together and ensure all are well-informed before departing. They must not leave until they are knowledgeable of their roles in the defense strategy. Aichu, see to the security until they are finished. Soul Searcher, we depart."

The two turned and walked away, followed by the remaining deity who stood in the background. They simply walked through an unseen doorway as they vanished from sight. The entire group of warriors and Jeremy looked after. It was difficult to believe what hand transpired, in which the spirit was now so strongly felt. Only Aichu and his six men remained, turning outward as if defending against as yet, unseen threat. Everyone stood as though they did not know what to do. Sky Thinker nudged Jeremy.

"I believe that we are all a little overwhelmed at what has transpired," Jeremy said. "I would like all of the tribal leaders and heads of your warriors to gather over in the west open area next to the large kiva. Take some time to compose yourselves and contemplate what we have seen. We have tables set up and food. The rest of you warriors please proceed to the food area if you wish or talk amongst yourselves while we meet with your leaders. And everyone, I need not admonish you, but what you have just witnessed you are to keep among yourselves only and other warriors not present. You may not discuss it with anyone else until after the battle. General Bardos, the President and rest of our entourage will meet you at the planning area. Let's move.

The leaders and warriors gathered around as they managed to squeeze everyone around the tightly packed tables.

"General Bardos and I have been planning this for some time, along with Lunadi, Erin, Stone and Austin," Jeremy said. "In favor of secrecy, we will outline the plan and draw the surrounding geology. The location will not be given until later. It is imperative that this information remain among us and not come to the attention of others."

All nodded and voiced agreement for they, better than anyone, understood circumstances developed out of treachery.

"I'll turn the meeting over to General Bardos and he will explain the basics," Jeremy said.

"Thank you, Jeremy," Jason said. "Let us move away from the tables and form a large circle. It will be easier to see the map that way, which I'll just draw in the dirt."

The general marked each end of a line to get the scale correct from northeast to southwest and then on a ninety-degree angle. Then he drew in some hills, mountains and open areas to represent plains.

"Okay," Jason said. "I have the scale right, so gather around and I'll begin with explanations."

"Before we begin," a Tribal leader began, "are we going to have military assistance?"

"Excellent question," Jason remarked. "The answer is yes to an extent. I will be leading that, working your units in with ours. We will provide logistics to get you where you need to be, as well as support throughout the battle as much as is possible. I would like you to envision yourselves as guerilla fighters supporting a larger mission because you're great at it. Lunadi has one thousand warriors to bring. That is why this plan is so important. We know their main objective, which is crucial in terms of logistical transport to the southwest and the nation. Because of your guerilla warfare capabilities, we will coordinate with you to begin attacks one hundred and forty miles from the Chinese objective, here. As they close to within forty miles of the objective that is where we will hit them with everything we have. You may be wondering how we know this. As you just witnessed, we will have superior guidance and assistance if we perform our duties.

The intent is to develop a psychology of fear among their troops. It is going to be a formidable task. Additionally, their Russian allies will be moving up through this region. Here we will also mix our forces and with the help of Aichu and his men, we will meet the Russian force here, about seventy miles out. That force will not be as large since they need most of their troops to drive up the east coast. They also likely will not have air cover due to proximity to their main force coming in at Houston. We will attack from the high ground all along this valley front. I will be relying on our combined expertise to defeat this enemy. Guerrilla warfare tactics will be particularly important. We will discuss manpower requirements, as well as capabilities and make assignments accordingly. These tactics will all be focused on cutting the logistical supply lines of both approaching forces. One problem we will have is the air superiority of the Chinese force, however, we have a plan to combat that. If successful, it might give us the small advantage we seek."

"Will we have tank and air support?" a leader asked.

"Yes, I have managed to create a mission capable command," Jason replied. "But they may not be enough. As far as anyone knows, it is just a training exercise, even the troops in the command know no different. We have over three hundred tanks, A-10 Warthogs, Apache helicopters, artillery units and other weapons at our disposal. Make no mistake, we will be outgunned, but we have some surprises. With constant pressure on their supply lines, we should be able to outmaneuver them and keep them from reaching their objective. While we will conduct ourselves professionally, it will be up to you to determine how you wish to deal with an enemy in your sights. I would like all the leaders and those who will be leading your warriors on the field to make suggestions and changes to our overall plan based on where you will be assigned."

The general continued to explain the battle plan and answer questions from the leaders and warriors. As he learned their capabilities more and how many men they would have, he grew more pleased with their potential ability to control the battlefield. Time would tell, but it looked more promising. He, Jeremy, and Lunadi began explaining the finer points of the plan as the others looked on. Lunadi escorted the lead warriors away from the main group to begin discussing melding their skills into the overall plan for supply line disruption.

"I must admit that I'm impressed," Phil said. "It has gone much better than hoped, although the appearance of deity did not hurt any."

"If we do not win, it will not be because we did not try," Austin remarked.

"Any word on your Canada exploration?" Phil asked.

"Yes, we just received word before we arrived," Stone said. "It turns out based on our information that our asset gathered in Nicaragua, that there are likely many more of the systems present than we discussed."

"How many are you estimating?" Phil asked.

"Based on agent feedback, we are thinking about four hundred, perhaps more," Austin said.

"Wow," Erin whistled. "Can we deal with that many?"

"That was going to be my question," Phil said. "What are your thoughts?"

"We need more men, it's that simple," Stone said. "There are too many of them for just our assets to sort out and sabotage."

"Quite right," Austin said. "With that in mind we wanted to get your permission to activate what we will call Shockwave Brigade out of Delta Force."

The President eyed them both warily. "I am not sure we can keep a lid on that."

"If you don't mind me saying sir, we can list it as a search and destroy training exercise with our other units under General Bardos. That should provide the cover we need to keep it off the radar of our friends in DC."

"Yes," Stone said. "I agree. We just need to ensure to select men we can trust. The general will know most of them through previous assignments."

"Agreed," Austin said. "Because there are so many potential systems, we are going to need to mix our men with others to cover all the potential locations within our projected timeline."

"Do we have enough special operators," Phil asked. "Four hundred units means there are at least one hundred launchers."

"We have thought about that," Stone said. "In that regard, Austin has spoken with Lunadi who will lend us one hundred of his best men, more if we need; all are prior military and most with special operations or counterintelligence experience. If we combine them with the Shockwave Brigade and our own assets, we should be able to cover the projected number and locations."

"That sounds reasonable," Phil said. "Make it happen. Any other help that you need?"

"Well sir," Austin began, glancing at Stone, "given the nature of invading location of the Chinese at Long Beach Port and in an effort to cripple their supply lines, we were thinking of putting up our own systems for anti-ship and land-based attack on San Nicolas Island and on Channel Islands National Park."

"That will take some paperwork," Erin said. "We will need to classify it under maintenance, upgrades, or surveys of some sort. How large are these systems?"

"They are housed in CONEX containers, the standard eight by forty-foot size. Sitting in place, they just look like a regular container to most people," Austin replied.

"Can we just think of them as containers housing tools and equipment?" Erin asked.

"Exactly," Stone said. "It should be easy to say we're doing surveys for park area, environment monitoring, or the like."

"Yes, we can make that happen," Erin said. "How many are you thinking?"

"Probably ten on San Nicolas and fifteen to twenty in the national park," Austin replied. That will give us a total of up to one hundred and twenty missiles, which should be enough to take out their carriers and transports, as well as the port."

"You are going to take out Long Beach Port?" Phil asked.

"We do not have a choice Mr. President," Stone joined in. "It will be their major supply point and it is imperative that we remove that capacity. Besides, they own the port anyway."

"Hmmmm," Phil mused. "Good point. Let's make all this happen as quickly as we can. I'm thinking, based on a briefing from the secretary of agriculture that they'll soon be out of food. We are also in a tough spot in that regard. They won't wait until they're completely out, else the people may finally take over."

"What are you thinking timewise?" Erin asked.

"I'm guessing we have two to three months at most," Phil said.

"That means we must hustle," Stone said.

"Whatever it takes," Phil replied. "Link up with us on everything you need. We will get everything in place we have now and add as we go, but quickly."

"One other thing," Austin said. "We will have land-based missiles, predators with hellfire missiles, and other weapons all along the route. We have found various locations but may need some permissions from your office."

"Erin, make sure they get what they need as quickly as possible," Phil said. "Let's start working the phones and getting this moving. You have cart blanc permission for whatever you need. Contact myself or Erin for anything."

"What if we start getting prying questions?" Austin asked.

"Then we will brainstorm between the four of us and the others," Phil responded. "Defray the questions to Erin who can delay a response from me and give us time to come up with a credible explanation."

"Do you want me to continue working with the Chinese and Russians, sir?" Nick asked.

"Yes, they're likely stalling, but continue your discussions."

"Will do sir," Nick responded.

The group walked back to the general who was just completing explanations to the tribal leaders.

"Remember," Jason said. "I need to know within the next four days how many warriors you'll have. We will charter buses and trucks to pick them up, whatever it takes. The drivers will be our own. Once we have those numbers and the pickup location, you will stand in readiness until we call."

"Do you have any idea how long we will need to wait after pickup before the battle begins?" Ferni asked.

"Jeremy?" Jason, queried.

"We want men to be in place to receive about three weeks training on site," Jeremy replied. "Our current timeline indicates that pickup should occur in seven to ten weeks, perhaps sooner. We will update you as we narrow the time frame. It could be as little as three or four weeks. Be prepared for the unexpected. I encourage you to return home now and prepare immediately. The fate of our nation is in your hands."

The leaders and warriors all nodded, murmuring agreement as they walked off talking among themselves. The President's entourage watching them go. Jeremy walked over to Aichu who kneeled on one knee to be closer to him.

"I know this is going to sound like a dumb question," Jeremy said. "How do we contact you when we need you?"

"Contact the Mediator," Aichu said. "He will summon us to your side. I heard your plans and am familiar with the place."

"Great," Jeremy said. "We are done until then."

"Very well," Aichu said. "I will see you on the battlefield."

Aichu waved to his men as the seven of them gathered next to the large kiva. A large column of light appeared directly in front of them. The brightness caused all the warriors to turn. Suddenly, the column opened like a scroll and the Rephaim walked through, the light disappearing behind them. The sun was just tipping the eastern horizon.

"Well," Phil began. "Saying this was exciting would be an understatement. Jason, how do you feel about our chances?"

"When we first arrived, I didn't give us much of one," Jason said. "Now, after seeing this and talking with the leaders and warriors, the Chinese will get much more than they bargained for. Our chances are good Mr. President."

"Great, let us be on our way and continue preparing."

The group began walking to the southeast entrance of the pueblo. As they crossed the opening, the pueblo began rumbling. The group ran toward the other warriors, turning to see what was happening. As all the leaders and warriors watched; the pueblo returned from its renewed state to its ruined state. It was as if nothing had happened during the night — another miracle. For a moment, they all thought they heard the beating of drums.

CHAPTER 7

Searchers

The Politburo of the Chinese Communist Party was in a heated session in a conference room close to President Jin's office, tensions were running high. China's food supply was running out and their backs were against the wall as they tried to work out a strategy that would get them out of the problem. The looming food shortages would cut into every sector in the country – manufacturing, energy, water, retail, government continuity – nothing would be left unscathed. Minister Gan was talking, attempting to gain reason among the other five ministers, President Jin, and General Qiang.

"I'm telling you this is a mistake," Gan said. "It would be better to work out a deal with the Americans than to go down this path. If we lose, there is a good chance that the people will revolt, and the party will be destroyed. It is lunacy in my view to succumb to the desire for more power and control over a nation no one has ever defeated."

Minister Gan, in his mid-sixties, had been a staunch party supporter since his youth. He believed in his country and the men who ran it. He was barely five years younger than President Jin. Both had grown up in the Hanan Province and both were persistent in pursuing goals. It was a rare disagreement between the two men. Gan was the premier of the State Council of the CCP, and the head of

James Tindall

government and leader of the CCP's financial, economic and foreign affairs, as well as national security. He was a man of great power being the second ranked member of the Politburo. The group of seven men in the meeting, which General Li was sitting in on, were the top decision-making body of the CCP. Their decision was final, regardless of issue. On a global basis Minister Gan was among the top twelve most powerful people in the world. Thus, it was with intent that the other members were listening to him, their eyes fixed upon his face. He was a fit man and by Chinese standards, larger in stature than most and had a commanding presence.

"Your reasoning is misplaced," Li replied. "We can beat them. With Russia as our allies, we can beat the Americans and colonize the country. All non-Chinese will be forced into labor camps or put to death."

"I believe it is the only way to ensure our future," President Jin said calmly, nodding in agreement with Li. "It will give us continual resources forever. We could ship one third to one half of our population there and alleviate our resource problems in a single instance."

"But you are risking global war," Minister Gan said. "As head of foreign affairs, I am telling you that we can get all the food we need from the Americans, Brazil, and other countries as we have done in the past. Hell, it's how we get it so cheaply by subsidizing labor for manufacturing to produce products those countries and corporations want."

"Normally, I would agree," President Jin stated firmly. "But this time, we are in a position of utter failure. And what of the future? The entire Yangtze River Basin was flooded this year resulting in a one hundred percent loss of crops."

"But that was our own fault," another minister joined in, looking directly at General Qiang. "If the military wasn't monkeying around with weather modification programs, that would not have happened. At the very least they should have tried it on another country before experimenting with it here. And had it not been for that we would not be in this critical food shortage predicament."

"Perhaps," Li said. "But the Americans and Russians have been playing around with it for years and it has worked."

"Yes, it worked for them because Russia used their system to park a high weather front off the coast of California for years causing a drought and water shortage," Minister Gan said, the other ministers nodding agreement. "At least they didn't do it to themselves."

"Gentleman," Minister Kian blurted out. "The minister is correct. You promised us that when you began such a program it would deliver disaster relief, suppress hail, increase agricultural production through more artificial rain and snow, as well as mitigate current high temperatures and reduce grassland fires. But what we received for all the money spent on technologies was destroying our fertile breadbasket. I must agree with Minister Gan, there has to be a better way to solve this problem than starting a war with arguably the most powerful country on earth."

"We can beat them at every scenario, especially with help from Russia," Li chimed in. "We have run scenario after scenario, and it is a no win for them."

"Are you using scenarios by those who developed your weather modification system?" Minister Kian asked.

Li visibly grimaced, anger on his face.

"You're missing the main point," Li responded. "We need food for the next nine months or more. We cannot grow it and next year's crops won't be available until the end of that time. If we are going to move, we need to make that decision now."

"President Jin," Minister Gan said. "If you will give me a couple of weeks more, I can close the deal to buy more food from President Weld. Secretary of State Fabiani has been talking closely with us, attempting to make sure that we have what we need, even though it will stress their supplies as well. Also, I know President Weld through conversations we have had. He is a reasonable man and will not turn us down. More importantly, he will not use food as a weapon."

"I agree," President Jin said. "However, we have a great many on our payroll within the opposing party. They want him out and we want in. He has been a thorn in our side, and it would be better if we could deal with someone else. Besides, after having discussed it with General Qiang, I believe this is a perfect opportunity to implement this project and attack. We would have the upper hand and the party now in control of the house and senate want Weld gone. They would practically invite us in without resistance if we could help them. All of this could be done as we negotiate falsely with them. Don't you agree?"

"Yes, it could," Minister Kian joined in. "But again, I remind you that I believe food purchases are better than war. Why would they not retaliate with nukes at the first sign of a sneak attack? There is no way we can stop that. Even with an EMP attack to initially cripple communications, they will still maintain contact with their nuclear submarines, only one of which is needed to destroy all major cities in China."

"They will not use nuclear weapons," Li emphasized, looking around at the ministers. "They are totally against that, especially the ruling party. And if we helped them, they would move forward with the possibility by impeaching Weld and control of the nuclear suitcase would pass to the VP who would become President and, he is on our side as well, a sleeper if you will."

"That is a lot of ifs," Minister Gan said. "Buying the food is more logical and far less costly than war, which if something goes wrong, will be even more costly than we anticipate. And, if General Li is so convinced that our weather modification program is what it is claimed to be, there would be absolutely no sense in going through with this operation."

"Enough," President Jin said. "This is getting us nowhere. We have two choices, either a go or no go. Minister Gan, how long can we survive with our current food supply?"

"About four months."

"How long would it take to get a food purchase complete?"

"Likely three months if all goes well."

"That means that we are cutting it too close for reason," President Jin said. "General Qiang, if we launched, how long would it be before we could get food supplies from the U.S. after you have consolidated military power?"

"With our current strategy, I anticipate not more than four weeks of fighting," Li said, looking around at the ministers to see how his words were being accepted. "After that, we could have food shipments on the way via air and boat within seven days."

"That is a much shorter time frame," President Jin said, eyeing all the ministers, letting them know that was the way he was leaning.

"We do have another option," Minister Kian said. "We could simply apply for humanitarian assistance through the U.S. and NATO because of our agricultural loss along the Yangtze. It would be a perfectly logical thing to do."

"I heartily agree," Minister Gan said, all the ministers nodded basic agreement.

"I see," President Jin mused. "But suppose, we do so and find ourselves in the same position next year when we could have moved to prevent it and have a more than adequate supply of food. What would we wish we had decided in that case?"

The ministers looked around at each other. Despite not wanting to wage war, they clearly understood the message. They knew from experience that the future brings no guarantees. The meeting had fallen silent as what the President proposed sunk in. Almost one and a half billion people depended on their decision. And, like all government officials they were after all, narcissists, whose primary goal was to gain power and control and keep it. Money always flowed to those who did. The loss of power and control was something they could not bear to lose, no matter the cost! All these thoughts were going through their minds. What seemed like hours, was barely more than a minute of elapsed time. Looking up, Minister Gan looked the President squarely in the eyes and made an ever so slight affirmative nod.

"President," Minister Gan said. "We see your point. You know that we all have the party's goals at heart. What we do is for the country and the party. We would never presume to stand in the way of moving the party and country forward."

"I know that Minister Gan," President Jin replied. "General Qiang, how long will it take you to be ready for engaging the Americans?"

"We can be completely ready and launch the attack eight weeks from today," Li replied.

"Ministers," President Jin began. "Who votes yes?"

The ministers all raised their hands, nodding affirmatively.

"General Qiang," President Jin said somberly. "Make final

preparations for eight weeks exactly from today. We will meet again three days before to give final approval. Comrades, this is a great undertaking. Think on it some more. Any thoughts you have you can direct to Minister Gan or myself. We must be of the same mind in eight weeks because there will be no turning back if we engage."

Sam and his crew were going over final issues before seeking out all the launchers they could find. They were in a CIA safe house in the industrial section of Ottawa. There were enough trucks and vehicles coming and going that little attention was paid to small flat-bed trucks and vans as the teams pulled down the alley beside the building and drove through the steel, roll-up door. Sam, Rob, and Samantha had gotten in later than expected and had to wait only a few hours before all the team was assembled.

"Welcome everyone to Operation Eider," Sam began. "This is an overly critical mission with just several parameters. First, it is imperative that you not be seen near the location. Second, do not kill any security guards or sentries, we must be totally invisible. Third, you must make certain of your GPS coordinates. Fourth, all operations will be done at night."

"What is the target boss?" one of the agents asked.

"The targets are all containers of the standard eight foot by forty-foot size at the locations listed in your assigned areas." Sam replied.

"What, are they smuggling guns and drugs?" another agent asked.

"Worse," Rob replied. "Each container has four, medium-range missiles in it."

"Whoa, what are they doing, planning to start a war?" an agent asked.

"Exactly that," Sam replied. "It is the Chinese and we believe they are going to try to invade the U.S. from Canada. This is important; our lives are on the line."

The team looked around at each other, consternation on their faces. They hadn't realized the mission was of such importance. But then, it was always like that when you were in the field. You never quite knew how important something was until it was too late.

"We need to be like ghosts as we perform the mission," Sam continued. "We only have three days. The containers are located here, here, and here, pointing at a map. "You have it in your assignments. We have intelligence to that effect, but there may also be others, especially within Lakes Superior and Michigan. Samantha will take a team of six to the Port of Chicago. We have a contact at the Illinois International Port District that will set you up with two, twenty-seven-foot, Defiant boats to accomplish your tasks."

"Are those the ones made by that metal company?" Samantha asked.

"Yes," Sam replied. "They will be fully fueled and have a small, enclosed cabin to keep you temporarily out of the wind and rain until you need to get into the elements."

"Can you tell us what we're looking for more specifically?" an agent asked. "I mean all of these containers look the same."

"Rob, hand out the pictures," Sam commanded. "You will notice that the front of the container will have an electrical mount directly in the center about ten inches or so from the bottom of the container. To the left of that is an access door. You will not be able to see that until you are directly in front of the container. It almost looks like it was cut out and glued back on its so precise. The back of the container looks like a standard container."

"Is there anything else that will help us?" an agent asked.

"There are a couple of other things to look for," Rob joined in. "The missiles need to lift to a vertical position to launch, which takes about thirty minutes on the outside, but likely much quicker. However, because they need to lift vertically, the back doors of the container must be swung open to allow the lift and launch. Because of this, the container will not be able to butt against another container but must have a four and likely eight-foot distance to the container behind it and at least a few feet in front to allow access to the launch control panel. Our guess is that for each container there will be at least one operator around to launch the missiles. Oh, and one other thing, we believe the main color of the container will be blue, perhaps red as they appear to be the two dominant colors for containers out of China."

"So, from what you're telling us, a container will either need to be on the ground or if on a container ship, on a top row so it can open to fire," an agent responded.

"That is correct," Rob said. "It will also need to be supported where the backend doors are since the missiles lift vertically on that end. Because of this, there will need to be a container beneath it or the ground otherwise, it would fail. This is nice to know when you check the ports because you won't need to look at end containers at the end of an aisle or row."

"Any other questions?" Sam asked, no one saying anything. "Time is of the essence. Your equipment will be minimal. You need take only a logbook for location, your GPS unit to precisely mark the target location, as well as how many containers you find, a camera and of course your trusty pistol and suppressor and a knife. If you do end up shooting a sentry or security guard, you must get the body back to the closest city and dump it in a back alley. Make it look like a mugging. But I must reiterate, be like ghosts. If the Chinese get wise to what we're up to, they may jump the gun and our defense will be compromised. Okay, let's get going to your assigned areas. Oh, one more thing. If you find containers on a ship, make a note of the ships name so we can immediately get eyes on it and begin to track."

The six-man team Samantha was leading arrived early in the morning and had already secured the two boats, fully fueled, and marked with the identity of the port authority. They were cruising down the southernmost edge of the lake. The wind, coming out of the north about twelve miles per hour, whipped up mist from the shallow waves of Lake Michigan that shot backward above the bow and constantly struck the plexiglass on front of the cabin. Abruptly, the boats split to assume their separate search routes and cover the multiport area, as well as check for nearby, anchored container ships. They would be surveilling Dougherty Harbor, Iroquois Landing, and Harborside International. Because the port linked inland canal and river systems to the Midwest part of the country to the Great Lakes, giving access to the global shipping market through the St. Lawrence Seaway. They had another four teams searching the seaway and any river passage that a container ship or barge could navigate up. It was a lot of work and missing even one container could result in the deaths of hundreds.

The team had set up a search grid to make sure they didn't miss anything. Already they had identified several targets they would inspect after darkness fell. The day was long and grueling as they wound their way through the multimodal port system. To remain obscure, the helmsman followed the grid pattern as the two other members of the three-man team used binoculars from inside the cabin to surveil each ship, port area and any other place containers were sitting. They made notes in their logbooks as they toiled throughout the day. The breeze, now blowing more briskly, would help obscure sounds of their movement.

Sam and Rob had split up, along with the multiple teams searching for the missile launch systems. Driving through the night, Sam had reached the furthest of the Chinese camps near Dryden. He and his team took highway 601 north to Dryden Regional Airport. The area was not huge, the airport being under one and a half miles long. They were in a work van with darkened side windows so no one could see in. They continued along highway 601 around the far end of the airport to get the lay of the land. It wasn't long before they noticed the construction that had been going on and was now finished, for lengthening the runway, as well as the Chinese camp. It was late afternoon when they found a place to stash the van along a sharp curve on the north side of the airport. The woods were a mixture of mainly jack pine, mixed with lodgepole pine and occasional maple trees. The trees were close together and kept in moisture from rain and snow making the ground soft and silent. Sam new that while perhaps difficult to travel through, the woods would conceal their movements as they surveilled the area. The Chinese camp was at the far eastern end of the airport and slightly north a few hundred yards. It was about a quarter mile to the airport and then, three-quarter mile parallel to the runway to the camp.

Sam split his team into two groups, one to cover the airport to get an inventory of planes belonging to the Chinese and potential missile launchers; his group would get the location of the missiles and determine what was going on in and around the camp. The group continued easterly for about a half hour and reached a point where they could observe the Chinese. As they walked through the woods, they could smell the musty odor of the forest and feel the dampness rising to meet them from the forest floor. Picking a spot that gave them a clear view of the entire camp, they watched for several hours and drew a map of the layout. Sam had made sure they had satellite overwatch during the day for better analysis. The camp, alive with activity, was completely fenced with chain link that had razor wire attached to the top. Trucks were moving about, along with armed soldiers, AK-47s slung over their shoulders. There were multiple guards stationed at the main gates who appeared relaxed as they puffed on cigarettes. Each of Sam's team had thermal binoculars and began scrutinizing the outskirts of the camp. They panned their binoculars for almost an hour and discovered two roving foot patrols making their way around the camp perimeter, which was about a two-mile distance. They sat for another hour as the other two members of Sam's team timed their route. Sam busied himself searching for the containers that if, not neutralized, would rain death upon thousands of Americans. He finally found them on the far side of the camp, situated about midway along the fence.

"How fast are the patrols?" Sam asked. "Do they have any dogs?"

"No, no dogs," Vic replied. They are about twenty minutes, give or take two minutes apart. "Once we locate a portion of the fence we want to penetrate, we will not have a lot of time before the next patrol is on us, maybe fifteen minutes."

"That's enough," Sam said. "We need to get midway along the fence on the other side. I spotted the containers there.

Let's move, quietly."

The team backtracked their location for about a quarter mile to make sure any potential noise they made wouldn't be picked up by the patrols. Then they headed north until they were sure they had cleared the end of the compound before slowly circling back to find the fence on the opposite side. An area about thirty feet had been cleared outside of the fence all around the perimeter. They knew the backside would be the least likely suspicious guards would suspect anyone of nosing around, which meant they would not be as attentive. The team slipped along the inside of the trees, like a deer skirting the open ground for concealment, crossing shallow eroded gullies as they moved silently through the woods. Looking across the compound toward the airport, they could tell that the elevation dropped toward them about one hundred feet.

"Hmmmm," Sam mused. "If we are were lucky, we may not need to cut the fence."

"Pssss," Jake whispered. "Patrol."

The group stopped and squatted down, their dark clothing blending into the eerie shadows of the forest, cast by a quarter moon set among a star-studded night sky. They waited quietly, their hearts pounding with excitement as the patrol passed. The two guards were talking and laughing as they walked, looking more at the ground to avoid tripping than at the fence and cleared area beyond. After three or four minutes, Sam's team continued to creep along the inside of the tree line, relieved that the guards were unlikely to hear their footsteps. It wasn't long until they team was adjacent to the containers.

The second patrol was passing by as they again ducked down among the cover of the trees. Sam was silently counting the containers; twelve in all. That would be forty-eight missiles. A lot of firepower that just looked like storage containers for equipment and supplies. They were set far enough away from the fence to easily open and launch when the command was given. The three men sat, studying the containers, and looking along the fence line. After the next patrol passed, Jake and Vick scouted along the outside of the fence, looking for a way in without cutting it. Almost in the middle of the twelve containers was an eroded gulley grown over with weeds that they could use to crawl under the fence and along until they were among the targets. They hurried back to Sam.

"There's a small gulley there," Vick said, pointing. "We can get through and up close to the containers to inspect and get coordinates for each one."

"Okay," Sam said. "Let's do this in stages. Vick take the coordinates of each container and log it. Jake, you're the lock expert so look at the access door and see if there's a way in. I'll cover you. We'll begin three minutes after the next patrol passes and you'll have ten minutes to work."

Right on que, the two passed under the fence minutes after the next patrol passed while Sam stood watch. Vick marked the GPS location of each container and knelt by the fence waiting for Jake. The two could see him going from one container to another, first along the back near the fence line and then, to the opposite end where he disappeared for a few minutes. They could just make out the faint glow now and then of his red-lensed flashlight. He made it back to Vick and under the fence in less time than they anticipated.

"What's the verdict?" Sam asked.

"It was easier than I thought," Jake said. "Both the rear doors and front access door are unlocked. While they can be locked, it's likely they will not as I'm guessing they're not expecting anyone here."

"Is there a way to plant a charge inside?" Sam asked.

"Yes," Jake responded. "We could put one under the control panel in the front, but beside the panel is another access door leading to the missiles, which I peeked into. There is four to six feet of space between the door and the end of the tubes."

"That would be a better location to place a charge," Sam said. "Is there a good place to put the charge directly on or beneath a missile so it is hidden?"

"Shhhh," Vick whispered, "Patrol coming."

The team waited for the patrol to pass but were disappointed as the two soldiers stopped at the nearest container to have a smoke. They were laughing and appeared to be telling jokes as they loitered and seemed to be in no hurry to leave. Sam's heart was pounding as they hunkered down not forty feet from the guards who just kept talking. The other patrol arrived, and all four guards started talking. "Great, a community talk fest," Sam thought. An hour passed and finally, the first two guards started their patrol. About twenty minutes later, the other guards, who had continued smoking cigarettes and talking, resumed their patrol.

"I didn't think they were ever going to leave," Vick whispered. "What next boss?"

"We need to make sure if these launchers are locked, we can get in, no matter where they are located," Sam said. "So, Jake, concentrate on that, for both the access door and rear doors. Vick, if we are going to place a charge inside where the missile tubes are, we need a sample of the paint so that we can paint the charges a matching color. Any suggestions?"

"Let's use a red light to take photos of the lock on the front access door," Jake said. "Don can hold the light and our bodies will shield it while I take a couple of pictures. Then, we can go inside; I'll investigate the locks on the inside of both front access doors while Vick scrapes paint. We can also check to determine how much room we have around the missile tubes and the best locations for charge placement."

"Sounds like a plan," Sam said. "What will you collect the paint samples in?"

"I can just place them between pages of my logbook," Don said. "I'll number each and the location where it was taken. If I can squeeze under or beside the tubes, I'll take a sample near the front, midway, and back."

"Think you can get all that done in ten to twelve minutes?" Sam asked.

"No problem," Jake replied. "If we cannot, we will stay inside the container and wait five minutes then, finish up and wait for your signal through the comm."

Once again, the team waited and watched until the patrol passed, still talking as they walked. Vick and Jake made it quickly beneath the fence and had the outside pictures taken in barely more than a minute then, disappeared into the far container. Sam busied himself watching and after a couple of minutes, broke off a branch from a nearby bush to eliminate signs of having been there. In less time than they thought, Vick and Jake were finished. As they approached the fence, Sam threw the branch over and Don brushed up the grass and small bushes where they had walked, scurried through the gulley under the fence and brushed it up as well. They just made it to the tree line as the next patrol drew near.

They were excited, their hearts racing as they hid themselves, lying low in the grass. They gave the guards a few minutes and without a word, crept silently through the forest, away from the fence and then west toward the van. When they arrived, the others were already waiting. Both teams took a nap until daylight to avoid suspicion from their headlights on a backroad so early in the morning. As the sun rose above the eastern horizon, they loaded up and were gone. A successful mission. Sam would send his report when they stopped to eat.

The teams Samantha was leading were certain they had discovered all of the containers with missiles in the port area and the lake. They found thirty containers on eight different ships, which they identified so they could track later and another twenty containers spread around the port, set off to the side, apparently awaiting a customs check, but only when they were moved into the que. Another one hundred missiles; 100,000 plus pounds of high explosives. There was but one last ship to check. They donned wet suits and snorkels as they began to pass the ship. Samantha and Joe slid off the boat into the cold, black water as the helmsman cut the engine.

They saw no signs of movement through their night-vision goggles as they crawled slowly up the anchor chain, hand-over-hand, to the forecastle above the bow. The ship was awfully dark excepting a few spreader lights around the bridge and crew quarters. The two had removed their fins and were stealthily creeping along the starboard side of the foredeck that they were unable to observe from the lake. They found four missile containers then, crept past the bridge and crew quarters to examine the last containers on the stern area. As they passed the crew quarters, dim lights from within shown through the portholes. Joe motioned to Samantha to pause and watch while he peeked through a porthole. What he saw didn't surprise him but was a concern.

"What did you see?" Samantha whispered.

"I'll explain later," Joe said. "Let's finish up the other side."

They found another missile container on the stern and began moving up the port side, past the bridge and along the port side foredeck above the deck along the bottom row of the top containers.

"Something is odd about these rows," Samantha said. "See how every other row on top is empty? Stand watch while I check them out."

Samantha began walking across the empty container rows, noticing that they were also shifted back so that the containers above slightly staggered those beneath. She kept wondering why. Like an epiphany, it hit her. She was on the end that would need to be opened to launch the missiles, so she walked to the opposite end of the containers. They had staggered them just enough to allow access to the control panel. Damned ingenious she thought as she made her way back to Joe.

"What did you see?" Joe asked.

Samantha explained then said, "We need to count every container up here that has an empty row then, check to see if the opposite end of the container has space to access the control panel. The two separated, staying in the shadows as much as possible. Their night vision goggles making exploration much easier. They finally met back where they had started, off to the side of an access door of one of the launchers. They were a few feet apart. Joe was about to tell Samantha what he saw when, without warning, he heard a metal-on-metal creaking as the access door swung open toward him. A Chinese soldier, speaking and laughing, stepped from behind the door, smoking a cigarette as he clanged the door shut behind him. He was face-to-face with

Samantha. His mouth opened wide in surprise as he froze. Quickly realizing what was happening, he began raising his AK-47 as Samantha raised her 9mm suppressed pistol. The soldier had gotten it to the ready position when there was a sickening small pop and the sound of bone breaking. Joe had responded quickly, stepping forward as he reached around grabbing the soldiers chin in his right hand, bracing the head in a reverse palm heel grab as he pulled. He instantly snapped the neck, the soldier crumpling, dead at his feet.

Samantha's heart was pounding, adrenaline flowing as she holstered her pistol. Joe squashed the still burning cigarette out with his foot, as quietly and together, the two picked up the dead soldier and dragged him out of the way to the port side of the containers. Samantha climbed down to the deck as Joe took a coil of rope and lowered the soldier to her. He quickly descended and looking about, throwing the soldier overboard. The wind had picked up and the splash of the dead man hitting the water made little sound in the darkness, seeming surreal after what had happened.

"Thanks," Samantha said. "I owe you one, we would have shot each other, and I'd be dead too if you hadn't acted so quickly."

"Not at all," Joe replied. "You'd do the same for me. Let's get out of here and back to the boat."

They had to swim about two hundred yards to reach their craft. As they climbed aboard, the helmsman cranked the engine to life and they crept along at slow speed for a few minutes before, revving the engines and heading back to the docks.

"What did you see through the portal?" Samantha asked.

"Well, it didn't surprise me but is a concern," Joe said. "The crew all had on Chinese military uniforms. I think the entire crew is comprised of military personnel."

"I suspected that too when the soldier stepped out of the container," Samantha said. "How many launch containers did you count?"

"Sixty on my end," Joe said. "You?"

"Fifty, so that gives us a total of about one hundred fifteen," Samantha said. "That's four hundred and sixty on one ship."

"A lot of heat," Joe said. "No wonder there are not as many troops as we would suspect for an invasion. What if they find the body?"

"Since we didn't shoot him, they'll just think he fell overboard and drowned, even if they find his body," Samantha said, breathing a sigh of relief.

The two sat silent, listening to the drone of the engines as they skipped across the small ripples in the dark water, lights of the docks reflecting off it like a mirror as they realized what they were up against. They shuddered to think what would happen if there were that many more of these things."

"God help us," Joe blurted out.

Samantha slowly nodded her head in agreement as she pondered what the future would bring. She wondered if the invasion happened what the U.S. would become and, as during the time of George Washington, if they could count on the same ten percent of the armed population to help repel the enemy. The way the government treated the people, like prisoners and second-class citizens, she wasn't hopeful. Already the government had weaponized a hoax virus as a source of power and control resulting in a hatred by the people of them and an almost zero-approval rating. The future looked bleak. Somehow, she couldn't help but think that if the country made it through this, the elected officials that had played their games of power and control for so long and had stolen the people's money year after year, would pay for what they had done, and a different breed of politician would arise. One could always hope.

Major General Lorenzo White was awaiting a secret meeting with Jeremy, Lunadi, Jason, Austin, Sam, and Erin along with two hundred of his Shockwave special operators and one hundred of Lunadi's men. True to his promise, Nick Fabiani had recruited fifty Mexican Army Special Forces, the Grupo Aeromóvil de Fuerzas Especiales or GAFE. Beside him stood his most trusted aide, Colonel Ronnel Scott, every bit his equal in combat. As African Americans, they had fought a hard fight to rise through the ranks. The President had called him personally on a burner phone that a colonel had passed to him in an envelope. The traitors in the government had to be very numerous and or powerful for the President to contact him in such a manner. But, like Jason and the others, he knew the President to be an honorable man and therefore he would do what was necessary to defend the United States.

Shockwave Force was developed from years of experience from wars overseas and organized within Delta Force. Both officers and enlisted men were sought that had a leadership style characterized by instinct and strategy for operational planning, seemingly the wilder the better on the latter. Much like the Apache, you were either an enemy or not. If you were an enemy, no mercy was shown. Lorenzo had been their leader for a long time within the group now, he was the commander of Shockwave and Delta Force. During operations under his direct command, which were many and perilous, he had earned the name 'shadow' because he was like a shadow, sometimes revealing, most of the time not. He was able to engage a sentry at will, killing them proficiently without a sound. Shadow had proven himself capable many times over and was a legend, having moved from Special Forces at Ft. Bragg into Delta Force and then, as commander of Shockwave.

The command itself was never public knowledge although among foreign militaries and terrorist groups, the name Shadow was well known and brought fear into their hearts at the thought of him coming after them. Once the group had been reorganized into a smaller elite counterterrorism unit, codenames for members was instated. The first test of Shockwave came during war in the Middle East, a scientist had been captured by terrorists in Syria to help their allies improve upon bio and nuclear weapons delivery. The knowledge the scientist had would have advanced enemy weaponry by at least two decades. A call from the Joint Chiefs at the command of the President, activated Shadow and a fifteen-member squad to rescue the scientist. If rescue was not possible, termination with prejudice was ordered. That meant to kill the scientist no matter what.

Time was of the essence, necessitating rapid planning. After two planning days, Shockwave moved into Syria on a hunting mission for the scientist. Satellite surveillance and HUMINT quickly narrowed down where the scientist was being held. Shadow moved his team into position under cover of darkness, quietly taking out twenty-three terrorists himself as they made it into the facility and back out. The only thing the enemy discovered was over sixty dead bodies the next morning, the scientist missing. Shadow and his team proved themselves and their tactics. Afterward, they were assigned the most difficult and dangerous missions. Members of Shockwave were the epitome of the best. Each had the ability to adapt to changing combat conditions, think quickly on their feet, and were agile whether it was diving, running, forced march, mental recovery, endurance, concentration, fortitude to overcoming demanding situations, marksmanship, intelligence, foreign languages, technology, or a host of other skills. Shockwave members excelled in all of them.

They were meeting in a large warehouse on the west side of Fayetteville, North Carolina. It would prevent the team leaders from being recognized since they wouldn't need to check through the main gate at Ft. Bragg. The location had just enough traffic not to attract attention as the men filtered in slowly; they would go out the same way. The general and colonel noticed several inconspicuous cars had passed the building and then pulled up in front. The occupants got out of the cars slowly as they looked furtively about. Noticing the colonels hand wave motioning them inside, they proceeded into the main part of the warehouse.

"Sargent," Ronnel yelled. "Our guests have arrived. You and your men secure the premises."

"Men," General White said. "Come to order. We are about to begin."

The men immediately quit talking and situated themselves, taking seats on the floor. The general and colonel were at the front of the group, facing them as the guests filed in quietly behind them and began walking toward the front.

"Geez," Lorenzo said.

"What general?" Ronnel asked.

"You see that fellow bringing up the rear?" Lorenzo asked.

"Yeah, I see him, but don't recognize the man," Ronnel said.

"But he walks with purpose and his eyes catch everything."

"I saw a picture of him long ago," Lorenzo said. "They

called him the specter, we patterned some of our training after his tactics. My commander told me of his exploits as he was put out on loan to some of the special units. I'll tell you about him sometime."

"What's so special about him?" Ronnel asked.

"You know they call me the shadow," Lorenzo said. "That man ghosted one hundred twenty-two enemies, mostly by hand and that's only the ones we know about."

"Damn," Ronnel exclaimed! "In other words, he's lethal."

"And then some; he can be quite literally a ghost."

"It may be wise to introduce and out him just a little," Ronnel said. "You know some of the men can be quite arrogant."

"Good idea."

As the group met, they all shook hands and introduced each other, the men looking on. It was decided the general would introduce them and they would begin.

"Group," General White said. "I'd like to introduce this group to you, some of whom you may know. They have tasked us with a special mission assignment that is our eyes and ears only. This is Jeremy Yazzi, advisor to President Weld. Erin Shaw, the President's Chief of Staff; General Jason Bardos whose role will be explained later. Austin Murray, Director Operations, CIA and his colleague Sam. And finally, Lunadi who I am going to reveal just a little about. His exploits are what we based a lot of our training on. You will not find his name mentioned anywhere, but he is called among our former operators, 'the specter' and is in my opinion, the best of the best. He has removed more enemies than all of you combined. You have met some of his men. They have been trained comparable to you and if I know anything from Lunadi's reputation, likely better. I do not wish to embarrass him, *it was obvious he was*, but I am telling you this because you will be working with one hundred of his men and their commander. They are here to help you because of the enormity of the situation. I expect full cooperation from all. Jeremy will begin to fill you in."

"Thank you general," Jeremy said, stepping forward. "It is an honor to meet all of you. I cannot stress to you how critical this mission is. But I'll give it to you in simple terms. If we fail, our nation will perish and fall under enemy rule."

A deathly silence fell upon the men as they looked at each other, whispering among themselves as they stared at Jeremy. They knew the mission was important but thought of it as just another mission as they were all important, else their group wouldn't get the assignment.

"I work directly with the President," Jeremy said. "The others behind me do as well in various capacities. He has sent us here to ensure you understand the gravity of the situation and to brief you on the crisis we face. The President has personally briefed your commander, General White. We will now fill in the pieces. Please pay attention and raise your hands for questions as we go. It is imperative there are no misunderstandings. With that, I'll turn it over to Erin.

"Thank you, Jeremy," Erin said. "Men, I'll be brief. We face a crisis unlike any this nation has ever faced. You all have secret clearances. It is vital that nothing we speak of leave this building today. If it does, we will undoubtedly fail. I will be the contact for your commander to the President and will do all in my power to make our mission a success. But make no mistake, it will be dangerous for all of you, our nations survival depends on your success."

"Hello men," General Bardos said, stepping up. "Some of you know me from work in various units you have been assigned to. After this mission, you will be working directly with us on the plan of battle we have drawn up and what your missions will be. As Erin insinuated, this is a hypercritical situation. Secrecy must be maintained and for the next few months, perhaps more, you will receive one assignment after another, all of which will be extremely dangerous. That is all I will tell you for now. Please give your attention to Lunadi."

"Thank you, general," Lunadi said. "As you have been told, one hundred of my men will be working with you. Their commander, please stand Freeman, is Freeman Motlow. The men are well trained in all military-style operations, guerilla warfare, and have much the same training you have. They may be a little less trained on the technology side, but they are here to help you, be your eyes and ears as it were to protect your back when you are doing your work and unable to see approaching danger. If needed, I will spare another one hundred men and their commander. That will be determined shortly. Just know that we are committed to help you in your mission. Now you must pay close attention to Austin and Sam."

"Thank you, Lunadi," Austin said, stepping forward with Sam. "We have been tracking the enemy."

"Excuse me," a soldier said, raising his hand. "Are we allowed to know who the enemy is?"

"Certainly," Austin said. "I apologize we have not mentioned them. We are led to believe we will be invaded by both Russian and Chinese forces within the next two months. This initial mission will be against Chinese weapons."

One could hear a pin drop. The soldiers just sat staring at Austin and the commanders in front. Several whistled in disbelief. On one hand it was incredible to hear, much less believe, but on the other hand, all these men knew that at some point they would be fighting a war with these two enemies. After all, it was just a matter of time when bullies are on the block.

"For some time, we have been tracking their naval movements and intercepting chatter through various intelligence apparatus. We have also had significant help from others I cannot disclose at this time. Suffice it to say that prior to their main attack, they will attack with weapons that have already been dispersed on U.S. and Canadian soil. We do not know about Mexico yet, but have field agents checking that country too. This has all been clandestine and yes, before you ask, we have located a great many missiles thus far. Sam will fill you in on that as well as your specific assignments."

"Okay," Sam began. "You've heard all the good news. Now for the bad. So far, we have uncovered about six hundred missiles that are in place and that they will launch prior to main task forces landing troops and equipment. We are still finding them. I am sure you are curious about the missiles. We have discovered a mix of two types with warheads of about five hundred and eleven hundred pounds of high explosives and a range of about four hundred and nine hundred miles, respectively. This means they can take out targets all the way to St. Louis from the gulf or from Canada. Every major city along the coasts, as well as from the gulf are vulnerable."

"Do we have an idea of their attack sequence," a soldier blurted out.

"Excellent question," Sam responded. "We are tracking their fleets constantly. It is proposed by the group behind me and others that they will launch the missiles taking out important infrastructure such as the power grid and military targets then, hit us with one or two EMPs followed by invasion while we are in a state of turmoil. This is why your mission is so important. If we can find and destroy most of these missiles, we have a chance. If we don't find most of them, we are in dire straits."

"Do we have any idea how many there are total?" another soldier asked.

"It is conceivable they have up to eight hundred or even more. Now that we have discovered what the weapons are, it would be better when we infiltrate to plant charges and not need to return for a second visit. Therefore, we need you. At this point, we have remained undetected. Our initial mission was simply to determine how many and how to destroy them. Based on what we have learned, our engineers have developed a way to do it, but not until the missiles are preparing for launch. Although this is risky, we have a three-pronged approach. First, we will target the missiles we know the location of with our own missiles, as well as their bases in Canada. In the event of an EMP and communications gets fouled, we have a second approach, which also involves a third component, just in case."

Sam pulled a small bomb from the inside of the briefcase he was carrying. The soldiers were surprised.

"The missiles are brought to an upright position before launch. And this is where you come in and where it gets hairy and dangerous. This bomb is set up for two methods of ignition, which brings me to the second approach. You will place it in each launch vehicle and flip the switch to arm it. Once armed, we can send it a signal to ignite the shaped charge inside it. Each bomb has one-quarter pound of C-4 explosive. Two will be placed in each launch vehicle. The third approach is that if the signal cannot get through, a mercury switch will trigger ignition once the missile begins to raise to launch position. Whether electronically ignited or by the mercury switch, ignition will be immediate."

"In other words, we need to make sure each bomb is in place before we flip the arming switch," a soldier said.

"Precisely," Sam replied. "If you make a mistake, it will be good night Irene. Also, each bomb you have is painted like this one so that it matches the color of the missiles in the containers."

"Where will we place them?" a soldier asked.

"You'll be briefed on that by our engineers," Austin chimed in. "The basics have been covered. With that, we will turn it back to General White. There's not much more we can divulge at this time. We already have several thousand of these devices. They have all been triple checked for quality control and will work."

"General White," Jeremy joined in. "That's our brief for now. Please let us know if we can help further. We will take our leave and see you again soon. Men, it was a privilege to meet with all of you. Good luck on your mission."

The men watched them as they made their way through the door.

"Men," General White said. "Now you know why you are already packed and ready. The engineers will explain how to arm and place the bombs. As mentioned before, there will be two per launch vehicle. The key to this operation is getting in and out without being seen or leaving a trace. No killing, simply stealth. I cannot stress that enough. We will send a batch of bombs to each location. Based on what you find, you'll take as many as you need to complete your mission. Sam didn't tell you, but they found over fifty launchers on one container ship. If you run into such a situation, it will require four teams or more, to plant the charges."

"What if we do have to kill someone?" a soldier asked. "How do we handle it?"

"Use your discretion," General White replied. "Hopefully, it would be only one or two at most. The best scenario is to make it look like they fell overboard and drowned if on a ship. We have been advised by the CIA that if you're on land and need to shoot one, take the body and dump it in an alley somewhere; make it look like a robbery. No matter what, it must not look like a professional kill. Use your best judgement. Ah, the engineers are here. They will explain the workings and you'll leave for stations immediately after."

An engineer and his assistants wheeled several large carts in filled with the bombs. They were already divided up according to location, anticipating that land-based areas would have fewer launchers. The engineers took their time demonstrating to all the soldiers as they gathered in groups to familiarize themselves with the devices. Once the commanders were sure the men understood, the engineers took final questions, and the men broke into their separate units. Colonel Scott performed one last personnel check working with each commander, and the men headed to an airport a couple of hours away where various military transports were already waiting to take them to pre-assigned destinations. Within two hours the soldiers were on route to Houston, Los Angeles, Seattle, New York, Chicago, New Orleans, Norfolk, and other locations. The big question on everyone's mind was if they could find most of the launchers. They instinctively knew there was no way they would find them all.

The Speaker of the House was a little worried because she had not heard whether or not the agent was successful. No longer able to contain her fears, she pulled a burner phone out of her purse and made a quick call.

"Any word on progress?" she asked.

"Madam," the voice replied. "I was just about to call you. The Secret Service reports an agent got lost in the desert and are searching for him."

"Ours?"

"It appears so,"

"Get rid of the loose ends. This must not come back to us. Dispose of the remains."

"Yes Madam."

Evelyn began to wonder if the Secret Service was onto her. She could not afford to take a chance; it was time to move forward with the press conference. She dialed another number.

"Hello," the electronic voice answered.

"Tell the asset to leak the information. Shortly after, I will schedule a press conference."

"Very well."

Evelyn sat back in her chair, an evil grin on her face. "Now I'm going to fry your ass Weld. You'll wonder who but you will never know."

Minutes later, the Congress Woman of Michigan, sitting in her office, received the call.

"It is time," the electronic voice said. "Begin the collusion story. Leak it to the press."

The line went dead.

Susan sighed aloud. It would take great care to release the story and not be associated with it. But the press didn't care, it was a story. Any lamebrain could call something in and if it were against the current administration, the press would run with it.

There was a soft knock on her door.

"Got a minute?" Big Rod asked.

"Sure," she replied, holding up a finger, pressing the intercom button on her desk.

"Nancy. Hold all my calls and visits for a while.

"Will do," Nancy replied, knowing full well why, her lover had arrived, the cheating bitch.

"What have you got for me today?" Susan asked, locking the door. "Let me see."

She led her lover over to her chair as she began caressing the front of his trousers, feeling his manhood grow, then began to undress him.

General Qiang was excited. For years he had wanted to take down the Americans. Now, he had a timeline, and he was going to launch the operation on time, no matter what. He picked up the phone in his office.

"Wen, my comrade," Li said. "How fast can you have the navy ready?"

"Do you mean for the task we discussed?" Wen asked.

"Yes," Li said. "We have the authority to prepare with final approval pending readiness."

"The new destroyers won't be ready for six months," Wen said. "But the five you saw while visiting are in sea trials and will be ready in two weeks."

"Can you get them to the staging area and be completely ready in eight weeks for launch day?" Li asked.

"Yes," Wen replied. "It's a close cut but can do."

"Great comrade," Li said. "You have eight weeks from yesterday to be ready and on station. I'll talk to you soon. Prepare as previously planned."

Li leaned back in his chair, looking out the window. He let out a long sigh, a smile creasing his face. It had been a long road and it was finally coming to a head. He would show the Americans and the world who was best. Despite his euphoria, there was a nagging doubt that would not go away. It was the words of one of his generals to him.

"A war on America would be difficult for one simple reason, there is a gun behind every blade of grass and the people know how to use them."

Li shrugged it off deciding not to let it dampen his spirits and ruin the day. Superior firepower would make those words irrelevant. He swiveled his chair away from the window and once again, picked up the phone on his desk, dialing a number from a small black book he had retrieved from his front shirt pocket.

"Comrade, we need to meet," Li said. "Yes, Las Vegas, two days."

Lunadi and Erin, were taking a two-day break at his place as they got to know each other better. They both knew this would be the last for some time. Now late fall, it was crisp and cool as they sat watching the snow capped mountains to the west. The view was majestic, breath taking. They had been sipping hot chocolate. Erin was looking softly at Lunadi as he gazed at the mountains, a faraway look in his eyes.

"What's on your mind?" Erin asked.

"Did you ever have a feeling you were meant for something greater in this life because you had proven yourself or did something noteworthy in another?" Lunadi asked. "The Japanese would call it karma."

"I have had instances of Deja vu of such," Erin replied. "But I have always just passed them off as a daydream."

"I used to do the same," Lunadi said. "But after seeing Sun God and Monster Slayer for the first time here and then our most recent experience, I've begun to remember things buried deep in my mind."

"Are they unpleasant memories?" Erin asked.

"No, quite the contrary. They are pleasant and I see faces there I know here."

"Anyone particular?" Erin asked, quizzically.

"There are the two generals, the President and the rest of our group. It is all sort of jumbled up, but I saw us planning something through the portal in the setting of the vision we were allowed to see. Then, *he paused.*"

"Then what?" Erin asked. "Don't keep me in suspense."

"Well then, I saw you and us," Lunadi said. "It seemed as if we are long-time friends. Do you ever think that?"

Tears began to moisten the edges of Erin's eyes as she looked up at Lunadi who was standing beside the railing looking down on her. There was something about her face, it was glowing like there was a deity inside her. It took her a minute to catch her breath before she replied.

"The first time I saw you I knew there was a connection," Erin whispered. "Every time since, I have had this strong feeling we knew each other. I had a dream a few nights ago of a modern-day warrior using a knife to take out what I perceived to be an enemy. All around the warrior was darkness. It was like the world was dark. I could just make out the pain on the face of the enemy being taken out, swiftly and precisely, with no emotion, just a duty to perform his task. The warrior however was glowing. It's hard to describe. It was like the outline of a man; an outline with streams of gold overlaying a lighter gold mist. It was much like an artist might draw, like a sketch, but in color. But all about was a darkness and then the warrior began changing from a gold color to a pure white. His back was toward me. Suddenly, as if he felt someone was watching, his head whipped quickly around looking over his right shoulder. He still glowed but his eyes were like a blue flame of fire and then, she was staring at him, they changed to a piercing hazel brown. It, it …, *she stuttered, looking at him.* It was you and you saw me. I was at first frightened and didn't know what to do then, the fear left as I felt your spirit. I smiled and the dream was gone. I have thought about it every minute since and when General White revealed you as he called it, I knew the dream was not a dream but that it was real and that I had seen you in the act of a warrior taking out another warrior. Somehow, it has made me more peaceful and calm around you. Not that I fear you, but you are the most intense man I've ever met, yet somehow, you have this great compassion that is constantly there, but rarely shown. I had no idea the kind of person you were."

Lunadi stood there then reached for her hand, pulling her up and close to him, staring into her gray eyes.

"I have a confession to make," Lunadi said. "I too had a dream about you. I was on the open plains and far in the distance I could see warriors who seemed to be celebrating after a successful hunt. They saw me and began to scramble to their ponies, and I could see one of them waving their arms in a manner to stop them. They stopped and they were all staring at me. Then the person waving them down, jumped onto a pony and galloped toward me. It was far away. All I could see was this person was dressed in a white buckskin robe. As the person came closer, I could make out more details. It was a female with her black hair swept back into a ponytail and a turquoise band around her head with one white eagle feather protruding from the back. Her features were very refined and as she rode right up next to me, her high cheekbones sat beneath the most beautiful eyes. She was stunning; just sitting upon her mount and staring softly down at me. Finally, she smiled, and I had such a feeling of warmth come over me. My vision ended." "Did you recognize her?"

Lunadi's voice trembled as he replied, "It was you!" The two just stood, embracing each other. Somehow, they knew that they had been together before, eons ago and they had become separated. He bent his head down and kissed her on the cheek and felt her body quiver all over. Before they realized it, they were fondling each other and kissing full on. She reached up to unbutton the top button of his shirt. Just as her hands released the button, they both noticed it was getting very bright. At first, they thought it was the sun coming out from behind a cloud before they realized there was a person standing next to them in the air. They both jumped back in surprise. It was the Mediator, staring down on them.

"You have discovered yourselves," Mediator said. "You did great things before and you are destined for greater things in this sphere. See to it that you do your duties. Obey Sun God's laws and all will be well."

As quickly as he came, the Mediator simply vanished, so swiftly that the two were left staring at where he had been. As much as they lusted after each other and wanted to make love in each other's arms, they understood now was not the time. Erin turned back to face Lunadi; her hands flat on either side of his chest as he emitted a huge sigh.

"There will be other times my love," Erin whispered, as both their phones rang.

They didn't need to answer because they already knew what the callers wanted as they both said, "hello" in unison. "I guess there's always a price to pay to save the nation," Lunadi said flatly, hanging up.

CHAPTER 8
Scouting Trip

The White House Situation Room was starting to become too familiar to the group, but was the only place they could be assured of privacy from prying eyes and ears. Present were Phil, Jeremy, Jason, Stone, Austin, Nick, and Erin.

"Here we are again," Phil said. "Stone, fill them in please."

"Very well Mr. President," Stone said. "Our satellites are picking up troop and naval activity from both the Chinese and Russians. Some ships are sailing, but not enough to signal a full assault."

"What are we to make of it?" Nick asked. "Is there something I should do, warn their ambassadors perhaps?"

"No, not yet" Phil said. "It is a bit early, but you need to think along the lines of how we may stall them as we discussed a Chaco."

"That may be difficult, but I will work on a plan," Nick said. "I think I may be able push the food-shortage issue."

"What else is going on?" Phil asked.

"We have been investigating the secret service agent killed at Chaco," Erin replied. "There are a lot of tight lips and no one is talking. We found his cousin dead in an alley and his brother and wife dead at a stop light, all shot."

"Looks like they were coercing him then," Stone said vehemently. "I've worked at this a long time and this looks like a professional hit. His wife and children are also missing. My guess is they were loose ends. Likely we will never find them."

"They will be dealt with in due time," Jeremy said. "The President has the NSA working on linking the entire network together. Once we find all, at least most of them, they will be brought to justice, unlike how the former President who stepped aside with all that information."

"I will enjoy the day when there is a full accounting of their treason," Austin said. "By-the-way, we have more activity in Lake Nicaragua."

Everyone was all ears as they leaned forward.

"From our new asset, remember that our last one was killed," Austin said. "At least a dozen more warships and a couple of supply ships have slipped into the lake. It appears five of them are the new 055D destroyers."

"That's a big problem," Nick said. "A whole lot of firepower."

"Agreed," Phil said. "I suppose there is no way to counter it without tipping our hand."

"Correct Mr. President," Jason said. "But there is something else we need to look at as well. As you know Austin, Stone and their team are digging into and tracking all the missile launchers they can. From what we can tell, many of them are being carried by cargo ships, anchored in various ports."

"What are you suggesting?" Phil asked.

"Well," Jason began, looking at Stone and the President. "Stone and I, along with Nick have been discussing the problem and we believe that we need to place submarines in the potential locations to take them out when it is time."

"That is easier said than done," Phil said. "They report directly to admirals who report to the joint chiefs. It will be difficult to get them on station without showing our hand to whoever the Chinese power broker is in congress. How many are you suggesting?

"We would need two off Seattle and Portland, at least one near Los Angeles, six spread in the Gulf, one off North Carolina, another off the Potomac and one in New York. That's a total of twelve sir," Jason said, reading the reaction of those around the table.

"Seriously?" Phil queried, looking at them. "We have the subs but using that many means we will not be able to mesh it into a land-based defense drill scenario. Any other ideas?"

"As you may recall sir, we have been working on getting away from multi-role ships because they need to prioritize work during defense duties," Jason said. "We have been working on developing barge-based missile launchers and have done multiple tests on them. They work great."

"Do we have any ready?" Phil asked.

"The former President stopped the program," Stone said. "However, about three dozen of these ships are anchored near New Orleans and Houston seaports."

"Do they work?" Phil asked.

"Yes," Stone said. "They have been maintained and all the missiles, they have twenty launchers each, with missile reloads of twice that below decks, are stored in restricted areas at the edges of the ports."

"We have both civilian and military crews that can operate them," Jason said. "We would just need authorization and then, ensure that the men are kept quiet about the mission."

"I recall some information on the missile-barge program," Phil said. "Give us all a little more."

"The premise of missile barges has been around for a long

time," Jason said. "It all began with the Russians and their Club system, which the Chinese copied and is the current threat. We realized we needed to be able to do more with less money instead of tasking all the navy ships with multi-role status that forces them to set priority engagements in battle. Not the best scenario. Thus, we, along with Israel, decided to take a page out of the Russian playbook and develop our own systems. We already had the missiles and just needed to test them from the deck of a ship. We did and the missiles worked flawlessly. They are simply modular systems we already had in service that could work when operated off the decks of ships. Just as we got the ships operational and ready to go to large test trials, the former administration shut it down. Everything is in place. We could have them at sea within ten days and then, have them run drills everyday against potential threats. There are more than enough of them to get the job done."

Stone and Austin, along with the rest of the group were nodding silent approval.

"Make it happen," Phil said. "Whatever it takes. Do it now! I see no reason we cannot pull this into a practice exercise to go along with yours. It's small enough it should not draw attention. If we do this, do you still need the subs?"

"We wouldn't need the missile launch subs sir," Jason said. "Since we anticipate where the Chinese and Russians will concentrate their ships, we would need some Virginia Class fast attack and Los Angeles Class hunter-killer subs."

"How many are you thinking?" Phil asked.

"We discussed this scenario earlier," Stone said. "Based on Nicks naval experience as an admiral and Austin's as well, the three of us worked out a scenario for three along the west coast, two in the Gulf and one off DC. I think Jason agrees. These would work primarily against enemy naval ships and the barges would target other container ships we are currently tracking, as well as some naval ships. We have enough barges to station some off Long Beach and some along the northwest seaboard."

"I concur," Jason said. "Our agents and troops are likely going to find quite a few more container ships and we need to coordinate all the strikes against these we can. This will leave the subs to work against Chinese and Russian ships."

"We can manage that under naval exercise protocols," Phil said. "I'll contact the Chief of Naval Operations (CNO); we go way back. Besides, he owes me. He will keep it quiet too."

"Awesome," Jason exclaimed. "We are pulling it all together."

"What have you, Jeremy and Lunadi been planning?" Phil asked.

"Well sir," Jeremy started. "We have been working on a plan to have most of our equipment hardened against EMP strikes and the rest will be shielded until immediately after the strike we know is coming. Jason has gotten us several wings of A-10 Warthogs, as well as multiple battalions of tanks and aviation brigades of Apache helicopters. It is coming together nicely, along with Lunadi's men, General White's Shockwave force, and other combat personnel, and tribal warriors."

"Are you going to be able to keep this quiet?" Phil asked.

"Not a problem so far," Jason remarked. "Even with the new missile barges and sub assignments, as long as the men think it's a drill, loose lips won't hurt us. When the time comes to flip the switch to active, none of them will be in a position to give the operation away."

"Good," Phil said. "I've been getting some questions, but had no problem handling them so far. Stone, any news of

Dragon and Red Star?" Phil asked.

"So far, all is…

He was interrupted as there was a knock at the door and a secret service agent stuck his head in.

"I'm sorry to interrupt sir, but I have someone here from D/CIA's office, says it's vitally important."

Stone recognized Sheila and motioned her in.

"What is it Sheila?" Stone asked as she quickly crossed the floor.

"I apologize for interrupting," Sheila said, handing him a manilla folder. "Urgent message for you sir."

Sheila was out the door as quickly as she entered, the agent closing it behind her.

"Hmmmm," Stone said, raising his eyebrows, handing the folder to Austin.

"Damn," he proclaimed.

"What is it?" Phil asked.

"Dragon and Red Star passports were just flagged in Las Vegas."

"Holy hell," Erin exclaimed.

There was dead silence in the room.

"What are you thinking?" Phil asked earnestly, his voice quavering.

"It's what we are all thinking," Jeremy said. "They are making a scouting trip, checking the battlefield. We already knew, but this makes the location a certainty. No more guessing."

"Do you have men on him?" Jason and Phil asked at the same time.

"Our best field officer," Austin replied. "He sent the message. We will get as much as we can."

"Gentlemen," Phil stated flatly. "Finish your plans this week. Time is short."

The plane touched down on the tarmac of McCarran International Airport in Las Vegas. It made a few bounces and then the sound grew louder as the pilots engaged the thrust-reversers on each engine to slow it down. Li had been looking out the window from his first-class seat watching Las Vegas Strip speed by on his right. It was not his first trip to Las Vegas, but this one promised to be not only enlightening, but exciting. He could already scarce contain himself. General Tyurin would meet him at the Bellagio Hotel later. He realized it was a bit risky considering the two thousand or more security cameras in each Las Vegas casino, but he was traveling under an assumed name and was certain he would easily blend in with other Asian tourists in this wild and crazy city that was in full swing 24/7. There was never an end to people, alcohol, gambling, women, or shopping.

Sam's team was in place before Dragon made it to the hotel. There were so many people about that it made it easy to follow the target. The bad thing was that it also made it easy for the target to elude them if they became suspicious. His team had several cars standing by because he had a real hunch these two had come to look over the battlefield. After all, they were field generals and would be the ones leading their respective armies. A voice spoke calmly in his earpiece, alerting him to the target. It was then that he noticed Dragon pulling up in an inconspicuous sedan, his Asian driver likely a CSB agent.

This was a place where they would want to be as inconspicuous as possible. Sam's friend, head of Bellagio security, had been alerted to keep cameras on Dragon and Red Star as much as they could and to make copies of the surveillance for him. His friend was only too happy to comply. He pulled his cell from his trouser pocket and dialed Robert.

"Robert," Sam said. "Yes, just arrived. Gray, four-door sedan at curb, just getting out. He's the first one."

"Roger," Robert said. "On him."

Sam couldn't help noticing the music playing as he watched the Fountains of Bellagio, the water choreographed to music and lights. An opera song was playing, 'the Last Goodbye' that took his thoughts back to years ago when he had first visited this city with a friend. He had always thought they would get married, but it was not to be. His eyes glazed over as he wondered how she was; they had not spoken for years but this place would always remind him of her as his eyes moistened from the sadness of happy memories.

His earpiece buzzed; Red Star was pulling up in a taxi. The agents could see him pay the driver in cash as he stepped out and walked through the main door. Once again, Sam called Robert to alert him. Sam knew that Dragon had already taken up a seat in a raised lounge kitty-corner from the front door, where he could easily see the reception area and information desk. Just as he had done, Red Star walked in with one bag, looking like a typical tourist. Li almost did not recognize him as he checked in and headed upstairs to unlock his room. As Li waited for him to come back down, he ordered a drink.

"What will you have," the cocktail waitress asked.

"Do you have Baijiu?" Li asked.

"I do not think so," the waitress replied. "If we do not, what would you like as a substitute?"

"A glass of your strongest white wine."

As the waitress walked away, Li looked about. There were throngs of people walking past in front of him going toward the main entrance, as well as in the other direction. Directly across the aisle was a wide variety of slots as the Americans called them.

He remembered the old days when all the machines had pull handles and three reels. Now, the more common ones used five to seven reels and were highly interactive with 3-D video and immersive sound. It was surprising how loud the giant room was. Looking to his left he could see the gaming tables—blackjack, craps, roulette, and more. He was so engrossed in the atmosphere; everyone seemed happy with smiles on their faces, quite opposite from his more serious nature. He was so wrapped up in his thoughts he didn't realize the waitress was back.

"Ah, you have it," Li said, as he pulled cash out and paid her, a smile on his face having found something he enjoyed.

He was sitting in a prearranged spot because both men had been here before. Li noticed Panu walking toward him across the main foyer. Panu stepped up the three steps and grabbed a seat opposite. The waitress was beside him almost as soon as he sat down.

"Can I get something for you?" the waitress asked.

"Two shots of vodka please," Panu said.

"So, comrade," Panu whispered, leaning forward. "How was your trip?"

"Uneventful, yours?"

"The same, I took a first-class flight and slept most of the way. I didn't want to miss the excitement of Las Vegas. It gets so in one's blood."

"Yes," Li said. "I was just thinking the same. Too bad this place will get shut down when we take over, you know how our government feels about capitalism."

"Yeah, they hate it, unless they are the beneficiaries." Panu said as they both laughed.

The waitress had brought his drinks and they waited for her to leave before continuing.

"What do you want to do first?" Panu asked.

"It's too late to start today," Li replied. "I thought that first thing tomorrow morning we could drive out and look over your route then, head west to Long Beach, stay overnight there, and check out my route on the way back. That would put us back here late afternoon, day after tomorrow."

"I agree," Panu said. "That will allow us to shop for our wives when we return and fly out the next day."

"What games are you up for?" Li asked.

"I prefer the sportsbook, the horse races," Panu said. "If you don't mind, I'm going to walk over to Caesar's to the sportsbook and bet on the races. How about yourself?"

"Ah, too tame for me," Li grinned. "I prefer Baccarat and Pai Gow poker; they are much more strategic than horse betting. I see some of those down to our left."

"True," Panu said as he winked. "But they do not get your adrenaline going."

Both men had a good laugh. They would not admit it, but they were stressed and full of tension. Although Panu had always wondered if they were doing the right thing. It was only now that Li had some misgivings which he kept pushing out of his mind. Having some fun would keep those feelings at bay.

A man walked up the steps approaching Panu from behind. Li eyed him warily. Panu picked up the concern on his face as he turned in his chair.

"Oh, Dimitri," Panu said, reaching out to shake his hand. "How are you?"

"Well, thank you comrade," Dimitri said.

"Li, this is Dimitri, one of our FSB," Panu said. "His partner across the aisle is Gorgov. They will shadow us in the casinos while we are here, keeping back far enough to be unnoticed. I hope this is acceptable."

"Yes," Li replied, looking up at Dimitri and then across the aisle at Gorgov. "Your men blend right into the crowd. I will have our men shadow us in Long Beach since they blend in better there."

The Speaker of the House was all smiles as she stepped behind the podium, looking across the dozens of reporters.

"I have a brief announcement only," she said. "We will be offering more evidence in the next few days."

The reporters were in a tumult, all of them trying to ask questions at once.

"Settle down please," she said. "What I will tell you is what we know we have. Further proof will be presented later. This is the news. A source inside the CIA has recorded phone calls and emails to support our charges. Based upon this evidence and the fact the agent has come forward, we are charging the President with soliciting foreign interference by the Chinese in his election campaign and hiding that information from Congress. More evidence, as I said, will be forthcoming. That is all."

The reporters exploded with questions as she waved at them and walked away, a large smile on her face. It would soon be her turn.

Erin was watching the pony show as was the President inside the Oval Office.

"Can you believe that lying bitch?" Erin asked. "And the Chinese of all countries, what a joke."

"We know she's lying, but the perception will become what she wants," Phil said. "The media is against us and this will whip them into a frenzy. Get on your phone and quell as much as you can. It's gonna be another shit storm of lies that we have to prove our innocence."

"I will sir," Erin said. "On another note, have you kept abreast of the food shortages?"

"No, I've been too involved in this other mess," Phil replied. "What's going on?"

"Brazil has just suffered the worst drought in over one hundred years," Erin said. "Their main reservoir is totally dry, and people are evacuating Rio to try to find water where they can. The drought, creeping hazard as some experts call it, is beginning to have cascading failure effects in power and agriculture. It won't be long before it affects all their infrastructure as the failures filter down and could collapse their economy."

"Damn," Phil exclaimed! "That's bad. I know that we are not far behind. Let me work on it with our Secretary of Ag and DHS. We need to come up with some emergency measures or we will have rioting in the streets. You may want to know since our last meeting, that food shortages are growing. It won't be long before most of the country hears about it. We need to do something to offset the potential riots. Let's put our heads together about that later. For now, try to douse the fire the Speaker has started.

The two men sat chatting as Sam and his team watched from various positions nearby. It was so easy to blend in here Sam thought, so many people and so many things to do.

"Stay on your toes teams," Sam said through his mic. "They can move at any moment. Follow them, but not too closely. They appear to have two agents with them. One is talking to them now, the other is across the aisle in the khaki pants and floral-patterned shirt. It is not clear what they will be doing. If they separate, I want Rob's team to follow Dragon and Samantha's team to follow Red Star."

Sam was an old hand at covert surveillance. His team did not wear the traditional coiled earpiece that most tactical units and even secret service personnel wore. Instead, they had selected an earpiece designed by an audiologist. The speakers were so small they didn't block the ear canal, which gave his agents the ability to literally talk on a separate phone or to a person in front of them, as well as hear sounds coming from all around them, without removing it. Minus the coiled tube prevalent on most types of such earpieces, they were virtually undetectable and allowed his team to have total situational awareness, which they needed now.

Briefly, the two men stepped down from the lounge and walked along the main aisle going north. It was not more than one hundred feet when they found the Baccarat tables and baccarat bar on the left.

"This is my stop," Li said. "I will leave you to your horses."

"Enjoy your cards," Panu said, smiling. "I can't wait to place some bets. You know, it's in my blood."

Parting ways, Panu continued walking north down the aisle as it turned right briefly and after a bit, turned back north and angled off to his right as he approached a few restaurants and upscale lounges. Passing them, he found himself among high-end shops selling handbags, men's clothing, and other items. He could not help but think that most people, even in the U.S. could not afford the items in these shops. A working-class person would be paying off one of the expensive handbags for a year or more.

Nearing the end of the shops, Panu turned left exiting the hotel onto a walkway across West Flamingo Road and down steep steps to the main walk bending around left into Caesar's Palace main entrance. As he passed through the door, rounding the corner onto the main gaming floor, he suddenly became aware of how loud the casino was. He could hear the constant sound of slots, people talking and laughing and celebrating as they hit the jackpot; it was a din of noise. He split to the right and was making his way past the Omnia night club, his FSB security agent directly behind him, over his right shoulder. He stopped and paused as he looked across an expanse of the casino; directly in front of him was the Race and Sportsbook. It had a bar in front and directly behind in a slight, curving semi-circle, monitors along the top edge of the ceiling — high-definition televisions. The betting patrons were sitting in wide, leather gaming chairs, sipping drinks and relaxing.

A broad smile spread across his lips as he watched horses racing on several of the monitors, a wave of euphoria sweeping over him as he was barely able to contain himself. Since growing up with a couple of horses in Russia in the rural area around Moscow, he had always been fascinated by them. As a kid, his pet was a horse, black as the night and fast as the wind. He had gotten into horse racing early and had won quite a few as a young man until he became more involved in the military. The fun of his youth though, always came flooding back into his memories whenever he was able to be around horses or in a place where he could bet on them. Here was such a place he mused as he passed into the betting area, his eyes glazed with the excitement seen generally only on the face of the young.

Behind him, Sam's agents had taken positions along the wall, one of them next to a statue of Mohammed Ali.

"We have eyes," the agent said into his mouthpiece.

"No, he's just gambling," the agent replied. "He looks like

a kid in a candy store. We'll let you know if anything changes, out."

In the Bellagio, Li had seated himself at a Baccarat table and was having the time of his life, a smile on his face, drink in his hand, and cigar upon his lips. It was as if he didn't have a care in the world. Just outside the gaming area, the other FSB agent stood watch, trying to be as inconspicuous as possible. Unnoticed, one of Sam's team was playing a celebrity slot, within easy view of both the baccarat tables and the FSB agent. Sam sauntered by and gave the impression he was going to play one of the games next to his team member but paused long enough to whisper.

"Let me know if he goes anywhere. I'm heading over to Caesar's."

It was a Friday afternoon and Caesar's Palace was already crowded. Weekends in Vegas brought many more people than weekdays, flooding in from Los Angeles and other California cities, as well as around the country. Already, they were roping off the nightclub area in expectation of a busy evening. Sam walked by his first team member, by the statue of Mohammed Ali and gave him a slight nod. After a few seconds, the agent followed, turning left into the walkway leading past various restaurants, leaving the other team member to keep an eye on Red Star. Certain that they were no longer in view of the casino floor or prying eyes, they stood aside to let others pass.

"Any change in his activity?" Sam asked.

"No," the agent said. "He seems very content just to sit and bet on horse races from what I can tell. At least those are the screens he keeps looking at."

"Very well," Sam replied. "Let me know if there are any changes. Be discreet, change your location now. I need to make arrangements for tomorrow. Things could get a bit hairy."

As Sam walked away, he immediately got on his phone with his Las Vegas CIA safehouse personnel. He arranged for six cars for the next day and longer if needed. It was imperative they stayed close to Dragon and Redstar. Everything had to be precise, no mistakes.

One of Sam's team was slowly walking through the valet area in the Bellagio parking structure. He had made a pass twice and did not find what he was looking for. Naturally, he veered away to the bordering parking spaces. Looking down at a note in his small book, he made sure he knew what he was looking for. He was walking slowly, smoking on a cigar and slowly exhaling. Anyone watching would have thought he was just casually walking off the stress of losing money in the casino. After all, the business was all about relieving one of all the cash they had, the reason a nickname of Vegas was City of Lost Wages.

The agent was beginning to wonder where the hell the car was that he was looking for. He had already looked down several rows. Using patience, he kept slowly walking, pausing now and then to blow smoke and look at it, as if he didn't have a care in the world. Looking like just another gambler, a weekender in Vegas, was important because he was on camera everywhere he walked. He finally spotted the car in the last space, two rows over; it was in the valet overflow. Looking again at his small notebook, he verified color and plate number. Hoping that the car was not on camera, he looked carefully about. Unfortunately, a camera was pointed directly toward the car; it was almost directly in front of him. As he continued to walk, he stopped directly under the camera and looked in the same direction. Ah, there was a support column between the camera and the sedan. He knew from experience that one side of the vehicle would probably be visible on camera, so he continued to walk to the end of the row he was on and circle to the next, where the sedan was parked, rear out.

As he neared the car, he reached into his right pocket and retrieved a small tracking device. Putting the cigar to his lips again, he pretended to be burned by it as he let it drop from his hand, coming to rest directly beneath the rear bumper. Shaking his hand and sucking the outside of one of his fingers to reinforce his act, he deftly and quickly, knelt to pick up the cigar with his left hand, as he rapidly placed the tracking device between the bumper and the side of the gas tank with the other. A passerby, or even if caught on camera, would see nothing out of the ordinary. It looked as if he had simply dropped his cigar and picked it up again as he kept walking, brushing the cigar some and shaking his head.

The tracking device was attached via magnet, one so strong it would not be vibrated off, even if the car were racing in the Baja 1000. Without losing a step, he maintained the same pace as he rounded the end of the rows and made it back to the main vehicle curb in front of the Bellagio. He looked carefully about and spotted one of his agents as he put his cigar out, with a thumb up in the process. Unless you knew exactly what to look for, even a pro would have missed the gesture. The other agent did not.

"Sam," the agent said. "Team one here, equipment arrived and in place."

Sam smiled. No matter how risky it may get, the location of the car would always be known to them. He was hoping that they could listen in on the conversation, but circumstances were too volatile for placing a bug on either of the generals or the car. He had thought about having Samantha pose as a tipsy hot babe, because indeed she was, and place a bug on one of the agents. With no way to retrieve it, eventually it would be discovered, placing the operation in severe jeopardy. It was not worth the risk. Sam made a brief call with a quick update.

"Austin, everything is in place," Sam said. "Tomorrow will be the big day. Will send full report directly after."

"Sam," an agent said. "Chief one, off grid."

Dragon had retired for the evening.

Panu and Li knew it would not pay to be seen together too much. At least not in the casinos. Once they hit the road tomorrow, they could talk in the car. This helped them to relax as they contemplated the enormity of the task they were undertaking. Li, finished with gambling and having grabbed a quick bite, made it back to his room on the nineteenth floor, overlooking the fountains. Standing on his balcony in the darkness, he watched the lights begin to glow in the water, first a shallow arc then, several circles as music began to play. It was quite a show as the louder the music became, the higher in the air the water shot. Within a few minutes the show had ended, white mist floating across the water, as it finally subsided into the darkness, leaving reflections of the Paris casino across the street and the large Bellagio sign, along with Bally's, reflecting on the water surface, seeming so close one could reach out and touch them.

As Li attempted to sleep, he was overcome by all the doubts he had tried to fight off. While their navy was close to being the same in size of the Americans, he was not able to transport troops and ships as well as they had. But even in their wars in the Middle East they had to rely on commercial transport for troops and it took a long time to move tanks and heavy artillery. The key he knew would be having air superiority to make sure his objectives were reached and that strategic locations were kept. He knew the routes and plans, and everything looked perfect on paper, but in real battle, paper often went out the window as one improvisation after another had to be used. What worried him most was if he had enough tanks, planes for air superiority, and logistical supply lines that would function long enough to take Las Vegas, to gain a foothold and maintain the advantage once gained. A disturbing fact was that Panu, while having a great military, would have little air support. They would need to blitzkrieg across Texas and Arizona quickly to support the south flank. One good aspect was that the American navy would be occupied overseas, that was guaranteed and had been set in motion. To overcome troop logistics, they had been pouring in supplies into California for months, their weapons already on docks in containers. The thoughts consoled him as he drifted to sleep.

The trip had been a long one coming out of Washington. Jeremy had been up for over thirty-six hours and was beginning to feel it. Everyone he had recruited was doing their part, to save the nation if it could be done. There were too many whose lights had already dimmed. Saving them was no longer possible. They had sided with those spewing mindless political propaganda on the news and across social media. It was like they were possessed, incapable of thinking and making decisions about any important matter. None-the-less, he would try to save them, to give them more time to shed their disloyalty to Sun God.

He had returned to the familiar spot that was the

favorite of his father and grandfather and now his. Jeremy was going to attempt to send a warning to those who would attack the nation. The sun had just fallen below the mountains as he finished his sand painting, a uniquely special one. As far as he knew, only he and his father knew how to perform it. The sand painting depicted those from the dark path, the underworld, haunting those still living. Like most sand paintings it was circular but split into two halves, the bottom, being black, and the top, being white. Two figures stood in contrast to each other in the bottom, the serpent god of darkness in bright green and a servant standing out in dark blue. The serpent god was pointing upward to the center, where a fire burned in the white portion. On the left side of the fire was the depiction of a figure laying on its side, sleeping, tan in color. On the other side of the fire was a figure standing in the air, spear in hand, simulated rays coming out of its eyes toward the sleeping person. At the top was a depiction of Sun God and around the white border was a continuous line in red color signifying a boundary.

Jeremy waited until all that was left of the fire, beside the painting, were hot coals, glowing a bright red orange. He slowly began to hum and then, chant, softly at first, calling a name, over and over. He would stop abruptly and then, begin again. About half an hour later, the area around him was shrouded in a golden dome, a mist from the realm of Sun God. Jeremy was in a trance now as warriors danced around the mist amid the sound of beating drums.

General Li Qiang was startled out of his restlessness, awakened to a bright green glow appearing in his room, the source emanating from the end of his bed. It was a column of light that slowly turned from green to white to reveal a warrior figure within that became clearer as his eyes adjusted to the brightness. His eyes widened as a great fear fell upon him, using his hands to push his body back, away from the figure until his body hit the headboard with a bang. Li's face became pale as the blood drained from it, the figure now fully visible as the light, still present, had moved away from the warrior's personage.

The warrior stood in the air looking down upon him. His eyes were penetrating, with ruby red pupils glowing brightly, surrounded by an abnormally large white area. It was as if his eyes were lasers, cutting deep into Li's soul. On his head was a wolf's head, the pelt dropping behind the figure. Atop his cheek bones, down to his chin, were three inward pointing triangles. The top triangles pointing toward the nose on either side were white and turquoise, split down the middle, the middle triangle pointing toward the lips was bright yellow, the bottom triangles pointing to the chin were black. Around his neck was a necklace of gold and silver, made of four strands falling to the bottom of his chest, above a ripped abdomen. Around his biceps were three rows of the same material, as well as on either wrist up to almost the elbow. In his right hand was an iron tomahawk. A sheathed long knife hung on his right hip atop buckskin leggings that were covered at the bottom with knee-high wraps of what appeared to be animal fur.

Li was barely breathing, thinking desperately about what escape as his fear grew. The warrior was still, his eyes unblinking as he continued to stare at Li. His forehead appeared to be painted in blood as his eyes, unnerving, continued to look through Li, as if he were transparent. Finally, he spoke.

"I am of no consequence," he said. "The war gods Ahayuta and Achi have sent me. This is Sun Gods hallowed land.

Depart and do not return or we will send many warriors to fight you. And we will send the Skinwalkers, Kachinas, and others you cannot comprehend. Such fear as they can create you know not. Your hearts will feint as you fall before them. Give up your desires and return home in peace or die! This is your only warning."

Immediately after delivering his message, the light in the room drew into a small ball at the center of the warrior's chest and he vanished.

Li's back was still pressed against the headboard of the bed as he let out a long sigh. This couldn't be he thought as he finally got his wits about him and crept to the window to look out. He checked the lock, which was secure and sat down in a chair, looking around the room and out across the fountains toward Bally's and Paris casinos. A matter-of-fact type of person, he was led to believe if what he had seen was real, it was supernatural. Leave or die? That was not going to happen. Years ago, his mother had come to America to get a better life, while he had to make the best of his in China. Climbing the ranks, he swore one day he would have revenge. His mother was denied political asylum and being extremely ill when she arrived, had died in an American hospital. His father had returned aboard a ship. Heartbroken, he died in Shanghai two days after he arrived home. Li, a young man at the time, swore he would get revenge. He would not now be stopped by some apparition.

He flipped on the lights and pulled a counter-measure device, bug sweeper, from his suitcase and began to sweep the entire room, for the third time. Again, nothing. He looked behind every picture, piece of furniture, light fixture, and any place a projection or listening device could be planted and came up empty handed. As he sat back down in his chair, satisfied there was nothing, a sneer creased his face. Indian folklore and legend are no match for my high-tech military he thought as he arose and flipped the lights off then, sat back down in his chair looking across the Vegas skyline. As he kept pondering what he had seen, he finally passed it off as a dream; it was the only thing that made sense. He had felt especially tired after the baccarat game. Probably due to the excitement of being in Vegas, the game, and more importantly, making final plans for the battle that would advance his rank and climax in revenge for his parents. He slowly dozed off into a troubled sleep.

Jeremy was still humming, his eyes looking forward. He was listening to the feint beat of the drums, which suddenly stopped. The dome around him disappeared. He prayed that he had accomplished what he had sought to do. Slowly, he arose, found a short stick and destroyed the sand painting using counterclockwise circular movements. When complete, he covered the few remaining coals with sand as he stood fully upright, stretched, and yawned. To the east, evidence of the sun rise, as the sky slowly turned a noticeably light blue, above an orange hue. Satisfied he had done all he could, he climbed onto his horse and slowly rode down from the mesa. He would be back in Washington by the next morning.

The air was crisp and cool as Panu and Li met in the lobby. Although the sun had not shown itself, daylight revealed a full spectrum of colors from the buildings surrounding them to the fountains in front and the fauna surrounding the hotel.

"Good morning comrade," Li said. "Let's get something to

eat. Any ideas?"

"There is a small restaurant in the front of Caesar's that is open," Panu said, as the two began to walk. "How did you sleep?"

"Not well, tossed and turned all night and had the strangest dream,"

"Oh."

"Yes, it was about a warrior who stood in front of me at the end of my bed saying leave this land or die."

"Hmmmm, interesting," Panu said, eyebrows raising. "Did it scare you? Do you think it was real?"

"Yes, it scared me at first," Li replied. "But afterward, I got up and swept the room for bugs and looked everywhere for potential projection equipment. I found nothing. But I must say it was the strangest dream I've ever had."

"You sure it was a dream?"

"There is no way it could have been real. The only other explanation is supernatural, and I do not believe in such things."

"Me either," Panu said.

"You have not seen anything suspicious, have you?" Li asked.

"Nothing," Panu said. "It's been quiet and fun. Not often we get to enjoy such things."

"Agreed."

The two continued to walk, unaware that Sam's team had picked them up and were keeping close tabs. Having anticipated where they were going, Sam already had a couple of agents in the restaurant just inside Caesar's main entrance. It was one of the few nearby places open so early. Panu motioned for his FSB agent who quickly was at his side.

"Pick up the car and meet us at the main entrance to

Caesar's," Panu said, looking at his watch. "Give us one hour. Grab yourselves a bite and get us some snacks and drinks for the day."

The FSB agent nodded, motioning for other one as they strode quickly away. Sam's agent picked them up, shadowing them. It was routine because they knew where the agents would likely go but decided to err on the side of caution never-the-less. Sam had already positioned himself and was near the end of the fountains at Caesar's, a building between him and South Las Vegas Boulevard, better known as 'The Strip,' by the locals and all who visited this bustling city. He had picked up a breakfast burrito wrap and a cup of coffee and sat casually eating and sipping on the steps as the two men passed and disappeared into the door near the check-in area. He was far enough away not to arouse suspicion and why would he, looking every part the average tourist recovering from a night of gambling and other vices. He retrieved his cell from his pants pocket.

"Teams listen up. They just sat down in the restaurant. I need team one to position three cars spread out along Interstate 15 south toward Long Beach. You may be in for a long wait. We will know shortly. Team two, pull three cars up to the main entrance and we will follow from there. Take care not to get too close to their car if they arrive before you. Be casual, have a coffee and donut, look at a map or something. Whatever you do, avoid suspicion. I'll monitor you from the safehouse."

Dimitri and Gorgov pulled up on que. Panu and Li were already waiting for them as they climbed into the car and were off, pulling out onto the strip and turning right. About a block down, they turned left, going east on Flamingo Road. The roads were already choked with workers coming and going as the shifts of the 24/7 city changed. The work never stopped. After a few minutes they headed south along Highway 515, which merged onto Interstate 11. Just a few miles later, they picked up Highway 95 veering south heading past Searchlight and Palm Gardens toward the junction with Interstate 40. With the tracker on the vehicle, the three cars behind them kept their distance about a half-mile back. Just before the junction, they pulled off the road and laid their maps out on the hood of the car. To passerby's they simply looked like lost tourists trying to find their way.

"At this point, we are about ninety miles from Las Vegas," Panu said. "We could go up this route and meet you in the city, driving through and clearing the way to meet you on the outskirts where I-15 enters or, we could meet up with you as a combined force by heading along I-40 west to the junction with I-15 at Barstow. That is about one-hundred and thirty miles."

"Hmmmm," Li mumbled. "That's a long way for equipment to go and we are not that far from our supply lines in Barstow. I think it would be best to take the first route and meet in the middle. You essentially flank from the south and us from the west. We would create a spearhead with our combined forces."

Panu stood looking, first to the north along Highway 95 then, west along Interstate 40.

"From Houston to Las Vegas is almost fifteen hundred miles. There is no way to have air cover for that distance. We would have tanks on flatbeds, as well as helicopters. Even with those in tow, we will not have air cover if we meet a substantial force. That is a grave concern."

"Do not worry my friend," Li said. "Our missile launchers are already in place and set to target all military installations and airfields before we move an inch. They will not know we are coming until it is too late. Many will also be targeted by our ships."

"What about bases further away?" Panu asked. "They could be a significant danger as well."

"My friend," Li said. "We have over one thousand missiles targeting everything from St. Louis to Washington to Ft. Hood to New York and Miami, not to mention our fleet and air force coming in from the west. You also have many missiles on your ships that will target some of the same installations along with many different ones."

"Understood," Panu stated. "With that in mind, I will move two mobile divisions along this route. I estimate forty-eight hours to meet up with you given light resistance. My main concern is that once we leave Houston, the people in this country will be aware and there are far too many guns to deal with. Snipers will be a real problem."

"Yes, I believe so as well," Li said. "We will have counter-sniper teams continually roving, much like the Americans Marine Scout-Sniper units. They will be a pain to some extent, but there will not be enough of them to stand up to our armored personnel carriers. They are wheeled and can take up front and rear to be ready to engage light infantry or civilian snipers. Once we locate one or more, we will send those after them and annihilate them one by one. Whether by counter-sniper teams, machine guns, or mortars, these snipers will not be military, and I doubt they'll stand up against us for long."

"I'm not so sure," Panu stated. "While we can handle them, I do not believe they will just lie down and give up, but will be constantly harassing us. But, as you say, they shouldn't delay us. If it gets too intense, we will launch a helicopter attack against them."

Sam's team was not far away. They had stopped just over a quarter mile behind Dragon and Red Star, feigning a flat tire and watching them through binoculars. Another car was not far behind and the third car had moved ahead and turned east onto Interstate 40. The lead agent was on the phone.

"Sam," the agent said. "They have stopped ahead and have a map spread out on the hood. It looks like they are surveying the I-40 route coming from the east."

"Very well. Keep an eye on them and don't get spotted."

"Roger that, out."

Sam leaned back in his chair trying to ascertain what the generals were up to. What would he be looking at if he were them? He had a large U.S. map on the table beside him. As he stood up, he began looking at the southwest area from Texas to Nevada. Austin had mentioned something about Houston being a potential starting point. As he looked, it was as if the freeway were marked in red. Of course, he thought, they would naturally want to send a support group up to reinforce the Chinese flank assuming the Chinese were coming in from Los Angeles. The route made sense, but the expanse did not. How were they anticipating they would have air cover? Sam got back on the phone.

"Watch for them to take I-40 going west once they finish with their map. I'll have the other team pick you up near Barstow. I have a strong suspicion they are headed toward Los Angeles."

Sam kept staring at the map, as he pushed numbers on his phone.

"Yes, General White, this is Sam Malone. Would it be possible to have some of your men meet us in Los Angeles tomorrow?"

"Certainly, I have a group there now. Tell me where and

when. Oh, and just so you know, we have found over fifty of the containers so far in the Long Beach port area. I'll keep you posted and update you when you give us the location."

Sam decided to go mobile and took the map with him. This is getting interesting. He would report to Austin once he found out for sure where they were headed.

General Qiang was thinking about the vision he had last night. He kept shrugging it off, but still, it gave him an ominous feeling. He pushed it to the back of his mind. Nothing was going to stop him or sway him from his task. They had headed west on I-40 and had passed Barstow. They stopped just outside of Long Beach and switched cars. The security detail was now Chinese; CSB agents. With Li's connections, they had entered the main port cargo area where ships loaded and unloaded. It wasn't difficult since the Chinese owned the port. They, along with their two-man security detail, had walked a long way down the container yard. Sam's team, along with members of Shockwave Force, had scattered themselves about and had a keen eye on the two.

"Panu," Li said. "I want to alleviate your doubts about our preparedness. Look there toward the end and up on the left. All of those containers are missile containers, at least two hundred missiles, more are arriving shortly. I have been building them non-stop for almost five years waiting for this moment. And look there, across to the west, see those tankers and container ships." Li motioned with his hands. "Most of the tankers are ours, they are actually supply ships and the container ships are ours too, with more on the way; many are full of troops. We have more troops scheduled to arrive by cruise ships, full infantry divisions. I have two divisions here already. They all have missiles, as well as supplies to ensure we are completely ready."

"So, you're telling me that you have over one thousand missiles in containers?" Panu queried incredulous.

"And then some," Li replied. "We need those to take out everything we can before we engage. We can strike targets in San Francisco from here with ease, as well as all the military bases in Nevada and Utah, Arizona, and parts of New Mexico. We will own the soil and the air because we will take out all their aircraft first."

Panu was in deep thought as he looked toward the containers and then, across the port to the Pacific beyond.

"I did not realize you had such in place," Panu said ecstatically.

"Not only these, but we have many containers inland. They are strategically placed so that we can take out all military infrastructure."

As Li's words fell upon his ears, for the first time Panu the doubts he had before vanished. He kept surveying the port and the container and tanker ships at sea. A broad smile creased his face as he turned and laughed, Li laughing with him. This was going to be fun.

Unknown to them, Sam's agents were recording the conversation with a laser mic. As the two generals began walking back, the agent recorded the conversation onto his phone and sent it to Sam.

"Austin, we need the group assembled on teleconference immediately. Call me when you have them."

As he waited, Sam began circling every airport and military installation he knew off the top of his head, all over the U.S. There were so many. It was stressful. Not being a military man, he wondered how many missiles they would use to strike each target. His thoughts were interrupted as his phone buzzed.

Austin had gathered everyone on a secure teleconference. Present were the President, Erin, Jeremy, Generals Bardos and White, Stone, and Nick.

"What is so important?" Phil asked.

"We have been surveilling Dragon and Red Star as requested," Sam began. "I will not reveal the location, but you need to hear this."

Sam played the audio, which had been cut to the essentials. There was no indication of who was speaking in case someone was listening in. Those present needed no explanation.

"Holy God," Jason whispered. "When did you pick this up?"

"Three hours ago, sir," Sam replied. "We still have eyes on. They appear to be heading back to start point of last communique with you."

"What was the six weeks mentioned, do you know?" Stone asked.

"From what we can tell it is time to initiation," Sam responded soberly. "From today!"

"Keep us posted," Stone said. "Out."

"Gentlemen and lady," Jeremy said. "We need to meet immediately, securely."

"Agreed."

The generals had switched cars again and were headed back to Las Vegas, heading east on I-15. They had discussed logistics and timetables the entire way. Along the way near Cajon Junction, Victorville, and Barstow were canyons and bridges that could pose problems for the army in its drive to Las Vegas. These were of concern to Panu who had more experience in combat and with heavy artillery and tanks than Li did.

"These bridges, here, here, and here," Panu began, pointing at the map folded across their laps, could pose problems for us."

"I agree," Li said. "But only if they know we are coming. If it were you or me, we would blow them, but they have no clue. Besides, Americans are dumb, they won't do anything until the last minute. By then it will be too late."

"I would not be so sure," Panu said. "It's not only the bridges, like the one we are crossing now, but look at the high ground along this route. It wouldn't take but a few tanks to stand off a large force in some areas and bog us down."

"Again," Li said, frustration apparent. "Those only work in the Americans favor if they know we are coming. They do not and how are they going to know. Besides you and I and a few of our most trusted generals, even our own men have no idea yet what we are preparing them for."

"I suppose you are right comrade," Panu responded, a tight knot in his stomach.

"Dimitri," Li said, pointing at the map. "Pull off here."

Dimitri nodded affirmatively as Gorgov took the map and directed him. A short while later, the car pulled off at Baker and the junction of Highway 127. The two generals got out again and placed the map on the hood, which showed the geography of the surrounding area all the way to Las Vegas.

"This comrade is where we need to be ever watchful," Li said. "By the time we reach this point, they will know we are coming and where we are. It is here, if they have any manpower to stop us that they will begin making their defense. At least I would."

"Yes, I agree," Panu said. "Lots of room for maneuvering

tanks, artillery, and special operations. It is a large space to defend, but also a large space to attack. We must not get bogged down here or we fail. I suggest spearheading forward with scout tanks and armored vehicles on our forward and rear flanks."

"Good idea," Li said. "With that and presumably air superiority, even some heavy resistance should be overcome."

Sam had made his final report to Stone and Austin. The group was gathered in the conference room. It was late at night, prying eyes were gone for the day. There were sobering looks around the table.

"Do we have enough troops to stop this?" Phil asked.

"Well Mr. President, we should have enough," General White said. "Although, from what Sam has said, they likely have many more troops hidden here already. If they do, we will be seriously outnumbered. Our biggest task right now is finding the rest of the missiles they have stashed. We will not find them all but will continue searching."

"How many have you found so far?" Stone asked.

"Over eleven hundred," General White replied. "I talked to General Bardos who helped we with Lunadi. He gave us another two hundred of his men. With that, it allows us to search hundreds more places more quickly. After the initial report, we found all the ones in the port."

"Alright generals, what is your best scenario?" Phil asked. "Where would you put the missiles to take out our military if you were the enemy."

"We have been discussing that Mr. President," Jason said. "Let us show you."

As the two generals unrolled a large tactical map they had made of the area, the group stood to see.

"Due to the range of the missiles, they could be anywhere," Jason said. "But because they would want us to have little warning they will likely be within one hundred miles of the targets, maybe up to three hundred miles."

"In that regard sir, we have our intelligence sources seeking all rental areas for containers in all of these circled locations. As they report back, the information will be relayed to General White and Shockwave will check each location. We are looking for all possible leads. Our biggest problem will be container ships so, we're tracking everything from China, the Middle East, Africa, and Latin America, comparing typical length of trips, putting to port, travel time, and other fields. We are using cluster and neural-network analysis combined with data mining to uncover any variance from past times and routes for each ship and any newer ships. That information will be relayed to you as well."

"We will find as many a possible sir," General Bardos said. "The big question is, do we let them strike first once we have all in place?"

"As we have discussed before, is there any way to determine when these containers will launch?" Phil asked. "General Bardos?"

"From our own experience, the container has to be opened and depending on missile type, it can take up to thirty minutes to raise to launch position. We have that time down to fifteen minutes overall."

"If that is the case then, Shockwave and Lunadi's force can keep eyes on," Lorenzo said. "I say we watch then, blow the missiles once we see them being raised."

"General Bardos?" Phil asked.

"Agreed," Jason replied. "We are assuming they will contact the launchers first and launch them and afterwards, immediately set off and EMP, engaging with troops and heavy weapons one to two days later."

"Is there any way to keep our military intact for missiles that do get through?" Phil asked.

"I am reminded of what the Medicine Man used to teach us," Jeremy said. "We would work in guerilla tactics presenting a target and then make it disappear."

"But we cannot make a military base disappear," Jason said.

"That is not the point," Jeremy replied. "Have you ever seen a shell game, where the shells are moved, and you try to pick where the pea is? That is what I mean. For example, look at Ft. Hood. What are the most valuable assets there?"

"Air calvary units with their Apache helicopters and tanks," Jason said.

"Ah, I see where you are going," Lorenzo said. "We move our assets in and out."

"Exactly," Jeremy said. "Like search and destroy. One minute they are there, the next they are gone with some dummy assets to make it look like they are in place."

"For us to accomplish this, we would need to move the assets in and out on drills," Jason said. "The goal being to make sure they are out when the attack comes."

"That sounds fine," Phil said. "But can we make it work and do we have enough manpower to stop these armies in the desert outside Vegas."

"We can make it work to an extent," Lorenzo said. "But to avoid showing our hand, I recommend only doing it with the biggest bases."

"That would be wise," Jason said. "As for the manpower, they will have more than us. We will likely be completely outgunned."

"Might I remind you that a small group of focused warriors can accomplish almost anything," Jeremy said.

"And we will have ample help, not from our military. Please trust me."

"I have confidence in you, my friend," Phil said. "We need to move as quickly as possible. As you are aware, they are going to try to impeach me for that cooked up collusion scenario with China and Turkey. It's not true, but it will result in more prying eyes and ears. So, take care what you say and who you say it to. Nothing should leave this group and no open communications."

"The President is correct," Erin said. "The Speaker of the House has been snooping for information. I have been able to keep her at bay, but I believe it was her that sent the secret service agent to assassinate the President at Chaco. I have no hard evidence, yet, but it seems she has extraordinarily strong ties to the Chinese. She's deflecting and will thwart the President as much as she can. Already she is asking for him to give up the nuclear suitcase. Now why do you suppose she would do so?"

"That is a matter of concern," Nick said. "Let me do some digging of my own behind the scenes. We need to nip any possibility of her interfering with this endeavor."

"Very well," Phil said. "Mums the word for now. Generals, how long will it take for you to make final preparations?"

"I don't know about Jason's group Mr. President, but we can be fully ready in three days."

"I have positioned all my resources based on our previous discussions and messages from deity. Jeremy and I will be going out to make final preparations. I anticipate, Lorenzo and his men to join us after they find as many missiles as they can and also all of Lunadi's men, as well as the tribes and their warriors. We will be fully ready at that time."

"General White, how long before you finish your search and sabotage?" Phil asked.

"Given current manpower, another week sir."

"So, with that clarified, General Bardos?"

"Okay, with that information we should be fully prepared in two weeks." Jason replied. "All our resources will be in place and we can run maneuvers until they launch. However, I would suggest going quiet for five to seven days prior to anticipated engagement. I'm sure they will have their satellites scrutinize the attack route."

"I agree sir," Lorenzo said. "We must take every caution not to expose our hand."

"Very well," Phil said. "Generals make final preparations. Erin, you and Nick dig into the traitors. We will need to make a final decision on them soon. If you need anything, let me know. I want all our container ships locked, loaded, and conducting missile drills. Our subs also need to be on station, let's get the shell game going immediately. Our forces are our pea with the three shells. What did you call it Nick?"

"The formal name is thimblerig sir."

"Ummmm, let's show the enemies at our gates what a few good men can really do. Start moving the shells."

Evelyn Rutledge couldn't let a crises go to waste as she stepped up to the podium smiling; she could scarce contain her glee.

"Ladies and gentlemen of the press," Evelyn said. "As I told you two days ago, more evidence has surfaced. We now have corroboration showing collusion of the President with Turkey and the Chinese. The CIA informant has stepped forward and is giving closed-door testimony to a House panel right now. I'll answer a few questions."

"Madam Speaker," a reporter said. "Why would the President collude with China? I thought he didn't like them?"

"The simple answer is he is deflecting, pretending to disagree so that he is above suspicion."

"You're telling us that you have evidence to that effect?" another reporter asked.

"That is correct. We will be drafting the formal charges soon and have a vote of impeachment as well as no confidence. I'm sure that the vote will be a majority; we will walk the impeachment to the senate immediately after."

"What is the collusion with Turkey?" a female reporter asked. "How are they involved with China, I thought they were an ally of Russia."

"It has to do with illegal arms sales," The Speaker said. "The evidence is there, but we do not know the full extent at this time. We are still digging but have enough evidence to sustain charges. That's all for now. I will give you another briefing tomorrow."

One thing every politician knew was that once reporters smelled blood in the water, they were like sharks and would dig continuously until they uncovered every detail. This was getting better by the moment the Speaker thought, smiling to herself.

CHAPTER 9

The Desert

The day was cool and crisp, a slight breeze blowing from the north; the soil temperature was climbing fast. Already, before noon, it was a hundred degrees. It wouldn't go much higher. The three men stood atop Hollow Hills Peak in the wilderness area. They were looking south southwest toward Baker, about ten miles away. Each had a pair of binoculars, assessing the route and terrain the enemy generals had stopped to observe.

"What do you think general?" Lunadi asked.

"Well," Jason said, lowering his binoculars. "We must be painfully careful. Whether defender or attacker, it will be difficult not to be exposed."

"Agreed," Lunadi said. "We need to harass them all along the route beginning at Victorville."

"I was thinking along similar lines," Jason said.

"I'm sure they'll have many tanks," Jeremy said. "How are you going to stop them."

"It will not be easy," Jason said. "But, given the distance they are coming, while they may have some Type 99 tanks with 125mm guns, it's more than likely the majority will be Type 15 with 105mm guns. They are not as armored and can be transported two at a time aboard their Y-20 transport planes. And from what Sam has told us, they have been flying them in almost daily to Port Brito in Nicaragua. That means, they'll be flying them up, likely to LAX, so that they can gain quick control of the airport for a base supply."

"So, even if they launch their missiles, they won't just hit the road right away," Jeremy said.

"That is correct my friends," Jason said. "What? I see that look in your eyes Lunadi."

"I have an idea, so hear me out," Lunadi said. "We have been preparing to do the major defense from this area up to the edge of Vegas. We know that their supply line is their life's blood. And given the Type 15, even Type 99, they would want full tanks of fuel going into Vegas to guarantee maneuvering until they could secure the city. But, to get there intact, they will need to have their staging areas at Long Beach Port and LAX before they push out. They will naturally assume that their missiles will take out the opposition. I suggest we camouflage whatever weapons are needed and strike the airport and the port, before they hit the road."

"That could work," Jason mused, rubbing his chin. "We have just the weapons. The army has been revamping the M142 and M270A1 truck-based multiple rocket launchers. Both have been designed to devastate huge areas using a massive barrage of 227-mllimeter rockets, each of them loaded with over 500 cluster bomblets. Now we can do the same, but with much better precision."

"They will have aircraft that will come looking once we fire," Lunadi said. "How close do we need to be?"

"Hmmmm, as I recall, they both use the M31 GPS-guided rocket munitions, which has a range of forty-three miles and a little easier to handle," Jason said. "But each can swap out the standard rockets for the MGM-140 advanced tactical missile. Those are large and they can only utilize two per vehicle. But the range is one hundred eighty-six miles. And if we ignore INF rules, we can use missiles with a three-hundred-mile range."

"Then we should use the shorter range here and the longer range to strike the staging areas," Lunadi said.

"Precisely, let's add that to our defense," Jason said. "As far as their tanks, regardless of type, we can use the Javelin anti-tank missile to take them out. It is shoulder fired, man portable, and has a range of one and three-quarter mile."

"This is getting very interesting," Jeremy said. "Sounds like you're going to be using asymmetric warfare."

"It is the only way that we have a hope of stopping them," Jason said. "We'll be outgunned so we need to take out their air and heavy guns for a better matchup."

"I have a surprise for them," Jeremy said.

"Oh yeah," Lunadi replied. "What's that?"

"Well, I don't know the warfare part like you do," Jeremy said. "But I have my own team players who they won't like. If you have ever heard of the psychology of fear, they're going to experience the greatest fear they can imagine. I will call in the Skinwalkers against them."

Jason and Lunadi looked at each other.

"But aren't those like evil?" Jason asked.

"True, but in league with Sun God, they will obey, so the evil will be focused on the Chinese and Russians," Jeremy said. "And do not forget, we have Aichu and his fellow giants, as well as the war gods Ahayuta and Achi. Let me handle the supernatural. It will work, you'll see."

"They could definitely make our work easier," Jason said, smiling.

"Make no mistake my friends," Jeremy said. "We must do all we can before we ask for their help which will be given sparingly. We are the servants to perform our calling and duties. They will not let us off lightly whether we try to shirk our duties or not."

"Yes," Lunadi said. "It is up to us to fulfill our accountability."

"Understood," Jason said. "I just get carried away, after all, I have never had the gift of a supernatural helping to fight one of my battles for me."

"Come," Jason said. "We must survey the other areas for final preparations."

Santos, wearing camouflage clothing, crept carefully around the airfield, staying inside the tree line to avoid detection as Chinese sentry's roved around the perimeter. The roar of the jets was deafening. All day and night they came. Large military cargo planes bringing all types of supplies — artillery, rockets, tanks, helicopters, armored personnel carriers. He had been there all night, taking pictures from various vantage points. Despite the time of year, it was sweltering, sweat dripping into his eyes. His surveillance revealed an enormous number of supplies and weapons. He circled the airfield and military compound for almost the entire day and made his way back through the thick trees to his small truck late in the afternoon. As he neared his truck, he crawled up a small, bougainvillea crowed embankment. Gaining enough elevation, he was able to clearly see his truck and began glassing with his binoculars around the entire area to make sure no one was around. After an hour, he was satisfied and made his way down. Cautiously looking about, he crawled beneath the truck and opened a small hidden compartment, retrieving a satellite phone. He moved a little way away and took up a position in the shade beneath a pink butterfly tree. He was no expert, but he knew the buildup of an invasion when he saw it.

"Hello, yes, I have them. Many pictures, worse than we thought. I will send in one hour."

S am eagerly anticipated the report and was waiting at his computer for it to come in. As he sat, his foot began to uncontrollably bounce up and down, the ball of the foot anchoring it as the heel of his shoe tapped the floor. He suddenly realized what he was doing and stopped. His computer dinged as he eagerly opened the secure email.

Gazing at the photos as he read Santos's report, his heart began to beat faster.

"Damn," he thought. "I need to get this to Austin and Stone as quickly as possible."

He hurriedly wrote his own assessment of Santos's report, coupling it with what they already knew and with the container launchable missiles.

"This is not going to be a walk in the park," he muttered to himself as he pressed the send button.

A ustin was sitting at his desk when Sam's report came through. He had already gotten a phone call and was prepared for its critical nature. As soon as the report came through, he immersed himself in it.

"Holy shit," Austin half shouted.

He hurriedly stuck the report together and went running down the hall.

"Sheila, he in?" Austin asked. "It's most urgent."

"He's on the phone. Let me see if he'll see you."

Sheila walked to Stones office door and gently tapped, opening it. Austin sir, says it's most urgent."

"Look, somethings come up," Stone said, motioning for Sheila to allow Austin in. "I'll call you later."

What's so urgent?" Stone asked as Austin rushed in, out of

breath.

"Just this," Austin exclaimed, as he passed the folder and took up a seat!

Stone hastily opened the folder and began perusing its contents. Opening his desk drawer, he pulled out a large magnifying glass as was his habit and looked from one photo to another. He raised his eyebrows quizzically as he examined them. Looking over his glasses he eyed Austin then, read the report quicky again, shaking his head back and forth.

"Have you sent these photos to the analysts?" Stone asked.

"The first thing I did," Austin said. "They'll have them on your desk in about half an hour."

"I'm sure you understand how critical this is becoming. We cannot afford to make any mistakes at this juncture."

"Understood."

"Where are we on Operation Eider?" Stone asked.

"Unfortunately, we are finding more of the launchers than we thought," Austin said. "With the extra help from Lunadi's men, who are doing quite well I might add, the process is ongoing."

"What are your thoughts?"

"Well, even though there are more than we thought, we will find most of them. But .... his voice trailing off."

"But what?" Stone asked.

"I'm worried about the ones we don't find and how many that may be," Austin replied. "They could do a hell of a lot of damage."

"It's collateral damage," Stone replied. "It cannot be helped. We all know we are going to get bloody on this. It just appears that it may be much bloodier than we thought unless the generals and Jeremy can pull some rabbits out of their hats."

"Should we notify them?" Austin asked.

"Absolutely," Stone said, frowning. "Get this to Jeremy, General Bardos, and General White as quickly as you can. I'll inform the President."

Stone was already picking up the phone as Austin left.

"Erin, Stone here. I need to talk to Phil briefly."

"Can he call you back? He's in a meeting."

"Yes, but it's important."

"I'll let him know."

"Thank you," Stone said, hanging up. Not many things worried Stone, he was like steel, but this was one of those times that despite his skills, things appeared to be getting out of hand. His was in the intelligence arena and now, the intelligence pointed directly to war with two powerful enemies. More importantly, it was a time when many in congress were paid stooges for one of the foes and they were tightening down almost every kind of aid to the military he could think of. It was like an administration years ago when the military was decimated. Now, they had entered a time in which they were fighting a three-front war — the Chinese, Russians, and his own government. He stood and walked to the window. As he looked out, he expelled a large sigh as he watched cumulus clouds float across the azure sky. He allowed himself to fall into a trance as he tried to relieve stress, jolted out of it by his phone, which he wasn't expecting, he physically jumped at the first ring.

"Stone," he answered.

"Yes sir," Stone said. "I received the report we were expecting. Yes, worse than we thought. What time? Okay, I'll bring it then."

Jeremy and General Bardos had been joined by General White. To remain inconspicuous as they drove about the soon to be battlefield, they had rented a large, gray SUV. Several others followed them with a variety of aids and staff officers, as well as supplies while they began to plan the defense strategy.

They had reached the peak of a mountain pass about one-third of the way between Baker and Las Vegas and were able to get close enough to walk a short distance to the summit. Their aides drug a couple of large tables up the hill; they sat them up and spread their maps and satellite photos atop them. Every officer was looking through binoculars toward Baker to the southwest and Las Vegas toward the northeast. A straight-line distance of about seventy-five miles.

"This is a big area," Jason said. "Lot's to defend."

"I agree," Lorenzo replied, looking toward Las Vegas.

"True," Jeremy said. "Lunadi will love this place."

"Why?" Jason asked.

"Because it is what he would call a funnel of death."

"How so?"

"The enemy will be constrained to the highway," Jeremy said.

"Ah, yes, I see it." Lorenzo said. "It's like a SWAT team that approaches entry to a building, they're all grouped together at the door until they can enter."

"Jason," Lorenzo said. "Jeremy brings up a good point. They can wander off the road into some of the valleys, but to reach their objective, they need to control I-15 from Baker to Vegas."

General Bardos had a brilliant idea.

"Look at these mountains and high areas along the path," Jason said. "Here, all through here and these."

All the staff officers had gathered around as they began to form a picture of the overall defense. Abruptly, Major Kenneth Price, General Bardos's aide, rushed over.

"Sir, you will want to look at this," Kenneth said, handing him a laptop. "It's addressed extremely urgent to the three of you."

"Thank you major," Jason said. "Hmmmm, what have we here?"

As he opened the electronic communication, quickly scanning its contents, a scowl crept across his face, his eyes began to widen.

"Shit," he exclaimed!

"What is it?" Lorenzo asked.

"Look at this," Jason said, passing them the laptop.

Both gathered around it and quickly perused the contents.

"I'm no general," Jeremy said. "But this looks serious."

"You damned right it is," Lorenzo said.

"It's going to be a full-scale war gentleman," Jason said. "You know that they understand they will need to take out our communications before they move all this."

"How long will it take to move their ships from Port Brito to Long Beach?" Jeremy asked.

"The average ship speed is about thirty knots," Lorenzo replied. "So, about three to three and one-half days."

"So, what tactic will they use?" Jeremy asked. "I mean how will they knock out communications for that long and still be able to attack without our intelligence and military groups being aware of it?"

"That is why there are so many of the missiles," Jason said. "If I were running their attack you need to be able to communicate with all your people first. That means they would launch the missiles, putting everything in chaos, hit us with an EMP, then, begin moving their ships. Or they could slowly put their ships to sea, a few at a time and utilize the scenario once they were about twenty-four hours out."

"Either way, it will put us in a difficult position," Lorenzo said, gazing out across the desert toward Vegas.

"Alright then, we need to think back on the Little Big Horn," Jason said.

"That did not turn out so well," Jeremy grinned.

"True," Jason said. "However, this time we'll be the Indians. No offense meant."

"None taken," Jeremy said.

"What are you proposing?" Lorenzo asked.

"We know the terrain well," Jason said. "We prepare it so that we make their numbers irrelevant if we can. Everything becomes a sniper in Lunadi's experience; tanks, rockets, everything. We will fill every nook and cranny of these mountains with hidden defenses."

"That could work if we use asymmetric tactics," Lorenzo replied. The real problem for us will be their air power. Do you believe we can nullify it?"

"That's been on my mind," Jason said. "I think partially, at least I have some confidence. Before we talked about their supply lines and in this case, we know they need a base for air operations. That means they need to take over LAX or a neighboring airport. I'm fairly certain the missiles we have on Catalina, San Clemente, and other islands off the coast, along with our land-based anti-ship missiles will take out their carriers and supply ships. If we can do that it will eliminate most of their airpower, maybe. Without it, it will become difficult for them to beat us. But we must be certain. Tell me Lorenzo, how long before your men finish their missile search?"

"I'd say a few more days," Lorenzo replied. "The addition

of more of Lunadi's men hurried things up quite a bit. All container systems we have found have been sabotaged. I'm just hoping it goes unnoticed. Likely it will because they have minimal men at each site and our intelligence tell us they avoid being around them to avoid suspicion. Why do you ask?"

"If I were them, I would be searching for weapons that could blow them out of the water," Jason said. "Wouldn't you agree?"

"Certainly," Lorenzo said.

"Then, let's begin an exercise along the California coast and Camp Pendleton," Jason said. "It may slow them down but will disguise any loss of men on their part from Shockwave. We need to deploy now and search and destroy. Anywhere we have anti-ship and land-based missiles is a threat they will seek out. Deploy your men around those and kill the enemy on sight. They may believe that they were killed by those on drill."

President Philip Weld was discussing the latest intelligence with Stone in the Oval Office. They were attempting to determine the best course of action as Nick and Erin joined them.

"We do not have the generals here to weigh options," Phil said.

"They have been alerted," Stone replied. "They told me they were working on some options and will get back to us shortly."

"I hope it is soon," Phil replied. "This is getting more serious and, faster than we had hoped."

"It may be even more serious than that," Erin interrupted. "The Speaker just informed me they are going to pursue impeachment against you. She listed basic charges in a press conference; collusion with China and arms deals with Turkey."

"What?"

"It's just a smoke screen sir," Erin said. "But we have a problem, tell him Nick."

"Well sir, I been sifting through State Department emails," Nick said. "As far as we can determine, there are lots of side deals going on behind the scenes with China, Russia and Iran."

"I'm not sure I want to know," Phil said. "What kind of side deals?"

"Weapons and information are being sold to the enemy," Nick said. "Not only that, but there have been major agreements between power brokers to greatly increase their wealth from the Chinese if you can be removed from office."

"I don't see how they think they can be successful."

Nick was looking at Stone. A seriousness washed across his face. Everyone in the room recognized it. Something was up. Nick raised his hands in exasperation.

"Tell him, Stone."

"I was going to bring this to your attention sooner sir, but we received the new intel and I decided to wait."

"What's up?" Phil asked.

"What Erin and Nick are telling you is the truth," Stone said. "But it's even worse than that. So far, we have identified that over half of the congress, more than 220 in the House and fifty-five in the Senate are on the Chinese payroll. This comes from our team in the NSA out of Salt Lake that have been monitoring all of them. And that is not all of them. It is clear they have committed treason and we can prove it. I'm not certain how we should move forward sir."

"Carefully, very carefully my friend," Phil said as he rubbed his chin, staring at the Oval Office door as if someone would walk through at any moment. It was times like these that made him wish he had not run for President. There was no one to trust but an exceedingly small handful. Utmost caution was necessary. The silence in the room began to draw on, becoming uncomfortable.

"Sir," Erin said, speaking softly.

"What can we do with this evidence?" Phil asked, turning his attention back to them.

"We could file charges on all of them," Nick replied. "But I'm not sure we could get a court that would convict them or even hear the cases. As you recall this happened to a former President and now these idiots have even greater control!"

"Why don't we just kill them all sir?" Stone queried. "It's not the right way necessarily, but it would be a permanent solution and the sentence for treason is death."

"Let's not resort to their tactics," Phil said. "At least not yet. I want to talk to Jeremy and sound it out with him. He seems to always come up with solutions but not sure any of us have a good strategy for this. Is there a way to arrest them under terrorism charges? If we could, we could send them to Gitmo privately or a black site and they would be out of sight and out of mind. No longer would they be able to do more harm to the country and its people."

"I'm not enough of a legal eagle to determine that," Nick said. "I'll have one of our people look into it discreetly."

"Good," Phil said. "I want an answer by this evening."

"I'll get right on it," Nick said as he arose and left the room.

The generals and men had a long day. The hot desert floor and cool breeze had taken a toll. Instead of going back to a hotel in Vegas, they had brought a few small tents to spend the night and rise early for more planning. They had made their way to the south side of the interstate into Mojave National Preserve. They pitched their tents, built a small fire, and set up a couple of camp stoves to cook on. Chili was the feast of the day. The men were sitting around joking as they watched the sky to the wet; there was still an orange red glow above the hills and mountains. It seemed so peaceful in a place that would soon witness a raging battle. Within minutes the last remnants of light blue disappeared to reveal a velvet sky full of stars. The wind picked up a little as the men bundled up in coats and made some coffee.

"Generals, I need you to come with me," Jeremy said, as he picked up a pack and slung it over his shoulder then, another in his free hand.

"Are we doing what I think?" Jason asked.

"Yes, you may want to tell your men."

"What are we doing?" Lorenzo asked.

"You'll see," Jason smiled broadly. "It will be something to write home about, only thing is, you won't. Major, he yelled."

Major Price walked over at a brisk pace.

"Yes sir, what do you need?"

"The three of us are going up the hill there," Jason said, pointing. "You may hear or see some strange things. We will be okay, just stay here. No one else is to come up."

"Yes sir," the major said. "Got it."

The three men began walking up to higher ground and found a small, bare clearing behind a rock outcropping. Jeremy, shining a flashlight, began smoothing an area. Once he was ready, he took the bag he had carried in his hand and dumped it against the rock wall about ten feet behind the area he had smoothed and prepared a fire. In no time, a nice fire was burning, which allowed enough light to prepare a sand painting. General White had not been around Jeremy before and was curious, watching him as he prepared the sand painting.

"What is this for?" Lorenzo asked, Jason looking on.

"It is to summon the Yee Naaldlooshii, translated as 'with it, he goes on all fours.' It is the Skinwalkers," Jeremy said, a seriousness in his voice. Let me finish and I will explain.

The sandpainting had a completely black background with one figure in the center and an animal head in each of the four corners. The animal heads were wolf, coyote, bear, and mountain lion. They all had extremely dangerous looking fangs. The figure in the middle was blood red with a white head wearing an animal cape, a wolf. Its arms were outstretched to either side, ending in sharp claws. From each arm, from wrist to shoulder were four crow feathers. The face of the lone figure was ominous, having sharp teeth like a wolf, but the representation of a man. Its legs were spread wide, between them, three spear points pointing down and ending in the chest of what looked like a prone man.

The two generals were looking over his shoulder, fascinated as he prepared the sandpainting. To them, the painting, about four feet in diameter, looked ominous. They looked at each other, eyes wide in bewilderment. Finally, Jeremy finished and stood.

"Let me explain what this is," Jeremy said. "The figure represents the Skinwalker, the feathers represent the dark spirit of the witch. The black background stands for the dark power these spirits have. The spear tips between the legs represent the power they have over the victim, laying on the ground. They are clawed creatures that are considered witches by the Navajo; they are volatile and dangerous. As far as I know, only me and my father know how to summon them. And they must never be summoned except under authority of Sun God.

Although they are dangerous to us as a people, sometimes Sun God uses them to carry out his purposes. For us, they represent witchcraft, a dark witchcraft, which is another part of our spirituality. One cannot have light without darkness and all of us, good or bad, have varying levels of a dark part of ourselves. There are places in us where the power of both good and evil are present. Think of it as Yin and Yang. These powers of both light and dark can be harnessed for either purpose. As a Medicine Man, I, as well as other Medicine Men, can utilize these powers to heal and aid members of our tribe and communities. Some Medicine Men use their power for evil.

I will seek to direct the spiritual forces represented by the Skinwalkers to cause harm specifically toward our new enemies. This is called the 'Witchery Way,' that uses human corpses for tools made from their bones, and potions that will be used to kill intended victims. A Skinwalker is a malevolent witch that can transform itself into an animal like those depicted in each corner. Ironically, these witches evolved mostly from respected healers that turned to the dark side, usually male, but they can also be female. To become a Skinwalker is like being initiated into a criminal gang. The initiation is into a secret society, which requires the person to do a very evil act such as killing a close family member, sibling, or other near relative. After they have completed this act the individual acquires supernatural powers that gives them the ability to shape-shift into any animal. The most common animals are those depicted in each corner, but they can also transform to dogs, foxes, and others. A Skinwalker typically wears the skins of the animal they transform into and look very evil, with sharp fangs and claws and other animal characteristics, but they still generally walk upright like a man. In shapeshifting to the animal, they inherit that animals' characteristics such as speed, strength, stealth, endurance, and other characteristics. It is taboo among the Navajo to wear the pelt of any predatory animal because of this."

"Are you telling us that these things can kill a person?" Jason asked.

"Absolutely," Jeremy said. "Not only that, but they can take possession of the bodies of human victims if that person locks their eyes with the Skinwalker. Thus, when he is summoned in a little while, do not even look at him above the chin. Their eyes have a way of locking onto yours whether you want to or not. I cannot stress this enough — do not look them in the eyes. If you do, I cannot help you."

"I presume they look like the animal they shape shift into," Lorenzo said. "Is there a way to tell them from the real animal?"

"Yes," Jeremy replied. "Their eyes are distinctly different than those of the animals into which they transform. Their eyes look human but turn dark red if a light is shown upon them. But then, when they transform back to a human, their eyes look like the animal they favor. They actually recruit people to their society."

"So, what you're saying is they are very dangerous, correct?" Jason queried.

"And then some," Jeremy said. "It is not only the shapeshifting and eye-lock you need to worry about, but they also have the ability to read the minds of others, control their thoughts, destroy things and kill."

"They sound like lots of fun," Lorenzo said, with a small

nervous laugh.

"Oh, but that's not all," Jeremy said.

"Are you telling us they can do other things?" Jason asked.

"Precisely, they can control all the creatures of the night and make them do their bidding such as owls, wolves, snakes, especially deadly ones such as rattlesnakes. And, to make matters worse, they can call upon the spirits of the dead and reanimate corpses to attack their enemies. So, don't go anywhere alone. They are deadly and will kill you."

"You have me convinced," Lorenzo said.

"Oh, sometimes I wish I had their powers," Jeremy said. "They can run fast as the wind and even jump high cliffs. The greed, anger, and revenge of our enemies will be their undoing. Without continual killing, they will perish themselves. I am not in agreement with many Medicine Men, but it is my opinion they live somewhere between heaven and hell in a third dimension we are unable to see. They are rarely seen but you will be seeing them, just stay out of their way and tell your men to do the same. Fortunately, in this venture, they will be in the service of Sun God."

Jeremy walked over to the fire and placed the few remaining logs on top. It glowed brighter and brighter. He then took out a few pieces of peyote and handed one to each of the generals."

"Chew this, slowly," Jeremy said. "I want you to sit here General White and you are here General Bardos. I will sit between you and slightly ahead. We will form a triangle facing the sandpainting; the power of three. Again, whatever you do, look not into the eyes of the Skinwalker you are about to see and do not be afraid. Most importantly, do not speak or move or you will be dead men. The general's eyes widened at the remark.

Jeremy took his seat as they chewed the peyote. The fire began to die down. It was then that Jeremy began his chant, to summon the Skinwalker. Each word was repeated several times in pitches ranging from low to high, repeated over and over in a softly spoken tone. The chant began to increase in intensity. At the peak of it, drums began to beat. The generals looked about and saw nothing. The drumbeats grew louder as the chants of invisible warriors took over. Without warning, behind the sand painting, the generals saw warriors beating their drums through a portal that had quickly opened; drumbeats gave way to howls from the wolves walking back and forth in front of the drummers.

"Major, that's the beating of drums," a captain said, walking over, the other officers crowding around. "Where's it coming from?"

"There," Major Price said, pointing to the glow of a fire high up on the ridge.

"You mean the generals and Jeremy are beating drums?" the captain asked.

"I don't think so, they did not have any with them. I think this is like supernatural. I heard the general mention some of the things Jeremy can do; he's a Medicine Man you know."

"We should investigate at once," the captain said, he and the other officers starting to move forward.

Major Price held out his arm, blocking the captains path.

"I have strict orders that no matter what happens, we are not to go up there. We will obey the command!"

"But...." the captain said, being cut off.

"There are no buts, captain, that's an order."

The officers slowly walked off and went back to what they had been doing. They were not keen on investigating anyway. Within a couple of minutes, they were all talking and joking again, looking nervously toward the ridge, uncomfortable at the ghastly howling.

The embers of the fire glowed red as the area around them darkened; the howls stopped. Slowly, a white gray mist began appearing in the sandpainting as it started to glow brightly. A column of light, mostly red and black emerged from the painting, from below the ground and turned almost black, which instantly changed into a Skinwalker. More terrifying than the one in the painting because now it was no longer a painting, it was directly in front of them in all its ferocity. Its eyes glowing a bright ruby red. It looked almost exactly as depicted, but its feet were very large, in human form with sharp claws for the toes and the same for the hands. It was evil and ominous. When it had finished transforming from the mist, the Skinwalker stood just above the sandpainting, looking down on Jeremy.

"I am Death Feather," the Skinwalker said. "Do you not wish to look me in the eyes?"

The generals were shaking their heads no, remembering what Jeremy had told them.

"Very well. Why have you summoned me?"

"I am under direction of Sun God to give a command for help," Jeremy replied.

"Then, I am bound to obey," Death Feather said. "What help do you seek?"

"We have enemies making preparations for war, to invade us," Jeremy said. "This is the area where the battle will be. They will kill all they can, including us."

"More White Eyes?" Death Feather said.

"No, they come from afar."

"Why do you need our help when you have the White Eyes? Why should we help them?"

"These enemies come to take our country and to destroy tribal lands as well. The White Eyes do not have enough power to stop them because of traitors in their midst."

"We will let no one take our land," Death Feather said. Who are these enemies?"

No sooner had Death Feather said this than directly to his right, a bright light appeared. It was shaped like a diamond. The Mediator stepped out.

"Death Feather, these are your enemies."

From the diamond shaped portal behind him, appeared scenes of military units: infantry, jets, ships, tanks, planes, and submarines. As the images played, they were magnified clearly identifying Chinese and Russian military units and a global map showing the countries.

"These come to rob our land of its resources and colonize us," Mediator said. "When they are finished, neither the White Eyes, nor we will remain. Those not killed outright, will be sent to prison camps to work until they die."

"What would you like me to do?" Death Feather asked.

"Kill all you can," Mediator said, the scenes of the militaries still visible in the portal. "Have no mercy, work your darkest witchcraft and put such fear into them that the survivors will relate what they saw and put fear into their countrymen for centuries."

"What is my reward for this?" Death Feather asked.

"You will be allowed to recruit into your society any who fall before you," Mediator replied.

"Our society accepts your offer," Death Feather said. "We await the appointed time. Is there anything more?"

"One more item," Jeremy said, pulling a picture from his pocket and laying it on the ground before Death Feather.

As Death Feather looked at it, his ruby eyes grew brighter, setting the picture afire.

"What is it you wish?"

"That grievous harm come to her," Jeremy said. "Death or craziness; the vilest thing you can imagine."

"It shall be done," Death Feather said, laughing with glee.

No sooner did Death Feather say this than his form became a dark mist again, swirling down into the sandpainting like a tornado and disappearing. The generals could not believe what they were seeing. Their mouths stood agape in stunned surprise.

"You may look up now," Mediator said.

All three were looking at the Mediator as the scenes of militaries in the portal changed to a peaceful splendor of mountain tops and green meadows with the most gorgeous flowers imaginable. Standing directly behind the Mediator were many warriors in a column of four that extended past their field of view.

"All is in your hands young Medicine Man," Mediator said. "I have directions from Sun God. You are to summon the war gods, the ten tribes, and use the transparency as the battle becomes fierce and there seems no hope. It is imperative you understand and obey. It is then that all forces will combine against your enemies."

The Mediator stepped through the portal as it began slowly closing, the scene behind him still visible. Once again, the sounds of drums could be heard, growing to a crescendo and suddenly halting as the portal turned to a translucent green and disappeared. The embers of the fire glowed dimly as the three sat, not speaking. Lorenzo stood, as did Jason, looking down on Jeremy who suddenly rose to his feet from a cross-legged position, coming face to face with them. There was just enough light to make out each other's faces as the wind picked up, making an unnatural sound as it blew across the ridge and rock outcropping. It seemed to foretell that which was coming.

"In all my life I never imagined such," Lorenzo said. "Are you telling me the supernatural will fight our battle for us?"

"Absolutely not," Jeremy said. "We fight as hard as we can and maybe, just maybe, they will extend a helping hand."

"Trust me," Jason said. "We are doing all we can, I just fear it is not enough."

"I know we are," Jeremy said. "Whether it is or not, all we can do is try. Remember that a small group of focused warriors can accomplish anything?"

"Given the intelligence we received today," Lorenzo said. "We are indeed small compared to the enemy."

"Yes," Jason mused, scratching his chin. "The number of supplies and weapons suggests much more than a couple of divisions of men, tanks, and armored troop carriers. Do you think Shockwave can help us take an edge off the enemy Lorenzo?"

"Yes, we can my friend," Lorenzo replied. "With our men and the one thousand men of Lunadi's, plus the one thousand of Sky Thinker's, as well as all the tribal warriors, we will put up one hell of a fight. It may be like the Alamo where one hundred and eighty stood against five thousand, but we will make our presence known."

"You guys do your part and I'll summon the demons as it were."

The three made their way back down to the other officers. Jeremy's cell phone rang.

"Great, let me give you directions," Jeremy said, walking off.

After a few minutes he returned to the group.

"News?" Jason queried.

"Good news," Jeremy said. "Lunadi and his ten commanders, as well as Sky Thinker will arrive tomorrow morning. They're in Vegas for the night, but will be up at 4:00 a.m."

"Awesome," Lorenzo said. "I'll look forward to meeting them."

They turned in for a restless night's sleep. Daylight came early as the officers took care of their morning hygiene and gathered around the map tables, eager to continue planning. They knew that some things were being kept from them due to security reasons, but they were enjoying the strategy sessions. Just as they were getting down to business, three SUV's pulled up. As they finished introducing themselves, they got right down to business. A captain finally asked the obvious question.

"General Bardos," the captain said. "It's great to develop this strategy, but it looks like only a small force is standing against a much larger force. Shouldn't we plan for the rest of our military to assist in this operation?"

Everyone was watching the two generals as they eyed each other and Jeremy, Lunadi, and Sky Thinker. There was an awkward silence because the generals were not sure how to respond as the uneasiness grew. Finally, when it reached the point of tortuous discomfort, General Bardos motioned toward Jeremy.

"Tell them. And men, this is above top secret. It goes no further."

"Gentlemen, this is the Alamo all over again," Jeremy began. "We have Chinese and Russian forces preparing to wage war against us. No one is coming to save you. It is only us."

"What do you mean?" Major Price asked.

"Just what I said," Jeremy responded. "There are traitors in our government at the highest levels, many of them. Over half the congress is on the Chinese payroll and they have cut back all military maneuvers, aid, and supplies from the Presidents control. What we are doing is only authorized because it is under standard military drills and maneuvers. This is the only way we have been able to hide it from those in Washington who are collaborating directly with the enemy."

The generals watched the officers as what Jeremy had said sunk in. It was as if they had been gut punched because it was hard to believe. They looked around at each other, almost in a state of helplessness not knowing what to do.

"What Jeremy has told you is true," General Bardos said. "We make a stand for the country here or it dies. If word of this reaches the traitors, it dies. Who will stand with us to beat this enemy back to their own shores?"

There was a resounding yes from all.

"Now you understand why what we are doing is necessary. This is not a drill men. It is us or it is them! Now that you understand the perilous nature of what we are trying to accomplish, it is time to split into teams within your respective areas of expertise. So, let's spread out to our areas and meet late afternoon at the dry valley east of Jean. General White, you and Lunadi's men will carry out your planning for this area, here, pointing to a map. Let' head out and plan like we have never planned before. Think asymmetric warfare. We have some great resources, but we will be outmatched, at least initially and it is there we must hold."

General's Qiang and Leung were meeting at Port Brito for the last time prior to operations. They were standing outside, looking at Lake Nicaragua through their binoculars. Even knowing where they were, their ships were difficult to spot. There was a smile on Li's face.

"My friend," Li said. "You have done an outstanding job. Pulling the warships in by tug and camouflaging them like you did. It is amazing. I am looking right at them and they are almost invisible."

"I have done all I can," Wen said. "Do you have a date set yet?"

"Yes," Li replied. "But I need to meet with President Jin, MND Dong, Minister Gan, and the rest of the Politburo for final approval. How much preparation time do you need once they say yes?"

"Why Li my comrade," Wen said with a huge grin. "My navy is ready to commence operations immediately."

"Outstanding my friend," Li said as he gave a traditional Chinese greeting out of respect. "I knew you would not let me down."

"I need to ask you again," Wen said. "Are you sure this is wise? Like I said before, there is a gun behind every blade of grass in the United States. Are we prepared for that?"

"Do not worry comrade," Li said. "With our initial barrage followed by an EMP, we should be fine. We will do an old-fashioned blitzkrieg on them; it will be over before they know it. After all, they showed us how to do this very attack in Desert Storm. And those foolish leaders in Washington have allowed us to train with their military for years."

"I always wondered why," Wen said.

"It is because we own most of their politicians," Li said. "They will do anything we ask. The only thing they care about is money and power. Well, I will show them power very shortly."

Wen stood, looking at his warships in Lake Nicaragua. As he gazed across the calm blue green water, he could not shake the feeling of apprehension that washed over his body. He had known Li for an awfully long time and trusted him and his judgement, still, to attack the United States would be a formidable undertaking, whether they initially had the upper hand or not. He feared greatly lest they awakened the reprisal of all patriots because he knew that the patriots would fight to their last breath, even if they had only stones for weapons. Regardless of his feelings, he was under command of the MND and would do his duty as required. A cloud of anxiety was visible on his face.

Li, also looking at the ships, turned to look at his friend. It was apparent he had misgivings but there was no doubt he would do his duty. Looking at his friend caused a relapse of his own feelings about what they were about to do and about the vision he had while in Vegas. He had pushed them to the back of his mind and had been so preoccupied that he had forgotten about his fears. He too felt a twinge of trepidation. However, he was certain with his control of much of the congress that they would do his bidding to shortchange supplies to the military and keep most of them off the battlefield. To ensure this, he had a card he was ready to play that would make certain of it.

"My friend," Li said suddenly. "I leave you now and return to Beijing. Expect to hear from me soon. They will give approval; I am certain of that. When they do, I will send you a final date. It will be open communication, a string of fifteen numbers. Look at the first two and the last two for the launch date. That is when you will need to be on station. All other communications will be given through our secure military network."

General White along with Lunadi and his commanders, as well as a few staff officers, were looking out across the rocks and desert. It was here that they would stop the enemy or be overrun and the U.S. would fall. An awful feeling of the reality of their responsibility crept over them. Still, all they could do was the best that they could do. The general kept glancing at Lunadi and his commanders. Here were true warriors he thought. They were logical, pragmatic, cold blooded, and thorough. Their eyes showed no fear, and they were piercing; they assessed every detail and missed nothing. They were the eyes of natural born killers because that is what Lunadi had trained them to be and this would be their trial by fire.

"A penny for your thoughts," Lorenzo said.

"Hmmmm," Lunadi murmured, looking through his binoculars. "We have the funnel of death leading into the valley of death. We couldn't ask for a better scenario."

"How so?" Lorenzo asked.

"Suppose you were being engaged as an enemy force by Bardos and his tanks and air cover, but you needed to make your objective. What would you do?"

"The natural response would be to outrun them and secure your position as one of defense."

"Exactly. Do you see that large valley?" Lunadi was pointing at their map.

"Yes," Lorenzo said. "What of it?"

"It is twenty miles from Primm to this point. When they pass Primm, they'll likely break formation and scatter across the desert then, they'll join together again, creating a funnel of death before they pass into the last valley. It is the only path to their objective. We have six miles to stop them before they get to the outskirts of Vegas. General Bardos and his men will handle them out on the valley and continually harass their flanks as they start into the last six miles, the valley of the shadow of death. When they get here it is Shockwave and us, the general's men and tanks having fallen back."

"I think I see where you are going," Lorenzo said. "We deploy sniper teams all along the route and kill all we can."

"Yes, but not just sniper teams," Lunadi said. "Every weapon we can utilize becomes a sniper weapon against personnel, planes, and armor."

"What are you saying?" Lorenzo asked.

"Bardos said we would have access to the Javelin anti-tank missile so, we deploy them with our sniper teams. We will also have teams with stingers missiles for anti-aircraft defense. They won't be effective unless close, but they can help kill air support so, they kill equipment, we kill men."

"That's brilliant," Lorenzo said. "We harass them through this six-mile pass and kill all that moves. The range is certainly manageable. But there are some of these areas that are fifteen hundred to two thousand yards. That's a long way for a sniper."

"My men can hit ninety percent at that range," Lunadi said confidently.

"I had heard, but was skeptical," Lorenzo said.

"Everyone always is," Lunadi said.

"Commander Panther, come here please," Lunadi shouted.

"Yes sir,"

"General White, this is one of my commanders, Osceola Panther," Lunadi said, a look of pride on his face. "He is in charge of our long gunners. Those are our men that can shoot two thousand yards and beyond, accurately."

"Commander, did you bring your rifle as I requested?" Lunadi asked.

"Yes."

"Bring it please and let us demonstrate to General White your men's capabilities."

While Osceola fetched his rifle, Lunadi was looking through his binoculars, finding suitable targets. He ranged them with his binoculars – two thousand, two hundred and fifty-two yards; the second was twelve hundred and seventy-four yards. Osceola returned with his rifle ready to fire.

"Would you care to look through the scope?" Lunadi asked Lorenzo.

"Don't mind if I do," Osceola handed him the rifle and he looked through it. "This is an interesting scope, haven't seen one quite like it before."

"Quite," Lunadi said. "We can do rapid engagements from close to far. Let's demonstrate."

While they had been talking, Osceola had gotten into a prone shooting position.

"Ready sir," Osceola said.

"Okay, two targets, the boulder against the low-lying ridge directly in front of you. Second target is about twenty degrees southwest of that one. Range – 2,252 yards and 1,274 respectively. Wind is oblique right, six mile per hour; density altitude is 4.6."

"Both targets identified sir,"

"Send when ready."

All of the commanders and staff officers had gathered behind Osceola and also had identified the targets. They were shaking their heads. It was obvious they didn't think anyone could hit those, at least the far one.

"That boulder along the ridge is awfully far," a captain said. No sooner had he said it than the report of the rifle blasted their eardrums. A direct hit: six seconds later, the rifle sounded again, another direct hit.

"Wait a minute," Lorenzo exclaimed, "He didn't adjust his turrets."

"Like I said General," Lunadi remarked. "It's a rapid engagement scope. Once you have the range, wind, and density altitude you just shoot away."

"That's incredible," Lorenzo said. "Is there a chance we could get more of those right away?"

"I'll call and check on the supply," Lunadi said. "Better yet here."

Lunadi passed the general his cell. "Ask for David, tell him what you need."

"Hello,…" Lorenzo said into the phone as he walked away. The other officers were impressed.

"I can't wait to get my hands on one of those," a captain said.

"Here," Osceola offered. "Would you men like to try it?"

"Hell yes," the captain said. "Would we ever."

The officers gathered around as Osceola and a couple of his warriors instructed them on the use of the scope. Each fired several shots; it was obvious that they enjoyed it. More importantly, it helped relieve a building tension and apprehension for that which they had been asked to do. And yet one more time, patriots and warriors would put their lives on the line for an ungrateful government and large part of the populace. One often wondered how many people would step up and help save a country that they and their families called their own. Sadly, history has taught that it is few, though it always seems to be enough. The coming battle would determine if it were.

Minister Gan was meeting with the Politburo in yet again, a very heated session, redressing the general. Like a great many politicians, he was overweight from too many elaborate dinners at the people's expense and at this moment was attempting to get the President and General to stand down from what he considered a foolhardy and dangerous idea.

"I am telling you gentlemen that this is a foolish move," Gan said. "We can buy all the food we need from the Americans. I personally have set in motion a plan where we can solicit their help for greater food production for the future and they are even willing to fund up to an initial ten billion dollars to initiate the program. Their Secretary of State has guaranteed it. The current purchase will see us through until the agricultural season is finished and harvest is complete. Then, we will have all the food our country needs."

"Until when?" General Li Qiang asked vehemently. "At what point will we have all we need?"

"I understand your feelings general," Gan stated. "But we cannot let personal desires and hatred cloud our judgement. If we fail, a nuclear war could result. Their current President is not a wimp as has been most of them. He will not back down."

"Let me deal with him through our Washington contact," Li said. "We should not let his potential decision hold us back. I'm telling you, we can own and colonize their entire country, ChinaA. We should have no less a goal. For years we have been second to them, now we have the power to beat them!"

"Enough of this bickering," President Jin interrupted. "Do you have everything in order if we agree?"

"We can launch immediately," Li said. "There is no way they can stop us."

President Jin looked thoughtfully around the table at the other ministers. Privately, he was of similar mindset to Minister Gan, but he could not show it because it would be a sign of weakness. He swiveled around in his chair and looked out the window. Seconds seemed like minutes. Li was becoming impatient, but he held his tongue. More than anything he had ever wanted in this life, he wanted to wage war against the Americans. The other ministers were trying to determine whose side to be on. If things went south, the people would revolt because they knew President Weld would make them pay; a retaliation would certainly be forthcoming. If they played it safe, they would be on Minister Gan's side, but then, the future would be bleak because they would be going against the two most powerful men in the country. Still, they did not like the idea of going to war. Despite their belief in the general, Gan was right. It was to both countries interests that they cooperate. Ah, the greed of men was something that, regardless of the outcome of a potential war, could not be killed by a bullet. Finally, the President turned around to face them.

"Ministers," Jin said. "We are facing the most critical decision ever made by the Politburo. The decision we make today will alter the course of three superpowers and the destiny of the entire world. Your opinions please."

The ministers sat stunned. So, it was to fall on them. They knew they could be easily replaced, notwithstanding the consequences, not one of them wanted to go first. Minister Gan knew he was right, but he too was aware of the consequences. Awkwardly, he decided to speak.

"Ministers, President, General Qiang," Gan began. "You know my position on this matter. You also know that whatever is decided I will support it. With that in mind, I would notwithstanding, ask you to contemplate what I have said. As I see it, we have two choices. First, we can pursue the peaceful option, which I believe offers great rewards. The Americans will fund us to become more self-sufficient agriculturally, which will happen next cropping season. The food we purchase now, will adequately see us through until then, plus another quarter. Second, we go to war as the general is suggesting. Yes, we may beat them and if so, all our resource problems are forever over. But if we fail, millions more could perish due to a retaliatory strike. Those are our choices as I see them."

Minister Gan, was standing as he delivered his message, looking each Minister in the eyes, hoping to read what they were thinking and if, at this perilous moment, they would be men of reason. He sat down. Everyone was looking at the opposite end of the table toward the MND.

"Well comrades," Minister of Defense Yu Dong said. "Minister Gan is correct; those are our only two choices. Therefore, I will direct my questions initially to General Qiang. General, do your really believe that we can and will defeat the Americans?

"Minister of Defense," Li said. "Yes, that is without question. We have studied their tactics for years and we have trained with them. Not only that, we have also copied their best weapons and made them superior, especially our warships, fighter jets, and tanks. Our equipment and our moral are superior. Of that I am certain. If you doubt me, ask Admiral Leung."

"We do not doubt you comrade," MND said. "While we do have two choices, if we choose the second, there is no turning back and what Minister Gan has said is correct concerning them."

"You have my word Ministers," Li said. "Our PLAGF and PLAN will not fail."

"Failure is not an option, if we proceed down this path," President Jin said. "I need not remind you what will happen if you fail. Not only to you, but to your friends, family, and men."

Suddenly, the room was deathly quiet. Every man in it knew the price of failure at the level of stature they had risen to. At this moment, everyone's head on the chopping block and they would all live or die by their decisions today. Unlike other governments, loss of face was dealt with severely in their line of work. General Qiang stood, looking them directly in the eyes as he squared his shoulders, his uniform a perfect fit for his athletic frame. His eyes piercing and unyielding.

"I give you my word we will not fail," Li said. "We have superiority in every way."

"Tell us general," MND Dong said. "Describe your basic strategy."

"Minister, I will put it in simple terms for those of you who do not understand military operations," Li said. "I will demonstrate on the map, *walking over to a large map of the U.S. on the wall behind them.* We will strike from several locations, including the northwest from Seattle and Portland, from Long Beach in the southwest and from Ottawa and Thunder Bay area in Ontario where our troops will move southward into the U.S. The Russians, as per our agreement with them which you worked out, will be assisting from the Gulf of Mexico, landing at Houston and New Orleans."

"That seems like it will stretch our forces very thin," argued a politburo member.

"Under normal circumstances, I would agree," Li said. "Let me explain the plan of attack. As you know we copied the Russians in their efforts to manufacture and deploy container-based missile systems. As we did with the American weapons, we have made some major improvements. We have more than twelve hundred missiles ready to launch when we decide to move, plus hundreds more from our destroyers and container ships. They are targeting every major military infrastructure and the major hubs of the U.S. power grid and communications, including their major telecom hotels in New York and San Francisco and all major cities. We will launch our missiles then set off two EMP blasts in the upper atmosphere to disable most of their communications long enough for us to deploy and finally, take Seattle, Portland and Los Angeles for bases of operations as we move toward Denver and Las Vegas to solidify our power base. The Russians will move up the eastern seaboard toward Washington and secure it."

"The Americans have a large army," Gan interrupted. "Do you just think they are going to sit back and let us waltz in?"

"We have planned for that scenario," Li said. "May I, President?"

"Yes, inform them."

"Considering that scenario, we have been working with the North Koreans to increase hostilities along the 38th Parallel to a fever pitch, which as you know, they are good at. This will draw a major portion of the U.S. fleets and ground forces to South Korea, especially once they begin whining about potential invasion from the north. This will leave the Americans weakened allowing us to secure air superiority and take the major cities I described."

"That is all well," Gan said. "But what are you going to do about the east coast?"

"Our missiles will take care of all that from many container ships in their eastern ports; all of these are already on station, as well as separate, land positioned container systems. New York, Philadelphia, Washington, Norfolk, Atlanta, and many others are already targeted. All we need do is send the launch signal."

"Impressive," MND Gong said. "Gentlemen, is that a

satisfactory explanation?"

"Are you certain the North Koreans can draw out the U.S. military?" another politburo member asked.

"We have promised them all the resources they need to do so," Li said. "Not only that, once the Americans find out we are attacking their country, they will be forced to bring everyman to the fight. It will be too late, but when they do so, they will almost certainly remove their infantry from the 38th Parallel and then, North Korea will invade the south. It will be epic."

The ministers sat around the table looking at each other, talking about the map and the general plan; they were beginning to nod their heads in agreement. Li had given a fine presentation, allaying their fears and failure of such an attack on U.S. soil. Of course, saying it would happen and making it work were two different things. Without knowing the nature of warfare and how fluid and dynamic it was, they were convinced by General Qiang's explanation. They had no idea that the best laid plans in battle were often thrown out the window once bullets began to fly.

"I suggest we put it to a vote," President Jin said. "However, due to the nature of this plan and because I value all of your decisions, let us cast a secret ballot with only the words yes or no on it. We will go or no go based on majority vote."

The politburo members, the Politburo of the Chinese Communist Party, formally the Central Political Bureau of the Communist Party of China were about the cast the most important vote in their history. The President picked up his phone and a moment later, his secretary appeared, carrying a large ornate metal, Chinese bowl decorated with village scenes in enamel. She passed by each of the politburo members, including the President, as one-by-one, they cast their vote, written on a small piece of paper, into the bowl.

"Ling," President commanded. "Count each yes and no vote and lay them on the table please."

"Yes sir," Ling replied as she pulled each cast vote out of the bowl. She separated them into two stacks in front of her, near the President.

"What is the tally?" Jin asked.

"Four yes and three no, sir," Ling said, having no idea what the vote was about.

"Very well," Jin replied. "Leave us please and close the door."

"Gentlemen, the vote is cast," Jin said. "We launch upon General Qiang's orders.

As Gan left the meeting, he felt nauseated. This was completely insane, but he had no choice but to go along. He would support the vote, but knew in his heart a reckoning was coming, of that he was sure. But that might not be all bad. With his considerable influence, he may just become President. He would need to call in his allies, ready to move at a moment's notice if General Qiang's operation failed. A smile creased his lips, hoping it would, as he strode down the hallway and out of the Great Hall of the People, into Tiananmen Square. It was a sunny, cool day, and he began to revel at the thoughts of what lay ahead. He was wondering how he could better position himself. Deep down, he believed the operation would not succeed; in actuality, it was ludicrous to think that it would. Still, he needed to cover all his bases if he were to survive and challenge President Jin.

Erin was in the Oval Office with the President. She had just walked in and taken a seat on the sofa directly in front of the Resolute desk. President Weld held up one finger as he finished his phone conversation. The look on her face made it clear she was concerned.

"What is it?" Phil asked.

"The Speaker of the House is trying to get others on board to execute the 25th Amendment in addition to impeachment," Erin replied.

"She is going to make a push that you are unfit for office and unable to perform your duties."

"That will prove difficult, even for them. The entire country can see that I have no problem carrying out my duties."

"Everyone knows that, but they will concoct something. They will lie as they always do and get their propaganda media machine to push the narrative."

"That will not work."

"Be real Phil, half the people are duped into believing everything the media tells them, true or not. This will be all about perception."

"Hmmmm, I understand."

"How do you suggest we counter it?"

"Nick should be here any moment. Let's discuss options with him. He has been digging deep."

"At least everything else is on track."

"How so?" Erin asked.

"I have reports from the generals. All containers they could find have been sabotaged and all container ships found with missiles are being tracked, already placed in target status. They are out in the desert developing final strategies, our own missile systems are in place on land and at sea, submarines are on station doing drills, and everything has been planned out. The warrior leaders we met with at Chaco Canyon will be on site in the desert within the next ten days. I have every confidence in the generals, Lunadi and Jeremy. With a little help from our supernatural friends, we just may pull this off. If we do not, the Speaker will be of no concern."

The door opened and Nick walked in. The SOS had somewhat of a grin on his face.

"You heard?" Phil asked.

"Yes sir," Nick replied, taking a seat next to Erin.

"Erin has filled me in, what do you have?" Phil asked.

"Good news for a change," Nick said, smiling.

"Thank God," Phil replied, getting up from his chair and taking a position on the sofa across from the two.

"Tell us?" Phil asked.

"You'll be happy to know that we have gone through the servers of the State Department and the Congress and found substantial evidence of the Speaker working with one of our senior officials in State with both the Chinese and Russians. We are still decoding a lot of the messages, which were in those languages. There is, however, clear evidence of treason. The servers the information is on have been seized and replaced with new ones, which we continue to monitor. So far, no one knows except a couple of NSA technical gurus who are monitoring all of their communications, as well as on tech from State."

"How do you suggest we proceed?" Phil asked, a tremor in his voice.

"I believe the legal course would take too long and it would be a race of us against them and their rush to invoke the 25th Amendment sir." Nick said. "Thus, I suggest you have someone meet privately with the Speaker and lay down the facts. Either back off or be tried for treason. The emails and communications clearly identify her and her adherence to the enemies bearing down on us in the form of giving unlawful aid. Additionally, we have evidence of payoffs through banking transactions. If that does not work, we can always have her arrested under terrorism charges, which as you know are broad and will preclude a phone call. In other words, she disappears as long as you want her to."

"How do we charge her with terrorism?" Phil asked.

"It's simple really," Nick replied. "Under section 802 of the USA PATRIOT Act, one of the main acts is described as 'to influence the policy of a government by intimidation or coercion' and that will have some teeth combined with other evidence we have. Even though the act has mothed, the general public is familiar with it."

"If we arrest her, what is the best way?" Phil asked.

"Sir, it would need to be done discreetly," Erin said. "We do not initially want word of this leaking to the press. We make up some contagious illness and she just disappears at 2:00 a.m. She lives alone, her husband stays at their west coast property; we need only a few reliable officers to make the arrest and ship her ass to Gitmo or a black site."

"I'm damned tempted to do it right now," Phil said, wiping his brow. "Let's discreetly go the first route. If that does not work, we will go to plan B. Keep NSA monitoring her around the clock and make sure you have people you can trust. Also, it is time to keep her under surveillance physically, 24/7. She is cunning and we can ill afford to give her any breaks."

"Understood sir," Nick said as he arose to leave the room. "I'll get right on it."

"What are you thinking?" Phil asked.

"That's a good plan and in my opinion the only way to deal with that evil bitch," Erin said. "She would sell out the country and her own mother to get another ounce of control. We are in a shit storm aren't we sir?"

"No doubt," Phil muttered. "It's the perfect storm and will

result in failure or success. If the people knew what was coming, they would run or fight."

"But we are commanded by Sun God not to tell them sir," Erin said sadly.

"Yes," Phil said. "They must choose their own side, either loyalty to him or, death I suppose. It is a big burden knowing what we know and not being able to say anything."

"It is at that," Erin said somberly.

CHAPTER 10

Battle Prep

The dryness of the tan desert stood in stark contrast to the blue sky, not a cloud in it. It was great flying weather; General Bardos was busy making sure all his supplies were on the way as he watched a steady stream of cargo planes land at Creech Air Force Base, about thirty miles northwest of Vegas. General White and his Shockwave troops had arrived, as well as warriors from many tribes at predetermined locations in the desert west of the city. As the planes taxied to their preassigned hangars for unloading, there was a frenzy of activity; cargo was no sooner unloaded onto a truck than it was moving down the highway. General Bardos did not believe in keeping all his eggs in one basket thus, the supplies were being distributed based on personnel number and types of weapons and equipment. Everything was coming together, and he had a gut feeling there was little time left to prepare. To an observer, everything appeared as normal operations. Out in the desert, the arrival of thousands of men at different locations was out of sight of all but those in the know.

Lunadi had flown back home for a brief two days amid all that was happening. Staying in contact with his commanders and tying up loose ends. He was leaning on the railing of his upper deck, enjoying the view. Usually positive, he was suddenly apprehensive about what the future held and if he would survive the coming battle. His thoughts were interrupted by the sounding of a chime and then, several more. It was Erin; the chimes coming from motion detector activity as her car passed each one. He stood on the deck, watching a nearby curve in the dirt road intently as it wound its way through the ponderosa pines. A small movement caught his eye. He saw Erin's car and he watched the vehicle until it pulled up directly in front of the house. Erin was behind the wheel, smiling and waving at him as she pulled to a stop and slid out of the car.

"Hey there stranger," she said, a broad smile on her face.

"Fancy meeting you in a place like this," Lunadi said then, rushed downstairs to greet her. He opened the door and stood aghast at her beauty. Her raven hair fell below her shoulders and over a white button up blouse. She was wearing blue jeans that she filled out more than any woman he had ever seen. Her piercing gray eyes were looking directly into his, a softness to her gaze. He could not help admiring her beauty as her fit frame was damn near perfect in dimensions with full C breasts and olive-toned skin.

"Hello my love," Erin said, grabbing him.

The two stood hugging and kissing as if they had not seen each other for years; lovers who had been separated far too long."

"It is so nice to see you," Lunadi said. "Let me help you with your things."

"I only brought a small overnight bag," Erin said. "Phil needs me back in the office day after tomorrow. We are in a pickle, aren't we?"

"I am afraid so," Lunadi said. "We have good men, and they are focused, and we have good equipment, but they have more. The numbers favor them."

"True," Erin said smiling softly. "But all of us believe in you and Jeremy along with the generals. All our hopes rest on you."

"We will do all we can. And, we do have some surprises up our sleeve."

"I suppose this is the last time we will see each other for a while my love," Erin said. "We should make the most of it. Come, I'll make the coffee this time and we will enjoy it on your upper deck."

As Erin made the coffee and put everything on a tray to carry it upstairs, she looked around Lunadi's family room, kitchen, and dining room from where she stood at the kitchen counter. It was a beautiful place she thought as she looked up and out the windows at the Sangre de Cristo mountain range. She thought about the first time she had seen Lunadi in Washington and how her heart had jumped a beat at the site of him. He was a handsome man and determined. It was in his nature and anyone with an eye could see. He was a warrior, yet he was compassionate. There was something about him that drew her in. She felt the butterfly's coming again. Every time she thought about him now, they came, and it was pleasant.

She let out a sigh as she realized her feelings for him were unlike any she had before, including her ex-husband. As she carried the coffee upstairs, she knew in her heart that she would always have an undying love for this man. He was willing to put his life on the line for his country, even for people he despised and more importantly, he had let the guard down around his heart for her. She set the tray down on a the small stone table and began pouring coffee, black for her and cream and sugar for him. It was surprising how much she already knew about his personal habits. Lunadi came up behind her just as she was finishing and grabbed her around the waist, pulling her close. He could smell her fragrant perfume and breathed it in as he bent down and began kissing the nape of her neck as he slowly moved his hands up and cupped them over her firm breasts. A playboy bunny would have been second rate compared to her physique and beauty. A soft moan escaped her lips as she turned and looked him in the eyes. He melted because he could see the love in them. A love, like his, not easily given. She pulled upward and kissed him, her tongue exploring the depth of his mouth and his exploring hers. She could feel his manhood begin to throb against her thigh as she pulled away.

"Our coffee is getting cold," she whispered hoarsely. "We have time for this later."

She pulled away and picked up the coffee, handing him a cup. They leaned on the railing, looking across the mountains, another snow having just white-washed them.

"It is truly beautiful here," Erin whispered. "So peaceful; It makes me feel at home."

"To me, you are home," Lunadi said softly, looking into her eyes. "Your being here brings more tranquility."

"Thank you," she said, a single tear escaping and rolling down her cheek.

"What is it?" he asked.

"I fear for our future and I want to know what you think of our relationship?"

"You want complete honesty? She nodded. Very well. I find myself swallowed up by your beauty and character, by your intelligence and feistiness, everything about you. I promised myself I would not let my guard down again, but for you, it is an impossible task. I feel an attraction unlike what I have felt before."

"I feel the same my love," Erin whispered. "I have butterflies in my stomach every time I think of you and of us. All day, I long to be with you and too often I find myself in a daydream being with you."

Lunadi leaned against her, shoulders touching as he pecked her on the forehead, touching his to hers. Despite the predicament the nation was in, its fate to be decided by a live or die battle, a peaceful feeling overcame them as they stood, heads touching, the late afternoon sun beginning to sink low on the horizon. An orange orb emitting a faint aura around it as it hung above an orange strip of light basking the top of the peaks. They stood watching until the sun sank below the peaks, the orange glow giving way to faint blue as the stars above slowly became visible.

Both were filled with lust as Lunadi bent down and picked her up in his arms, carrying her downstairs and into the bedroom where he tossed her on her back onto the bed. She bounced a little as he climbed atop her, kissing with a passion they had never known. He began kissing her gently on the lips as he slowly unbuttoned her blouse, one button at a time, continuing to kiss her body on the way down. His anticipation was getting the better of him as he unsnapped her bra and unbuttoned and pulled off her jeans. She wore only a purple thong beneath. As he leaned forward to pull it off, she pulled him close, delivering a wet passionate kiss as she scratched his back with her nails. Slowly, ever so gently, he began to pull down her thong, kissing the area around the thin strip of fabric stretching from the front to the rear. Erin began to softly moan. She hadn't been touched in a while and it was obvious Lunadi knew how to caress in the perfect areas, his tongue ever so gentle. She began to writhe a little as he continued kissing and lightly licking around the thong near her privates. Gently, the thong was removed as she lay there in all her naked beauty, her nipples standing erect in her excitement.

"My turn mister," she said as she pulled him beside her and jumped on top.

She eagerly pulled off his sweatshirt then pushed him back on the bed as she began licking his nipples while she unbuckled his belt and jeans, deftly pulling them off. Next came his shorts and he too, lay naked before her. He was well built, better than she expected and in shape, the physical type. Her lust made her ache, tingling with a desperate need as she stared at his bulging cock, veins distended, his erection so hard it arched above his lean abdomen, pointing at his navel. Moisture beaded on the dark, plum-colored head. Unconsciously, she licked her lips, very nice she thought. She was about to go down on him when he tossed her onto her back like a doll and, slowly kissed her as his tongue migrated down her neck then atop her nipples one by one as he licked, tickled, and sucked first one then, the other, as his free right hand cupped her left breast and his left hand was softly massaging her flower box, occasionally letting one and two fingers insert themselves inside. Erin began to squirm almost uncontrollably at his touch. He moved down from her nipples as he gently ran his fingers through her pubic hair, then slowly began kissing her inner thighs, her legs spread wide. As he kissed, he slowly let his tongue drift to the skin surrounding her flower box. He began kissing it, little succulent smacks, lips pursed, no tongue. His first kisses were below the clitoris as he began to softly breathe hot air gently across and onto her vulva then, ever so slowly, began to blow it across her clitoris as he inserted two fingers to rub and gently caress her sensitive insides. Erin was writhing, her body undulating as waves of lust and pleasure washed over her, surrendering to ecstasy, spasms of satisfaction as she lost herself in the moment.

Lunadi was savoring every second; there was no rush, they had all the time they wanted. At this moment, there were no other cares. As he continued softly kissing and lightly blowing, he ever so gently began caressing her clitoris with his tongue, his fingers still inserted. Her scent was provocative and her taste powerful as he next plunged his tongue deep into her orifice. Erin began to moan, louder and louder. She had never experienced such ecstasy before. His tongue was mightier than the sword. It was like his kisses and licks were alluring, never knowing what would happen next as her excitement built. He backed off the kisses and began flirting with the inner lips of her vulva, tracing the edges with his fingertips as he squeezed and pinched them gently. He was making love to her as subtly and lightly as a feather. It was as if he could tell she was getting too excited and began to pull her back, to prolong the pleasure. He began to gently stimulate the smooth area just above the clitoris hood then, softly began to tap the region just below it and above the main entrance. He began to tease her again with his tongue, this time at the bottom of the lower entrance and slowly began to gently lick the area, stimulating the clit with his right thumb. He was wandering now with both fingers and tongue as he brought her excitement to a crescendo and then backed off again and again. Erin began to scream and moan, her excitement so great she was about to explode. He worked his way up again to her nipples as she suddenly grabbed his manhood and thrust it inside her.

Oh my god she thought as he began a slow rhythm. She was enjoying every stroke enormously as he slowly pumped in and out, probing eight inches deep. Wrapping her legs around and behind his waist, she began forcing him harder and harder into her, getting into a rhythmic motion. She was about to explode in climax but didn't want to. Suddenly, she twisted to the side, throwing him on his back and mounted him in the cowgirl position so she could control the pace. She began with a slow tempo at first and began to increase the pace with her excitement. Both were moaning, getting louder with each passing moment as their ecstasy became pure pleasure. Erin slowed just enough to change position to the reverse cowgirl and began a frenzied pace, as fast as she could. They were both screaming like one long moan as they came together. Lunadi thought his brain was going to explode. Erin fell beside him, quivering with an occasional spasm as both breathing hard, stared at each other in surprise, not believing they could have such joy. They spent the next two days in a love fest, not knowing what the future held, but knowing without a doubt they loved each other and didn't want the time to end. Whatever the future held, there was hope that it would be brighter than it appeared, that those things which were necessary they accomplish would be and that success would be won.

Panuftii Tyurin was in Hong Kong. He had arrived at a predestined restaurant where a private room had been reserved for the two generals. Today would be a momentous day. They would finalize the attack schedule and the victor would tell the tale. Like Minister Gan, Panu had his doubts about success. They would be a long way from home with little backup. Strategically, the plan looked good, if, an excessively big word, everything went according to plan. Panu had made his way to the Southern District of Hong Kong, overlooking Repulse Bay, the South China Sea beyond. It was an upscale area. The driver pulled off Repulse Bay Road and in front of the restaurant, Panu, without his two security guards, stepped out. As he reached the door, two plain clothes CSB security guards raised their hands. Panu raised his hands as one of them quickly patted him down. Signaling okay, the other quickly led him to a private back dining room. There he found Li, sipping Baijiu, a strong white wine distilled from sorghum.

"My friend," Li exclaimed, looking up! "Please join me. Have a drink. I have had prepared your favorite vodka."

"Nice to see you again," Panu said, shaking hands, picking up the vodka and giving a long sip. "So, we are close yes?"

"Very," Li replied. "Let's get down to business."

"I take it you have final approval from the Politburo," Panu said. "What have they given in terms of a schedule?"

"They leave it to us my friend," Li said, grinning. "They understand we know what we are doing. I suggest two weeks from tomorrow. Will that work for your forces?"

"Yes," Panu said. "We have everything in place and have been practicing drills for the invasion. Our last supply ships are on the way and should be arriving in Venezuela in three to four days. Are you ready?"

"You doubt?" Li queried, grinning. "We have been planning this for years, setting up resources. We were ready before Politburo approval. As we speak, our ships are sailing from Port Brito in random directions and will join off Long Beach at the appointed time."

"According to our intelligence sources, the Americans are overly concerned about North Korea," Panu said. "It has always been a hotbed and they've always sent fleets back and forth."

"Oh, but this time, it will be more than a hot bed," Li said. "It is arranged. North Korea is about to erupt, and the Americans will be compelled to send everything they have."

"If they do so, we will easily have the upper hand," Panu responded. "We couldn't ask for more."

Panu had no way of knowing that General Qiang, through his influence, had already devised a plan that would draw U.S. troops back to Korea, a repeat of the Korean War.

Outside, one of Sam's Hong Kong agents had watched Dragon and Red Star arrive but was unable to hear the conversation. He relayed the information back to Sam.

Panu and Li had brought charts and battleplans and went over them on final time, clarifying schedules, routes, manpower, and logistics. They planned everything to the last detail, acting as if they had already won.

"That covers all my friend," Li said. "Our next contact will be at launch. I will convey when we have done so, but you will likely see some explosions. When you do, move immediately, whether you have heard from me or not."

"Understood," Panu said. "Where will you be?"

"I will be on the Admirals flagship until just prior to launch," Li said. "Then, I will lead our divisions toward the objective."

"Very well," Panu said. "Have we covered everything?"

"We have," Li replied. "I will talk to you in two weeks. 7:00 a.m. is launch time, two weeks from tomorrow."

Lunadi had arrived back in the desert after an unbelievable weekend with Erin. They were planning their final defense strategy. It was complex, yet simple. If everyone performed as he knew they could, they may just have a fighting chance. General White, his Shockwave war fighters, along with Lunadi's and Sky Thinker's men, and warriors from all tribes had set up sniper positions all along the canyon through which Interstate 15 ran that would be the funnel of death. Tanks had been placed in various areas all along the route along with personnel with Javelin shoulder fired missiles, Stinger missiles, and over one thousand sniper teams. General Bardos was making final preparations for his tank battalions, A-10 Warthogs, Apache Helicopters, Cobra Gunships, and explosives of all kinds, all along the route from Long Beach to Vegas. All commanders were present for his briefing.

"We have everything in place," Jason said. "All of you have your assignments. This is going to get nasty. We are uncertain how many men they will have, but I'm expecting at least seven infantry divisions minimum with two or three armored divisions."

"Will we get any more support from the government," a war chief asked from the Cheyenne tribe.

"We must not expect any help from them," Jason said. "They are against the President and the people."

The chiefs, presidents, and leaders began murmuring as they cursed those who had been elected to lead and manage and yet, had sold the country down the river to the Chinese, UN, other foreign powers and the large corporations. He was right, there was no one coming to save them, it is only us. And, like all battles, this one would come down to boots on the ground as men fought, bled, and died to save an ungrateful nation who had caved to the liberals and their lunacy. This time however, if they won, when they won, those who would not support the fight and those who had committed treason would be removed from office permanently.

"Okay men, the way I see it, we have maybe seven or eight days to hone our maneuvers," General Bardos said. "After that, it is likely the Chinese and Russian satellites will take surveillance photos to determine if anything along their objective route has changed. They must not see any of us."

"Have you devised a way for us to efficiently practice?" A major asked.

"Good question," Jason replied. "Yes, we have arranged for a convoy of about twenty trucks, vans, and SUVs to travel from Long Beach along the same route that the enemy will follow. It's the only route. The convoy does not have military markings for a reason, but all of them have been wrapped to advertise a variety of sports drinks and products. The wrappings are in orange and bright green for visibility. The first and last vehicles in the convoy will be eighteen wheelers."

"Are we to treat them as enemy tanks, armored, and supply vehicles as they pass?" Colonel Ronnel Scott asked.

"Exactly," General Bardos said. "As they approach and pass, range them, mock blow bridges, set off charges, use them for sniper targets, etc. There will be four convoys, two from each direction, each identical to the other. You should have a practice target every hour. We will practice this for seven days. Hone your skills until you can do it in your sleep. These convoys will follow a towed crane that is moving at the same pace of armor, maybe a little faster to keep you on your toes. Take the rest of the day, inspect your equipment and men and get in place for the first drills at sunrise tomorrow."

The officers and chiefs all dispersed, talking among themselves, excited that the wait was almost over. Although they realized they could not count on help from Washington, they were upbeat and eager to get going. The generals were pleased to see that moral was high.

"This is going to work," Jeremy said. "We may be outgunned initially, but these men are determined."

"They are," General White said. "Tell me Jason, what have you devised out here in the desert once the enemy reaches your position?"

"We have some surprises up our sleeve," Jason replied. "Do you remember the attack techniques we discussed using small drones?"

"It's been a while, but yes. What of it?"

"We perfected the explosive charge," Jason said. "Our engineers developed an impact trigger mechanism. The drones will explode with any impact at twenty miles per hour or more. Not only that, but they have also devised explosives on them for anti-personnel and anti-aircraft, shaped charges for the latter. Imagine flying along and suddenly you hit one of these drones with a quarter pound of C-4 on it? No more plane."

"Interesting," Jeremy mused. "I tried flying a drone once but wasn't particularly good at it. How are you going to be able to anticipate when to launch these things based on the speed and maneuvering capability of their jets?"

"Not to worry my friends," Jason said, smiling. "These are both manual and computer operated. They use artificial intelligence systems and networking. And, we have arranged our pilots to fly along the anticipated routes so the drone operators can quickly anticipate when to launch. We will also have them airborne in some cases for easier and quicker targeting."

"Jeremy, you mentioned the other day that you had a vision of a second force helping the Chinese," Jason said. "Tell us more about that please. We do not want all our eggs in one basket."

"I saw a second force coming from the beach and a Phoenix flying above the desert. Then, the Phoenix flew away into a mountain and turned into a spirit. I could see both forces then, one coming from the west and one from the south."

"Hmmmm," General White murmured. "I was thinking something like this could happen and so was Lunadi. He is scouting the southern route now."

"Were you able to translate the vision?" Jason asked.

"Yes, and I spoke with Lunadi about it too," Jeremy said. "The other force will attempt a flanking maneuver from the south of Vegas, coming by Spirit Mountain and attempt to secure the city from that direction."

"That makes sense," Jason said. "If I had the manpower, that's what I would do, and it coincides with the intelligence we were given on the enemy generals scouting trip. Okay, Lorenzo, work with Lunadi and devise a defense against that route. Leave nothing to chance. It will spread our forces, but they will not be able to have air support, we need those in reserve of the larger Chinese force. Good job men."

The Oval Office was the perfect place to have the ensuing conversation because it was the office the Speaker coveted and promised to make her own, no matter the cost. She and the President were sitting directly across from each other on the sofa's in front of the President's desk. You could cut the tension between them with a knife.

"I want you to look at this Madam Speaker," Phil said, handing her a folder.

"Bullshit," Evelyn said, as she glanced over it. "Do you think you would actually succeed charging me with both terrorism and treason?"

"I certainly do," Phil replied.

"Do you remember a past administration?" Evelyn said, acidly. "They had more information than you do and are no longer here. I am. What does that tell you?"

"They didn't have the watch dogs I do Madam," Phil replied. "You are supposed to manage the affairs of the people, not get in bed with the enemy."

"The people are too stupid to know what to do," Evelyn said. "They must be controlled, managed, and then, told what to do, when to do it, and how to do it. Surely you know this. We have proven it over decades. They are fighting each other rather than us because they are too dumb to realize we are behind the segregation and hate that has engulfed the country. Divide and conquer and the elite in Congress controls all, including you. Indeed, our disinformation campaign is a success because the stupid populace believes everything we tell them."

"Therein is your problem Madam," Phil said, amazed at her arrogance. "You think you are above the law."

"I am," Evelyn said icily. "When you are gone, I will still be here. By the time I'm done with you on impeachment and the 25th, you'll wish you weren't here."

Her eyes narrowed as she looked at him, unafraid and on the attack.

"I'll tell you what Mr. President," Evelyn spoke vehemently. "You do this while I impeach you. Let's see who gets to the finish line first. I ….., voice trailing off as Erin rushed in.

"Excuse me Madam Speaker, Mr. President. I have urgent news."

"What is it?" Phil asked.

"The North Koreans have launched a missile across the 38th Parallel into Cheorwon, it appears to have been launched from south of Pyonggang. The joint chiefs are on the way."

"Mr. President," Evelyn said. "You have more important things to do. Mind my words. We will talk again. Then, perhaps you'll see things my way."

Phil watched her as she walked out of the Oval. What a bitch he thought.

"This is just great," Phil said. "Given the status of our other problem, this seems to be more than a coincidence."

"I would say it was planned, but then I'd sound paranoid," Erin said. "I have already let General Bardos and White know. They will stay abreast of developments."

"This is extremely critical," Phil said. "If it's a setup, we wouldn't know until it was too late. If it's real, then God help us."

A knock at the door interrupted them. General Roscoe Wilson was admitted, the Chairman of the Joint Chiefs.

"Mr. President," he said, shaking hands. "I assume that Erin has informed you."

"Yes, just a few moments ago general," Phil said. "Where do we stand."

"It's difficult to say sir," General Wilson replied. "We are trying to determine if it was intentional or an accident. It may take a few days to know for sure."

"That puts us between a rock and a hard place," Phil said. "What are our options?"

"We have only two sir," General Wilson said. "We either sit back and wait to find out for sure or, we send our fleets and troops to Korea. We can pull them back if it's a false flag. I have already ordered two task forces out; they will be underway within the next 24 hours. I have mobilized all troops to combat readiness along the 38th and the South Koreans are mobilizing as well. I have also ordered our two fleets in the South China Sea to move into Korean waters. They are speeding there as we speak."

"What happens if we wait," Phil asked, dreading the answer.

"Sir, if we wait and North Korea escalates, South Korea

could fall within seventy-two hours. I do not see that we have a choice."

"It is even less than that," Phil said, apprehension in his voice. He let out a big sigh as he looked at the ceiling.

"We have no choice, do we?" Phil asked, already knowing the answer.

"To reiterate sir, we do not."

"Very well, mobilize all necessary fleets, strategic bombers and other forces. We cannot afford to wait for a false flag. Call me with constant updates."

"Yes sir," General Wilson said.

"Never a dull moment is there?" Phil muttered to himself as he began thinking about how to deal with the Speaker.

L i Qiang was sitting in his office, talking with one of his staff officers when his phone rang.

"Sir, the American fleets are steaming toward the East China Sea. They started two hours ago," the intelligence officer said.

"Very well," Li said. "Keep me apprised."

"Yes sir."

Li hastily wrote a note on a piece of paper and called in his secretary.

"Send this immediately."

"Yes sir."

Panu was sitting at his desk when his aide walked in.

"Sir, something just came through."

As he read the note, he smiled. Li had been correct. The Americans were going in mass to Korea. Using few words, the note was concise.

"My cat stalks the canary."

It had been almost a week after news of the North Korea missile launch. No other missiles had been fired. The North Koreans had mobilized some troops in response to the U.S. troops movements along the 38th but all was quiet.

At the request of the President, Nick Fabiani had contacted the Supreme Leader Marshal of the Republic of North Korea and told them that if they didn't pull back and invaded the south, that the U.S. would launch ballistic missiles destroying all military complexes in their country, as well as Pyongyang. Other targets were also being selected and nuclear weapons would be used if deemed necessary. It would be a no-win scenario for North Korea. The discussions with Nick and the North Koreans were not going well, although they appeared to be having second thoughts.

At Jeremy's request, General Bardos had already spoken to the House Intelligence Committee warning them of a possible attack from enemy forces with almost all troops out of the country. He needed more supplies but knew deep down he would not get them. The committee had ignored the request. He knew they must be in on it and did what any real combat commander would do, he sent a dispatch to Congress.

I direct this open dispatch to the Senate majority leader and Speaker of the House of the U.S. Congress and all your members and constituents, also to all those who have been chosen by the people to govern and manage the affairs of this nation — to be dispersed to your collective bodies, whether in Washington DC or elsewhere.

You were elected by the constituents in each of your various districts, regions, and states to manage the affairs of the people of the United States. Why have you not performed your duties to the people? You have sent most U.S. troops to Korea and left us defenseless despite my warnings to you of likely invading forces. We need immediate assistance for supplies and arms.

I remind you of the following words written when this country was founded. *"We have reached the Course of human events, when it becomes necessary for one people to dissolve the political bands which have connected them with another, and to assume among the powers of the earth, the separate and equal station to which the Laws of Nature and of Nature's God entitle them, a decent respect to the opinions of mankind requires that they should declare the causes which impel them to the separation."* I do the same now for the patriots of this nation to fight the Liberal Fascists at our head.

Article 1, Section 10 of the constitution states that no title of nobility shall be granted, but that is what you have done for yourselves — appointed yourselves as nobles over this people, you are fascists. You have broken the laws you swore an oath to uphold.

Behold, our enemies come swiftly upon us, to take possession of our country. I await assistance from you and except you begin immediately to support our armies against those about to invade this nation, I will come to you after the battle and remove you with extreme prejudice so that you no longer have power to impede the progress of this people in the cause of their freedom. I close my dispatch.

Evelyn was on the Delaware Shores browsing the fish market. It was crowded as she strolled down the marketplace, steadily glancing at her watch. The scheduled time arrived. Looking around, seeing she was alone, she pulled a small bundle from her purse. It looked like a simple handkerchief, but as she unrolled it, there was a small silver bag inside. It was a Faraday bag that blocked all wireless signals to the phone she pulled from it. There was only one number in the contact list, which she pressed as she raised the phone to her ear, glancing furtively about. She was wearing a scarf and a hat; sure no one would recognize her.

"What do you have for me?" Li asked.

"All is going according to plan," Evelyn replied. "The President gave authorization to the Chairman of the Joint Chiefs to move all free military assets to the Korean theatre. Many are already on the way."

"Yes, my intelligence is showing that," the electronic voice said. "If you were to estimate, how many of your troops and fleets will be tasked for this?"

"It is the bulk of our fleets, along with strategic bombers, submarines, and soldiers," Evelyn said. "You should have no problem. Oh, one other thing. General Bardos has requested more supplies and men because he thinks there is an imminent threat of invading forces."

"I have heard of him, he is very good," the voice replied. "Is he a threat to us?"

"Not at all. He has been running a few drills here and there around the country, but they are scattered."

"What kind of supplies did he ask for?" the voice asked, concerned.

"The usual," Evelyn replied. "It didn't look like anything big, but do not worry, we are ignoring him and will continue to do so. We will dispatch a letter to him in four or five days telling him we will authorize it at our next meeting. That will stall him until you have accomplished what you desire."

"Very well," the voice crackled confidently. "How are you

coming with the President?"

"We had a meeting yesterday," Evelyn said. "He brought up the same idle threats, but nothing I cannot cope with. I have drawn up plans for both impeachment and removal under the 25th Amendment and, I have enough support in the Congress to pass it through, as well as that of the VP. Your money has greased the skids quite nicely. The only thing left is to present it to the floor of the House and then the Senate for a vote."

"Excellent," the voice said. "I want you to call an emergency session two weeks from tomorrow at 10 a.m. for the votes to be cast. By then the North Korea deal will be more heated and such a meeting will distract all from our operations. Put it out in your propaganda machine. Be careful with the timing."

"Excellent," Evelyn said. "I will release our intent to the media at the appropriate time. Remember our deal. Once the President is out of the way, the VP has agreed to step down, he has no choice given the dirt on him. I will become President and be in control of our new nation."

"The deal is solid," the voice said. "Complete the last few tasks."

L i sat, relieved. At last, his goal was going to be achieved. He could hardly contain his excitement. He picked up his phone and dialed his old friend.

"Wen, how are you old friend?" Li asked. "I have great news."

"You have a date set?" Wen asked. "When?"

"Yes, approval has been granted," Li said. "Have the PLAN ready and on station two weeks from tomorrow. We launch at 7:00 a.m. on that day."

"It will be as you request."

Everything was coming together perfectly as Li cupped his hands behind his head. He rarely smoked but had saved a cigar for just this occasion. He pulled it from his desk drawer, clipped the end and lit it. He loved the aroma as he drew the smoke into his lungs and exhaled large puffs, watching them ascend like a fog toward the ceiling with a smile. At last, he would have his revenge and one day, he too, would be leader of his people.

Commander Lawton Wills was at the helm of his container ship, the SS Arvus. On it he had twenty container launchers mixed with the other containers, invisible to any who may think the ship was anything but an everyday average container ship headed to harbor at Houston or New Orleans.

"Sir, you have a call," an ensign said.

"Commander Wills," Jason said. "I wanted to check on your progress as we believe time is very short."

"General Bardos," Lawton said. "I have twenty-four ships in the Gulf, each with twenty launchers that we can also reload. I have sent a dozen more up the eastern seaboard to target container ships that Shockwave identified. In the Gulf, we have an initial launch capability of nineteen hundred and twenty anti-ship missiles for the first salvo. The key will be range."

"Excellent," Jason said. "Our intelligence suggests the enemy will be coming through the Yucatan Channel from Venezuela. Position your ships based on range to protect the Port of New Orleans and Houston Seaport. Scatter them as you deem necessary. I will contact you once I know more."

"Is there anything else sir?" Lawton asked.

"Yes," Jason replied. "Assume stations as quickly as you

can and continually run drills of mock attacks on enemy ships to hone your men's skills. Set target tracks for all identified shipping ahead of time."

"Yes sir, out."

Lawton had already mapped out a plausible scenario for protection of the entire Gulf as much as he could with his meager number of ships. He began altering it to position a couple of ships northeast of the Straits of Florida, a few more near Port of New Orleans with the potential to strike toward the south and west toward Houston, a few more scattered in between and out in the central Gulf and the rest in a line along the 95th longitude from Galveston area on down. It would take the furthermost ship only twenty-four hours to be on station. This was going to be fun. As soon as he had re-mapped areas, he sent a communication to all ships. They would begin drills late tomorrow and continue around the clock. He would hone the crews to a razors edge.

Evelyn Rutledge, true to her word, called a press conference. The capitol was buzzing with anticipation. "This press conference will be very short," Evelyn said, standing behind a podium clustered with microphones.

"I will give you more information later, but this is what I can tell you today."

All the reporters were screaming questions at her as she stood soaking in the attention. She raised her hand; the reporters grew quiet.

"I have only one small announcement," she said. "Two weeks from tomorrow, due to incontrovertible evidence of collusion with the Chinese and unlawful arms sales to Turkey, we will be filing both impeachment charges and removal from office under the 25th Amendment of President

Philip Weld."

She let it soak in for a moment, knowing that the less she talked now, the more the wheels of the media would spin. Within a few days the entire nation would believe the narrative because they were too stupid to investigate anything themselves. The Internet and smart phones were the most powerful educational tools on the planet and all that most people used them for was 'look at me, I'm on social media.' The press and social media would try and convict the President before the House and Senate met. She could not smile outwardly, but inwardly she was as giddy as a schoolgirl. Finally, she would be President. She had labored for decades to make this happen. She would savor the moment.

"That's all I have for now. I will give you an update in a day or so."

Of course, she wouldn't do that because she wanted the media spin. She calmly walked away from the podium, away from the clamor of questions and down the hall, inwardly glowing.

Jeremy had found a location on a peak, about eight miles north of where the main battle would be, but close enough to see it. There was a small sandy area in a pocket of rocks with a rock peak to the north and an open view to the south. It was perfect he thought, as he began preparations for a series of sandpainting's he would need to call upon those in the other realm. On this trip, he had brought all the necessary supplies and slowly began hauling them up from the truck he had borrowed. Last night he had a vision that showed him the exact time the launch would occur. He had relayed that information to the President and Generals Bardos and White. They would have a couple more days to drill before they had to shut everything down and wait. The years of planning were quickly culminating into what would become a chaotic frenzy pitting nation against nations and soldiers against warriors. Those who would not pick up their weapons of war were showing great disloyalty to Sun God. Jeremy did not tell the generals or the President the remainder of his vision showing millions perishing. Tragically, they had made their choice. He finished his preparations and waited. The next few days for him would be spent praying and fasting. Nearby, he had a radio to stay in constant contact with the Generals, Lunadi and Sky Thinker.

Sky Thinker was with General White and his Shockwave troops along with about one third of Lunadi's men and half of the 50,000 warriors the tribes had gathered. The rest had gone to Spirit Mountain area to await the arrival of the Russians.

"What do you think?" General White asked. "Can we do anything more?"

"We have done all we can sir," Sky Thinker said. "All is in order and the drills have went very well. When we asked the convoy to speed up to double the pace, the men had a difficult time initially zeroing in on the targets. Now they are perfect and when the convoys slowed down to a normal pace, we achieved a ninety-five percent success rate in hits."

"That much?" Lorenzo queried. "That's amazing. Let the men stand down for the rest of today and tomorrow then pick it up again after that. We'll see if they still have their edge after the break. I'll feel better if they do."

At their Spirit Mountain base camp, Lunadi and his commanders had planned a trap for the Russians.

They also had Aichu and his giants who would help them and 25,000 warriors from the tribes. The giants had been fitted with steel shoes that would crush a tank. This would prove interesting.

"We need to stop them before they reach Needles," Lunadi said. "We do not know if they will try to flank us to support their Chinese counterparts or if they will attempt to join into a larger force at Baker. Given they will have tanks and helicopters, I would think they would want to save the wear and tear and fuel and head north to take Vegas from the south."

"Where do you propose we should take them?" Commander Oconee asked.

"Here," Lunadi said. "Between the road bend south of Yucca to the bend south of Needles. That gives us about twenty-five miles to stop them."

"That should work," Commander Guale said. "But how are they going to get here from Houston. Isn't that too far to move their tanks and heavy weapons?"

"Yes, it is," Lunadi said. "But we have men watching because we think they will use the passenger train route and move equipment on flatbeds from Houston to San Antonio, then, through El Paso, Tucson, up through Phoenix and Flagstaff and finally west from there to Needles. We will blow the tracks over the Colorado River here just south of Catfish Paradise. Also, set charges to blow the interstate bridges as well. If we have difficulty stopping them, they will need to find a place to cross, costing them valuable time. They can't just roll into town on a train, they need to organize first. We will also blow this bridge at Happy Jack Wash once they cross. As you can see, it is just north of the freeway at the bend south of Yucca. This will allow us to hem them in close to the foothills and ridges, giving us high ground advantage. Let's set up all our defenses along this route."

"What about air support?" Commander Yamassee asked. "Do they have any?"

I'm guessing they will have some helicopters with them but won't launch them until the last minute. Aichu and his men will attempt to take them out first, along with our stinger missiles. However, if the Chinese have air superiority, they will be close enough to call them in. Commander Yuchi, you be ready for that scenario. Any more questions? Alright then, let's get to work."

General Bardos had double checked his men; everything was as ready as it could be.

"Sir," Major said. "You need to see this."

It was a weather report, which the military had always kept track of since World War II when General George Patton moved three divisions in sixty-six hours through extreme snowy weather and counter attacked the Germans in the Ardennes. Now, weather reports were much more accurate. The general sighed as he looked at it.

"If I were the enemy, I would take advantage of these fronts and move in behind them," Jason said. "Pass this along to all commanders. Tell them to expect the attack as these fronts pass by. I calculate we have three days max."

As the major left, the general picked up his radio.

"Scott, make sure everything is protected against the EMP, move it deep into Yucca."

The generals had also devised a defense force on the outskirts of Vegas, just in case. He had a growing excitement; he and his men and those of the other commanders were warriors, this is what they were born and trained for.

Both Admiral Leung and General Qiang were on the bridge aboard the admiral's flagship, the carrier Denang. They were sailing with the front and would be on station at the appointed time, where the bulk of the Chinese Navy was meeting off the coast of Los Angeles. The meandering course each ship had been following was changing to a purposeful one as they joined forces off the U.S. mainland. This storm would be their greatest ally.

"How fortunate to have such a storm just as we begin our final leg," Li said.

"Yes, most fortunate," Wen replied, looking through his binoculars at the rough seas as they tossed about.

His carrier crashed down atop waves that were at least fifteen feet high, white froth falling from the crest down into the dark trough. He could barely make out the outlines of his heavy cruisers and his three other carriers. All was well he thought. They had one hundred twenty-eight J-15 fighters. If plans worked according to Li's strategy, it should be more than enough. Although everything was going better than expected the apprehension, he felt months, earlier returned.

Panuftii Tyurin was aboard the Russian main carrier. They were following the storm toward Houston. A part of the navy had already split off and was headed toward the Port of New Orleans, arriving just off the coast. They stayed at the twelve-mile border so that they were in international waters. The storm was expected to subside about daybreak; they would be in position before then. Looking at his watch, he could not believe how fortunate his fleet was. Just like the Chinese, the bulk of Russian naval forces had sailed quietly into the Gulf of Mexico. With the Americans now having most of their troops around the

Korean peninsula, they were almost defenseless at home. They had been thrown to the wolves by their own government and didn't know it yet. One of the problems with capitalism he mused. If they could not defeat the Americans, there would be hell to pay. He would be held directly accountable and to save face, his government would execute all involved claiming they were rogue generals. It would be the saner course of action than potentially losing millions by nuclear retaliation from the U.S. He also feared lest they were about to waken a sleeping army who would not follow any rules in combat, let alone the Geneva Convention. No, he was about to move his men into harm's way into a state known for its guns. What the hell had he been thinking?

E velyn called the majority whip from her car. As luck would have it, she needed to drive herself today, but she would have anyway because she didn't want any listening ears around to eaves drop onto her conversastions.

"Mike, I'm running a little late," she said. "Is everyone there?"

"Yes, Madam Speaker, we are waiting for you."

"Do not wait. Get the vote in process. I will be there before it gets too far. As you know, I'm just going to rubber stamp your vote."

"Yes Madam Speaker. I will start the vote now. I will tell them know you will be arriving shortly.

As she hung up, glancing at her watch; 9:55 a.m., she eagerly anticipated the vote. Finally, after years of surviving Washington politics, she would be the big gun. President Weld would be removed, and she already had a plan in place for relieving the VP. Within a month, she would become President. Her party would never have elected her, but this had been twenty-five years in the making. It was her time. Her way or the highway, there would be no dissension. She was so excited she began humming.

Timing had worked out perfectly. Li had dispatched multiple teams of the Navy's Jiaolong (Sea Dragons), to seize and hold LAX until reinforcements could arrive as transport planes had already left Port Brito and would be landing in waves every five hours. It was 7:00 a.m. Pacific Time as Li gave the command to launch all container missiles.

"Launch immediately," Li commanded. "All unit's, all missiles."

The officers in the command-and-control center immediately relayed the general's orders. Every container system began their launch.

Captain Zhang had arrived from Shanghai about 2 a.m. into the Lower Bay of New York Harbor. His executive officer brought him the orders. It was time. He had already prepared the launchers.

"Launch now." Captain Zhang said. "He watched from the bridge as thirty-two missiles launched into separate directions. twenty of them tracked to the southwest. The captain watched them closely as they arced high into the air and then dropped back down to only a few hundred feet above the ground and disappeared. He did not know where each of the missiles were headed, but he felt sure he knew the destination of those.

CHAPTER 11

Valley of the Shadow of Death

Evelyn Rutledge had just hung up her phone, giving instructions on how to do everything to the last detail to her crew in the Capitol Building. She was headed northeast and had just crossed over the Potomac on Interstate 395 when she heard the initial blast of large explosions, her car beginning to vibrate, picking up shockwaves from the shaking earth, almost like the aftershock of an earthquake. She glanced at her watch; it was 10:23 a.m. In front of her on the horizon about a mile away she saw multiple large plumes of black and gray smoke that slowly turned white, her stomach tightened. In her driver-side mirror, she saw the same thing almost directly behind her, but much larger; it was the Pentagon. People were stopping their cars and pulling over, getting out as they watched in shock. She had no time for that; the sinking feeling in the pit of her stomach driving her forward. Circling northward on the 395, she was about seven hundred yards away. The smoke had subsided clearly, and she could see that the U.S. Capitol building was gone. It was now a pile of rubble and even on the freeway, small and larger pieces of concrete were scattered from the outward force of eight missiles hitting the building almost at the same time. Already emergency responders were arriving on scene and blocking off roads to prevent entry.

Suddenly, she realized what had happened.

"That son of a bitch," she screamed. "He never had any intention of keeping his word. He eliminated all of us."

As she stared at the scene in anger, she knew that they had all been pawns in a larger scheme for China to seize the U.S., that she would never be President. Suddenly, panic and fear seized her, chest heavy, finding it difficult to breathe. Quickly, she pulled over to gain her thoughts. She was startled almost immediately from a tapping on her window. It was a first responder directing her to pull forward, motioning to loop around and back onto the freeway. She was back on the freeway in no time in a blind panic. As she drove past the Pentagon, she realized it was also gone, the impact of many missiles had mostly leveled it. It was then she began to realize the enormity of her situation.

The panic gnawing at her turned to pure fear, like that of an animal fleeing a forest fire. She came to a growing realization that the evidence held against her by the President would not be shoved aside. The American people would want a scape goat and she would be one of many. The nation would scream for her head. Without hesitation, Evelyn headed home to pack. Realizing her normal military flight would be unavailable, she called an air transport company on the way. She needed to be out of the country tonight. She turned on the radio to hear reports already coming in. There were expected to be no survivors from the Capitol Building, even the press corps that had been at hand to cover the proceedings were all presumed dead. The Pentagon was projecting total damage and a seventy-five percent loss of personnel.

"My God," she thought. "What have I done? The country would now be at war with China, but with the fleets in

Korea, could they hold them off? Her mind began to think through every scenario and possible route of escape as law enforcement and government agencies would execute emergency operations plans almost immediately and begin to shut down air and even ground transport in many areas, especially the larger cities. It was highly likely all air flights would be canceled. She needed to think of an alternate way to get out of Dodge."

The President was in the Oval, in discussions with Erin. He had come to a decision about the Speaker.

"I want you to send the Secret Service to arrest the Speaker," Phil said. "Be discreet. Do it immediately."

"Yes sir, I'll take care of it right away."

"What else is on the agenda?"

"As you know, congress is meeting and will be voting shortly on impeachment. But more importantly, what we have been fearing. Riots are erupting in Chicago, Dallas, Portland, and other major cities due to food shortages. Looting and killing is occurring in Chicago and New York, it's as we …."

Erin's voice trailed off as the explosions rocked the building. They rushed to the window to look out then, quickly up to the veranda overlooking the Rose Garden. To the left they could see the smoke rising from Capitol Hill, to the right, from the Pentagon. Instinctively they knew the attack had been launched.

It had been a long night and General Bardos was just waking. Staring at the ceiling of his tent, he started thinking back over his career. It had been a good one and he was hoping this wouldn't be the end of it. He dressed quickly, shaved and did his morning hygiene. His first order of business was to check in with Jeremy and Generals White and Shockwave. Having done so, he grabbed a quick cup of coffee, it was then that the reports began coming in. Major Price came running over, gasping for breath.

"Sir, you should see this. The Pentagon and Capitol Building are gone." Major price said, handing him a one-page report.

"Damn," Jason exclaimed! "I wasn't sure they would go to this extent. Damned bold of them. Get on the horn to all units. Today is the day, be prepared. Also, shield all electronics in the next few minutes. It is imperative."

"Jeremy, it has begun," Jason said, hanging up, quickly beginning a new call on his radio.

"Scott, make sure all is shielded; they just struck first targets."

Major Price had contacted all units who began making final preparations.

Reports continued coming in of strikes on multiple military bases and cities — Chicago, Detroit, Philadelphia, St. Louis, Miami, Dallas — the list continued to grow.

Unknown to the nation and its inhabitants, the destruction of the Capitol Building and Pentagon was the start of the Battle for Las Vegas. A nation would fight against two well-armed adversaries to decide its fate, whether it would survive or whether it would perish. It was a battle that had been planned for decades. Traitors and enemies within, because of their greed and lust for power, had set the nation on a course from which there was no turning back. The attack came almost immediately after the people began learning there was a looming food shortage and to prepare for the worst. Now it would be much worse, millions would starve at the least.

General Bardos ordered the launch of all targeted missiles on GPS recorded targets of all Chinese military units in Canada and tracked container ships. Within fifteen minutes, missiles began striking their targets.

Captain Zhang was smoking a cigarette as he leaned against the railing, awaiting additional launch orders. He caught a motion in the corner of his eye. He turned to look just as the Tomahawk missile struck his ship; his body exploded like a ripe melon hit with a heavy caliber bullet as its bloody pieces were thrown through the air, across the water, to become fish food. All along the Great Lakes, New York Harbor, off the coast of Los Angeles, Seattle and Portland, container ships were struck with missiles, sinking so fast few noticed.

"Should we launch against their ships?" Major Price asked.

"No, let's wait," Jason said. "If we launch now, it's likely our missiles will be caught in the EMP blast, if they use that scenario. Better to be safe than sorry."

"Roger that."

Enemy missiles continued striking targets all over the country, both civilian and military.

Reports were coming into the command center about containers exploding as missiles were launched.

"Do we know how many have malfunctioned?" Li asked.

"No sir, we have reports of only a few so far but communications are sketchy, dropping in and out," a captain said.

"Very well, we knew some were untested," Li replied. "What else?"

"Intelligence confirms Capitol Building and Pentagon taken out sir."

"Excellent," Li said, smiling. "Launch EMP strike

immediately."

"Yes sir," the captain said, as he turned and began barking orders.

"The fools," Li thought. "They had betrayed their own country for money and power. Did they really think that the Chinese would keep them around? Anyone who would betray their own people for money would certainly betray them. He had fired them all!"

He couldn't help laughing aloud, his staff looking toward him, wondering what was so funny. Thirty minutes after launch he calculated all missiles had reached their targets. Now, the Americans were about to be thrown into a communications blackout.

Sam Malone was sitting in the emergency operations center, hovering. Somehow, he had a gut feeling that things were about to get dicey. The missiles they had found in Ottawa and near Thunder Bay had opened and then, exploded. He was getting reports from his teams all over the country of similar instances and was hoping they had found most of them. He immediately called Austin and filled him in. Within minutes they were on their way to see the President, witnessing the attack on the Capitol Building. The White House was bustling and in lockdown mode. The two were led by Erin down to the PEOC, Presidents Emergency Operations Center. She had a grim look on her face, despite that they knew something like this was coming.

"President," Stone said. "I would tell you that it has already begun, but you know that."

"Yes," Phil said, looking at reports as they came in. "This Korea thing is a ruse correct?"

"Definitely," Stone said. "I would recall all fleets and

aircraft immediately. We need them here."

Earlier that morning, General Wilson had come to the White House to brief the President about Korea. It was his good fortune not to be at the Pentagon, the rest of the joint chiefs were not so fortunate.

"General Wilson," Phil said. "Recall all fleets and troops home immediately. We need them here, now. Tell them to make all possible speed."

"What else do you have?" Phil asked.

"The missiles we discussed are blowing up everywhere sir," Austin said. "Our agents have confirmed and are keeping us up to date. We didn't get them all, but most, I think. However, their ship missiles are many and devastating. We failed to make a full accounting of them."

"No shit," Phil said. "That's an understatement looking at our current losses. What else can we expect?"

"According to Generals Bardos and White sir, the initial attack will be followed by an EMP," Stone said. "Then, they will begin their assault."

"Any idea on timing?" Phil asked.

"I'm not sure sir," Austin replied.

"Sir," Erin interrupted. "According to Jeremy, Lunadi, and General Bardos they expected the initial assault and as soon as the missiles reach their targets, about a half hour, they expect an EMP then, the assault."

"So, we can expect the EMP in the next half hour, great," Phil said. "Erin, get on the horn to the Department of Homeland Security, have them warn all critical infrastructure sectors to prepare for an EMP as much as they can. Go, now!"

Erin moved over to one of the control consoles and began issuing orders to its operator. She knew it was a long shot to get everyone notified in time, but every little bit helped. She also knew from working with Lunadi and the General that the major hubs were the most important and they had a list of those whom they contacted immediately, some had been destroyed. They worked feverishly and were making good progress. Erin also suggested each of the infrastructure groups contact others directly connected to them. This left Erin and her small team more time to contact everyone else they could in what little time remained. In the back of her mind, Erin knew that what was happening within the PEOC paled in comparison to what the boots on the ground were preparing for. She worried about Lunadi for there were few against many. But she trusted in Sun God to protect them all because they were doing what they could to protect the nation and those with light. She said a silent prayer.

Two Jin-class (Type 094) submarines had reached launch depth. One was approximately one hundred miles east of Washington DC in the Atlantic; the other was about fifty miles west of Los Angeles. One missile bay door opened on each as the captains gave the order to launch an JL-3 SLBM, a submarine-launched ballistic missile. More than enough to do the required damage. They were set to explode two hundred fifty miles up in the atmosphere above St. Louis, Missouri and Provo, Utah. The effects would encompass most of the United states. The crews of both submarines were in a joyous mood as they launched against America. Their joy was short lived. Having been warned by General Bardos, and expecting this very scenario, orders from Admiral Rodin had been sent to two Los Angeles Class attack submarines that had been shadowing them. Because war had not been declared, that was all they could do until the subs made an aggressive move. The American subs had detected the missile bay doors open on the Chinese submarines and immediately launched their torpedoes. It was too late; however, the ballistic missiles had already cleared the water on their way to their targets. Within seconds after launch, both Jin-class subs were blown apart as their ruptured hulls settled to the ocean floor. The commanders of the attack subs reported in. About ten minutes later, both ballistic missiles, carrying 1.5 megaton nuclear warheads, exploded above their respective targets.

The Chinese and Russians hoped the damage they sought from the EMPs would occur although there had always been confusion of the effects of what such explosions would have. This was because the initial tests by both the U.S. and Russians had been conducted in the late 1950s and early 1960s were at best inconclusive, although the potential effects were known. When the two ballistic missiles exploded, gamma rays produced by the fission process were directed downward, colliding with the electrons in air molecules of the thin upper atmosphere ejecting the electrons from their parent molecules at high energy. Traveling at the speed of light, a sonic boom was created by each, electromagnetic radiation arriving virtually simultaneously to the ground. The first pulse was short, called E1 by the experts and quickly followed by an intermediate pulse called E2, like a lightning pulse, and finally a late pulse from the explosions, followed by E3 and much like a geomagnetic storm. The effects of the explosions were instantaneous as all three pulses occurred in mere nanoseconds — the damage was done. Little known to the General Qiang and his forces was that the main effects of the EMP on the electrical power grid would not be as damaging as hoped. The greatest damage would be disruption resulting from induced voltage surges in connecting cables and by direct exposure to the initial pulse. The digital protective relays in the system, devices to help detect faults in the grid, remained resilient to direct exposure to the initial pulse, although still vulnerable to surges induced on control and communication cables.

The energy companies, from years of research in the laboratory, had discovered what a few bomb tests could not, that initial pulse impacts could be mitigated using various options that included shielded cables and proper grounding, low-voltage surge protection devices, use of fiber optics cables for communications, and enhanced EMP shielding of electric substation control houses and grounding and bonding enhancements. The result would be, not the wide-ranging catastrophic effects General Qiang wanted. Several regional service interruptions occurred but a nationwide grid failure didn't happen because damage to large power transformers was minimal. The biggest problem was the loss of cell phone communications, vehicle issues, and social media blackouts, catastrophic due to the psyche of those immersed in social media who were already suffering from hysteria, more than from blast damages.

Power grid supervisors, immediately upon the warning received from the Department of Homeland Security, began flipping electrical switches and relays to America's power grid. Energy, the Achilles heel of an advanced nation, was shut down to prevent cascading failures through all critical infrastructures: water, communications, banking and finance, defense, emergency response, agriculture, shipping, and more. Without power, nothing worked and without news of what was going on, people were left guessing.

Critical thinkers were preparing for the worst; social media addicts were tearing their hair out in a frenzy because life as they had known it, immediately changed. Shutting down the grid meant that the nation would be able to save most of the critical components from damages due to electrical power surge. Unlike the 2003 blackout of New York City that cost over fifteen billion dollars in damages, the long-term fate of a nation hinged on critical infrastructure managers.

News feeds coming out of Washington were severed; there was no power to broadcast. A nation in darkness now began to fear that which they had barely received a glimpse of. The emergency broadcast system was put into operation, but there was little news, and few heard it due to electrical outages.

Anxiety began to cause panic as mobs in large cities started looting stores and killing anyone who got in their way. The food shortage had already caused mass riots and now, the anger of the people intensified. Most law enforcement officers stayed home to protect their own loved ones as a deep, dark despair gripped the country. Numerous militia groups began hearing of a coming battle in the west and knowing that most U.S. troops were in Korean waters, instinctively understood the grave ramifications. They began immediately making their way toward Nevada to lend any assistance they could to the few remaining combat personnel in the country.

The nation was back where it began. In the blink of an eye, it had digressed to the same state as 1865. And, as in the days of George Washington, who courageously stood against the British with only ten percent of the people supporting him while the other ninety percent sat on their ass waiting for the outcome, so it was now. The day that

President Weld and his team had been preparing for was here and the only thing to do was deal with it. It would be bloody and cruel.

L i Qiang, general of the Chinese army had said goodbye to Wen and deboarded the carrier right after the EMPs were set off. As much as he thought he was prepared for the aftermath, he was having a good deal of trouble communicating with his command. He pushed forward as quickly as he could because he knew time was his most precious resource.

"Sir, we are getting spotty communications, but it seems that many of our container launchers malfunctioned and blew up as they were launching," a major told him.

"Did you find out how many yet?" Li asked.

"We do not know yet sir, but so far at least a dozen reports, more than at last account."

"Find out as quickly as you can and report back."

Li began to wonder if the malfunctions were sabotage or if they had rushed production so fast that errors had crept into the manufacturing process. He desperately needed to know which ones malfunctioned to reassess his battle strategy. Assuming the worst, he made his way into Long Beach Port. Three battalions of T99 main battle tanks were already being offloaded. With 125mm guns, they were no slouch and as good as the M1A2 Abrams. His Dragons special operations group had seized LAX. Transport planes with helicopters and troops were already landing, coming in from Nicaragua. Planes from the four carriers were in the air as well but there seemed to be a nagging communications problem between all command groups and with the Russians in the Gulf. The same thing had happened to the Ariel-1 during Russian and U.S. testing.

Still, that satellite had not failed until four days after the U.S. detonated a nuclear warhead two-hundred and fifty miles above the Pacific. If communications were being hampered this early on, what would the EMP do to their low earth orbit (LEO) military communications satellites? He pushed it out of his mind. He had a war to win.

General Bardos was getting updates from surveillance personnel on the ground in and around Long Beach Port and Los Angeles. Thus far they had counted up to five divisions of troops, sixty thousand men. Where the hell were that many men coming from? They couldn't airlift them in so short a time. He was beginning to feel like General Custer at the Battle of Little Bighorn.

"Sir," Major Price said, approaching. "This is just in from the missile commanders. They want to know if they can strike?"

"Not yet," Jason said. "We have too many glitches in communications. If it is affecting us, the guidance systems on the missiles will be affected as well."

"What do you propose sir?" Major Price asked.

"Hold off for a while," Jason said thoughtfully. "Let the enemy mass. Once they are in larger units that's when we hit them."

"Yes sir," Major Price said, walking off giving orders through the radio.

The Russian fleet had moved stealthily into the Gulf of Mexico. They were standing off the coast of Houston as they began launching missiles into military and commercial targets along the coast. Some of the missiles dropping into the ocean after launch, their tracking radar affected from the EMP. His men were already landing on the shores along the Houston Sea Port and three divisions were landing around New Orleans. All was quiet. The American Navy was conspicuously absent. The only ships showing up on their radar were scattered container ships. Their surveillance drones had picked up some explosions in and around Ft. Hood, so he guessed the container missile launch Li had devised worked well enough. Despite how smoothly things were going, he had a sinking feeling in his stomach; it was all too easy. If it had been this easy, America would have been invaded long ago.

"Sir," his aide said, walking up and disturbing his thoughts. "Our Spetsnaz have secured the Port Terminal Railroad head in Houston sir. We can move our transport ships up the Houston Ship Channel for good access."

"Good," Panu said. "Make it so. Get our tanks and helicopters on flatbeds as quickly as possible. Oh, and secure all the oil and chemical storage yards. It will be a big boost to our supply chains. We need the fuel."

Chinese troops and ships had taken both Seattle and Portland and were moving south out of Ottawa toward Washington and south from Thunder Bay, along highway 61, picking up Interstate 35 toward Minneapolis. The Canadian Prime Minister's agreement to allow Chinese troops into Canada could be the downfall of both countries. The container ships that had moved in from the Pacific were operational and the missiles made their targets. Both Seattle and Portland were heaps of rubble. The goal was not to capture these port cities but to overwhelm and destroy them, making way for more troops that stood offshore in their transport ships. There were no troops to protect the people. The entire goal was to take the west coast, move inland and take Denver and Las Vegas and destroy

Washington and all military infrastructure along the eastern seaboard. The Russians were masters at logistics and soon had troops and helicopters moving north. Like the Chinese, everyone they encountered, they gunned down. Anything or any person that moved was shot. There would be no prisoners. The shear brutality of what they did was overwhelming. Militia's had taken up the fight and were sniping at the troops as they moved, but the firepower against them was overwhelming. While they managed to kill many of the Russian troops moving toward Washington, they simply didn't have the manpower to slow them down. Thousands of militia members were killed as they fought to their last breath. The enemy within had left the country vulnerable and now, the price was being exacted.

Russian divisions moving up the eastern seaboard had separated, heading in two forces, one to Jacksonville, the other through Montgomery, Atlanta, and Charlotte on their way do DC. The large cities were left in ruin as they passed through. Some people had been out with signs, welcoming them. They were cut down with heavy machine gun fire, their bullet riddled bodies left bleeding and dead in the streets. Militia forces and average everyday American, patriots, shot at them until they were out of ammo, many of them dying as the Russians sprayed their locations with intense gunfire. There simply was not enough firepower to counter the enemy who rolled onward to DC.

The invasion was going like clockwork, there was little to stop it. It was now or never, while they could do the most damage.

"Get me Admiral Rodin on the horn," Jason said, looking at the intelligence reports in front of him.

"Admiral," Jason said. "It has started. Please order an immediate attack from your subs on all enemy ships. Primary targets are the carriers and supply ships. We have done the same with the container ships in the Gulf and all our land-based systems.

All submarine and ship commanders, as well as land-based launchers received a green light to commence firing. Within a few minutes, they had their targets locked and fired their missiles, torpedoes, and shells at every target they could lock onto. The order was a little too late as the Chinese and Russian destroyers had already launched all their missiles at land-based targets, hundreds of them. Curse the dam EMP and communication glitches.

L i had his command in good control as he moved toward Victorville and Barstow beyond. Given the number of troops he had and lack of armored transport for all of them, he would make slower time than he had planned, but he knew he had a superior force in both numbers and technology. They had picked up the 405, California 22 not far from the port. Here and there, along overpasses were lots of people holding signs that said 'Welcome China' as they passed beneath. The people were cheering them on, and his troops were smiling and waving back then, opened up with machine guns as they killed all they saw. Oddly, none of the welcome parties had guns. That would change. Li wondered how people in a country could do such a thing. Wasn't it obvious from their formation that they were an invading force and not American? Were they that sick of their own government? Likely so, given what he had seen in the media. Like his troops, he smiled devilishly and waved back, watching their blood-soaked bodies fall to the ground. They would feel fortunate to have died if they knew they were destined for work camps until death.

Major Stratford had just received his orders. They had the greenlight to fire. He got on the radio to his batteries on Catalina, San Nicolas, Channel Islands National Park, and a couple of other small islands and his shore batteries, all missiles. His primary targets were the four Chinese carriers and LAX where they had planes landing and were massing more troops and supplies. He would target each carrier with three anti-ship missiles. Because they were the platform for major firepower and mobile, he would use his long-range anti-ship missiles, LRASM. The one-thousand-pound, blast-fragmentation, penetrator warhead, would slam into the carriers at close to five hundred miles per hour. Each had the capability to home in on enemy targeting radar without sending out its own signal. As it approached the target, it would seek out the hottest parts of a ship using infrared tracking; it also had the capability to swarm attack. The other ships would be targeted with improved Tomahawk Block V cruise missiles from all his batteries, as well as missiles from two offshore submarines.

Just as they were launching, Chinese Dragons moved into position, firing from cover in an attempt to stop the launch and blow the missiles. Expecting this, they were countered by hidden special forces groups. The firefight was blistering as men fell on both sides, the missiles continuing to launch. The last Chinese were dispatched as surviving personnel began to run, knowing they were already targeted by the enemy ships. They had just reached cover when the launchers blew, not knowing that the ships that had launched them had been targeted by subs and were already lying on the bottom of the Pacific.

Wen Leung, Admiral of the PLAN had watched Li until his force was out of site. The gnawing at his stomach had finally subsided. Perhaps his friend was correct; Li had always told him the West was weak and decadent. It was then that he saw explosions in the direction of the Los Angeles Airport, LAX, which they had secured to supply their troops. Most of his own naval aircraft were there instead of on the carrier because he deemed it safer. Training his powerful binoculars on the airfields, he watched the explosions, they were not large single ones, but multiple smaller ones. He realized that it was cluster munitions, designed to do the most harm to personnel and airplanes. Hearing an explosion behind him, he quickly turned, the gnawing at his stomach became a huge sinking hole as he realized they were finished.

He immediately relayed orders to all ships to assume combat formation; it was too late. Already, two of his carriers had been struck by multiple missiles and were afire, sinking. The third was struck and crippled. It would never leave port. How could this be? Wen thought as four missiles slammed into his carrier. It was his last thought as his ship exploded, one of the missiles having hit the munitions storage area amidship.

Los Angeles Airport was hit by multiple barrages of missiles and cluster munitions. Almost all Chinese forces and over seventy percent of the carrier fighters were destroyed in one major attack. Other fighters had managed to take off and survive the barrage, but without carriers, they would need to find another airport. It would not be hard, but their effectiveness would be reduced until they could regroup. The explosions on the runways left the airport inoperable, as inbound transport planes were targeted with Stinger missiles.

Notwithstanding the success of the strike, Chinese destroyers and submarines had counterstruck. Almost all the land-based batteries were knocked out. Los Angeles attack subs had been shadowing the Chinese subs and were able to sink all of them, but not before they had launched against the missile batteries. Huge losses of men and equipment had occurred on both sides. The Chinese would be forced to cope with their remaining supplies and forage for more as they moved toward their objective.

The Chinese divisions were moving steadily toward Vegas as they amassed more men and equipment, which had been stored in the Free Trade Zone where nothing was inspected. They were too far away to see what was happening at the port and LAX, but Li, riding in the lead tank, began receiving reports of the damage. The fleet was lost, the airport was lost, and he had only about fifty planes left for air support. If he lost them, all was lost. Communications was less spotty now as he checked on his forces moving from Portland and Seattle.

He was thinking quickly. How had they known we were coming? Did he have a traitor in his midst? More than enough troops remained to get the job done. The Russians were coming up from the south and he had his troops pushing from the northwest after destroying both Seattle and Portland. They had met no resistance although the container ships had been blown out of the water, but they were irrelevant since they had launched most of their missiles and completed their missions. He would divide the forces coming from the northwest into two groups. One group would push for Denver and the other would join him. They had two hundred attack helicopters, tanks and five divisions of men. Taking half of them would give him almost ten divisions. And with the combined firepower of his remaining jets, he would yet see his objective. He gave orders for the split. He would have their air support reassigned to his unit. Instead of Denver, the smaller group would now target Salt Lake City. They would be closer if more assistance was needed. Li would await arrival of the other troops at Barstow before pushing forward. He relayed orders and made haste to the rendezvous point. He had been unable to reach Panu.

Major Price was getting tired of being the bearer of bad news, but someone always got stuck with the task he was thinking as he found the general surveying troops and defensive positions through his binoculars.

"Sir, I have reports from the coast," Major Price said.

"Any good news?" Jason asked.

"Well sir, some. We took out most of their fleet and the airfield so, they'll need to find a new airfield to operate from. Our scouts are busy scouring the surrounding airfields now, but I'm afraid there are quite a few to check."

"Good, keep them at it," Jason remarked. "And the bad news?"

"It looks like they are still massing more troops. We also have communications from the Seattle and Portland areas. It appears those troops have split and half of them are headed south, presumably to reinforce those headed our way."

"Damn," Jason muttered. "We just aren't going to get a break. Ok, keep an eye on them, find the new airfield and don't be surprised if they split their airpower into multiple groups. If we can find them, we have enough missiles with cluster munitions to take many of them out. Find their helicopters too."

"Yes sir," Major Price said, walking away.

The odds were not in their favor, outnumbered three to one in tanks at least and about even, maybe, in helicopters. The good news was the A-10-Warthogs held in reserve. They were good tank killers, but no match for the Chinese J-15 jets. They were also facing about ten to one odds in troops. Yes indeed, they were in a bind. The one good thing going for them was the enemies supply lines were being stretched. If they could continually harass them, they could slow them down.

The Arvus was sailing halfway between New Orleans and Houston in the Gulf. An AWACS, the military standard in Airborne Warning and Control Systems, was relaying ship positions of the Russian fleet as it passed through the Yucatan Channel and into the Gulf. Commander Wills contacted all his container ships and made target assignments for each. When word came to attack, they would launch in unison. Without being told, he knew the primary targets would be the carriers and supply ships. He had enough missiles for the first volley to target each of their two carriers and six missile cruisers with four LRASMs each. They would never know what hit them.

He was also in contact with Admiral Rodin; U.S. subs in the Gulf were on station. There were two U.S. Los Angeles Class attack subs searching for any Russian subs and two Seawolf Class subs who would target all Russian ships. Commander Wills hadn't been waiting too long when the orders finally came. He wasted no time ordering all ships to fire. Within minutes the bulk of the Russian fleet within the Gulf of Mexico was sunk or sinking. They had returned fire and half his ships were obliterated, as well as one sub. Other targets east of Norfolk had survived, his container ships there being sunk. Due to sporadic communications, the Russians had managed to get all troops ashore before the fleet was destroyed. They had also launched a large number of land-attack missiles, which the commander presumed targeted military bases. The situation posed a significant military problem for the country, they were seriously outgunned.

General Bardos was rethinking his strategy. With their ships destroyed, both enemy forces would need supplies, especially fuel, which their ships could no longer provide. Looking at his maps he saw the World Oil Terminals at Long Beach, along with LBC Tank Terminals and other oil storage facilities in Houston, crude oil storage in Corpus Christi, and the Louisiana Oil Port in New Orleans. They are likely already under enemy control, at least he knew Long Beach was.

"Major Price," Jason yelled. "Get me Commander Wills and Admiral Rodin."

"They're online sir," Major Price said, handing him the radio.

"Gentlemen, we have a problem," Jason said. "As you are likely aware, the enemy far outnumbers us on our own turf. But they need fuel supplies. Major Price has informed me our missile batteries in California are no longer operational. We need to cut fuel supplies to the enemy. I need you to immediately target and destroy the following oil and fuel storage terminals, reading off a list. I will take full responsibility."

"We agree with your assessment," Admiral Rodin said.

"Give us a few minutes and we'll take care of that for you." About four minutes later, each of the targets were completely destroyed. The enemy troops protecting them were annihilated. The explosions of the main storage tanks were massive, catapulting fireballs hundreds of feet into the air as black smoke from oil and fuel began blanketing the area, obscuring visibility.

General Tyurin had finished loading the last of his two divisions onto the train. It was pulling out of the station when the first explosions rocked the ground. Glancing quickly up, he knew instinctively what had happened. The Americans had destroyed the oil and fuel supplies that were of such great value to his forces. He knew scrounging for fuel would take more time, but war wasn't easy. He had his aide contact the Spetsnaz groups and ordered them to look for more fuel sources.

"They know we are here," Panu remarked to his aide. "Let us make haste to the rendezvous with General Qiang. I want all the speed you can muster out of this train. Let's go, now."

"Yes sir," the aide said, talking into his radio.

The train slowly picked up speed as it left the station. The general had deliberately kept his force smaller for greater speed and agility, if two divisions were considered small. The strategy of his force was to protect the flank of the Chinese into Vegas or to make a southward attack, whichever was most necessary. He would be unloading his forces about twenty-four hours later. They would stop only long enough to refuel the train. The engineers had already mapped out the positions. With his combined four dozen Mi-24 and Mi-28 helicopters, along with three battalions of ninety-three T-14 Armata, next generation main battle tanks, who was going to argue with a refuel?

"Sir, I have bad news," Sergi said, his aide.

"What is it?" Panu asked, inwardly grimacing.

"They took out our fleet sir," Sergi said.

"That's impossible," Panu said. "They would have had to know we were…, his voice trailed off."

"Get General Qiang or one of his men," Panu said. "We need to know what the hell is going on."

A few minutes later, Sergi was finally able to get one of General Qiang's men on the radio. Communication was still spotty. They were informed the Chinese fleet was in ruins and that the oil fields and airfields at LAX had been destroyed as well. It confirmed the sinking feeling in General Tyurin's gut. The only way they could have taken out our fleets was if they had been prepared ahead of time and the only way that could happen is for someone to inform them. Even if they had seen Russian and or Chinese ships in Venezuela and Nicaragua, they wouldn't have been able to develop a plan to thwart them on such short notice. Someone had to be leaking from the Chinese side. Perhaps the congress members that were supposed to be on the payroll were not so traitorous as Li assumed. On the other hand, if they knew they were coming, which was obvious, where was their military? He knew the main American forces were near Korea, although now he was certain they would be headed back. It would take about two weeks to arrive. There would be enough time to achieve their objective but what other surprises lay ahead? It was much easier to hold a city than to take it. He must prepare. Achieving their objective was now going to be more difficult.

With the power out and the gray skies over Fairfax, Virginia threatening rain, the inside of the Speakers condo was gloomy and dark. Evelyn had pulled a suitcase from her spare room and thrown it onto the bed. She was frantically packing as she went from one dresser to another, into the bathroom and back, moving with great purpose. Suddenly she felt the hair on the back of her neck raise and had goose bumps all over her arms, not from the cold, from fear. She felt uneasy and frightened as she tried to shake it off. Her mind was racing, were they here already to arrest her? She hurried even faster. There was precious little time. It was then that she saw it, in the recesses of her large walk-in closet, almost completely dark, the brooding skies seemingly hastening nightfall. A pair of ruby-red eyes staring at her. Evelyn Rutledge had always been in control, until now. Her breathing became short and sporadic as she backed away from the figure slowly approaching her. Tripping over her shoes, she found herself on the floor, staring up into those ruby eyes, finally getting a good look at the figure towering above her.

"Who, who, are you?" She stammered.

"It is of no importance, but if you must know, I am Death Feather. You have been disloyal to Sun God, a traitor to your own people and to mine."

"A dialogue," she thought. "I can gain the upper hand."

"Who do you think you are?" she asked. "You trespass into …, her voice trailed off as she found it difficult to catch her breath.

Death Feather was waving his hand as a red glistening dust settled over her hair and face. At the same time, orange beams of light shot out of his eyes into hers. Evelyn's eyes widened as she began talking incoherently.

"I have the authority to kill you, but for a traitor such as yourself, I have decided that death is too lenient. I commission you to live out your life in the torment of your own mind, unable to communicate with another."

Death Feather waved his hand again and a pale green light draped over the Speaker's entire body. She stripped herself of her clothing piece by piece, mumbling incoherently as she made it to the front door, exiting naked just as two Secret Service agents began knocking. She fled past them, into the pouring rain, babbling unintelligibly. The agents were taken by surprise, watching her run down the sidewalk.

"You don't see that every day," an agent said.

"No, you don't. I'm not chasing her; guess we better call the EMTs and let them round her up."

About a half hour later Evelyn Rutledge, Speaker of the House of Representatives, was lying in the back of an ambulance, on the way to the hospital, still babbling incoherently as her pale, sickly green eyes, stared into space. She would die a long, lonely death, trapped in the recesses of her mind, her worst fears imagined over and over as she fell further into the never-ending abyss of insanity.

Jeremy was still sitting in his observation area when the General, Lunadi, and Sky Thinker made it up to him. There was a series of sand paintings laid out in the sand before him. He waved his hand at them to stop as they approached. They stood looking down upon, what to them, looked like artwork, better found in a museum than atop a rock and sand outpost in the desert outside Vegas.

"Tell me my friends," Jeremy said. "What brings you here? Do you have news of our enemies?"

"Unfortunately, yes," Jason said. "There are many more of

them than we anticipated. We have taken out their fleets and ability to supply themselves from our reserves, but I'm afraid they outnumber us ten to one in personnel and at least three to one in tanks and aircraft."

"Do not worry my friends," Jeremy said, smiling and waving his hand. "These will help us. All is going to plan. You have done all you can, now you will receive our help."

"Do you mean to tell me we have done all of this for naught?" Sky Thinker asked.

"Not for naught," Jeremy said seriously, the smile gone from his lips. "You have done it to show your loyalty to Sun God. Is that not enough? You have proven yourselves up to this point. The battle will wage sore, but your valiance in the fight will prove your worth."

"You speak as though Sun God could do this himself," Jason said.

"He can indeed," Jeremy replied. "But he must test us and often, even the wicked serve his purposes. Though they know it not, they have a place of service, but not one of loyalty. Sun God could simply release Monster Slayer to kill all, but that would remove our agency. Come let us meditate as the sun falls."

The group sat down away from the sand paintings, meditating, a calmness falling over them. The sun had set, the faint glow of light blue still washing across the horizon when Jeremy stopped his chanting and the others looked at him, wondering what he was about to do.

"As I understand it, the Seminole have the ability to transcend from the physical to the spiritual state," Jeremy said. "Is this not true Lunadi?"

"It is true," Lunadi said. "Only a few of us can do it. Our spirit can leave our bodies to do good or bad. Mostly we use it to understand our enemies or to do good deeds for our people."

"Then you must use it now," Jeremy said. "You will be doing a good deed for your people and the Earth Surface People by helping them to survive and to understand our common enemies."

"That is incredible," Jason said. "I had no idea. What can we do to help?"

"Normally, we do not perform it in front of others because it is sacred," Lunadi said. "However, given we are involved in a sacred undertaking to save the country, I trust the Great Spirit will not be offended."

"What do you need?" Jeremy asked.

"I need all of you to sit in a larger circle and to protect my body while I am out of it. First, we need to build a small fire three feet from my head and the same distance from my feet. I will lay flat on my back between them. Do not say anything and do not move. Do you understand?"

The men nodded affirmatively. Lunadi lay down and they marked the spots where the fires would be lit as they gathered wood Jeremy had brought, fires in the correct places. Again, Lunadi lay down. As the others sat, the wind died completely, he began an unbelievably soft hum, the others watching him. Instead of the hum becoming louder as they expected, it changed to a staccato rhythm and abruptly stopped. There was a sound in the air, indeterminable yet pleasant, almost like a woman's voice whispering. A white mist began to gather atop and immediately around Lunadi's body, growing thicker and brighter, hovering over the body in an undulating fashion. Abruptly, there was what sounded like a sigh and the mist took the form of Lunadi, looking just like him, standing above his body. The men looked at it and at each other, captivated what they were witnessing. The mist slowly turned from white to a darker gray and then a black color, fading as it moved quickly away, too fast to follow with their eyes.

They watched in the direction it had gone and slowly looked from one to the other, wanting to say something, but they dared not as they followed the instructions Lunadi had given them. The fires cast eerie shadows on the rocks around them as they waited patiently for what they hoped was Lunadi's return.

The general's aide had spread out several maps on the back of the armored vehicle. Under red lighting, the general, and several of his higher-ranking officers, were attempting to determine the best attack strategy given the damage to his fleet and supply lines. He was looking at the latest satellite images first. The area around Vegas had not changed, except that in one of the photos was a truck out in the middle of the desert.

"This concerns me," Li said. "Odd that a truck should be out in the middle of nowhere."

"I agree," a colonel said. "But there have been no signs of any movement in the area for the last week and none yesterday. I think it's just some teenagers four-wheeling as the Americans say."

"Ah," Li mused. "You may be right as there are no other vehicles."

"Besides, wouldn't they have put up some sort of defense and attacked us near the port if there were military present?" The colonel asked. "We have seen no sign of anyone other than the missile attacks."

As they talked, the spirit of Lunadi stood just beyond the glow of the light behind them. He had maneuvered his form to merge with the shadows and had a clear view of the map, able to hear and see what they were planning.

"Okay," Li said. "Our reinforcements will be here tomorrow giving us a full ten divisions. We will leave immediately upon their arrival and press toward the target. The only choke point appears to be this canyon. We could go around it."

"Do you think that is wise?" a general asked. "Going around it would take several days and scatter our forces over very rough terrain. With no sign of the enemy, I say we move quickly through it to our objective."

"I would normally agree," Li said. "It is just odd that we have seen nothing."

"That is because all their troops were sent to Korea," the general said, the other officers nodding in agreement. "Even the Americans can no longer fight a two-front war."

"I suppose you are right," Li replied, feeling a little better about reaching their objective. "We will press forward past Baker and then through this mountain pass, pointing to the map, once we get through it, we will mass at Primm and then circle left and right through the desert and then mass again as we speed through this last canyon then, we will be on the outskirts of Las Vegas once we push through."

"Is it wise to disperse after Primm?" the colonel asked.

"Humor me," Li said. "Just in case there is an enemy force, we will fare better if spread out. With ten divisions, they will have little chance of stopping us, assuming there are combatants in the area."

The clack, clack, clack of the train passing over the rail joints made a familiar rhythmic sound as General Tyurin conferred with his aide.

"We will disembark here at Needles station," Panu said. "That will put us within easy range of Vegas and likely no resistance. However, if General Qiang needs us, we will continue on to Baker, here."

Lunadi was standing against the wall, away from the nearest light, again listening and watching. Several other officers sat about in the club car, tired from an already long journey. The strategy Lunadi had guessed was the correct one. He knew where they would stop, and his forces were at work planting explosives along the route. Now, he would modify where they were. If they could derail the train, it would almost completely nullify this force. They could take it out quickly.

About three hours later, the spirit form returned and hovered over Lunadi's physical body as the color changed to a dull yellow, then black, followed by red and finally, a white mist that settled back onto Lunadi's unmoving body in the same manner it had formed, embers glowing red in the darkness. In an instant, the mist was gone. Lunadi sat up. So intent were these men on trying to figure out what was going on that his movement sent a jolt through them.

"Damn," Jason said. "You scared the hell out of me."

"Sorry about that," Lunadi said, grinning as he stood.

He looked out across the vast expanse of the desert toward the west and then back to the south. He was contemplating what he had just seen and heard while transformed.

"Were you able to get any information?" Sky Thinker asked.

"Yes, I was," Lunadi responded. "It is what we expected. The Chinese are waiting in Barstow for their reinforcements from the north, which will boost their forces to ten divisions. The Russians are on the rails as we speak, quickly moving toward Needles."

"Are you telling me that you visited both enemy positions?" Jason asked incredulously.

"Yes," Lunadi said. "When in the spirit form, I can travel at the speed of thought. The key is to remain undetected. This is what I found out."

Lunadi began to draw a large map in the dirt, explaining to the group what he had discovered. They discussed strategy until the sun peaked above the eastern horizon, casting its familiar orange glow across the sky. They didn't realize how long they had been planning, but rather than being tired, they were invigorated at what they now knew. Jeremy stayed behind as the others made it back to their assigned areas. One thing that greatly troubled the general was the firepower the enemy had with ten divisions: 130,000 men, maybe more.

President Weld was sitting with Erin in Cheyenne Mountain within the NORAD communications center. Erin had never been to the complex. It had been little used since the Cold War until the day of 9/11, when it was brought back to the mainstream of military operations. They were one mile inside the mountain and two thousand feed down from the top in a network of thirteen, three-story, and two, two-story buildings that housed the offices and communications of NORAD and NORTHCOM. They had taken a bus into the facility and were protected from EMP and nuclear blasts.

The circumstances in Washington made it necessary to vacate and run the government from a more protected area. Only General Wilson had survived the Pentagon bombing because he had been visiting Stone and Austin at Langley. All members of congress had been killed except a congress woman from Michigan and a congressman from Georgia who were as yet unaccounted for. General Wilson was briefing the President and staff.

"Sir," General Wilson said. "As I mentioned before, we are in fairly good shape. We have no military forces to deal with the enemy forces."

"Why?" the President asked.

"Well sir," the General said. "All our troops were shipped to Korea along with our fleets. Although Shockwave and the accompanying forces were able to find and sabotage a great many of the container launch systems, enough remained so that they were able to knock out all military bases and remaining forces, along with our fighter wings, though we had few left in the States. According to sketchy satellite feeds, the Chinese forces are stopped currently at Barstow, California. We believe waiting on reinforcements from the Portland area, which appear to be headed that way. The Russians have a couple of divisions on trains moving toward Las Vegas, the rest of the Russian forces, the bulk of them, are moving out of New Orleans up I-95 and along the Eastern Seaboard and through Atlanta and other major cities. It seems they've split their forces for greater effect."

"Is there any way to stop them?" Phil asked.

"No sir, unless there is an act of God," the General replied. "Not until our fleets arrive back from Korea; that's ten days out at least. By then, the enemy will have made it to Washington and gained control of Las Vegas, Salt Lake City, potentially Denver and no telling what else. There are also the two Chinese contingents moving down from Ottawa and Thunder Bay toward Philadelphia, New York, and Minneapolis. We are developing a strategy for our National Guard to engage them and slow them down until we can reinforce them."

"Is there any good news?" Erin asked.

"Actually, there is. We have knocked out both the Chinese and Russian fleets so that their logistics are temporarily cut off. They will be able to forage for fuel and other supplies as they move, but it will slow them down. The real problem is that if they succeed in taking the cities I mentioned, we will pay an awful price taking them back."

The President sat, looking about the room at the staff. They were all looking to him for leadership. He had to be strong because the fear and anxiety on their faces was evident. It was likely that none of them had ever contemplated the scenario they were facing. It was time to give them some good news, which he had held back not knowing who he could trust and who he could not. Because the congress had all been killed, who comprised the bulk of traitors to the country, this small group of men and women, because their very lives now depended each other and on a handful of others, could be trusted, at least short term.

"General," Phil said. "Do you know General Jason Bardos?"

"Why yes," General Wilson replied. "We went to the Academy together. He's brilliant. Most of his commanders didn't like him because he is unpredictable, but I wish the hell he were here now."

"He is, at least in voice," Phil said. "I'm about to tell you something that may seem incredible and impossible to believe. I want all of you to take a seat for a few moments."

The President and Erin rehearsed all the things that had happened in the past few months and his first meeting with Jeremy in college. They also gave an accounting of what happened at Chaco Canyon and the attempt to assassinate the President and the role of the tribes in what was about to happen in the desert. When they had finished, some of the staffers had tears running down their cheeks. It was like the spirit whispered to them the truth of what they had heard. "I have only one question Mr. President," General Wilson said. "How can I help General Bardos and his troops?"

"He would be the best one to answer that," Phil said. "Erin, hook the general up with a radio and get him and Jason talking."

Susan Grisham had planned on voting from her office in Michigan. The bad news had reached her from a confidant and then she watched it very briefly on the news until power died. News of the tragic event had filtered down to many, at least in various state houses across the country. For a couple of hours, she had mulled over the course of action to take. There was a knot in her stomach as she packed her suitcase, her husband sitting in a chair across the room.

"I do not understand why you need to go," he said.

"Our country needs me," She replied. "I am to go to Colorado to help what remains of the President's and Chiefs of Staff."

Considering the circumstances, it was the perfect lie. Did he believe it she wondered? Once she was gone, he would not be able to contact her since cell towers were out and now, too many hours after the EMP blasts, phones were out of juice.

Her husband kept staring at her, wanting to believe what she said, but for months he had suspected she was having an affair. Was this yet another lie to rendezvous with her lover? Although he knew the capitol building had been destroyed and the Congress killed, the trust was minimal.

"I suppose you're right," he said. "Now more than ever the nation needs its leaders. Don't leave me hanging; keep me in the loop."

He kissed her on the cheek as she headed out the door. The look in her eyes was telling, it was one of indifference. Susan hurried downstairs to a waiting limo. As the driver took her bag, she climbed into the back seat, waving back at her husband throwing her a kiss from the living room window. She had called Big Rod to meet her at the office with her last remaining cell power. They would spend a hot night of lust as they planned the best strategy for leaving the next morning. It would not take the NSA and FBI long to put the trail of breadcrumbs together. Had her party remained in power, they would be under control, but now they would be looking for someone to blame. She had stashed away over ten million in an offshore account and all she left behind was, in her view, a worthless husband. She smiled at the thought of sunning on the beach with Big Rod.

A non-descript van, disguised as a plumbing contractor was parked a block away. The two occupants had been surveilling her for over two weeks and watched the Congress Woman as the limo slid into light traffic. Staying several blocks behind, they tailed the car to its destination. Susan's burner cell was ringing.

"Hello," she said, apprehension in her voice.

"You have done well," the electronic voice said. "Where are you headed?"

"I am not sure yet," Susan said. "I will call you with the destination once determined."

"Very well. I will await your call."

General Li Qiang was hovering over his maps and satellite photos when his aide brought him a radio.

"One of those who escaped will call with her destination," the electronic voice said. "What do you want me to do?"

"Let her reach it then, make it look like an accident," Li said.

"Do you think she knows you are one of us?"

"She has no idea," the voice said. "She only cared about the money and her lover."

"Good," Li replied. "Eliminate her before their FBI find her."

Hanging up the phone, Li smiled. Two had gotten away, but they would not make it far because treason bore a price.

Li had all his forces gathered and was on the move toward Las Vegas. As they went along the route, there was occasional gunfire as patriots took aim and began killing as many of the enemy as they could. This was coupled with Javelin missiles that managed to destroy about thirty tanks before helicopters took them out. Although a feeble attempt against such a large force, with a few men killed here and there, General Qiang became more certain that there would be no defense of Vegas although harassment by the militias, Shockwave, and tribal warriors was unrelenting. The warriors were becoming more difficult for his choppers to target as they adapted to hiding from the helicopter's infrared. Thus, the death toll of men and equipment continued to mount. In response, he made bolder moves with his men than ordinary. The force maintained a steady pace; twenty miles per day forced march. The troops who rode on tanks and other vehicles one day, marched the next. They made it to the first major mountain pass west of Primm on the fourth day. Li was worried because he had not heard from General Tyurin in more than two days. Still, his jets and helicopters had seen nothing and encountered no resistance. He was making all haste toward his objective, maintaining constant air cover, convinced the City of Lost Wages would soon be his.

Looking through his binoculars to the southeast, he noticed about one hundred men dressed in wild, brightly colored clothing. Curious he thought, they don't look like military and are too far away shoot us.

The men of Lunadi's STS force under Commander Agnew had his men lined up along a small ridge when the Chinese came into view. As they advanced, his men continued to range the distance to target. They waited patiently as they settled behind their rifles. The lead tanks stopped just inside their two-thousand-yard marker; a few small boulders set atop each other went unnoticed. Commander Agnew could see a couple of the officers looking at them through binoculars.

"Send it," Commander Oconee yelled, along the line of fifty sniper teams.

No sooner had General Qiang thought the distance too far than several men fell from their tanks, dead, mortal wounds to the center of their chests. A few dozen infantry were also killed. Having quickly ducked below his turret opening, Li wasted no time sending a helicopter to annihilate the small group.

The helicopter reached the position quickly, flying low along the ridges and lower-lying sands before radioing back to the general's aide who was watching the helicopter move back and forth in a grid pattern, searching.

"Sir," the pilot said. "There is no sign of the enemy."

"What do you mean?" the aide screamed. "They were there, we saw them; they killed almost three dozen of our men."

"We will continue to look sir, but so far, there is no sign of them."

For the next few days, the same scenario was repeated. To the enemy it was like STS and the tribal warriors were ghosts.

Chairman of the Joint Chiefs of Staff, General Roscoe Wilson was inside Cheyenne Mountain coordinating as much as he could with other military groups. All forces had been ordered back to the U.S. from Korea, but it might be too little too late. He was doing what he could to get satellite coverage for General Bardos.

"I wish I could send you more forces General," Roscoe said. "But we haven't any. What is the best thing I can do for you?"

"Aerial surveillance with whatever you have would be best," Jason said. "I have some Warthogs that can help take out their tanks, but they cannot match the J-15s. Do you have any land-based launchers that can help us?"

"No, they were knocked out by the Chinese," Roscoe said. "We do have a few in Texas and some in California. The ones in Texas will arrive too late. We have not been able to communicate with California yet."

"Understood General," Jason said. "Okay, so let's focus on two items. First, find where their jets are located. I have some missiles and will send a SOF group to take them out, at least as many as we can. I could also use a couple of Apache's, but I do not want to give away anything yet. Second, give us updated aerial surveillance as often as you can. I'll let you speak to Major Price who will be in control of that. Thank you general."

"No, thank you," Roscoe said. "We will do everything we can for you."

General Wilson understood the gravity of the situation. Ten divisions, well-armed and motivated, along with two divisions of Russian troops on their way were about to go to battle with a much lesser force. The odds were not good; time for guts to take over. God help those men. He began snapping his fingers signaling for all his officers so they could come up with a plan to help General Bardos.

Lunadi had spent the day with his commanders along the ridges and foothills east of Needles. He had set explosive charges to blow the train trestle across the Colorado River and all along the tracks for the length of trains he expected which for two divisions, was miles. He assumed five to seven miles but extended it for twelve. Several trestles ran across washes; those were set with explosives as well. He also set charges across Happy Canyon Wash so that if the rear locomotives remained working after the explosives went off, they would not be able to return eastward. The force would be confined within that space. Combined with his men, he had the giants, a couple of thousand militia and about 25,000 tribal warriors.

Lunadi was speaking to Major Justin Roth, officer in charge of the combat engineers. He was a matter of fact type and burly as they come. His physique was unmistakably built for hard work and he was strong as an ox. His barreled chest straining to burst the seams of his shirt. He was chewing on a half-smoked cigar protruding from his lips and had a mischievous gleam in his eye.

"Major Roth," Jason said. "Let's go over this once more. You have all the charges set on the trestles and along the tracks here, here, here and along here correct?"

"Yes sir. They are set to go off at the same time once you give the order."

"The last item is the I-40 overpass," Jason said.

"Yes, as you instructed, it is wired, but we will not blow it unless we see the Russians start to move across."

"Very well, carry on Major," Jason said.

For the past several days, militia groups had been pouring in from Arizona and Texas, a couple of thousand of them so far. They had heard a big fight was going to happen and they wanted to be a part of it. Lunadi needed all the help he could get so he was compelled to speak to their leaders one last time and had his Commander Lucin Oconee assemble them. Along with Aichu and his giants. They were on the east side of the Colorado River. Lunadi had a megaphone so they could all hear.

"Men, welcome to hell," Lunadi said as they all laughed.

Aichu and his men walked around the edge of the foothill behind them as Lunadi spoke, the men had never seen them and began to push back in fear from their gigantic size.

"It is okay," Lunadi said. "These are our friends and will be helping us. I will explain about them later."

"What do you want us to do?" a leader asked, eyeing the giants, not quite sure what to make of them.

"I'll put it bluntly as I can," Lunadi said. "We are going to be up against a tough, combat proven Russian force. They're headed up these tracks. I have lookouts posted out to one hundred miles so, once they are spotted, we will have maybe ninety minutes to wait. As I told you before, I cannot guarantee your safety but at the same time, your country needs you. There is no one coming to help, it is just us. We have a simple game plan. When they approach, we are going to blow the bridges and tracks. You must remain concealed until that happens. Once the explosives have gone off, get everyone of the enemy you can in your cross hairs and pull the trigger. We cannot afford to let them move into Vegas or to join the Chinese forces to the west."

"Do you think the explosives will damage the tanks enough not to work?" another leader asked.

"We should get many of them," Lunadi said. "But that is why we need you. Once we set off the charges, it is important to kill every man before they can get into a tank or armored vehicle. It is imperative."

"How good are most of your men with their rifles?" Commander Oconee asked.

"Most of us can kill up to one thousand yards," a leader spoke out. "A few up to fifteen hundred or so."

"Good, you will come with me and we will assign your positions based on your skills."

"Okay, remember," Lunadi said. "Watch out for your fellows. Do not shoot Aichu or his men and do not begin firing until the explosives go off. Remain completely hidden until then. Once you begin firing, keep shooting until your barrels melt down if need be, you won't get a second chance."

"I have a question," a leader said, holding up his hand. "I'm sure they will have helicopters; how do you plan to deal with them?"

"We have men with Stinger missiles along this entire route and at the train station in Needles," Lunadi said. "They will be like snipers such as yourselves, except with missiles, and will take out all they can. My guess is that they will only have a few flying ahead of them as they approach. We will all remain hidden until we spring the trap. I hope that satisfies you."

The men murmured in approval as they followed Commander Oconee and some of his men to their positions. Without a doubt it was going to be a long, nerve-racking day as they prepared to live or die at the hands of yet, an unseen enemy moving swiftly toward them. A loaded train would be moving faster than an empty one, seventy miles per hour so, it wouldn't take them long to arrive.

It was late afternoon when word came of the Russian approach. Flying ahead of them flew a dozen, Mi-24 helicopters, a tank of aerial death. Each had eight troops, likely Spetsnaz, and had a speed of two-hundred miles per hour but were keeping tight formation a few miles ahead of the trains. In the lead helicopter was General Panuftii Tyurin, supervising operations for his forces. His troops were minutes behind him as he checked the route into Needles. Two of his helicopters flew on into the station and landed, disembarking their men near the main terminal, which was busy with a few workers who looked at them in astonishment, not sure what was going on. They could tell these men were not U.S. troops and fled.

Commander Oconee had placed a few dozen of his men around the terminal, obscured by the cars on the tracks. They were in six teams, all armed with stinger missiles. When the helicopters landed, they shut their engines down as their eight-man Spetsnaz troops sat around them in a semi-circle, guns at the ready. The warriors zeroed in on them and waited for the explosions before opening fire. The anticipation was making their adrenaline pump. The remaining helicopters had held back near the river, scouring every inch of the terrain. Panu did not see anything out of the ordinary. He directed his chopper to the river so they could inspect the trestle.

"Drop us down and let's look at the trestle and overpass," Panu directed the pilot.

"Yes sir."

The pilot hovered the helicopter and then descended

close to the water's surface as they looked for signs of explosives to determine if it were safe for the train to pass. So far, they had a few snipers shoot at them along the way, but no sign of military movement or troops. They naturally, had let their guard down a little. As the helicopter hovered and went back and forth several times along the trestle and then the overpass, they saw no signs of explosives and were satisfied. The choppers hovered on either side of the river as Panu told the officers to speed up the train. He wanted to unload before nightfall, few hours remained. As he hovered above the river, he looked about at the stark beauty of this barren land and yet, it flourished with agriculture thanks to the mighty Colorado River.

The train approached swiftly, without slowing down as it started across the river. The locomotives had just made it across when the explosives went off. All along the tracks for miles, the ground shaking as if a major earthquake had struck. Two of the hovering helicopters were struck instantly by Stinger missiles as they went down in balls of fire. General Panuftii Tyurin, a great Russian warrior, was dead before the battle began.

Hearing the explosions, the troops next to the two choppers in the station jumped up as the pilot began starting the helicopter. Without warning, two Stinger missiles slammed into each, exploding them into a mass of twisted metal and shrapnel. The men left standing that were not killed by the explosion were killed by Commander Oconee's men, who afterward rushed back to the river to help secure the I-40 overpass.

Lunadi's men lined both sides of the tracks from a higher elevation of about twenty feet, enough to give them the high ground. Reinforcing his men were 25,000 tribal warriors; their faces painted. The explosions had sent the rail cars crashing over each other. Many had turned upside down; others lay on their side. Many of the tanks had also turned upside down or had rail flatbeds laying on top of them.

The remaining helicopters came in firing with a vengeance and were killing hundreds of men. Heavy thuds were felt by the men as Aichu and his giants jumped from their positions and began swinging their fifteen-foot swords. A sound, like a hoarse, high-pitched whistle was heard as each sword sliced through the air. The low flying helicopters were so focused on killing Lunadi's force they did not see the giants until just before the swords sliced through them, chopping them in half.

The explosions from the charges had ignited fuel in many of the armored vehicles on the flatbeds; fires were burning all along the tracks. Thousands of soldiers flew through the air as the trains soared off the tracks, colliding with flatbeds ahead of them. Many were killed but there was still a large force. Dust blowing from the explosions and wreck had not settled when the first volley of bullets struck the Russians. Chaos and mayhem reigned as the Russians, fear taking hold of them, fought back aggressively. Aichu and his giants had affixed the steel shoes on their feet so they could stomp on tank barrels and other equipment as they ran amok from one end of the trains to the other, beginning at different locations. They ran like the wind, close to fifty miles per hour as they crushed men and equipment beneath their feet, the ominous sound of their slicing swords heard above the din.

A withering barrage of bullets plunged into soft flesh as thousands perished. Somehow the Russians continued to fight back, filling the air with lead. In less than an hour, all sides had run out of ammunition. It was then that the 25,000 warriors, all along the tracks, rushed in. Hand to hand combat followed with knifes and bare knuckles as men fell under the knives. Blood soaked into the dry earth in rivers. Men were falling, exhausted, covered in dirt and sweat and blood.

The battle raged for almost two hours. A few tanks had been manned and cut down hundreds of militia members before they were taken out by Javelin missiles, one by Aichu's giants, two of whom were seriously wounded. Shoulder-fired missiles from Lunadi's men kept striking armored targets all along the length of the train as Commander Oconee's men, along with several other commanders and the militia groups kept firing until the barrels of their rifles turned cherry red, the rounds in the chambers beginning to explode before the trigger was pulled. Throwing their rifles aside, they followed suit with the other tribal members and plowed into the Russian soldiers, slicing and dicing as they moved forward. White flags on the end of empty AK-47s began to appear all along the tracks. The Russians surrendered. Lunadi's and tribal warriors moved in, rounding up the prisoners who were immediately marched to the Needles station and put into box cars to hold until General Bardos decided what to do with them.

"General Bardos," Lunadi spoke into the radio. "We have eliminated the Russian force and taken the remainder captive."

"How are your men?" Jason asked. "Sir, we have at least two thousand wounded; the militia lost hundreds, killed. We are still counting sir."

"I'm sorry to hear that," Jason said. "And the Russian's?"

"We locked the remainder into box cars at Needles," Lunadi replied. "I'm estimating their losses at sixty percent or more. They wouldn't quit sir and we could not afford to."

"Understood," Jason said. "Okay, do what you need to do to wrap it up, talk with the local police to help you and get the remainder of your group here as fast as you can.

"Sir, the only way to move as many men as we have is by flatbed," Lunadi said.

"Do you have a suggestion?"

"Yes sir. Given the strength and position of the enemy, we can move via train to Goffs then, basically northeast and flank them."

"That will take several days."

"We will do it in one and a half sir."

"Very well," Jason said. "Good luck. Keep me advised, out."

Lunadi and his men were tired; adrenaline flowing a mile a minute tended to do that. Once the prisoners were rounded up and locked away, he left a contingency of his men to work with local law enforcement to help control them. The rest loaded up on train flat beds and headed to Goff. They would travel through the desert at night as they sought to flank the Chinese on the south while General Bardos engaged them on the east. The familiar rhythm of the rails was a welcome sound as he dozed; he was proud of his men. They had performed well, and everyone knew it. His eyes closed as he fell into an uneasy sleep thinking of Erin, wondering how she was.

The AWACS overlooking the battle of Needles, relayed the images back to Cheyenne Mountain and General Wilson's staff.

"Damn, those guys are good," General Wilson said as he watched the battle. "It's like every weapon is a precision sniper. We may get out of this yet."

Summoning over one of his Flag officers, he ordered him to get images to General Bardos at once. Next, he was on the line to Admiral Rodin.

"Admiral," Roscoe said. "We may have found the base the Chinese are using for their jets. It is about two hundred miles inland. Do you have a sub around Long Beach equipped with LRASM or similar?"

"Yes, all of our subs are," Admiral Rodin replied. "We can launch as soon as you give us the coordinates."

"Very well," Roscoe said. "Let me speak with General Bardos, out."

General Wilson knew they would only get one shot at this. If they didn't take out the majority of those fighters, Bardos's, White, and Lunadi's forces would be decimated. He also knew that the Chinese were already flying sorties up to Vegas, surveilling the terrain and reporting back to their commanders. So far, the small number of forces under General Bardos had remained undetected, but it could not remain so. Soon they would attack and then, well, time would tell.

Communications across the U.S. remained sporadic. News media outlets and television networks could not get their signals out beyond the local populace and then, only to those who had antenna's and older tv's. The Internet was shut down except for essential government communications, which were strangely quiet. Those remaining, mostly military, felt it unwise to create more panic. Some people were having anxiety attacks because their phones no longer worked, and they were unable to login to social media sites that were also down. Most phones had run out of power after the first twenty-four hours and would not be working again until power was restored. It was like the U.S. was in a vacuum. Everything was strangely quiet excepting locations around the enemy forces moving up the eastern seaboard. The Russians had moved through Alabama, north Florida, Georgia and kept moving toward the Norfolk naval base and DC. There was no one to stop them as they left dead bodies and a wake of destruction. Atlanta had been almost leveled by missile bombardments from their ships off the eastern coast. Missiles raining down on the city like hail stones.

Jason Bardos was briefing his commanders over the radio. A squadron of Chinese J-15s had just done a flyover, looking for potential threats. The general and his forces would now need to contend with them and try to escape their instruments of death until they figured a way to take them out. Their combat radius would only allow them twenty to thirty minutes over target, but that was too long for them to survive and at the same time, defeat the Chinese forces.

"We need to find that damn base," Jason said emphatically.

"Sir," General White said. "We have our men working on it. We believe we are closing in."

"The sooner the better," Jason said. "The enemy is here, approaching the mountain pass," Jason said, pointing to the map. "We will let them get near our end, the eastern end and we will strike them. The combat engineers have set shaped charges along the seven-mile route to help damage and destroy tanks, as well as Claymore's for anti-personnel defense. Our scouts say they are just entering the western end of the pass. That's why they are scrambling their fighters, they don't want to get caught in a trap. This general is shrewd. Once we attack, they will know they have a fight on their hands."

"What are you anticipating General?" Lorenzo asked. "I wish I could tell you it was all going to be peachy but that's not my style. This will be the best chance we have to kill as many of them as we can at one time. Once they exit the pass on the eastern end, it's open desert and they'll fan out until they come to the next choke point. Their fighters will be providing tight cover, along with their helicopters. I'm open to suggestions."

"Sir," Sky Thinker said. "I would attack with our aircraft first, then set off the explosives. If we do the latter first, the armor will spread quickly and become more difficult to target."

"Excellent idea," Jason said.

"Yes, agreed," General White conceded.

"Very well," Jason said. "May Sun God be on our side at this perilous time. Jeremy, any help you can get from the other side is most welcome. Attend to your stations men, the fun is about to commence."

"General Wilson sir," an aide said, hustling up, out of breath. "We found the air base sir."

He laid a map and images out in front of the general who promptly called General Bardos to confer. The sub had a greenlight to attack. Shockwave personnel were close enough to observe. Three minutes later, two Ohio class submarines off the coast of Los Angeles launched a series of Tomahawk Block IV land-attack, subsonic cruise missiles carrying one-thousand pound-class unitary warheads. They were fondly called TLAMs by the navy, Tomahawk Land Attack Missiles. Even though it was against the Cluster Munitions Convention the U.S. signed in 2017, four of the missiles were the Block III TLAM-D carrying one hundred, sixty-six combined effects bomblets. The base was one hundred seventy-nine miles away. Twenty-one minutes later, the missiles began to strike the airbase. All Chinese fighters and transport planes on the base and runways were destroyed. The submarines were out of TLAM's, but the mission was a success.

The Chinese divisions were nearing the eastern end of the mountain pass when General Chiang received word of the airbase bombings. He began to wonder why he was not yet attacked. The missiles must have come from submarines, it was the only explanation. They knew where the airbase was, so they obviously knew where his troops were. They had been moving slowly but steadily toward the objective. Apprehensive of an enemy attack. It had taken almost two days to move from the initial staging area at Baker. He gave orders to spread out and speed up to get through the mountain pass.

"How many squadrons do we have left?" General Qiang yelled into the radio.

"About sixty planes sir, three squadrons," his aide yelled back. "But we have four more squadrons arriving from our troops moving toward Minneapolis."

"Have all of them land at the secondary base, refuel, and return to cover us immediately."

The divisions of men and armor were about one-half mile from the western end of the pass when it happened. Thirty A-10 Warthogs had flown at near ground level from the north, through Sandy Valley and up over the mountains at about five thousand feet when they dropped from the sky in groups of two and three, segmenting the route. The armored columns were caught like sitting ducks on a pond. They had nowhere to go. The Warthogs came in skimming the sand, launching their Maverick and Sidewinder missiles. Armored personnel carriers, tanks, and men tried to elude them but had little success. The planes then began dropping their incendiary cluster bombs. To the soldiers on the ground, it was as if everything was on fire. They panicked, fear on their faces as they tried to escape the blistering attack. It was then that the Warthogs opened with their 30mm cannon, a gatling gun firing up to 3,900 round per minute, puncturing holes in armored vehicles and tanks like a hot knife through butter: turning men into piles of bloody sludge.

General Qiang was yelling orders through the radio from his lead tank. Near the end of the pass, a dozen Apache helicopters rose just above the ridge high enough to fire their 70mm guided rockets in a salvo that halted the front of the moving column. General Qiang's driver had managed to run into the gully along the edge of the freeway as several rockets shot just over their tank, exploding into the hillside beyond them. The Warthogs were making a second pass with their 30mm cannons. A dozen were shot down from machine guns on the tanks. Suddenly, it was quiet, like nothing had happened. The drone of the planes and the Apache's was gone. General Qiang looked behind him. He knew he had lost a large number of his force. Anger welled up in him as the explosives set by the combat engineers went off along the seven-mile stretch of road running through the pass. He ducked and closed the tanks turret, riding out the next wave of the attack. The effect on the armored vehicles was not nearly as devastating as on the soldiers. Blood from those killed by the explosives and Claymores ran down the interstate like water.

Everyone that could move was ordered to take what wounded they could and get out of the pass immediately. By the time they were out of the pass and regrouped, they had both fighters and chopper cover. General Qiang and his officers busied themselves strategizing their next move and boosting morale among the men. The attack had been devastating and still, there was no sign of an opposing force. Li would never admit it, but it was becoming unnerving.

His aide, a loyal major, walked up beside him and handed him some images he had just received from surveillance of one of their fighters who had been sent to contact the Russian force. The images were of the devastation of the trains and equipment. There was no sign of anyone living. Li motioned his aide away as he sat pondering, looking across the desert. The enemy, despite lack of visible forces was out there. They had reverted to asymmetric warfare and yielded a valuable clue, that they had insufficient force to deal with him so, his attacks would be short and fierce. Knowing this, he would put large numbers of his personnel out front, along with armored personnel carriers to scout every inch of the desert. He was going to crush the enemy. To prevent another major loss, he split his command into three main groups, separated so the enemy could not target all at once. They would move, flanking the lead group.

"Colonel," Li yelled, motioning him over. "Is there news of the Russians along the east?"

"Yes sir," the colonel replied. "They are making good speed and are currently in Norfolk and have secured the naval base there and have more ships on the way. Our troops are moving down from Ottawa and New Brunswick. Assessing the route and speed, both forces should reach Washington at the same time. Intelligence says it is all but deserted."

"Thank you, that is all," Li said.

It appeared that Washington and Vegas would fall into

their force's hands at the same time. Regardless of setbacks, it was going to be fine in the end. He would achieve his objective. Night had fallen as an unnerving calmness settled.

The glow that usually lit up the night sky above Las Vegas was gone; the power having been cut. The stars seemed to shine more brightly as the forces from both sides took some solace from the anxiety and stress of the day. Far out into the desert, both sides could see the glow of a small fire through their binoculars and softly at first, they heard the beat of drums. The sound was feint but recognizable to all.

Lunadi's group had unloaded from the train the night before and force marched through the desert, quietly moving up undetected along the Chinese southern flank. He had only men, no armor and would be forced to use hit and run tactics. He had contacted General Bardos with his position. About 2:00 a.m. he sent in several dozen of his men along with the warriors from the tribes. They selected small groups and creeping up to them, slit the throat of only one and fell back to the safety of the dark desert, back to the main forces as they awaited sunrise.

Jeremy had lit his fires, three of them. He began to chant and pray as he conjured Death Feather. It was not long before he appeared as a black mist, taking form into his frightening shape right before Jeremy, looking down on him with his ruby-red eyes.

"What is it you wish?" Death Feather asked.

"We need your help," Jeremy replied. "We have insufficient forces to contend with the enemy."

"I will help as Sun God has commanded," Death Feather

said. "All is not lost."

Death Feather left more quickly than he had come. Jeremy kept chanting asking for more help. The forces of both sides could hear the feint sound of drums watching the dim, fiery glow that seemed miles away. They witnessed what happened next as a red column of light shot down to where the fire was burning, obscuring it as the drums stopped.

The red bolt of light slowly dimmed to reveal Monster Slayer in the midst, standing above Jeremy.

"The time has come young Medicine Man," Monster Slayer said. "Those who have lost the light will be no more."

"Will you not spare them?" Jeremy pleaded.

"It is too late," Monster Slayer replied. "Even now they cheer on the enemy into our chosen land. They had their agency and have proven their disloyalty. No, my servant, they will not be spared. One cannot live their life constantly slapping the hand of the master that feeds them."

"Is there no way to save them?" Jeremy asked, his eyes glistening with tears.

"None," Monster Slayer said tersely. "Tend to your duties and worry not about those who are traitors. On the morrow you shall see that the wisdom of Sun God is above all and that his patience has run its course."

The column of light became as bright as the noon sun as it turned at first a bright white and then, a blood red, matching the blood-red color of the full moon shining down upon them. A blood moon, never a good omen. Both generals had an uneasy feeling about what they had seen as the dim fires again became visible and the drums beat softly once more.

It was 2:00 a.m. when the Chinese sentries first noticed the ground moving but it was not the ground. Looking up they were surrounded by thousands of sets of glowing red eyes from the bounds of darkness away from the security lights they had set up. Soldiers began to scream, running to and fro as their AK-47s made their familiar clacking from automatic gun fire. The general ran out of his armored vehicle to witness a scene of complete confusion. All around the encampment me were running and shooting at the ground. Out of the corner of his eye he caught the movement as he jumped backward into the vehicle, just missing the strike of a diamond-back rattlesnake. The ground was alive with them. He shut the door to keep them out. The screams continued, as well as the shooting, soldiers killing fellow soldiers as they shot at the snakes and the Skinwalkers. The lights went out one by one until there were none left, leaving the light of the blood-red moon to reveal the horrid scene of death and terror.

The soldiers kept running, panicked and fear stricken. They climbed atop tanks and anyplace they felt safe as the snakes seemed to grow in number. But it wasn't the snakes they feared, it was the wolf-like figures moving faster than they could keep track that frightened them. It was the Skinwalkers. They grabbed the soldiers one by one, as many as they could and stared into their eyes with their ruby-red look, revealing their past sins and driving them insane. After the look, the soldier took no thought of the snakes or of the Skinwalkers as they ran out into the still night air of the cold desert.

A team of Shockwave special operators were close enough to the encampment to observe some of what was happening. They could not see the snakes and looked back and forth at each other.

"Is this some kind of exercise?" one of the asked.

"I don't think so, those men are scared to death," another

said. "Look at them, they are running everywhere, dropping their weapons and just running. Look there, those figures with red eyes; they are chasing them."

As the men continued to watch, several of the soldiers ran right past them. At first, they were going to shoot them, but kept their fingers off the trigger as they noticed the awful look of fear in the soldier's eyes, the whites as large as golf balls. They ran right past them without care. The gunfire and craziness went on for several hours and slowly subsided.

"Never seen anything like that in all my days," the squad leader said, as he called in his report.

The next morning, the Chinese encampment looked like a scene from a zombie movie as dead soldiers and rifles lay scattered about, troops fearful of coming out into the light as they saw their comrades on the ground dead from snake bites and gunshot wounds. Many others were writhing in pain, unable to function. The general and his officers ordered the men to get a grip as they began to haul off their comrades and stack their bodies in piles. Dozens had their throats sliced by Lunadi's men, which blended into the chaos.

Li looked toward where he had seen the fire and column of light the night before and wondered if there was a connection. Get a grip he thought, it was just a freak natural accident. It took hours to get the troops calmed down and back in order. His aide came walking up, a fearful look on his ashen face.

"How many did we lose?" Li asked quietly.

"About six hundred dead sir and another four hundred incapacitated. There were quite a few others with their throats cut. I think the enemy crept in while they slept."

"So, they wish to create fear and panic. Thank you."

The aide knew better than to loiter and walked off murmuring about what had happened, shaking his head in disgust. The odd thing was there were no snakes to be found, not even dead ones. For the first time, he had doubts that he would ever return home to his wife and kids. He had served the general for years, but now he was fearful to follow him another step. The only reason he would continue he determined was to be able to return home to his family. It was 10:00 a.m.

More than fifty-five hundred miles away, Monster Slayer hovered above Cumbre Vieja, an active, yet dormant volcanic ridge on the ocean island of La Palma in the Canary Islands, Spain. There was no longer any question about what must be done. To save the good of the nation, the disloyal would be sacrificed. They had made their decision. Cheering on enemy troops as they passed only cemented their bad judgement. They hated the country that had given them education, riches, and the world as their oyster. Patience was at an end. Monster Slayer held out his hand, pointing his fingers at the heart of Cumbre Vieja as white-hot energy beams shot from them, igniting the volcano, collapsing the earth beneath, causing a huge landslide as it fell thousands of feet into the blue-green ocean below. At the same time, Monster Slayer pointed his spear below the volcano as a red beam emanating from the tip, hit the water like a bolt of lightning, generating a 9.7 earthquake.

As the rapidly moving landslide entered the water, combined with the force the earthquake, the water behind and ahead of the mass was rapidly displaced. Within minutes a seventeen-hundred-foot tsunami was moving westward toward the United States at five hundred miles per hour.

It was 6:45 p.m. with the last light of day fading in the eastern sky. The streets of New York were fuller than normal since there was no electricity, people were wandering around the streets, enjoying daylight while they could. Most were returning home when they heard the sounds of rushing water. Looking toward it, they began to run, but it was too late; the water was too fast. Millions were drowned in an instant as the tsunami hit all along the coast of the eastern seaboard from New York to Miami. As the wave moved onto shore it dropped in height to one hundred thirty-five feet. The Statue of Liberty was washed from its foundation, as were buildings, boats, homes, almost everything. The Jersey Shores were obliterated. There was no escape from the angry sea as it came crashing landward. The Chinese troops in New Brunswick were wiped away as if they never existed.

Washington was flooded and wiped out. It was like the wave was adding insult to injury. In Norfolk, the Russians had secured the naval base and killed all military personnel, and were unloading supply ships when the wave struck. The ships and men were instantly swept away, into the dark, sand-filled waters of the wave. Not a single person survived.

Most of the buildings in South Beach, along the Miami shoreline were removed from their foundations and collapsed in the wave as it swept across the entire state. The satellite view looked like the nose of a deer broken off, as Seminole Medicine Man Buffalo Jim had said many years ago. The state was under water from Orlando southward. Every town south of Orlando, including Miami and Key West were obliterated. The few remaining Russian ships still afloat in the Gulf were capsized and sank. The damage was on an unprecedented scale. All remaining emergency electricity for hospitals and other critical facilities was gone. There was not one light along the entire eastern seaboard. It was truly a black night and the next morning, those left alive awoke to the most devastating natural disaster the U.S. had ever known and still, there was no communication.

President Weld, Erin, and the rest of his staff were deep inside Cheyenne Mountain, monitoring the battle outside of Vegas when one of the generals aides came rushing in.

"It's a disaster," he was screaming. "Look!"

He had piped into the room onto the large monitors the latest satellite image of the morning.

"A tsunami hit the eastern coast, stretching from New York to Miami sirs, lady."

"My God," Phil exclaimed. "What happened to our early tsunami warning?"

"The communication to the buoys must have been knocked out with the EMP." General Wilson exclaimed. "Holy God."

"And the nation doesn't know sir," Erin said. "We do not have communications back up yet."

"Get everyone on it you can general," Phil said. "We still need to focus on helping Bardos or nothing else matters."

"Major," Phil said. "Is there any good news to this?"

"Not much," the major said, his face ashen gray. "The best news is that both the Chinese forces and Russians were wiped completely out. The worst news is that the estimated death toll is about seventy million and climbing; more will die in the next couple of weeks due to lack of food and potable water. We have no resources to deal with such a massive-scale disaster sir."

"The tragedy of a nation," Phil exclaimed. "When it rains it pours."

It was then that he remembered the words of Sun God and his servants, that those who would not help would perish. He wondered if this was a part of that. He sat looking around at the entire staff who were in shock. The workload that needed to be done had just become overwhelming. The irony was that the battle was the only thing that mattered now.

General Jason Bardos and his force were awaiting the Chinese. As they made their way across the desert toward the last pass that blocked their way to Las Vegas. The Chinese jets had discovered a few of their positions and taken them out with rockets. There was no doubt the Chinese knew they were here; they had infantry in front, behind a forward spearhead and air cover. He got on the radio.

"Scott, can you see the enemy?" Jason asked. "Good, what can you do to them with the drones?"

"We have one-quarter pound shaped charges in each drone," Scott replied. "I have them all hooked to an artificial intelligence network. They are programmed to get in the path of fast-moving jets or seek out openings in armor such as turret hatches. They can penetrate up to about six inches of steel sir, not enough for a tank, but can kill most of the armored personnel carriers they hit."

"When can you start?"

"I can initiate on your command sir."

Jason sat looking over the terrain. The enemy had their tanks in diamond formations a mile apart, spread along a three-mile attack front with three major groups headed his way. It looks like they have attempted to copy our maneuvering from the Middle East, he mused. The problem was defeating the air cover to have a fighting chance. He knew that if he could keep his Apaches immersed in ground clutter, they would be hard to detect by the jets and difficult to engage, unless the Chinese pilots were foolish enough to drop down to low altitude, otherwise the jet would be invulnerable to the helicopter's weapons. The trick would be to lure the jets down low enough to take them out. The Warthogs could lure them out, but in making a run for it, they wouldn't escape, not most of them anyway. But it was the only way to knock the jets out. If they could do that, it would still be nasty, but would give his forces a slim chance. He would first need a squadron to work in from the southeast, attack the tanks and armored vehicles then, the Apaches would lay in wait along the ridges of the peaks east of Mountain Springs. Lure the J-15s by them and let them blast away. The drones would serve as the initial diversion. He didn't want to expose his men or armor until absolutely essential. No sense in creating a killing field out of his own men. He kept watching the tanks and armor of General Qiang. They were advancing slowly, protecting themselves and their infantry. In about an hour they would be in the right place.

"Scott, how many drones do you have?"

"Two thousand and a bit more sir."

"Good, on this initial attack, do not use more than five hundred of them. Can you see the armor?"

"Yes sir, they're coming around the mountain southeast of Jean."

"When they get to the small valley near the end, launch your attack on the tanks."

"Roger that, out."

The general got back on the radio and ordered an airstrike on the tanks in an hour and a half, coinciding with the end of the drone attack. They would be the bait for the jets. His other men and the tribes, hidden in the mountains, would remain in place until the final assault by the Chinese.

Lunadi's forces stood ready to attack with small-arms fire when the drones and A-10s did their work. They waited patiently for the signal.

General Qiang was confident he would succeed. His formations were just past Jean, beginning to spread into a wider formation when his tanks started exploding. He was amazed when he saw why. It was a drone attack, sometimes in swarms. The drones were entering the turret hatch of the tanks and exploding inside, setting off the munitions and tearing the tanks apart. He had lost two dozen more tanks. He quickly radioed all units to close hatches. The drones, no longer effective against them, shifted targets to less hardened vehicles. The battlefield was filled with explosions and black smoke. Some of the personnel carriers had been successful in downing quite a few of the drones, their buzzing no longer heard. Almost immediately from the southeast came the familiar sound of the Warthogs, flying low in attack formation, three abreast as they pounded the tanks with rockets and 30mm cannon fire. Zipping across so close to the ground that the props from their engines threw up dust from the desert floor, making it almost impossible for the gunners to target them although they managed to down seven of the planes as they continued northwest, the general's aide quickly calling in air support.

The J-15s dropped altitude down to about three-thousand feet in chase. Being much faster, they caught up with the Warthogs about ten miles later, firing air to air missiles and downing twenty-three planes. As they had been ordered, the Warthog pilots ejected once the missiles locked on.

The Chinese pilots didn't realize they were in a trap until a squadron of Apaches rose just above the ridges to their left and fired, downing the entire squadron of twenty fighters. Not one escaped. According to intelligence, that was a third of the enemies' planes. Back on the battlefield, Apache helicopters had engaged the Chinese Z-18 helicopters, each side losing a dozen before they retreated to safer zones, after firing all their ammunition.

The STS force with Lunadi and the warriors of all the tribes began firing as soon as the drones attacked. Having only rifles, they could only effectively engage infantry units. Almost immediately, they were spotted as they spread out to keep explosives from catching too many at one time. The Chinese engaged them from heavy machine guns from their personnel carriers and sniper fire. slowly advancing toward them, protected by tanks behind that began lobbing 125mm rounds their way. The force moved, separated into small groups foothills and ridges south of General Bardos's position. Several Apache helicopters provided cover fire so that the force could make it to safety. The warriors lay down a devastating barrage of sniper fire forcing the infantry to take cover behind the tanks. Small groups of men were difficult to target as rounds from the tanks fell short of the target or passed overhead, though a great many were wounded, and hundreds killed before they made it to the safety of the rocks. The Chinese withdrew back to the main force; guns fell silent.

Each side was licking its wounds as they pulled back to regroup. Chinese forces had been whittled down, but they still far outnumbered General Bardos and his men by at least five to one. The good news was that a great many tanks were out of commission and much of the airpower had been diminished. The loss of the Warthogs was regrettable, but they had served a good purpose and there were still two squadrons remaining. The general kept them hid, away from enemy view. Their extended combat radius of about thirteen hundred miles, kept the enemy guessing where they were. While the Chinese had been delayed, they were making slow but steady progress toward their objective.

Lunadi, Sky Thinker, and General White had come to the side of General Bardos as they watched the armor of the Chinese approach about five miles away as darkness fell.

"Any suggestions men?" Jason asked.

"We prepared as much as we can," General White said. "The tribes, along with some Shockwave squads and Lunadi's men have pits dug in the desert. Once they pass them, they will shoot the tanks with Javelin missiles, as many as they can. They will be in range for support fire from our snipers and we will have some Apache's attack them as well."

"That could work," Jason pondered. "We will have our tanks engage them at the same time from the front. Once we open fire, their air support will lock onto our positions. Where is Major Roth?"

"Here sir," as he came trotting over.

"Do you have this canyon rigged like the other?" Jason asked.

"Yes sir. I also have and entire explosive line toward the eastern end that will go off killing anything it encounters if they manage to pass."

"Very well men, get ready to drop some lead on those sons of bitches," Jason said, grinning. "It's been an honor."

Everyone took their positions. As darkness fell there was no sound, not even a bird or coyote. The stillness was broken by the beating of drums and chants of many warriors that was clearly heard as before by both sides. This time however, the fire was more visible to General Qiang and his forces, being almost parallel with Jeremy's position in the rocks. He sent several squads of his Dragons to investigate and to capture or kill whoever was there.

Jeremy had lit his three fires as before, summoning the war gods Ahayuta and Achi. The two rode through the air on horses of flame, like a rainbow arch. The soldiers of both sides were amazed, not knowing what was happening. The soldiers of General Qiang began to be as fearful as before. The encounter with the Skinwalkers and rattlesnakes had shaken them to the core. They knew deep down that they should not be here in this country.

The soldiers of both sides stood, amazed as a fiery arch appeared across the sky, descending to the flames at Jeremy's position. The flaming horses of the War Gods stopped in front of Jeremy, perched on the rocks as if they were statues.

"We are here to assist," Ahayuta said.

"Command us as you will," Achi stated.

"Tomorrow we win or lose the battle," Jeremy said. "We cannot let them reach the city. We have prepared all we have left. You must make sure the enemy does not proceed one mile past the end of the small valley into Vegas."

"It shall be as you wish, young Medicine Man," Ahayuta

and Achi said in unison. "None shall escape to cause harm."

Without warning, several dozen warriors, gold in color and glowing as a flame, armed with bows and arrows materialized around Jeremy facing outward. Arrows, as it were a gold flame, flew outward in a circle as they shot one after the other. The arrows hit the Dragons in the chest, killing each one. No sooner did it hit than the arrow disappeared. Looking around, the warriors vanished.

"We take care of our own Medicine Man," Achi said.

"Our own are taken care of," Ahayuta screamed, whooping.

The two war gods rode in a giant circle, above the Chinese and American forces, their steeds aflame with a fire so hot the soldiers could feel it. They rode northward as the soldiers followed their flaming arc until is disappeared into the stars. There would be no sleep this night as the soldiers retired to their bedding areas, wondering what the hell they all had gotten into.

Just as the soldiers were retiring, two columns of gold shot upward into the night from the heart of General Bardos's camp. He came running, just in time to witness the two seriously wounded giants, turn into a gold mist upon the ground, the mist turning into a golden column like a plume of lava shooting from a volcano.

"What happened?" Jason asked.

"My brothers have passed on," Aichu said. "The color signifies they have been accepted back into his presence."

"I am sorry for your loss," Jason said. "I know how it feels."

"Do not be," Aichu said proudly. "For us, it is an honor to die in the service of Sun God so that we have the chance to be with him again. It is proof of our loyalty and penance of our past."

The ground trembled as Aichu and his four remaining

comrades walked away, the soldiers nearby staring in amazement. In a way, General Bardos knew exactly how Aichu felt; it was the same way a true warrior felt about the country and giving his or her life for it.

In the City of Lost Wages, fiery red wisps circled cemeteries spread within and without the city. The wisps came down out of the sky and began making rapid, clockwise circles above each cemetery, so fast that the air above turned red, blocking out the night sky. Within the wisp could be seen a ghostly figure with red eyes and a mouth like the jaws of death reaching out from hell itself, an evil laugh as it passed. The graves began to shake at the top as spirits emerged from each. They began to march in unison down the streets, their spirits in the shape of their own bodies before they had gone the way of all the earth. Slowly, the walk became a run and then, they moved like a scavenging horde of locusts turning a dull red on the outer extremities as the inner became a brighter red, the shape of a person clearly visible in spirit form. Those on the street jumped away in fear as they passed. By the time they had reached the outskirts of Vegas, they were moving almost seventy miles per hour. As they glided along the road, hitting I-15 headed west, they made a noise like a roll of heavy thunder that grew louder as they moved. Above them were ominous red lightening bolts, crackling and moving with them.

"What the hell is that?" a soldier asked, pointing, watching the approaching hoard from high up the ridge. He grabbed his radio. "General, you need to see this, coming from Vegas sir, a wave of red."

Jason, along with many of the other commanders had scarce gotten a view of the red hoard as it passed, running toward and into the enemy camp. They could hear faint screams of terror in the still night air.

"What the hell is that?" Jason asked.

"It must be some of Jeremy's work," Sky Thinker said. "I've never seen anything like it.

"I'm glad it's them and not us," Lorenzo replied.

Immediately in front of them emerged Death Feather.

"Fear not the dead who have arisen at my command," he said. "They collect but one soul each as they pass."

He had no sooner spoke than he vanished.

"What the hell did he mean," Jason asked.

"He meant that for each of those risen from the dead, they would take one soul of the enemy," Lunadi replied, staring toward the Chinese camp. "They will separate the soul from the body, taking it with them as the body falls to the earth, dead.

The group stood shaking their heads as they watched the dim red glow within the enemy's camp, saying a silent prayer, thankful it was not them.

E very soldier was awake to see the orange orb of the sun peak the horizon. A thick haze hung in the air; so thick the sun emerged as a round, orange ball. As the haze began to dissipate the soldiers wondered if this would be their last sunrise. The Chinese camp was locked in fear as they recalled the night. Not a one of them had slept as the red hoard had moved through the camp at a lightening swift pace, leaving several thousand of their comrade's dead. A weeping and wailing could be heard as they walked among the dead bodies. Their commanders, on orders from General Qiang, quickly got them focused back on the mission at hand. The sun was lifting ever so high as the Chinese began their last push for Las Vegas. They must reach it at all costs before reinforcements could arrive. Both generals knew this day would be decisive; it would be victory, or it would be death — the Chinese took no prisoners.

"Colonel," Li said. "See the ridges and walls of that canyon, pointing. "Line up all our howitzers and blanket it on both sides. Fire until your barrels melt."

"Yes General."

The Chinese armor had reached the point where there was little maneuvering room as they took up both sides of the interstate, moving east toward the city. The last stretch, a combination of a valley and canyon that was merely a gap in the foothills running north to south west of Vegas, was now the valley of the shadow of death. This day would witness the death of many. The Americans struck first.

As the Chinese reached the first quarter mile marker set by the combat engineers, the first wave of Javelin missiles was fired, destroying every tank they shot at, but there were many more coming. Lunadi's men, and what remained of the militia from the Russian encounter, lay down a withering fire on the Chinese infantry, joined by the thousands of warriors from all the tribes. Blood spray burst from their chests as most were shot center of mass, the bullets passing through the body and impacting the dirt behind the enemy. A .338 round at less than one-thousand yards tended to do that. At the same time, Chinese artillery began falling on them, taking a huge toll, a great many wounded, decimating their ranks.

Many of the Chinese troops, already panicked and fearful because of the Skinwalkers, began to flee. General Qiang ordered them to stand firm or their explosive helmets would be activated. As many continued to flee, the helmets on their heads began to explode. While they watched the heads explode like a melon, sending brain matter and blood everywhere and as several dozen headless, lifeless corpses fell to the earth, the troops became more afraid of their own general than the enemy and returned to the fight.

General Qiang ordered in his Z-18 helicopters that started laying down a withering fire on Bardos's men. They returned fire with Stinger missiles and machine guns.

"Roger that, bring in air now from the east end," Jason yelled into the radio.

Within two minutes, the enemy tanks and armor, as well as personnel were being strafed by 30mm cannon fire from the A-10s. More armor was lost as the fight raged. Helicopters were battling it out in the air, bursting into huge balls of flame as they were shot down. It was Apache versus Z-18 doing aerial combat in their attempts to rid the battlefield of the enemy. Bullets, rockets, 120mm and 125mm rounds were ripping men, equipment, and the desert apart at they collided in a hail of death.

Tribal warriors were firing as fast as they could acquire targets, oblivious to the bursting shells falling around them, their comrades wounded and dying. It was keep firing or die!

Lunadi and some of his snipers had crawled to a position where they could look down from high ground as they began to take out officers on the tanks, who quickly closed their turrets, several had been killed. They next focused on infantry officers and other soldiers. Lunadi had teams of snipers with dynamic targeting scopes with four of his men constantly calling our range and wind speed as the snipers went from one target to another. The other warriors were firing at will. The soldiers were dropping like flies as not one sniper seemed to miss his mark. It didn't take long for an armored vehicle to spot them and lay down a covering fire with its 12.7mm caliber heavy machine gun. The rocks around the Lunadi began bursting from bullet impact, sending clouds of dust into the air, rapidly whisked away by the east wind blowing down the canyon.

"Damn, let's move," Lunadi screamed. "They're zeroed in. Move, move, move."

As the men ran, several were wounded. They had barely managed to get to better cover when a Z-18 buzzed their position, firing a rocket. The battle scene was pure chaos as Chinese Z-18 and Apache helicopters continued to square off against each other and against opposing forces. Bullets continued to rain down like hail. Another squadron of A-10s came down the valley, again wreaking havoc on Chinese armor. The mission was short lived as J-18 jets, not getting suckered in again, delivered their payloads of rockets onto the Warthogs and personnel. They crashed into the sides of the hills and into enemy armor and infantry; the entire squadron was lost.

"Make your push now," Jason yelled into the radio. "Target all enemy tanks."

General Bardos had held his armor in reserve until the last quarter of the valley. Heavy duty battle tanks roared westward down the interstate in a five-by-five alternating formation, directly toward the enemy. Smoke and fire obscured their approach at first and then, they unleased hell on the Chinese. Gun turrets leapt into the air, from the impact of the 120mm rounds. It was tank against tank as the Chinese began finding targets of their own. Lunadi, Sky Thinker, and Shockwave were along the ridges of the hills and began firing at will. Chinese troops were falling by the hundred, but they were so large in number, they just kept pressing forward, stepping over fallen comrades killed by the snipers and others turned to mush by the impact of a tank round. The men around Lunadi and his STS force, along with the warriors were falling like flies, most wounded, but unable to continue fighting. Lunadi was moving with his men when a round struck him in the left shoulder. Two of his men immediately bandaged it, but he could only fire one-handed.

The combined warriors of the tribes were shooting everything that moved. Many of their leaders had fallen, but they didn't stop. The war cries they let out, many thousands yelling at once, could be heard above everything else. The Chinese infantry visibly sank lower to the ground, crouching as they relentlessly moved forward, not know what to expect.

To attack the American tanks, the J-15s were forced to come in low, it was then that the hidden Apache's, hovering just below the ridge tops, engaged them, along with the last squadron of A-10s. The valley was in complete chaos as fire and smoke rose from the valley floor, when Chinese jets, helicopters and Warthogs came crashing down upon both sides armor and soldiers. As the black smoke rose, leaving bursting flames and exploding armor beneath it, it revealed soldiers running for their lives. The battle had been raging for six hours as tank fought against tank and man against man, aerial combat serving as the backdrop.

The late afternoon sun, bathed the combatants in an unnatural orange glow as its rays tried to penetrate the smoke rising from the desert floor strewn with carnage of men and destroyed equipment. A heavy toll from both sides had been exacted as General Bardos lost his remaining air cover and tanks.

"Now Scott," Jason screamed.

Within a few seconds, over fifteen hundred drones fell

upon the enemy as they swarm attacked the armored personnel carriers and troops. The one-quarter pound, shaped C-4 explosive in each drone did significant damage as they exploded on impact. The attack only lasted a couple of minutes but seemed to make no difference. The number of Chinese troops were simply too great. General Bardos was high up in his command post. He realized they could not stop the Chinese as his men continued to rain down hell upon them and the last battalion of his tanks had fallen to the enemy. He said a silent prayer. He had lost all his armor and all his helicopters and planes. His men, thousands of warriors, and Shockwave were at the mercy of the Chinese who were regrouping to make their final assault.

At his location, Jeremy had just finished the last sand painting. He could not see the battle from where he was, but the rising smoke and sounds of explosions filled him with apprehension. He knew they were hopelessly outnumbered.

He sat down and began to hum and pray then, chant as the sandpainting in front of him started to glow a fiery red. It was in the shape of a circle with the figure of Monster Slayer in the middle, encroached by five structures on either side, with a name above each. It was a large painting, eight feet in diameter. Monster slayer was a red figure, the structures were all white. Beneath them were small symbols: bows, tomahawks, spears, and other weapons of war. The symbols began to glow a bright yellow as the red swirling mist formed a single, dense column that appeared almost like red concrete. The column suddenly shot like a bolt through the air directly toward the battle, but a few thousand feet above it. Jeremy followed it with his eyes as he stood and tried to make out what it was, he had conjured from the supernatural. It was not something his father or grandfather had prepared him for.

Commander Osceola Panther of Lunadi's force was behind his rifle. He was no longer just a commander; it was all hands on deck. His men had been fighting all day and were covered in dust and gunpowder, their faces blackened except for small flesh colored creases from sweat running down their faces, blood also trickling from wounds from exploding rocks. Gunfire rang out all around him along with bullet impacts from the enemy below. The sounds from both sides were deafening. He was watching the giants run amok through the Chinese armor, as one by one they fell, their bodies turning to a gold dust then, columns of gold shooting skyward. The warriors and other soldiers saw it, watching briefly in awe as Aichu's men fell. Only Aichu remained and even he had fallen.

Osceola was looking through his scope for his next target when he noticed an armored personnel carrier away from the others and what appeared to be several officers looking through binoculars and pointing in different directions along the valley, east, toward Vegas. He measured the distance to be 2,150 yards. He quickly lined up his target, a man in the middle that appeared to be giving orders. He was concentrating so hard that he didn't notice his men turn and gasp, looking behind him. The group of men next to his target also saw it, dropping their binoculars and staring east. Perfect Osceola thought, everything was absolutely still; he leveled his crosshairs, let out half a breath and squeezed the trigger of his .338. He didn't watch the impact as the men behind him started to gasp and murmur. He quickly turned to look.

"What the hell is that?" one asked.

Behind them at the exit to the valley, Vegas just beyond, a strange cloud formation had begun to appear. It was like cumulous clouds, but dark blue gray that formed the shape of a broad base, thousands of feet across with a central column emerging above, smaller columns of cumulous clouds to the left and right of it. From the central column, pushing out of the clouds was Monster Slayer in all his glory, his spear in his right hand, his eyes a piercing ruby red staring at them from beneath his headdress, the war gods on either side of him, riding their flaming steeds. Below him in the foundation of the clouds were ten black stallions, a war chief upon each. They were fearsome looking, their faces colored white with two broad black stripes running vertically on either side of the nose. In front of the ten stallions, sat Ocatu, head of the ten lost tribes, riding a stallion as white as snow under full sun. They began to ride toward the valley of the shadow of death at a dead run, descending on white roads of clouds, a twin column behind each chief. As they reached the end of the valley, the chiefs stopped, five on either side of the valley, looking toward the center, toward the brave soldiers who had attempted to stand off so many, Monster Slayer and the war gods above them. Ocatu rising beside them as he directed the battle below.

The columns of warriors kept coming, swift as the wind, flinging arrows at the Chinese. Soldiers were dropping to their knees as the warriors rode past. The arrows were red, with ten white stripes around the bottom of each shaft. They struck the Chinese with such force; each soldier was knocked several feet into the air and away from the blow as each that was struck fell dead upon the earth. The remaining Chinese helicopters and planes were hit with giant spears that flew faster than bullets, disintegrating them in midflight.

Lunadi's men had tears streaming down their faces as they witnessed the spectacle before them and began screaming and yelling as they pumped their rifles up and down in the air. The thousands of warriors from all the tribes began their war cries as well. It was only then that they noticed the beat of drums that became louder and louder as the rows of warriors kept coming, flinging arrow after arrow at the fleeing troops.

The armored personnel carrier was idling as the officers outside it gazed in fear and amazement at the columns of warriors. They quickly loaded their fallen commander into the carrier and made all haste toward the west. General Li Qiang had been struck just below the left ribs in the outer abdomen by Commander Panther's bullet. He was alive, conscious to see what was happening. His thoughts quickly drifted to his family and how very wrong he had been.

After a few minutes, the entire Chinese force was on the run. General Bardos commanded his troops to follow them but to stop at Victorville. Jeremy had driven rapidly across the desert and was kneeling by the side of Aichu, who was coughing up blood, dying. He had been hit in the shoulder by a 125mm round. Almost instinctively, the men knew where they should go as they walked down the hillsides and from the canyon floor, circling Aichu.

The cloud formation changed from a formidable dark to white as it moved its center above the fallen giant, all the ten chiefs riding their black stallions hovering in a large circle above the men and Aichu, row upon row of warriors stacked in the clouds above them, their horses neighing, trying to run like the wind as the drums still beat, the sound lessening then ceasing.

"I am sorry my friend," Jeremy said. "Is there anything

I can do."

"Do not be sorry Medicine Man," Aichu said, coughing. "I did what I needed to do to demonstrate my faith."

The clouds above them opened into a portal as Monster Slayer descended, standing above the two. Without warning a white column shot down, beside Monster Slayer; it was Sun God.

"You have been valiant in your service to me Aichu," Sun God said. "You have proven yourself. Come with me."

As Sun God touched his hand, Aichu turned into a white spirit, of normal size and the two shot up into the portal, where could be seen thousands of warriors to greet them as the portal closed. The drums beat once more and faded in the distance as the cloud rapidly moved northward. Monster Slayer and the war gods remained, standing in the same spot.

"I am commanded to tell you to remind your President to honor his commitment to the tribes."

"I will do so," Jeremy said. "Who was that who just helped us?"

"It was the ten lost tribes," Monster Slayer said. "Be grateful to them. While you call them lost, they are not lost to us. Stay well young Medicine Man. Continue to teach our people. One day you will be welcomed back like your friend Aichu."

Monster Slayer, the war gods following, shot skyward, following the cloud formation, now nearly out of site. The men had all fallen to their knees showing great honor to Jeremy. The leaders of all the tribes had surrounded him, paying respect and tribute. The stories they had been told of him were true. And this moment was something they would be telling their grandkids; generations would hear of it. During the gathering, General Bardos had made his way back down the hills and had heard and witnessed the event. Incredible he thought that those whom the U.S. Government had treated so brutally had been our saviors.

"Well done my young friend," Jason said, holding out his hand to Jeremy, who shook it. "Our nation owes your people a great debt that I do not know how we can repay."

Looking about, there was not a face without a tear. The men knew as well that their lives had been spared because of a young Navajo Medicine Man and the warriors from many tribes who stood about them now drenched in sweat, blood, and dust, teary eyed at what they had just witnessed. The white soldiers turned to their new Native American friends, helping them, dressing their wounds, laughing, making new, lifelong friends.

James Tindall

CHAPTER 12
Aftermath: The Reset

The valley of the shadow of death had proved just that; in the aftermath, there was nothing but dead bodies, burned out armor and downed planes and helicopters. There were so many that it was difficult to walk among them without stepping on one. Thousands had perished in the fight to save a nation and a way of life. The City of Lost Wages remained intact; electricity was being restored, and the nation was waking to a new day.

Bardo's troops stopped at Victorville, determining there would be no need to follow the enemy further since their fear of what they had seen drove them onward like a rabid dog. The forces had been stopped for a few hours when in late afternoon, they felt it. A giant earthquake that lasted twelve and a half minutes. Scientists reported it at a 9.5 level, it was the San Andreas rupturing and ripping California a new one, running off the coast to the connecting Cascadia fault and up along Oregon and Washington, triggering multiple volcanoes.

Ninety minutes later, a tsunami stretching from Seattle to San Diego hit the western shoreline. It was moving at over four hundred miles per hour when its one hundred fifty-foot wave hit. The damage was even worse than along the eastern seaboard. The Los Angeles basin was completely submerged as the wave washed up against the

Santa Monica Mountains to the east and northeast of the basin and then, quickly retreated to the Pacific. The estimated death toll along the west coast rose to thirty-five million. They too, had made their decision. Scientists had long discussed the 'Big One' and when it would strike, always when least expected. The wave had taken all Chinese ships with it. Their soldiers now lie at the bottom of the Pacific, including General Qiang. What they had witnessed would never make it home; there would be no stories to tell. Perhaps it was for the best. Qiang would be made out to be a rogue general, along with those who served him, many of whom would be publicly executed so that China could keep its lie, the public none the wiser.

Secretary of State, Nick Fabiani, had discussed with the Chinese what the reprisal would be. They had been given twelve hours to evacuate their shipbuilding yards, primary naval bases, and four largest military bases, which had been obliterated with ballistic missiles. Any further Chinese aggression would be dealt with by nuclear strike. A similar deal was offered to the Russians. Minister Gan became the new President, much to his liking and he had already apologized to the world and the President, explaining how a rogue general and four Politburo members had conspired with the president; his words were, "they had lapsed into insanity." They were put on display for public execution to save face.

The plumbing truck was sitting in the west parking lot of the Michigan Hall of Justice. The two Death Commandos had gotten access to the building and were on the roof, one sitting behind a takedown .338, while the other ranged the target. They had been waiting since early morning. Being a Sunday, there was no one about, especially since electricity was out, everyone was anxiously waiting for it to come back on for any morsel of news.

"Let's go," Susan said. "We have clearance for a small, twin engine jet to Bermuda. From there we'll take an immediate departure to Chile. We'll figure the rest out as we go."

"Okay," Big Rod said.

"The two walked out the west entrance of the building. Susan stopped, taking a last look at what had been her throne of power and then, turned facing the Hall of Justice. The three hundred grain bullet, from eight hundred forty-five yards away, struck her center mass. The energy of the impact on a closed system so violent it blew her hands off. Big Rod watched, frozen in surprise as her body flew back onto the concrete, blood flowing from it like water. By the time it dawned on him what had happened, a second bullet found it mark, striking him in the back of his head, exploding it like a cantaloupe as he fell lifeless atop his lover.

"That's what happens to traitors," the Death Commando said. "They reach a Dead End."

"Who's next?" the other Death Commando asked.

"Judges," the warrior said. "Call it in."

Miles away, in Atlanta, a second team had followed Georgia Congressman Ray Hunt who had pulled up to a stop light; as it turned green, a male passenger in the pickup truck that had pulled up next to him threw a grenade into the congressman's car. It exploded four seconds later.

A ir Force One was on its descent when Erin hung up the phone and made her way to the President.

"I'm afraid there is more bad news Mr. President," Erin said. "The New Madrid fault went off, 9.5 intensity. It changed the course of the Missouri and Mississippi Rivers.

All bridges along the Mississippi are down from New Orleans to the Great Lakes. No word on death toll, but another major disaster. It also cut all the trunk lines for fuel, natural gas and power grid. Electricity on the eastern seaboard will be out for at least several months. Almost all critical infrastructures are down sir."

"I guess when Sun God said he would sweep the country, he meant it," Phil said, looking out the window as they drove on until, a short while later, they reached the battlefield. The nation would fall into immediate economic collapse. All he could do was let out a huge sigh as the wheels touched down on the tarmac at McCarran International Airport. The President and his team were whisked to the battlefield to meet with General Bardos, Erin and of his staff in tow. They had mustered air cover from the return of two aircraft carriers and now had constant air support overhead.

"I'm sorry that we couldn't help in the Midwest Mr. President," General Bardos said, saluting.

"That's alright General," Phil replied. "From what General Wilson says, our air support and the locals stopped the enemies three divisions just before they entered Minneapolis, it appears there are lots of patriots there."

Erin had spotted Lunadi who was wearing a sling. She made no pretense of their relationship as she ran to his side, tears in her eyes, wearing a giant smile, grabbing him and planting a long, deep kiss.

"I worried so much about you," she said. "I'm glad you're safe. I'll take good care of you."

He just looked down on her with a huge smile, pinning her to him with his good arm around her waist.

As the President looked at the men who had gathered round, along with all the tribal chiefs, tears ran down his cheeks. The overwhelming scene of dead and wounded and burned-out equipment made him realize how lucky the nation was. His view of people and the world had changed. "Our nation owes you a huge debt," Phil said. "I will honor the commitment I have made to you but feel that it is terribly inadequate. "

"It is our land too," Ferni said. "We will always help our people keep it."

"How many men did you lose?" Phil asked Ferni.

"Almost all have been wounded, about twenty percent dead," Ferni replied. "Lunadi's and Sky Thinker's forces are mostly wounded; none dead."

"How can that be?" Phil asked, surprised.

"Their mothers taught them to keep the faith — they did!"

"We will honor all of you," Phil said, feeling guilty so many that had been treated so badly had died.

A week later, in front of Caesars Palace, the President addressed the nation from behind a podium set up at the main doors, the fountains in front. Only tribal leaders and commanders, as well as General Wilson were allowed to attend. Those watching on television were amazed at the information given. The President updated the nation on the catastrophes that had befallen the country and all the events that had led up to this moment, showing scenes of the battle and troops from the west to the east and in Minneapolis as proof of what occurred. He also showed pictures of the aftermath of the natural disasters. The charges against those who had helped the enemy were also given, as well as their names. A few on the Chinese payroll had managed to disappear, but they would be found; their names and pictures were posted as he spoke. He spoke of a new beginning for the country, a reset, to make sure such a thing never happened again and urged the people to help each other in this time of great need. And, to pray for us all.

He profusely thanked the tribal chiefs and apologized for the use of the name, but that it was used in the most profound respect. The President informed the nation of the valiant effort the tribes had put forth and their great sacrifice. And had it not been for them, the U.S. would now be under Chinese rule, headed to death or work camps. He also outlined the reward the tribes would receive for saving the country and had already signed a Presidential directive to that effect, to begin immediately. The President also thanked Mexico for their special force's operators. The loss of life was staggering, one hundred seventy million dead, the count still rising. The country would overcome as they always had, except now, there would be a great reset. Because of the help of the tribes, the nation had survived once again. A constitutional convention would be called to adjust a few amendments so that political officials could no longer become an elite group, ignoring the needs of those they served.

Jeremy, Lunadi, Erin, Sky Thinker, and Generals Bardos and White were standing off to the side, in front of the entrance gate to the west parking garage, which had been closed. They had become fast friends. The comradery of battle unlike any other. Jeremy quietly led Lunadi and Erin aside.

"Lunadi and Erin, I need to tell you something," Jeremy said. "I wanted to earlier, but our duties got in the way. Look there, in the shadows. Go to them. Listen to them."

The two could see White Shell Woman and the Mediator standing in the shadows above the asphalt. They walked over, bowing their heads in respect, Jeremy staying behind."

"You have done well warrior," the Mediator said. "You helped our young Medicine Man save a people and our hallowed land. You will be called on again. See that you keep the faith."

Jeremy walked up beside them, pulling a superbly made Seminole bead string from his pocket.

"In your tradition," Jeremy said.

He wrapped it around Lunadi's right wrist as he grabbed Erin's left and wrapped it tightly around, binding the two together.

White Shell woman waved her hand. A sparkling white dust settled upon their heads drifting from above. For a brief instant, it was as if they had halos.

"Yours is an undying love," White Shell Woman said. "Keep it strong, you are bound forever."

END

ABOUT THE AUTHOR

James Tindall is the author of Jagged Grass, Sun God's Treasure, Alas Omega, and other books, including two best-in-field textbooks. He grew up on a Florida reservation wrestling alligators and training horses to earn money. He is a U.S. Army veteran who served in intelligence and is an expert in sharpshooting and hand-to-hand combat. He has five martial-arts black belts of advanced rank including a 9th degree in Kenpo, as well as four college degrees. As a federal scientist, he specialized in water, energy, and food security, engaging him in the areas of homeland and international security and counterterrorism. His assignments have taken him from Latin America to Brazil, Mexico to Alaska, Turkey to China, and many points between. When not writing, he consults to solve tactical and strategic problems for international governments and SOGs.

James Tindall

NOTES: